THE BOOK THAT
HELD HER HEART

BOOKS BY MARK LAWRENCE

THE BROKEN EMPIRE
Prince of Thorns
King of Thorns
Emperor of Thorns

Short Stories
Road Brothers

THE RED QUEEN'S WAR
Prince of Fools
The Liar's Key
The Wheel of Osheim

THE BOOK OF THE ANCESTOR
Red Sister
Grey Sister
Holy Sister

Short Stories
Tales of Abeth

IMPOSSIBLE TIMES
One Word Kill
Limited Wish
Dispel Illusion

THE BOOK OF THE ICE
The Girl and the Stars
The Girl and the Mountain
The Girl and the Moon

THE LIBRARY TRILOGY
The Book That Wouldn't Burn
The Book That Broke the World
The Book That Held Her Heart

THE
BOOK THAT
HELD HER HEART

———

THE LIBRARY TRILOGY:
BOOK THREE

MARK LAWRENCE

ACE
New York

ACE

Published by Berkley

An imprint of Penguin Random House LLC

1745 Broadway, New York, NY 10019

penguinrandomhouse.com

Copyright © 2025 by Bobalinga Ltd.

Penguin Random House values and supports copyright. Copyright fuels creativity, encourages diverse voices, promotes free speech, and creates a vibrant culture. Thank you for buying an authorized edition of this book and for complying with copyright laws by not reproducing, scanning, or distributing any part of it in any form without permission. You are supporting writers and allowing Penguin Random House to continue to publish books for every reader. Please note that no part of this book may be used or reproduced in any manner for the purpose of training artificial intelligence technologies or systems.

ACE is a registered trademark and the A colophon is a trademark of Penguin Random House LLC.

Excerpt from *Arm of the Sphinx* by Josiah Bancroft, copyright © 2015 by Josiah Bancroft. Reprinted with permission of Josiah Bancroft.

Library of Congress Cataloging-in-Publication Data

Names: Lawrence, Mark, 1966– author.
Title: The book that held her heart / Mark Lawrence.
Description: New York: Ace, 2025. | Series: The Library Trilogy; book 3
Identifiers: LCCN 2024035598 (print) | LCCN 2024035599 (ebook) |
ISBN 9780593437971 (hardcover) | ISBN 9780593437995 (ebook)
Subjects: LCSH: Libraries—Fiction. | LCGFT: Fantasy fiction. | Novels.
Classification: LCC PS3612.A9484 B65 2025 (print) |
LCC PS3612.A9484 (ebook) | DDC 813/.6—dc23/eng/20230714
LC record available at https://lccn.loc.gov/2024035598
LC ebook record available at https://lccn.loc.gov/2024035599

Printed in the United States of America

1st Printing

The authorized representative in the EU for product safety and compliance is Penguin Random House Ireland, Morrison Chambers, 32 Nassau Street, Dublin D02 YH68, Ireland, https://eu-contact.penguin.ie.

To libraries, bookshops,

and everyone who works in them

THE STORY SO FAR

For those of you who have had to wait awhile for this book I provide brief catch-up notes to Book Two, so your memories may be refreshed, and I can avoid the awkwardness of having to have characters tell each other things they already know for your benefit.

Here I carry forward only what is of importance to the tale that follows.

- The library is effectively eternal and infinite. It reaches into many worlds and contains a truly vast collection of books (or the equivalent) from a great many species, spanning all periods of history. It comprises square chambers two miles on each side and is staffed by gleaming white assistants that stock and restock the books. The door from one chamber to the next opens for every member of some species and not for those of others. The further you travel from an entrance keyed to one particular species the rarer become the doors they can open.

- The Exchange is an in-between kind of place whose appearance is shaped partly by the expectations of those visiting it. The Exchange can change the appearance of others to suit visitors' expectations and it makes the speech of everyone in it understandable to everyone else. This translation-and-disguise effect can follow, for a limited time, the people who use its portals.

- The Exchange contains many doors. Those doors lead to the past, present, and future, and to different worlds. The furthest forward time a person visits becomes their present. If a person leaves the Exchange by a door that leads to their past they appear there as a ghost, invisible to the people of that time and unable to touch anything or communicate with anyone. They will regain their normal form in the Exchange and in any place in their present or future. Left to its own devices, the Exchange brings things together and creates coincidences.

■ The Mechanism is a small building into which a single person can take a single book. It will then allow them to experience and interrogate the book as if they were walking through the world in which it's set or talking to the author with the advantage of all manner of solid illusions to illustrate the text.

■ Escapes are the blood of the library and can take physical form. They can manifest as a person's fears and often mirror the violence around them.

■ There are many mythologies concerning the library's creation. All of them are true. The one that is used by Livira, Evar, and the others in order to make sense of the situation concerns two brothers: Irad, who created the library, and Jaspeth, who wants to destroy it. The current library is an imperfect compromise resulting from a fragile peace between the two brothers. A low-level war between the brothers' proxies has been flaring back and forth across history. It appears to be coming to a head again in the here and now. In the library's war, Yute is championing the current compromise. Mayland has sided with Jaspeth and wants to destroy the library.

The main characters we have already met in this story are:

Livira: a human from a settlement on the Dust, now a librarian aged around twenty. She spent around two hundred years trapped inside an assistant (known as the Assistant) that raised five canith children trapped in a library chamber.

Evar: a canith in his early twenties who spent a decade in the Mechanism with Livira's book. Last seen failing to save the assistant in which Livira was trapped from being destroyed by skeer.

Clovis: raised as Evar's sister. Dedicated to the arts of war. Until recently she hated all humans since humans—specifically King Oanold and his soldiers—slaughtered all her people in the library chamber when she was a child.

Starval: raised as Evar's brother. Dedicated to the arts of stealth and assassination.

Kerrol: raised as Evar's brother. Specialises in understanding and manipulating others.

Mayland: raised as Evar's brother. Thought to be dead, but turned out to have escaped the chamber a year before Evar did. Specialises in history.

Arpix: a male librarian, early twenties, companion to Livira, studious and serious.

Jella: a female bookbinder, early twenties, companion to Livira, timid, kindly.

Carlotte: a female house-reader, early twenties, companion to Livira, vivacious, adventurous.

Leetar: a rich trainee diplomat, early twenties, sister to Livira's recently deceased friend Meelan.

Yute: deputy head librarian, former assistant, married to now-deceased head librarian.

Yolanda: Yute's daughter, a child in appearance but has spent years "lost" in the library.

Lord Algar: a one-eyed nobleman who has tried to put an end to Livira's career at every stage.

King Oanold: ruler of the now-destroyed Crath City. Stirred up hatred against the peoples who live on the Dust (including Livira) for political ends.

Salamonda: Yute's housekeeper and cook. A woman in her late fifties.

Celcha: a female ganar. The ganar were enslaved by humans and by canith. Celcha and her brother, Hellet, were manipulated by Mayland (and Starval) to help create an assistant that would work to destroy the library from the inside. Celcha wrongly blamed Livira and Evar for the harms done to her and worked to destroy them using mechanical ganar.

Wentworth: Yute's artificial cat that has many powers but seldom uses them. The most powerful library guide.

Edgarallen: an artificial raven created as a library guide.

Volente: a large very black artificial dog created as a library guide.

———

THE BOOK THAT Broke the World ended with three portals in the floor of a reading room side chamber within the library.

The three portals were created by the blood of an assistant (Hellet—Celcha's brother) when a giant mechanical ganar (made by Celcha) beat him to death on the floor. With the mechanical on fire and about to explode, the portals offered escape routes to those gathered there.

Through the first portal went the canith, Mayland, Starval, Clovis, and an unconscious Evar, who had earlier been shot trying to save Arpix (plus Salamonda and Livira's friend Neera). Mayland is heading the effort to destroy the library, effectively championing Jaspeth. Livira tried to go with them to be with Evar, but Mayland stopped her.

Through the second portal went Livira, Yolanda, Jella, Leetar, and a dozen or so survivors from the city. Yolanda is trying to fulfil Irad's vision for the library, fighting the restrictions on it.

Only Kerrol followed Yute through the third portal, both of them seeking some kind of compromise that will stop the warring parties.

Arpix, Salamonda, and Neera were captured by King Oanold's soldiers and are now his prisoners. Lord Algar has Livira's book and wants Arpix to help him use its power. King Oanold's group is still trapped in the library and his soldiers have resorted to cannibalism, killing and eating some of the civilians with them.

THE BOOK THAT
HELD HER HEART

The alphabet of scars exists so that those lessons need not be carved into our flesh a second time.

Holocaust, *author unknown*

CHAPTER 1

Anne

As a baby, Anne had taken her first ever steps among the aisles of what her grandfather called his library but was in fact a second-hand bookshop. It wasn't even his, since his mother, the Hoffman matriarch, was still alive, though you wouldn't know it to look at her. Anne had been told that Great-grandma Ruth was ninety-three, but she had seen, in one of the huge encyclopaedias that had to be lifted down for her, an engraving of an ancient queen embalmed with forgotten skill and preserved against the tide of nearly fifty centuries. Nana Ruth looked every bit as old as the queen amid her wrappings.

In any case, it was within these musty aisles that Anne had taken that first step, and later read her first word, which in retrospect had been a step of more significance, carrying her over an invisible threshold into a world much larger than that occupied by those who rarely choose to exercise their imagination.

As a toddler, and in fact until she was older than she was now prepared to admit, Anne had thought her grandfather's shop to be endless. She had believed that there would always be another corner to turn, another previously unknown aisle to discover, the shelves overfull, spine crowding spine, other books pushed in horizontally to rest atop their more orderly fellows.

She had of course, in the intervening years, discovered the rear wall and traced its entirety, which was unbroken but for a single door leading to a workshop where her father had once been employed repairing any book of sufficient rarity and value to deserve such attention. The shop stretched back much further than a casual visitor might imagine, but it most definitely had its limits. A fact that had simultaneously comforted and disappointed the young Anne, the balance between the two emotions varying across years as she grew older, or even from the morning of one day to the evening of the next.

At sixteen, she watched the shop when her grandfather's other business took him across town. Watching the shop mainly meant watching the door, since once a potential customer had disappeared among the shelves there was no telling where they might be. "Count them in. Count them out." This was her grandfather's instruction, written in a faded hand on yellowing paper pinned behind the till. The shop had to operate on an honour system since there was no way of knowing if someone were spiriting out a book under their jacket. Though if the person emerging from the aisles appeared considerably fatter than the one that entered, this was a pretty clear sign that they should be hoisted by the ankles and shaken until evidence of their crime presented itself.

Sadly, in Anne's view, no shaking took place, and any thefts went largely unnoticed amid the uncatalogued plenty of their stock. Replenishments for the books sold or stolen came largely from house sales where the occupant had died, and their descendants wanted easily divisible cash rather than awkward reminders of the lost relative. In the past, Grandfather had jokingly called himself and the others who converged on such properties "vultures." The unwanted furniture would go to Wagner or Fischer, the carpets and rugs to Hersch or maybe Wolf, and so on. Most often, Grandfather's offer on the books would be the best and he would return with his cart laden, a modest private library sheltering beneath the tarps.

But such joking had long since been abandoned, now that the townsfolk were stirred up against the tribe, and more than ready to throw the word as an allegation rather than the self-deprecating label originally intended. Anne had grown up with dirty looks and name-calling in the school playground. She'd become used to attending the birthdays only of the children who shared her temple. But more recently it would be a stone that was thrown at her rather than merely unpleasant words.

She tried to tell herself that it was because she'd grown into a bigger target, almost a woman now, but the Wagners' children came back from lessons crying or bruised or both often as not. Her grandfather said that evil men sought to use any difference to create fear, distrust, and hatred, all of which they would employ to advance their own position.

Anne had often wondered at the contrast between the way mankind divided its books and the way they divided themselves. For the former, they looked beneath the cover and considered what was written there, finding shelves for histories, for romances, for biographies, and for mysteries. For people, each far more complex than even the most profound of books, the cover often served. They saw her hair, the shape of her face, and they knew exactly how she fitted into their lives, regardless of her character. She was beneath them, unclean, an intruder into the town where her forebears had lived for many generations.

ANNE SAT AT the counter, the mechanical crank-operated cash register hulking in front of her. They didn't need a register of course. The customers came in twos and threes, or more generally these days in ones, with long, silent gaps in between. But Grandfather had inherited the register from one of his uncles' shops and installed it with an owner's pride, insisting that it made the place look modern and busy, even though the device was the best part of fifty years old, and the shop was largely deserted.

Despite the family's business being concerned primarily with old books, their takings run through an ancient register, it was the future that fascinated Anne's grandfather. His favourite topic of conversation was the pace of change. He would list the things that filled Anne's world, and which were wholly absent from his own childhood. It wasn't, he insisted, that he was jealous of the marvels she now had access to, be it mechanical adding machines or lights that burst into life at the flick of a switch, but that he envied her the next fifty years. If technology had delivered so much over the course of his own life and was still accelerating, what wonders were to come?

A familiar but unexpected noise startled Anne from her thoughts, tumbling the neglected book in her hands to the dusty floorboards. She stood up sharply from her stool. She'd been on edge lately—well, more than lately—her nerves tight-strung. A glance at the windows showed a gloomy, rainswept street, empty save for a lone figure in a raincoat, bent against the wind, quickly gone from view. The board that covered the hole from last week's half-brick rattled in the wind. The cracks spread beyond the board, catching whatever light escaped the clouds, glimmering, letting her know that the violence couldn't just be covered up, promising more.

Anne tore her eyes from the street. The noise had come from back among the aisles. It had been the sound of a book hitting the ground, much like the sound her own book had made a few seconds later. *Count them in—count them out.* She had done just that and knew herself to be alone. But still a book had fallen.

"Hello?" Her voice sounded small. She coughed and tried again. "Hello!"

Nothing. Just the peculiar silence of books. Fresh rain suddenly pattered against the window, spattering the legend *Hoffman's Books*, the painted letters offered to her in reverse. It seemed too dark for barely after noon, even for November. The electric lights struggled to fill the space. Two bulbs had blown earlier in the month, filling some of the aisles with sharply drawn shadows.

Another soft noise from the rear of the shop. Not a book falling, not this time. The scuff of a shoe perhaps? Anne lifted the divider and came out from behind the desk. She'd asked her grandfather why the shelves weren't arranged in long straight lines. A brief walk across the storefront would reveal any intruder were that the case. Instead, the arrangement was closer to labyrinth than linear.

"Mystery!" had been the old man's answer. People want to get lost in a book, he said. Let them get lost in the act of finding one too. Add some wonder and excitement to that part of the process in order to remind them why they should part with both their coin and their time. Choosing a book should be a private business, conducted in the secrecy of the aisles, not on display for strangers' judgement.

Anne currently had very specific views on the value of mystery. She was against it. "Come out!"

The sudden jangle of the bell above the street door made her jump. She spun towards the entrance, feeling almost guilty, as if caught doing something she shouldn't have been.

A policeman stood there, rainwater dripping from his shoulder wrap and beading on the gleaming leather bill of his cap. He pushed the door closed with his heel, the bell's jangling intensifying again.

For a long moment he stood, taking in the store with a sliding gaze that slipped across Anne as if she were of no more interest than the furnishings.

"Can I help you, sir?" Anne didn't recognise the man. He was young, tall, clean-shaven. But for the close-set meanness of his eyes he might be handsome were he to smile. The shop's infrequent visits from the law usually came in the rather portly form of Officer Muller who would pop in every now and then on sunny days. Or used to. Anne hadn't seen him for maybe two years now. Grandfather said the man's superiors hadn't approved of his fraternising.

This new officer clearly hadn't come to chat, and his silence unnerved Anne. "Have you come about the window?"

The question made the man sneer. "If a broken window is the limit of your trouble, you will have done very well."

"It's against the law to—"

"The *law* is made to serve the people. And the people don't want your kind here." The officer snapped at her as if she were a child in class. He wouldn't use that tone if her grandfather was here, Anne was sure. Though it was her grandfather who had told her never to talk back to a policeman. He'd given her a lot of instructions lately. Stay behind the counter. Don't argue with customers. Don't leave the shop.

"Where is your father?" Cold blue eyes fixed her.

"He's dead, sir." Anne remembered that her grandfather had also told her to be scrupulously polite. "My grandfather runs the shop."

"And where is he?"

"Out on business, sir."

"Business . . ." The officer removed his cap. He had a blunt head, his fair hair cropped short. "With your sort that means stealing." He advanced on her, an unreadable malice in his stare.

Anne stood paralysed by indecision. She wanted to run for the security of the counter, however illusory that might be. But running from a policeman in her own shop would be silly. But then again, whatever his uniform promised, she could see that the man meant to hurt her in some manner.

"How long do you think you can last here?" His head tilted with the question, a smile edging thin lips. "They piled the books higher than a man in Babelplatz and burned them all. Degenerate filth!" His eyes swept the shelves, perhaps imagining a similar blaze here.

Anne cringed as the man loomed above her, standing far closer than a stranger should. He raised a gloved hand towards her face, and, hating herself for flinching before him, Anne found herself filled with a strong instinct to bite the reaching fingers. Instead, she turned her head away as he touched her hair.

"How old are—" His voice fell to nothing, and he took a sharp step backwards.

Anne turned in the direction of his stare, and also took a step away. The figure emerging from the aisles was both impossibly tall and somehow alien, as if perhaps a lion had taken to its hind legs and come in search of a good read. She blinked and saw that her eyes had deceived her. The man was merely outrageously tall, so tall that she shouldn't have been able to miss him among the bookshelves, but not so tall as to defy reason. And the mane was merely an unruly expanse of darkly curling hair falling to his shoulders.

"Is there a problem?" The stranger's voice rumbled out so deep that at first it seemed as if he were speaking a different language, but a moment later Anne's mind rotated the sounds into something that made sense.

"You're so tall!" Anne hadn't meant to say anything so stupid. The words had just fallen out of her open mouth. She belatedly remembered to close it. She opened it again. "I'm so sorry. You surprised me. Us." She glanced towards the policeman.

The officer had retreated another step, his amazement equal to hers. Now, realising himself the subject of scrutiny, he drew himself up to his full height, scowling. "Who are you? A gypsy?" Contempt shivered through his words. "Is the circus in town?"

The tall man's clothes certainly had an odd look to them, a patched leather waistcoat with metal buckles, trousers seemingly made the same way. He looked young but something gave his face a peculiar gravitas, as if a king in rags had stepped among them.

The stranger advanced and the policeman retreated, running out of places to go. "You seem angry, my friend."

"Who the hell—" The officer shook his head. "Papers! Show me your papers!"

The tall man made a strange crooning noise, dipping his shoulder in an odd manner. Anne, fascinated, couldn't take her eyes from him. He set an overlarge hand to the policeman's arm, just above the elbow. "Come."

Astonishingly, the policeman let himself be drawn away to the far side of the shop, the other man, head and shoulders above him, like a father leading an errant son. He kept talking the whole time, his voice so low and deep that Anne couldn't separate the words.

Freed from the stranger's hypnotic presence Anne glanced away towards the street, wishing her grandfather would come. For a moment she thought she saw him, ghostly through the rain, only to realise with a start that she was seeing the reflection of someone behind her.

She spun around to find that a second stranger had emerged from the aisles, this one short enough that she could believe him to have passed among them unseen. In his way, this other man was no less strange than the first. What she'd mis-seen as a charcoal grey robe was in fact a sensible business suit of the same colour. The dark grey only served to accentuate the unhealthy whiteness of his skin. Anne had read about the condition but had never seen someone who suffered from it.

"Albino." Dismayed to find the word on her lips, she covered her mouth as if it could somehow be retrieved. "I'm so sorry. I was startled. That's no excuse. I thought I was alone in the shop and now . . ." She waved her other hand helplessly. She wasn't sure if the shop had had four people in it at once all year. "Can . . . can I help you, sir?"

The man inclined his head. In his right hand he carried a black umbrella. "I hope so. I'm looking for a book."

"A-any book in particular?"

"One that won't burn."

Most books require no key, and yet a closed mind cannot open them.
Dressed in Chain, *by Eli Nathan*

CHAPTER 2

Anne

The giant man, who must have in Anne's estimation stood close to seven feet in height, steered the young policeman back to the street door. The tight and vicious look that had commanded the policeman's face since he walked in had been replaced by a wondering confusion. The small but deep vertical lines between his eyebrows had smoothed themselves away.

"Be careful, Officer Schmidt," the giant said as the policeman pushed through the door and hunched himself against the rain. "It looks wild out there."

Anne closed the door behind him and stood there as the bell jangling above her wore itself out.

"That one," said the giant, "has many issues. It could take weeks to untangle him. But his main problem seems to be that he's fallen in with some sort of cult."

Anne covered the smirk that escaped onto her lips. It wasn't funny. None of it was.

"I didn't see you come in." It seemed the most logical place to start.

The albino bowed his head. "My apologies. I am Yute, and this is Kerrol. We came from the library." They were both foreign, they had to be. They spoke the language too well, their grammar too perfect to be from anywhere nearby, and yet untainted by any regional accent.

"Anne Hoffman." Anne felt she should offer her hand but resisted the impulse. She realised that she was staring and tried not to. Clearly neither man worked for the town's small library. Possibly the scientific library at Regensburg, but Anne found it hard to believe that the institute would employ such unusual characters, especially in the current political climate. Mr. Yute was at least respectably dressed . . . She wanted to thank them for putting in an appearance and somehow taming Officer Schmidt, but to do so would be to admit that she had been in danger from a policeman in her own shop, and that would make what had nearly happened far too real. Under the expectant gaze of her new customers Anne shook off her confusion and asked, "What was it you were looking for, Mr. Yute? I think I must have misheard you."

"And I think I must have misspoken." Mr. Yute inclined his head, his hair as white as Great-grandmother Ruth's. "We're here on a . . . what shall we call it? A discovery trip. And I think that our first task should be to learn what kind of place we've found ourselves in."

"The best bookshop in town." Anne folded her arms and grinned. Even though Mr. Kerrol had yet to speak to her, something about his presence made her feel safe, and that was a thing she'd not felt for a long time. There was no real sense to it. A dozen inches of extra height would do nothing to save you from a thrown stone, a club, a knife, or a bullet. But there it was, she took comfort from his being there.

"And how many bookshops are there in town?" Mr. Kerrol's voice rumbled out as he walked past her, so deep that it almost seemed to reverberate in her chest.

"F— Three." She had been going to say five, but Werner's went bust the previous year, and the Saveenys had left town only last week, boarding up the windows of their shop.

"Remarkable." The giant stood with his hand set to the window glass, his fingers splayed, the raindrops on the other side running past them. "An invisible barrier."

If it hadn't been for Mr. Yute saying they came from the library, or the way Mr. Kerrol had dealt with the policeman, Anne might have imagined the giant to be a native of some primitive country, brought to civilisation only recently by an intrepid explorer. But the explanation felt a thousand miles from fitting.

"Glass," Mr. Yute said, raising his voice slightly.

"Ah," Mr. Kerrol turned away from the window. "Glass. I should have known. I'm afraid I was the same way when I first saw fire. I thought it was some strange red flower."

Anne laughed nervously, not entirely sure that the man was joking.

"It occurs to me"—Mr. Yute rested his pink-eyed gaze on the street—"that we should perhaps visit these two other bookshops first. The manner of our arrival has . . . clothed . . . us appropriately, but it won't last. I'm afraid your uniqueness won't pass unnoticed for long, Kerrol."

"My impression from Hans was that this is not a time when differences are well tolerated in this kingdom," Mr. Kerrol rumbled.

Anne took the opportunity to retreat behind the counter and closed the divider. She wasn't sure she'd been following the conversation properly, but that last part she understood. She understood it to be understatement. "It might be dangerous for you to wander the town." She paused. "But you got here without trouble. Maybe I'm being silly."

Mr. Yute flexed his jaw. "I wouldn't say we had no trouble . . ."

Mr. Kerrol came and leaned on the counter with an easy smile. "Perhaps you could give us directions to these two other shops?"

Anne took a piece of notepaper and with the stub of a pencil began to sketch out a map of the streets the pair would need to take. "And don't go talking about the kingdom. Not where anyone will hear you. We've not had a king for a long time. Not since before I was born. It doesn't do to talk about kings. That will get you into politics, and that will get you into trouble faster than punching a judge in the face." She started to label the streets they would have to follow. First to reach Weber's shop, and then the antiquarian Madame Orlova whose upmarket emporium sold leather-bound tomes of the sort prized by scholars, collectors, and by bankers who bought them by the yard to fill their shelves with the necessary gravitas for men set in charge of vast sums of money.

"I would come as your guide," Anne apologised. "But I can't open that door." She nodded to the street.

"I'm familiar with such restrictions," Mr. Kerrol said, with no hint of complaint.

"I mean, I can, obviously." Anne felt the need to explain even if no explanation had been asked for. "Only, I promised my grandfather. He worries when I'm out. Says it's not safe for us these days."

"And where is your grandfather?"

"Out . . ." Anne shook her head and bent to finish the map. She handed it over. "There you go, Mr. Kerrol."

He accepted the page. "Just Kerrol. And my thanks." For a moment something seemed wrong with his hand. The shape? The way the fingers divided? The *number* of fingers? Anne shook her head and looked again. It was a perfectly normal hand, just very large. She suppressed a sudden desire to set her own hand against his palm and see how the size of his swallowed hers.

"Kerrol," she said.

"Just so." He straightened, waved the paper at his companion, and strode towards the door.

After a moment's fumbling they had the door open between them and a cold, damp blast rattled round them.

"Rain," grumbled Mr. Yute. "Better than the sun, I suppose." He led the way out, head bent, not choosing to pit his umbrella in an unequal battle against the wind.

"Rain!" Kerrol seemed delighted. "Another first!" And, dipping his head to avoid the doorjamb, he followed out, closing the door behind him.

Another first? Anne frowned as she watched the two men go. How did that make any sense? She watched them until the edge of the last window blocked her vision. One white as a ghost, the other tall as a beanstalk. They both had targets on their backs. There were plenty of brownshirts in town. Even out of uniform they'd spoil for a fight with a pair as clearly foreign. If Kerrol and Mr. Yute happened to pass by any of the factory yards they would draw trouble, sure as rain falls down. Any place where workmen would be coming and going, hanging out under the eaves of the machine sheds for a smoke, or standing in the shelter of a wall, any place like that could see them chased, beaten, driven out of town. Or worse, they might be arrested and taken to one of the new camps where all the communists were ending up these days. She should have sent them down that alley by the slaughterhouse, made them go the long way rather than past the lorry factory.

"Damn it!" Anne grabbed her coat and the key and ran to the door. She turned the sign to "closed," slipped out into the rain, locked up, and hurried after her customers, still struggling into her coat. "Wait!"

She caught them at the corner. "Mr. Yute, wait!"

"Just Yute," he said, turning with a surprised smile despite the rain which he very clearly wasn't enjoying.

"Yute." Anne felt uncomfortable calling an adult stranger by their first name. Kerrol wasn't much older than she was. Early twenties at most. But Yute . . . she couldn't tell how old he was. He had a face that made it hard to judge. He had to be at least forty, surely? But well-preserved. But equally he could be a youthful sixty. "Sir. I really should have just said I'd take you there. So, I will!"

"But your grandfather told you to remain in the shop," Yute observed. "I doubt he'd forgive me for inciting you to ignore his rules and to leave his livelihood unguarded."

"Oh, it's not much of a livelihood," Anne protested. "And the rule of hospitality trumps the other rule. You're strangers in town. Grandfather wouldn't forgive me if I left you to wander in such weather."

Kerrol smiled down at her, shaking water from his hands. "It might be nice to get somewhere dry. I never liked swimming in the pool, and I'm finding it just as unpleasant when the stuff falls from the sky."

Anne nodded uncomprehendingly. "This way." She crossed the street, aiming for Tanner Lane. Like her grandfather's shop, Weber's bookshop was tucked behind a high street where shops crowded elbow to elbow. Rather than keep other stores' company, the bookshop numbered lawyer's offices, accountancies, and suppliers of inks or stationery among its neighbours. Thunder rumbled in the east, like the sound of distant guns, and Anne picked up her pace.

She led them the long way, all the time praying that her grandfather's business kept him a little longer so that her dereliction of duty not be discovered. She took all her usual precautions, listening out for shouts or singing or raucous laughter, the hallmarks of the drunk, pausing at corners and peering around. It should have worked. Especially in the rain. But three streets shy of their target, and as the rain slackened to a scattered drizzle, a voice hailed them.

"Oi!" Hardly a threat but the lack of respect in the overfamiliar address was warning in itself. The confidence was another source of concern. You don't shout at two grown men in the street unless you have something to back it up. Particularly if one of those grown men has grown much further than probably any man within twenty miles ever had.

"Say nothing to offend them," Anne cautioned in a low voice, turning to face the speaker.

Four men in overalls had just emerged from one of the terraced houses they'd passed, men in their middle years, heavy bellies used to beer and sausage, sour expressions, a fifth emerging, closing the door behind him. Shift workers at the foundry, Anne thought, the four perhaps calling to pick up the fifth on their way in.

The largest of them, the oldest by the look of him, sported a handlebar moustache and the ruddy complexion of a drunk, though surely he wasn't currently inebriated at an hour that for him must be just after breakfast.

"Gypsies aren't allowed round here." The big man led his friends towards them with a swagger.

Anne would have run if she were on her own—the men didn't look fast, and they'd probably be satisfied with seeing her run. But it seemed unlikely that Yute in his smart business attire or the towering Kerrol would scatter like schoolboys, even though it would be very much in their best interests to do so.

"We are not gypsies," Yute said. "But since we are leaving, the point is moot." He turned to go.

"Don't turn your back on me!" the man barked.

Yute turned slowly back to face him. Kerrol said nothing, studying the men with a careful frown. He was far taller than any of them, but he didn't seem particularly powerfully built, and despite his height he didn't seem the fighting sort.

Looking pleased with himself, the man waved a hand at the three of them and glanced conspiratorially at his friends. "What have we here? A gypsy circus freak, a useless eater, and a Jew-rat."

The man behind him, bald and heavy browed, had fished a wrench from the pocket of his overalls.

"We should go." Anne tugged at Yute's arm.

"No." Kerrol's rumble was free of anger or fear. "They won't be satisfied without injuring us."

The leader's complexion darkened, flushing with more blood. With balled fists and a sense of impending purpose he closed the gap between them in swift strides.

"I—" Anne started to speak, but Kerrol moved so fast that the words were stolen from her tongue.

In one heartbeat he was towering beside her. In the next he had snatched up the biggest man in just one hand, carried him back to his fellows, seized another man in the other hand, and used the pair as clubs to knock the remaining three to the ground.

"My apologies." Kerrol threw the two men in his hands down onto the three struggling to rise. "With more study I'm sure I could have reasoned with you." He kicked the man closest to gaining his feet, knocking him flat. "Sadly, time is short, and I will have to employ fear." He glanced back at Yute. "If you could take our friend away. This will work better without an audience."

Yute reached for Anne's hand, encircling it with white fingers and leading her around the next corner. The blood-curdling growl that reached after them made Anne want to add her own scream and tear off at a flat sprint. Yute squeezed her palm and released her. "His bark is worse than his bite. His sister though . . . she is another proposition."

Kerrol emerged from the lane at a stroll a short while later, though wearing a frown once more. "I did my best. I don't think they will come after us or report us to any authority. Shame and fear are powerful motivators, but not ones I like to employ. They're unsubtle and apt to come back to bite you. And it seems that they have already been overused in this town for many years. Fascinating . . ." He brightened and looked expectantly at Anne. "Shall we go?"

"Y-yes sir."

"Kerrol."

"Kerrol." Anne had seen him pick up a man in each hand and wave them about as if they were mugs of beer. And the speed with which he'd moved. It didn't seem possible.

———

UNLIKE HOFFMAN'S BOOKS, which had four large windows with wooden pillars between them, Weber's boasted a single huge plate of glass. Or had. The whole window had been replaced by two tarps, flapping in the rain-laced wind. Anne stopped at the corner as soon as she saw it.

"I had read that glass was brittle stuff," Kerrol said behind her. "But if it's this fragile it seems a poor material to use, unless it's very cheap to replace?"

"It isn't cheap," Anne muttered.

"But one of yours was broken too," Kerrol said.

"Probably the same hands threw the stone." Anne stared, unsure whether it was safe to approach the shop. Was it still open to customers? A moment of fear seized her at the thought of grandfather's place left unguarded.

"Forgive me," Kerrol said gently. "Are the owners of this shop also worshipers of the Jew god?"

"Everyone here worships the same God." Anne glanced at him, wondering at his ignorance. "We just do it in different ways." It was too complicated to explain, or rather it was simple. It was about hate. Hate and difference. Difference only because it was something to hang hate from.

Kerrol nodded. "I know only what Officer Hans told me back in the shop, and Otto said in the alley. I doubt they are unbiased sources. But I'm keen to learn. It seems that persecuting a minority is a regrettably common trait among humanity. King Oanold chose the people from the Dust. He called them dusters. A racially identifiable group—"

"Sadly, it's not something unique to humanity," Yute interrupted. "Perhaps we should conduct our business while we still can." And so saying, he led out across the street, aiming for the bookshop.

Anne followed, glancing from Yute to Kerrol. *Humanity?* Both of them had used the word, and neither man had spoken it as if it were something they felt themselves to be part of.

"Let me go first." Anne set her hand to the door ahead of Yute. She turned the handle and pushed on through.

Immediately the familiar smell of books greeted her. Herman and Carl were both behind the counter, standing almost in each other's shadow. They slumped visibly on recognising her, the tension leaving them.

"Anne!" Herman smiled. He was the older of the pair, perhaps forty, slightly built, already starting to grey. At his shoulder Carl's smile was more strained. His left eye was blackened, his cheek bruised too.

As Yute followed in behind Anne, and then Kerrol stooped to fit beneath the doorway, both men pressed even closer together, their fear renewed.

"These are friends of mine." Anne sought to calm them. "Yute and Kerrol. They're interested in books." She turned to the pair she'd named her friends, though in reality they didn't even qualify as customers, not having made any purchase yet. "This is Herman, and this is Carl. They own the shop. But they're not Webers. That was the founder. He died a long time ago and his son sold the place to Herman." She realised that she was babbling and stopped. The image of Kerrol swinging a man from each hand returned to her.

The two owners stepped apart with a hint of reluctance. It was Carl who normally manned the counter, and Herman was more often to be found among the aisles, rearranging the stock. But clearly the attack had unsettled them. Anne had never quite understood what it was that singled the pair out for the town's disapproval. Her grandfather wouldn't talk about it and even seemed to share some of the same sentiment, though at a much lower level than those who spat at Carl in the street when he ran errands. People said the pair were too close. But Anne thought if you found a friend you could really trust, then that's exactly what you should do—keep them close.

"You had trouble." Kerrol approached the counter, making both men look like children. He touched his eye.

Herman shook his head. "The town's strung too tight. Something's going to give. It's going to be worse than a window or two. I think they're going to kill someone. I really do. They're saying something big's coming tonight. That's the rumour anyway. Lots of brownshirts in from Weiden. Activists in the beer halls . . ." He shook his head, and then his whole body gave an involuntary shudder. "How may I help you, gentlemen?"

"I'm not sure." Yute wandered to the nearest shelf and ran white fingers slowly across the offered spines. "I'm hoping it will become clear. The library never sends us anywhere without a reason. But those reasons can be obscure. Sometimes nothing more than coincidence." He followed the line of books, gaze sliding across titles and author names.

Anne shot an apologetic look at Herman. Yute seemed to be a bit of a mystic, and she was beginning to wonder if Regensburg or indeed any other library had really sent him to her town on this day.

For his part, Kerrol returned to the door and peered out of the small glass panes arrayed in the arch above it. "Forgive me, but I've really seen enough books to last a lifetime. I'm more interested in what's out there. I wonder if there will be snow? I'd like to see snow next. Or maybe a tornado. Do you have those here?"

The ghosts of our past dog each step but it's the future that haunts us.
Present and Correct, *by Colonel R. Sanders*

CHAPTER 3

Livira

S he fell through a night not made of darkness. The others plummeted beside her, a constellation of falling stars, all of them pitched into the void through the portal opened by Hellet's blood.

A flash of sight, gone too swiftly to register. It felt like falling through a gossamer web, or the thinnest of pages. Another barely sensed impact, and another, each with its too-brief flash of vision. Three more, ten more, scores, each barrier feeling a little firmer, glimpses of sky, grey ground, tall trees, white-topped waves, an endless desert of stones.

Livira understood they were falling through places, times, maybe even worlds. A flat greyness tore at her as she punched through it, a mountain range shuddered, almost managing to keep her as her velocity made a hole.

The next one stopped her entirely. She jerked awake from a dream of falling and found that she *had* fallen. She lay on her back, the others close at hand, each startling from their own nightmare.

Yolanda got to her feet beside Livira. Despite having lain flat out on the dusty ground, the child's white hair, white skin, white tunic, and white leggings showed no trace of dirt, even her shoes were pristine. All around them the refugees who owed their lives to Yute were beginning to stand. Despite their debt to Yolanda's father, they had followed her rather than him. Or more accurately they had followed Livira when she tied her colours to the white child's mast.

Livira was the last but one to stand. Seera Leetar only managed to reach her knees, and knelt there, head bowed, still shaking with grief. Livira knew she should also be floored by Meelan's death. The fact that she could stand felt like a betrayal of their long friendship and brief intimacy. And yet she had known tragedy and hurt on this scale before, and now, like then, she found she could push it from her mind, leaving only a raw wound, filled with the knowledge that the sorrow would dog her until she stopped running, and then it would have its way with her.

"We're home!" It was Acmar who said it. Acmar who Livira had barely had time to register among Yute's band, let alone speak to.

She turned to face the direction in which Acmar and most of the others were now staring. The bloody edge of the sun made lumpy silhouettes of the dome-like huts. The structures huddled together for company amid a mean scattering of crops, black against dawn's red warning. Livira could hardly distinguish one dwelling from the next, but she knew her own in an instant even after half a lifetime's absence.

Her eyes sought and found the rickety windlass above the well. The refugees all stood in silence for a long moment, broken only by the cry of the baby in their midst. A mother reached for her child's hand.

"I tried to aim for a place that I knew," Yolanda said, "but it seems the majority steered us here."

Livira understood. Of their number, a dozen, more than half, were from the Dust, and six, including herself and Acmar, were survivors from this settlement. "How is it still here?"

All of them, even the city dwellers who had probably never ventured from Crath's walls into the dry peril of the Dust, were walking slowly towards the small collection of buildings. Jella and her fellow bookbinders, Sheetra and Nortbu, followed them.

"No dogs," Livira muttered. The dogs should be barking at the approach of strangers. Silent during the day, the hounds were essential for the crops' survival during the nights.

Acmar, reaching the first of the jarra plants, bent his broad back to touch the leaves. He pulled back his arm and stared at his fingers in puzzlement, then tried again. This time he snatched his hand away with an oath. "It's bewitched!"

Livira understood in that moment. "We're ghosts." The miracle wasn't that the settlement was still here. It was that Livira and the rest of them had fallen back through hundreds of years to a time when the settlement still existed. She raised her voice. "You can't touch anything here, Acmar. None of us can. The people here won't see or hear us."

Even as she spoke, a figure emerged from the blackness of the nearest hut. Just from the shape of her, the way she moved, Livira recognised the old woman. Ella, whose clever fingers had defied age to keep on working the wind-weed, right up to the day that the canith came and ended her along with so many others. Livira had called them sabbers back then—"the enemy." The small band that destroyed her life in this place had held at least two of Evar's distant ancestors, and for a while it had been hard for her to rid herself of the belief that their crime ran through his veins. Now though, the sudden memory of him, stick-shot and bleeding out his life-blood, eclipsed her vision. He'd gone where she couldn't follow.

"Livira!" Breta, who had been almost a baby when they took her from the settlement and who was now barely into her teens, helped Livira back to her feet. Livira hadn't even known that she'd fallen to her knees.

"I'm all right." Livira wiped her stinging eyes. Benth had carried little Breta across the Dust when her legs failed her, and Acmar had carried Gevin. But Benth was dead, a victim of Crath's hungry industry, and Gevin . . . Livira could hardly bring herself to think of Gevin. She'd left him in hell, half-eaten by darker appetites than she had ever thought men might entertain.

Hypnotised, the refugees moved slowly towards the settlement, following Acmar. Those who had been captured when the canith raided reached the huts first, others from the Dust behind them, the city people almost last to go. Only Yolanda and Livira lagged behind the city-born.

A lone ball of wind-weed, no bigger than a fist, blew between Livira and the white child. They stood, watching the others go.

"We can't take them with us," Livira said. "I don't know where we're going but it's no place for babies and children."

"You and I were both children when we entered this war," Yolanda said. "By some reckoning, I still am."

Livira didn't buy that last part. Yolanda had bathed in strange timestreams. Whatever lies her body might tell, her mind was old. "I don't care about that. I want them safe, or you're on your own. And I think you need me."

Yolanda shrugged. "You're the author of the weapon with which Jaspeth intends to end the library. It would be easier to defeat his plans with your help. This is a war fought by proxies and Irad appears to have fewer of us than his brother does."

New figures were emerging from the huts' dim interiors. Soft cries of hurt and wonder went up from Acmar, Breta, and the others who had once made this place their home. Livira, knowing that she should not, let the same fascination draw her forward.

At Teela's hut she found her aunt already dressed and sharpening her hoe. She looked good, less stern than Livira remembered, the steel gone from her dark hair. Back in the hut someone was moving—a stumble—a fall!

"Cratalac shit!" Her uncle's legs waved in the air as he lay on the bed finishing the job of hauling his trews on.

Livira remembered her uncle, though dimly. He vanished in the night the year before the storm took her mother.

"Mother . . ." The force that swung Livira around felt external. Like magnetism taking command of the compass needle. She walked towards the place her mother had lived. To where there had been a family with Livira at its centre. She skirted Trayvon's hut, rounded the curve of the largest hut, where Kern, their headman, kept home with two wives and several children. Acmar sat outside that door, head on his knees, his weeping shielded by both arms, betrayed only by the quaking of his shoulders. A small boy chased a chicken close by. And the boy was Acmar.

"You shouldn't go." Yolanda had followed Livira. "Some things are best forgotten."

"I don't forget." Livira turned on the girl. They stood just yards from the hut—the home—where Livira was born into the world and given her first name. Her mother would be there, perhaps already shelling beans, her fingers crimson. Livira would see herself as a baby in the crib, or at her mother's breast, or crawling in the dirt, exploring everything, tasting the sour world into which she had been delivered. She knew now that the dust surrounding them was the stuff into which every past triumph of mankind had been pounded. Glorious civilisations pulverised by their own hubris, wrecked by the seeds of violence that they bore within them, and that technology could not erase.

Livira turned to meet Yolanda's pink-eyed stare. "Isn't memory what we're fighting for? The library is the world's memory? But you're telling me I should turn away here?"

"It's important that there is a memory, and that it *can* be visited. That doesn't mean that every memory should be returned to, any more than the existence of a library means you should read every book in it. Exercise discretion. I've walked enough of my own past to know it to be a path that will cut you. Even the softest recollection can conceal a blade, if only for the fact that it is gone, and those moments will never be yours again."

Livira glanced in the direction of her home, looked at Acmar then went to stand beside him, setting a hand to his quaking shoulder. "We need to get them somewhere . . ." She wanted to say "safe" but the place they were in wasn't dangerous to ghosts. ". . . somewhere they can live. This isn't their fight."

"It's everyone's fight," Yolanda said, looking up at Leetar as she came to stand, red-eyed, beside Livira.

"That's what people in wars always say." Livira shook her head. "Whatever happens with the library and however doomed this world is on the grand scale, there's still time to live out good lives." She looked at the settlement hunched around them. "People lived them here. They weren't happy all the time, but they laughed, there were games, they loved, children grew. I was loved. And yes, dammit, I want to see that, even if it makes me cry. So, send the others who haven't chosen this fight somewhere better."

"You overestimate what I can do."

Livira had already turned her back though, and her feet brought her to the open doorway of her mother's hut. The small dome was dried mud bricks, layered in a reducing spiral to a smoke hole that a tall man could reach without going to tiptoes. Her mother sat a little way within, the morning sun lighting her to her neck, face still shadowed. Crimson hands moved almost too quickly to follow, the action ingrained even now in Livira's muscle memory, shelling beans. The jarra bean had three skins to protect its moisture from the Dust's endless thirst. The innermost one was toxic and unless it was completely removed the bean stew would induce vomiting and diarrhoea.

Drawing closer Livira saw her mother's face for the first time since she was six years old, and the storm had taken her. For a moment Livira didn't understand why she couldn't breathe. The sound that burst from her was as ugly and raw as it was involuntary and unexpected. Like Acmar she found herself on her knees. The grief for Meelan Livira had been able to wall off though she knew it would find her later and hurt her all the more. This emotion was primal, like a fist striking up from within, and Livira could no more stand against it than she could stop her heart from beating.

She had thought that she might study her mother as an object of curiosity, then step by her to peer at her infant self. Instead, she crawled away, passing Leetar who stood bewildered but wise enough to stay silent. Once out of sight of her mother Livira rose, standing to continue her retreat, bent around a child's pain, bowed beneath the weight of a lifetime's unspoken words.

By the time she reached Yolanda, Livira had straightened herself and dried her face, walking now with the careful steps of someone cradling a wound. The girl offered no comment and an echo of Yute's compassion could be seen in her face, though perhaps she was still too young to inherit her father's seemingly all-encompassing care.

"We need to get them out of here," Livira said.

"I can't make portals." Yolanda raised a white hand to forestall what would have been unreasonable objections from Livira. "But"—and now she rose from the ground, flying just as Livira and Evar had learned to do as ghosts—"in this form our motion is not limited to up and down, or through. We can move in time too. Though it is more difficult."

"How difficult?"

"It requires something to push off," Yolanda said. "If I push the rest of you forward to a point where you will regain your present, it will push me much further backwards into the past."

"We'll do it together, if you show me how."

"You know how," Yolanda said. "You wore the white. You just need to remember."

Leetar, who had been following Livira silently, a ghost's ghost, spoke up behind them. "I want to go with you. There's nothing for me now. I don't know how to start . . ."

Livira opened her mouth to say that it was too dangerous, that Leetar didn't understand what she would be letting herself in for. She closed it. Even Livira didn't know what she was letting herself in for. And Leetar had seen the danger. A huge mechanical wonder had crushed her brother beneath an assistant. "All right."

"Should we tell them?" Leetar said. "The others?"

Livira looked out across the settlement and in that moment saw Jella, who was standing some way off between two huts, turn and stare in her direction. Gentle Jella, who only wanted peace, and had not long ago had only a rapidly failing door between her and a raging canith warrior. Jella would never forgive her for what she was about to do. Never forgive her for saving her.

Livira looked to Yolanda. "Can you send them somewhere good?"

"I can only send them some-when. They'll still be here. Right in this spot. Just like we will be. And good times are few and far between. In fact, in most of the better times, this spot is underwater. But I'll do my best."

"There's a baby." Livira stressed the word.

"I'll do my best."

"Should we tell them?" Leetar repeated. Jella was walking towards the three of them now, with purpose.

Livira stared at the dusty ground, seeking wisdom, or at least inspiration. She could tell them, but they would want her to go with them. Or they would refuse to go. Those that didn't know her would think she was using them somehow. Those that did would want to help her and want her help. Jella would want to help her. Already the guilt was eating at her, and yet all she'd ever done was try to save them. She could go with them, leave Yolanda to the quest. Spend her life shepherding the refugees through whatever future Dust they arrived in. As if not having abandoned them to the canith hordes made her somehow responsible for their survival forevermore. As if she were somehow more able to carve out a life for them than Acmar or Breta or any of the others were.

"No." Livira met Leetar's bloodshot eyes. Where dirt and panic had failed, grief had dented the girl's seemingly impervious beauty. It made her more real, closer to someone Livira could like.

Jella was almost on them. Livira raised her hand, asking her to wait, and Jella did, confusion in her eyes.

"Don't leave me," Leetar hissed. They'd trained her to be a diplomat, to falsify smiles, to flatter and deceive. But sorrow had pared all that away, leaving honesty. "I need to be with people who knew him. Who loved him."

Livira met Leetar's honesty with her own. "I did love him. I don't know what he would want me to do. But I'll take you with me as far as you can go." She turned to face Yolanda. "How do we do this?"

CHAPTER 4

Livira

Yolanda did the tricky part. With the eye of her mind, she found each of the refugees among the settlement and set her will upon them, making phantoms of the world and reality of the phantoms. Livira did, she believed, most of the pushing. She felt herself a blunt weapon wielded by Yute's daughter to strike the necessary blow. The impact sent more than a dozen people skipping through the years towards the day that Yolanda had chosen for them. In reaction Yolanda, Leetar, and Livira were sent hurtling back into a past even more distant than the one in which they'd found themselves. And true to Livira's word, they pulled Leetar with them. And though it tore at Livira, they sent Jella with the rest, her last expression one of disbelief.

The world changed around them. The sun and moons blurred through the sky, peeling back the days so swiftly that the heavens became a vague eternal twilight. Storms came and went, averaging to a haze of dust constantly in the air. The rare rains fell without pause, joined into a single parsimonious drizzle that slightly dampened the air.

Huts rose and fell, rose and fell. The settlement expanded and contracted like a beating heart, and then without warning was gone, the well taken with it. Trees resurrected themselves from the ground. Ancient tapwoods springing erect before starting to diminish. Grass hurled itself across the Dust, swallowing it in an instant. Trees continued to appear full-grown, only to be sucked into the ground as if the earth itself were inhaling them. Suddenly they too were gone, and the distant surface of a lake rippled high above, changing the quality of the light.

Twice the lake came and went. A road snaked past. A forest devoured it. The sun slowed its passage, light and dark blinking by faster than heartbeats. And with a jolt Livira staggered back, passing through the trunk of a tree before she caught herself.

It was daytime. Everything around her was green and soft and warm and moist and full of motion and the song of birds. If Livira had never seen the Exchange, she would have wept to see the forest. Even with that experience to steady her she stood in wonder. The Exchange had been order to this chaos. This was wild, untidy, crowded, cluttered, truly alive in a way that nothing Livira had seen had ever been.

"Where are we?" Leetar asked.

"Ten yards from the hut I was born in," Livira said. She still saw Jella's face and the first sense of betrayal dawning across it. But Livira had saved her. She had saved one of her classmates. Arpix lay in the worst kind of trouble, Meelan was dead, and Carlotte lost. But Jella she had saved.

"Ten yards and the best part of two millennia." Yolanda stepped between them. "When you travel through the blood of an assistant—or more generally, when the library is involved, as it is with any journey through the Exchange, your first question shouldn't be where, or even when, but why. The library associates, it organises. Not at the basic levels. It leaves the users to build shelves and arrange the books upon them. But at the higher levels it creates coincidence and brings together things which have consequence for each other." The girl turned, exploring the undergrowth as if a clue might be concealed there. "We chose the direction of travel, but there is a reason we landed on this specific day. I can almost guarantee it."

"What are we going to do?" Leetar asked, eyeing the shadowed forest with suspicion.

"We could go and see if the city is where we left it," Livira said.

"You can find your way through all . . . this?" Leetar waved her arm at the green confusion pressing from every side.

"Up is a good start." Livira rose smoothly through leaves and branches, reaching clear air within a few moments. An undulating carpet of treetops stretched away in all directions, but the mountains, seemingly as impervious to time as the library itself, could be seen in the distance.

Yolanda appeared below Livira, towing Leetar by one hand. Leetar's astonishment had shaped her mouth into an O and appeared to have overwhelmed any sense of fear.

"Curious." A break in the arboreal pattern beneath her toes snagged Livira's attention. She angled herself towards it.

Yolanda brought Leetar to Livira's side. "A literal trail of destruction . . ."

A path had been forced through the forest below by something, or somethings, that were larger than the gaps between the trees would permit. Anything from saplings and bushes to trees whose trunks were as wide as Livira had been broken, uprooted, or otherwise trampled. The path wound around forest giants and left islands of larger trees midstream, but generally proceeded with a focused intent.

Livira descended to draw level with the forest's upper limits and began to follow the path, taking her direction from the way the trunks lay. As she flew, she tried to imagine what had wrought such damage. It wasn't the work of some great mechanism. She couldn't see wheel tracks or the marks of saws and axes. And it looked to have been done some days ago. The greenery on snapped trees had wilted, but not yet become brown, let alone dried and fallen from the bough.

They followed the trail down a long slope, across a small river, and to a cleared area where a village lay in ruins amid trampled fields of crops. The devastation wasn't limited to the buildings. Many inhabitants must have run, forewarned of the approach, but some had chosen to defend their homes or been too infirm to leave. It was impossible to tell which since the bodies lay scattered, the pieces too small and flyblown to tell young and hale from old and frail.

The path of demolished trees continued on the south side of the clearing, heading off in a new direction as if the village had been the intended destination and following its erasure a new target had been selected.

Livira shook her head, shivering despite the warmth of the day. "We're days behind. We're not going to catch up in a hurry." Slowly at first, then faster, shrugging off the imagined bonds of gravity she rose into the air. If challenged she would have claimed to be seeking perspective and a broader view. The truth was that she just wanted to get away from the mangled homes and the remains of the dead.

The heights offered nothing familiar save the mountains. A change of weather had given the Dust new clothes and rendered it unrecognisable.

"Come on." Livira led off towards the valley in which Crath City would one day lie and whose rocky arms had cradled many other cities before Oanold's ancestors started piecing the rubble back together. Thinking of the city pushed out images of the broken corpses behind her and re-placed them with thoughts of Arpix, Neera, and Salamonda in the king's keeping. The horror of it suddenly spiked through Livira, causing her to drop a dozen yards, tumbling, before her conviction caught her once more. She reminded herself that she wasn't wasting time while the three of them suffered. Technically, they had not yet been captured and would not be for thousands of years yet.

Yolanda and Leetar caught up with Livira as she regained lost height. Leetar was still being towed, lacking the belief required to keep herself aloft. Treetops blurred beneath them as they arrowed towards the moun-tains faster than a galloping horse. Livira found herself wondering whether any limits were placed upon her in this form, or if the only bounds were her expectations and imagination. She had discovered flight by herself but was shamed that she had had to be shown that time was just another path to walk, another direction to take.

The world around her now seemed every bit as real as the smoke-filled reading room she'd left behind, but somehow the gift of godlike powers not only reduced it in scale but made it seem less important. The fact that she could span vast distances in inconsequential amounts of time, that she could soar to the heavens and see kingdoms spread below her like a map, that she could pass unseen, walk through walls, spy in the mightiest of halls . . . all of it sucked the importance out of the place. It made it into a toy.

Livira gained still more height, soaring so that the trees merged into one vast greenness and the limits of the forest came into view. She could see that no city sat where Crath City and its predecessors had laid their foundations only to burn time and again. However, before the mountains' feet, the forest surrendered to patchwork farmland, and on a plateau only a few miles to the south sat a citadel with the skirts of a city reaching out from the cliffs' base.

Livira angled herself down towards this unexpected metropolis. The plateau had been named Arthran in her time. Livira recalled the fact only from a map that hung in Deputy Ellis's office. Of the civilisation that once grew there, she knew nothing.

As she descended, the citadel opened itself to her, more of a walled city within a city than some fortress squatting above the masses. Rooftops resolved into buildings, flecks of green became gardens, lines broadened into streets, dots became carriages, horses, and people.

Despite being more city than fortress, the place appeared to have been recently called to arms. Powerful ballistae had been positioned at regular intervals on the citadel walls, with smaller ones stationed on every available tower and rooftop. Had she approached on foot, Livira might not even have noticed it. The oversized crossbows appeared to be aimed at defending the populace from the sky. Even knowing herself to be invisible and insubstantial Livira knew a moment's fear at the thought of one of those spears being launched her way.

She alighted in a small square off a crowded thoroughfare. Yolanda and Leetar dropped down behind her.

A woman walked by in dazzling colours, and unknown cloths. Livira stared in wonder. "What now?" The options seemed endless, but also somehow pointless. They couldn't touch anything. They could achieve nothing. To act they needed to find the present, their own particular "now," but that lay further away than ever—the price paid for having sent the others forward.

"In my experience it's simply a matter of waiting," Yolanda said. "Having a look around often helps too."

Livira had too much going on in her head to enjoy the exploration of a long-dead city. Malar had died. Meelan had died. Evar had been mortally wounded and then stolen away by his treacherous brother. Arpix, Salamonda, and Neera had been captured by cannibals . . . She drew a deep breath. None of that would happen for over a thousand years. Time was on her side, even if her heart wholly rejected the idea and even her brain couldn't properly accept it.

At any other time Livira would have chased her curiosity. Questions would lead her. But for once she had no questions. In one stroke Livira saw how power corrupted her. She had been given gifts—gifts to see more deeply into more lives than she could ever have imagined, to sample more views, more countries and cultures . . . hell, she could fly to the moons. And yet that power wouldn't bring her closer to the people of this time, it wouldn't make her care more. Instead, it had, even at this early stage, added a distance between her and those still bound by the laws of the place. She could neither touch the world around her nor be touched by it. She might be able to walk through walls, but there was another wall, an invisible one that stood between her and everything she would see, and that wall she couldn't breach.

To Livira's surprise it was Leetar who led off, skirting around a passing couple, turning left at the next corner. Livira followed at a slower pace, not moving to avoid anyone, overlapping strangers here and there, momentarily drenched in images of their lives, washed over by whatever emotion held the heartbeat before they were through and gone. She walked through the corner, glimpsing the interior of a house before emerging into the street.

None of it mattered to her.

Leetar followed the currents of the citadel and Livira followed Leetar, Yolanda trailing. Livira had only been in two cities, and this one was not like either of them. The differences would have fascinated her another day. She would have remarked upon and questioned everything from the architecture to the fashions, from the foodstuffs to the temple awnings. Today she passed by oblivious, wrapped too tightly in her own affairs to worry about the arbitrary point in history into which they'd dropped.

It wasn't until they entered a grand square lined with tall and many-balconied buildings that Livira pulled up short. Two huge statues stood at the centre of the square amid a collection of smaller, but still large, heraldic beasts in stone. A king fully as tall as the five-storey buildings bordering the square, and reaching to his shoulder, a queen.

Livira frowned. "She . . . seems . . ." Livira rose smoothly from the flag-stones, gaining height for a better view. She drew level with the rooftops, then dropped like a stone as the surprise hit her.

"Fuck me . . ." Livira picked herself off the ground and stared up at the stone faces lit by the morning sun. "That's Carlotte!"

The true value of freedom is revealed only in its absence. It is a structural ingredient whose removal takes with it the colour, taste, and substance of life. A similar effect is observed in gluten-free cakes.

Baking to Win, *by Joshue Shoe*

CHAPTER 5

Arpix

A rpix had no memory of the time between being dismissed from Irad and Jaspeth's audience within the Mechanism and coming to his senses amid the book towers of the adjoining library chamber. His waking view was of his own heels dragging across the floor. It had taken him a while to figure out that the source of his motion was the two large, ill-smelling soldiers. Each had an arm under one of his. He tried to twist free and, in failing to do so, reached the understanding that his wrists had been bound behind him.

Arpix had still been woozy, his thinking eclipsed by the mother of all headaches, when the soldiers' retreat across the chamber had been interrupted by yells, stick-shot, and the screams of the dying. Arpix hadn't seen the canith, but it had seemed that Clovis and all her brothers must have attacked, judging by the chaos and the death toll, which he later overheard to stand at twenty-one.

In the end the canith were driven back without Arpix seeing any of them. At least one was reported shot. Arpix hoped that was a lie, but if true he hoped it was neither Clovis, Evar, nor Kerrol, in that order.

Before long Arpix had found himself back in the chamber where he'd first encountered Yute's group and later been joined by Livira as she fled the very menace that had now snared him in turn.

Standing on his own feet, and being hustled along the aisles, Arpix was dismayed to catch glimpses of Neera and Salamonda. He tried to call out to Salamonda, wanting to know who else had been captured, but the guards shoved him forward, and he lost sight of her amid the crowding troops and narrow spaces.

Arpix stumbled on, wondering who else had fallen into Oanold's hands. It couldn't be everyone because the canith had attacked and the soldiers had been retreating at speed. It seemed they must have Livira though, or else why had Evar led his family against stick-fire with just one sword between them?

Livira had said the king's troops, unprepared to suffer the misery of hanging on to life inside the centre circle, had fallen to cannibalism. It had sounded both awful and unbelievable. But here, among the stinking, gore-splattered soldiers, beneath the cold hunger of their gaze, he felt it to be true. He'd never had much meat on him, even before the slow starvation of the plateau, but he feared for Salamonda who remained considerably sturdier than he did, and for Livira's friend Neera, who although slim, had enjoyed Yute's century-spanning pilfering from Salamonda's kitchen.

Arpix's concerns rapidly became much more personal when, still with bound hands and with the fresh addition of a gag, he found himself surrounded by three soldiers who proceeded to beat him whilst joking about "tenderising the meat." The fact that he was a head taller than the largest of his tormentors seemed to antagonise them. Arpix had never been punched before, not even as a child by another child. He was astonished how much it hurt. He wanted to reason with them, but even if he hadn't been gagged an early punch took all the air from his lungs, and the ensuing pain removed any ability to put words in order.

Blows landed from random directions, not so swiftly that one blurred into the next. They gave him time to feel each one. Letting the fear build. Letting him wonder just how badly they would injure him. A heavy fist slammed into his ribs and Arpix reeled back, crying out around his gag. How long would it last? It seemed to have taken forever already.

"Leave that man alone."

Arpix straightened painfully to see a figure almost as tall and narrow as himself approaching down the aisle, seated soldiers moving their legs out of his way. Even through tear-filled eyes Arpix recognised the man—Lord

Algar had come to his rescue and Arpix felt ashamed of how deeply grateful he was.

"Take his gag off." Algar stopped a yard short of them in his soiled finery, frowning slightly. "This is no way to treat a librarian."

Arpix winced as a bearded soldier yanked the gag away.

"What's your name, young man?"

"A-Arpix." Despite the unconvincing nature of Algar's concern, Arpix felt like crying. He could taste his own blood, and something was wrong with the vision in his left eye.

"Well, Arpix." Algar gave an unsettling smile. "I want you to tell me all about this book." The poorly bound volume he lifted into view was one that Arpix had never seen before.

"I . . ." The truth, Arpix felt, would deliver him back into the hands of the three soldiers and the continuation of their fun. Arpix had always been a great believer in the truth, but with his many sources of pain only now beginning to divide themselves into individual hurts, that faith was wavering. "Could I see it more closely?"

Lord Algar held it in front of Arpix's face, eyes narrowing.

Arpix searched in vain for a title or an author, but the covers were worn smooth by time. The faintest pattern persisted but he could make out no more than a circle occupying most of the front, filled with barely visible lines squiggling this way and that. "If I could . . ." He tried to bring his wrists out from behind him. ". . . look inside?"

Algar glanced at the bearded guard and gave a slight nod. "It came from one of your colleagues. Young like you, though not one of us." He set a conspiratorial hand to Arpix's shoulder as the guard untied him.

Arpix brought his arms forward and rubbed at both aching wrists. He sensed he might be being offered a chance to remove himself from the menu. "Livira had it?"

"The duster, yes."

"Where is—"

"She's safe enough and not far away. But what I'm interested in is what you can tell me."

Verification. Arpix was familiar with the concept. Librarians preferred to get the information in one book confirmed by a second source. Better still, many unrelated sources. Oanold's forces must have recaptured Livira and be holding her close by. If what Arpix said contradicted Livira's story, she would feel the consequences. The trouble was that Arpix didn't know what she'd said and didn't know anything about the book in the first place.

"Can I see inside?" Arpix moved his hand towards the book.

Algar drew it back. "If I give it to you, and you do anything I don't like, I'll have to ask Jons here to break both your arms. He's recently had a sword stuck through him and is in very poor humour." The aristocrat managed to wrap a diplomat's expression of regret around the bluntness of his threat.

Arpix glanced nervously at the soldier by Algar's right shoulder, a grizzled veteran, seamed by old scars, chest blood-soaked. His fatal-looking wound had presumably been healed by the centre circle; the pale eyes with which he regarded Arpix gave the lie to the grey in his short-cropped hair—this was a dangerous man.

Arpix took the book in trembling hands and opened it somewhere in the middle. He saw immediately that the pages were all of slightly different sizes and made of a wide variety of parchments and paper. The comfortable sprawl of Livira's quillwork greeted him. This was Livira's book, the one that she'd been writing for years but that had always been scattered inside other tomes in the library, a cuckoo book securing each new page in the nest of some other volume. She must have worked fast to collect the leaves into one manuscript on the day that the library burned.

He'd opened the book at the start of a new chapter, or more accurately the beginning of one of the stories that Livira was always going to weave into a coherent whole but never had. "The Phantom Queen"—it wasn't one he'd ever heard her talk about. Though from what Evar had said during his stay on the plateau it might be that some of the book had actually been written by Livira whilst in the body of the assistant that had raised the canith children.

What strange fiction Livira might have created whilst in that timeless state Evar couldn't say, but a familiar name at the foot of the page caught his eye. "Carlotte . . ."

Arpix, rather than starting at the beginning, began with the line that had snared his attention. *"'It does look a bit like Carlotte.' Leetar squinted up at the giant statue."*

And without transition Arpix was there with them. A wide square, bordered by tall buildings with balconies at every level where figures, made tiny by the distance, looked out from their dining tables, their hanging gardens, their soirees, and their gatherings. The light was different here, bright but gentled by some quality of the air. Moisture! Arpix breathed it in. Not the arid mountain air he'd always known, not the wind that leached the water from your skin as it skipped by.

"It *is* Carlotte," Arpix said, staring up at the familiar statue. In his time on the plateau only the head and one shoulder emerged from the ground, and the prominent nose had been damaged. Here it was perfect. "It's her."

"How would you know?" Livira was standing to his left, looking down at him.

"I . . ." Any attempt at an answer was lost in the realisation that Livira was towering over him. He'd been so dwarfed by the two statues in front of him, Carlotte and some unknown king, that he'd not noticed how almost everyone in the square loomed above him too. It was as if he and Livira had reversed their traditional positions where he stood head and shoulders taller than she did. He looked down at himself. "What?" He was dressed all in white, and where his arms emerged, his skin was as pale as the turns of linen that wrapped his body.

"Yolanda?" Livira knelt beside him. "Are you sick?"

"N . . . no . . ." Arpix shook his head. Somehow, he was a child. The same white child that had joined them just after Livira had escaped the king. Yolanda had been the one who led them to the Mechanism and the audience with the library's founder, Irad, and with Jaspeth, the brother who opposed him.

"Why would anyone build a statue of Carlotte?" Leetar asked.

It felt like the wrong question. "How did Carlotte get to be queen?" Arpix asked in a girl's voice. Asking how he got to be the white child seemed an even more pressing question, but something kept Arpix from posing it. The situation felt somehow fragile, like a page that might easily be torn. Arpix had nothing good to go back to. He wanted to stay. And to do that, some instinct told him that he should follow the rules of the piece.

He'd always liked rules. At least as far as they represented a vessel that could hold compassion as well as the order that he always sought.

Livira shot Arpix a look. "How do you even know who Carlotte is?"

"I . . . uh." Arpix could feel the story slipping away from him. Though suddenly he wasn't sure it *was* a story. Certainly, Livira couldn't have written it as her normal self. She could never have anticipated the statue. And if she wrote it as the Assistant then maybe it was real, seen across time. Because there definitely *was* a statue of Carlotte out on the edge of the Dust. "Is this real? You're really Livira? Oanold's men didn't catch you again?"

"What?" Livira stared at him. "You know that he didn't. Thank the gods." She looked so sad and scared and horrified all at the same time that Arpix was sorry he'd asked.

"But he got Arpix, Salamonda, and Neera, and who else?"

"Only them." Livira set her jaw. "But it hasn't happened yet. It won't happen for thousands of years. And that's plenty of time to figure out how to save them."

The square was fragmenting around Arpix now. As if invisible spirits were individually removing bricks, flagstones, rooftiles, and speeding away with them. The story was slipping through his fingers. He didn't belong in it. He half saw Algar's single eye watching from a hawklike face.

"We need help now, Livira! It's happening now! They've got your book. I'm reading it!" Arpix could hardly hear the voice of the girl he was speaking through. A wind tore around him howling.

"Me . . . ism . . . it . . . oo the mec—"

And with a convulsive shock that saw him drop the book, Arpix was back in the library amid the foulness that King Oanold had made of it.

Too many lack the strength for kindness. Too few are brave enough for empathy.
And yet the weakness of anger leads to where the Iron Crosses grow.

Decoration, *by Frederick William the Third*

CHAPTER 6

Anne

While Yute walked the length of Weber's shelves, tutting quietly to himself, Anne spoke to Herman and Carl.

"You think we'll have trouble tonight?" She thought of the policeman. If a broken window was the worst she got she'd be lucky—that's what he said.

Herman nodded. His gaze flitted back and forth between Kerrol and Yute.

"Did . . . did you tell the authorities?" Anne nodded at the window. The worst had been cleaned up, but shards stood like teeth in the frame and small fragments glittered on the floor.

"Who do you think hit Carl in the face?" Herman seemed too frightened for outrage or sarcasm, and since on a good day he was the most sarcastic person Anne had ever met, it worried her more than the window.

A shadow came up to the door, then retreated rapidly, presumably seeing Kerrol's height at the last moment through the rippled glass.

"I'm losing you customers." Kerrol stepped back. "Is it normal to carry a stick with you here?"

"A walking stick?" Anne asked.

"I don't think so."

Yute came from the shelves with a book in hand. "Remarkable!" He lifted it up. "This is a book about flying machines! Do you have one?"

Herman and Carl exchanged glances. "Another book?"

"An aeroplane," Yute read the word carefully from the page.

"Uh." Herman shook his head. "I wish I could afford one and had somewhere to fly away to."

"Oh." Yute looked a little disappointed. "How large is this city? How many people live here?"

"The town has ten thousand people, sir," Herman spoke carefully now. "About that number."

Anne wondered, like Herman must be, if Yute were a spy. The talk these days was always of war, of the many enemies the Fatherland had. Be vigilant, the newspapers exhorted. But surely even the least competent of enemies wouldn't send as the agent of their espionage an albino and a giant, to ask such blatant questions.

"Three bookshops in such a place." Yute gazed at the open book in his hands, still fascinated by the diagram of an old biplane from the World War.

"Five." Anne couldn't stop herself. "There were five."

"Five!" Yute looked up. "And how far away is the library?"

"The local library is on Aspen Street, just on the other side of the bridge," Herman said.

Yute's white eyebrows elevated. "I mean *the* library. The big one."

"Which one, sir?" Herman mirrored Yute's confusion. "There's the scientific library at Regensburg. There's the state library in Nuremburg, but that's forty miles . . ."

Yute shook his head and set the aviation book on the counter. He rolled his neck as if preparing for some feat of strength then placed the tips of his fingers and thumbs together and raised his hands so that he could stare down in the cradle they made. For several long seconds he studied the empty space there, pink eyes burning with intensity.

"It's not there," Yute breathed, astonished. "I can't find it. Remarkable!" He approached Kerrol at the door. "I believe we're in an original cycle. A first-cycle world, Kerrol, think of it! All these wonders dragged from the dirt by force of will. They're populating the library for the first time without any help at all."

Kerrol studied the smaller man speculatively, his curiously blue eyes flicking to Anne and the two men behind the counter. For her part Anne was wondering if Yute were touched in the head, or perhaps a mystic of some kind, and that maybe there really was a travelling show nearby.

"Ah." Yute shook himself as if suddenly remembering his audience. "My apologies. Sometimes my mind wanders. I really would like to see the third bookshop you mentioned. What we're looking for must be there."

Anne frowned. "It's on the main street. You're more likely to find trouble there."

"Even so." Yute fished out the map she'd drawn him. "I feel we must call in on"—he squinted at Anne's handwriting—"Madame Orlova. Kerrol and I will find our own way. We don't want to lead you into any danger, Anne, you've been more than helpful."

Anne knew she should really let them go this time. If the pair didn't fall foul of a larger group of townsfolk or a band of stormtroopers, they would certainly be in trouble with the police soon enough. But she couldn't. It wasn't charity. She would like to claim it was, but this was curiosity, plain and simple. With winter looming, the dark days of autumn had been full of a fear both sharp and dull. Anne had been overtaken by the conviction that whilst her life should have been on the final climb towards womanhood, filled with new possibilities, she was in fact, along with her whole world, on an ever-steepening decline, and that somewhere ahead, not so distant that she couldn't sense its hunger, an abyss waited for her.

"I want to come." The words burst out of her, surprisingly emphatic. She did want to. Yute and Kerrol were the first strangeness in her life—the first *good* strangeness—in forever. The first thing that didn't feel as though it were rolling down that sensed but unseen slope. She couldn't just let them walk out of her knowledge, any more than she could just let them walk out of her grandfather's shop. They were still searching for something—but it felt as if she had already found a thing that she hadn't known she was looking for.

MADAME ORLOVA'S BOOKSHOP sat on the high street amid a score or more establishments, uniformed by the broad green and white stripes of their awnings. The legend above her shop read simply: *Journeys*. Perhaps anyone coming to the door in the hope of booking passage to some foreign shore might be disappointed, or perhaps, being of a less literal mind, they would recognise the sign-painter's truth.

Anne was aware of a great many eyes upon her companions as she led them at a brisk walk towards their destination. The comments that passed between those shoppers braving the November wind were neither whispered nor spoken behind hands, but Anne was happy to find they weren't being shouted at them or replaced with heavier projectiles than words.

She had thought they would make it to the shop without challenge. But within yards of Madame Orlova's door, a policeman emerged from Weiner's tobacconist's, almost colliding with Yute. Both Yute and Kerrol stepped neatly past the officer and continued towards Anne.

"Papers!" A single word, snapped at their retreating backs, cracking the air like a pistol shot and potentially just as deadly.

It's almost as easy to think of reasons why books should be banned as it is to think of reasons why they should not be.

Health and Safety in the Workplace, *by Vyene Custodian*

CHAPTER 7

Anne

P apers!"

The demand froze Anne mid-step. Kerrol, though he barely had clothes, must have papers. He couldn't have moved around the country without them. But whatever was written on them would surely prove insufficient on Amberg's most prestigious high street. If there was one thing policemen seemed to dislike more than crime it was things that they disapproved of but that weren't actually crimes. Neither Kerrol nor Yute fitted in any box that an officer of the law would find acceptable. Kerrol they would label as a vagrant or worse. And Yute . . . she had no idea what they would make of Yute.

Yute turned with a smile. Kerrol rotated to face the policeman more slowly, pensive.

"Your papers." The policeman extended his hand, jerking it forward like a threat.

"Certainly." Yute maintained his smile, rummaging in the inner pocket of his jacket. He drew forth a yellowing square of notepaper.

The policeman took it with a frown, turning to shield it from the breeze as he unfolded it. His frown deepened, furrows corrugating a broad forehead. He glanced back and forth between Yute and the paper, as if comparing him to his photograph. Hints of alarm began to claim his face. He straightened suddenly and brought his heels together as if he were a soldier on parade. "Thank you, sir!"

Yute took back what still looked to Anne like a page from a notebook, free of any writing and certainly not bearing official stamps or a recent photograph. "Thank you, Officer." He refolded the paper and returned it to his pocket before joining Kerrol and Anne. "This is our next stop, I presume." He gestured at Madame Orlova's windows, all set in beautifully carved frames amid a polished wooden shopfront.

Without waiting for an answer Yute passed by and went in. Kerrol, following close on his heels and nearly forgetting to duck, muttered, "Do I have papers too?"

"I'm sure you do," Yute replied. "Disguise, translation, these are all the gifts of our means of arrival. If you know what you're doing, they can be adjusted for maximum advantage. Temporary gifts, I must stress, hence the need to press on."

Anne followed the pair in, shutting the door behind them, sealing out November. As magical as she had once found her grandfather's shop, it was Madame Orlova's bookshop that Anne would aspire to if she were ever to go into the business in her own right. The place smelled of old leather, and comfort, and care. Its bookcases were not the shelves of a business, but of a rich man's private library, the oak ornamented at the corners and heights with flights of a carpenter's fancy, spires on this one, gargoyles on that, carvings that might on a larger scale wait atop some Gothic cathedral grinning at the weather, or nestle in the vaults, beyond the laity's curiosity, a reward shared only with the angels or masons daring such elevation to carry out repairs.

The tomes that weighed upon such shelves were themselves works of art, leather-bound, embossed in geometric patterns, the titles, authors, the numbers of the volumes all inlaid with gold foil. The works of polymaths like Goethe, philosophers like Kant, flights of fancy from the Brothers Grimm, anything and everything of quality from the last few centuries.

Ahead of her, Yute and Kerrol both drew in deep breaths, as if the air outside had been too thin for them and they had returned to the atmosphere of their native land. A rumble of approval ran through Kerrol's chest. Yute stood, turning, looking for something.

"She's at the back," Anne said. It seemed crazy to her, but Madame

Orlova kept her counter back out of sight of the door. With the value of her stock so much greater than that they shelved at Hoffman's, the old lady still relied on mere honesty to keep her from being robbed blind.

Anne followed Yute towards the back of the store, watching him with fresh eyes. His papers had set that policeman back on his heels. The reaction, the instant respect, or fear, did nothing to instil confidence in Anne.

Madame Orlova never failed to make new customers stop and stare. Many years previously, nature had taken a very different path with the infant Ingrid Orlova. Where others had followed the broad path trodden by their peers and predecessors, the baby Ingrid had grown in strange ways, leaving the familiar trail far behind her. No doctor that her family's wealth could summon was able to coax her back to the agreed route. Her head sat crooked on a hunchbacked body, the skull too large for her frame, too misshapen not to draw the eye with its strangeness. She resembled, the children said, some creature of myth, a hobgoblin, an ogre perhaps, a troll even. A kindly one, but still a monster for all that.

Her family had hidden her away, ashamed. Locked her away, if the rumour was true. But one by one the years had claimed them. The father first, then the mother, two brothers, two sisters. All of them certain to outlive the sickly and deformed child who had never made it past the school gates. And yet there they were, lining up beneath impressive tombstones in God's Acre, whilst Ingrid inched ever closer to inheriting it all.

And in the end, she outlasted her entire family. With the Orlov fortune in her name and nobody left to object to her freedom, she left the institute they had incarcerated her in and moved into the family mansion. She set up her shop before the World War had come, weathered the winds of conflict, and had run it ever since, not requiring that she profit from the enterprise, but unwilling to hide the face that God had given her. Requiring only that if you wanted to see it you would have to come into her shop, not merely gawk in through the windows.

Even as Anne took Yute to Madame Orlova's desk she wondered if she weren't leading a snake into the old woman's nest. Yute held some sort of authority, and it was authority that had been tightening a vice on the Jews ever since Anne could remember. The chancellor was, if anything, a still greater enemy of Madame Orlova. If she weren't too old to bear children, the authorities would already have let some butcher operate to ensure she never did. To hear Hitler talk, you would think that any day he might just order that the disabled and the mentally ill be shot.

It was madness, of course, but when that man began to rant on the wireless . . . Anne could almost see the spittle fly, and in those moments, he seemed capable of anything.

Anne found herself before the lady in question. "Madame—"

"Whatever it is, there's more of it here," Yute said to himself, hardly looking at the woman before him.

"More of what?" Kerrol asked.

Anne had been watching them both. Everyone reacted when they first saw Madame Orlova. She always thought that no other heartbeat would ever tell you more about a person than the one in which they laid eyes upon the old lady. Yute and Kerrol didn't even seem to notice her deformity. It wasn't a matter of self-control. That might be imposed in the next heartbeat out of a sense of decency. But in the first moment, the honest moment, there was always a mix of horror, sympathy, disgust, compassion . . . a host of emotions, the mix varying from person to person. Yute and Kerrol paid no more attention to the woman's unique appearance than they would to an unfamiliar flower or previously unseen breed of dog.

"More of what?" Madame Orlova echoed Kerrol.

"More . . ." Yute raised a white hand, rubbing his thumb across his fingertips as if judging the quality of a piece of invisible silk. ". . . magic."

The old woman smiled. "You're very kind to say so." She got up from her chair and came out from behind her desk. "I can see you are strangers to town. Please feel free to look around. Let me know if I can help you." She turned to peer up at Anne. "How is your grandfather, dear? Is he keeping well? Safe?"

"Safe" was the real question here. With so many immediate problems crowding into their lives, hardly anyone not inside the circles that had been so clearly drawn had time to consider the lesser issues of health and wealth.

"He's well, thank you, madame." Anne nodded her head, resisting the urge to curtsey. She had always curtseyed when she was a little girl—only to Madame Orlova though—she wasn't sure why. Perhaps it had started as a joke between them. But she was older now and certainly not any kind of princess. It felt these days as if half the town would spit if she came near them.

Anne stood with the old woman and watched the two men wander among the shelves. Kerrol was always visible and seemed more interested in the shop itself and the street outside than in the books. Yute, often lost behind the shelving, walked slowly, looking as if he might be in a mystic's trance, or listening to the finest music, swept along by the currents of an orchestra in full spate. He trailed white fingers across the spines, and when he paid attention to a book it was as if his hands had alerted him to its importance rather than his eyes.

Yute paused, turned, a compass needle drawn by some new pole. He removed three books, two more, setting them atop the opposite shelf. Anne glanced at Madame Orlova. The old woman's cautious bemusement had vanished, she stood transfixed, gnarled hands trembling at her sides. Yute reached in, fiddled as if with an obstruction, something slid aside. He withdrew a slim volume, a drab item with paper covers, bound like a collection of articles rather than a proper book.

"Helen Keller? Is this author known to you?"

Anne went cold. Was Yute, despite all appearances, a government inspector?

"I . . . I didn't know that was there," Madame Orlova stammered. Anne had never known the woman anything but confident and calm. It hurt to hear the fear in her voice.

"Please," Yute said. "Just tell me what you know."

It didn't sound like accusation or interrogation. It was possible he genuinely didn't know. A random person on the street was unlikely to have heard of the woman, after all. Anne swallowed. "She lost her sight and hearing as a baby and grew up blind and deaf. They say she would rage and attack anyone who touched her."

Yute's face softened in sympathy. Anne resisted the urge to trust him, although it was very late in the day for such sensible caution. Had Yute and Kerrol been working with the young policeman, the whole thing a ruse to gain her confidence? Interrogators often pretended to be sympathetic at the start—her grandfather had told her that.

Kerrol loomed at Yute's shoulder. "Anger would be a natural reaction to the frustration of such imprisonment." His blue gaze shifted from Anne to Madame Orlova. "The world is cruel."

"A silent world, and a dark one," Yute said. He raised the book higher. "And yet . . ."

"And yet a teacher found her, and she learned how to communicate without words." Anne had been amazed by the story when she read about the woman, but now, retelling it to strangers, it struck her with more force quite how astonishing it was. "She learned to read and to write in Braille, a language of touch."

"And such a wonder is hidden away?" Yute tilted his head as if puzzled.

"Banned . . ." Anne studied her shoes. "Some of it. She wrote against war."

Yute looked up from the cover. "Socialism?"

"That too." Anne met his gaze, feeling suddenly fierce. "Are you going to burn it?"

White eyebrows lifted in amazement. "Burn?"

"You can't tell me you don't know that's what's happening!" Anne found that she was shouting but suddenly she was past caring. "Who are you? You haven't dropped into Amberg from the sky! How can you wander around like you know nothing? And what he"—she flapped an arm at Kerrol—"did to those men . . . How is that possible?"

"I'm a librarian," Yute said, voice calm. "I don't burn or ban books. Were I ever to let personal distaste overwhelm me, the most I would do is unfavourably shelve the offending volume. And even that I would consider a failing of character." He stepped aside and gestured to Kerrol. "My companion has lived within a library for his entire life with the exception of the last few weeks. Setting fire to books would be a suicidal habit for him to possess."

"How . . ." Strength returned to Madame Orlova's voice. "How did you find that book? Is it what you were looking for?"

"It isn't." Yute shook his head. "It's one of the more important works in your shop, but it's not the reason we came." He turned to Anne. "Forgive me. Kerrol and I have travelled a great distance and any offence we give derives from our ignorance rather than our intent. Something called us here. I am trying to understand why."

"Maybe some tea would help?" Madame Orlova turned away and shuffled towards the door behind her desk. "Come. The samovar is hot. Or schnapps. I have schnapps if you prefer."

Living in the past is all we can ever do. The future has yet to be forged, and the now is gone too quickly for anyone to notice it. The only choice is how far to lag behind the quill tip as it records your story.

The Story of U, *by Pauline Retro*

CHAPTER 8

Livira

"We need help now, Livira! It's happening now! They've got your book. I'm reading it!"

The words were coming from Yolanda's mouth and the voice was hers, but someone else was speaking through her, Livira knew it.

The girl's pale lips writhed as if fighting to say more, but no sound escaped. Confusion filled her pink eyes.

"Don't let them take it to the Mechanism!" Livira couldn't even begin to imagine the harm it might wreak there. "Don't take my book to the Mechanism!"

Yolanda shuddered and looked around, suspiciously. Leetar watched the pair of them, wrapped in her own confusion.

"I am myself again." Yolanda patted her upper arms with her hands as if checking she wasn't lying.

"Are you all right?" Leetar came closer, reaching out tentatively as if the girl might be wounded somehow.

"Who was talking through you?" An awful thought seized Livira. "Was it Arpix?" Saying it out loud made the answer obvious. It had been Arpix, scared and begging for help. She knew exactly what sorts of terrors Oanold's camp held, and the thought of Arpix at the mercy of those monsters left her fighting not to be physically sick. "Get him back!"

"Get him back?" A rather put-out look managed to escape Yolanda's normal imperturbable façade.

"Yes! Let me speak to him again!"

"That isn't something I can do." The girl gave her a withering stare. "I felt the book at work. This is one of what I fear will be many dangerous side effects of the damage you've wrought."

"But we can still go back to when we left and save him?" Livira wanted to leave now. Whatever tricks time might be playing on her, the need felt too urgent to ignore until some more convenient day.

Yolanda shook her head. "Your friend has given you a new present. If you return to a time before he spoke to you, you will be a ghost. You can only have physical form from the moment that conversation ended. If he makes contact again the same thing will happen, and you will lose the ability to stop anything that has happened to him by that point."

Livira wanted to object but realised that she didn't understand enough to know what to object to. She paused, trying to wrap her thoughts around what Yolanda had said. Leetar just looked bewildered. "Each time he talks to me like he just did . . . everything that has happened to him is locked into the past. His past becomes my past. I can't go there."

"Except as a ghost to watch what has happened." Yolanda nodded. "Yes."

"Let's do what we're here to do and get back to where . . . to when I need to be." Livira returned her gaze to the statues at the centre of the square. What had happened to Yolanda had been so strange that it had managed to drag her attention from the possibly even stranger thing standing before them. "That's Carlotte!" She pointed at the queen. "My friend Carlotte, from the library." It hadn't been until she was level with the statue's face that Livira was sure of it. From the ground it was hard to tell, though there was still something very familiar about the nose, the hair, the shape of the jaw.

"Impossible." Yolanda still sounded distracted. "Whatever queen it represents must just look similar to your friend."

"It's her," Livira insisted, though her confidence wavered now the face wasn't immediately in front of her.

Yolanda shook her head. "It's difficult to get a good likeness in stone. Especially at that scale."

Livira continued to stare, her neck already uncomfortable from looking up at such an angle. It was true, she'd seen a number of very unconvincing statues, but better sculptors had produced work that looked as if a real person had been caught between moments and turned to stone. Though, she had to admit that she had never seen the live subject on whom those works were based . . .

"It's her. You said we were here, now, for a reason. This is too much coincidence not to be that reason."

"If she came to this time," Yolanda persisted, "she would be a ghost just as we are. How would anyone make a statue of a ghost?"

Livira's frustration spilled out and anger coloured her voice. "I'm not saying—"

"We could just go and see?" Leetar interrupted before Livira got into full flow. She had one arm extended, finger aimed at two vast bronze doors sitting atop a flight of steps on which guards in plumed helms stood to attention. "Whoever the queen is, she lives in there."

Livira shrugged. The palace Leetar had pointed out would be their best option. She gestured with an open hand for Leetar to lead the way.

Yolanda followed on after Livira. "They tend to make statues of people after they die."

"You don't know Carlotte. She'd want to see it for herself." Livira climbed the steps behind Leetar, all three of them passing unseen between watchful guards.

Livira opened her mouth to add what was both obvious and at the same time a revelation—namely that Carlotte must be married if she were queen. That she must be sharing her bed with a king. But as her lips parted, a sound like the cracking of the world ran through her, a knife of noise, as agonising in its volume as in its discordant sharpness. She felt immediately fractured, her mind in different places, too many images filling her eyes. Arpix bruised and bloody, head hung in defeat. Yute standing in some lesser library beneath an unwavering light, a slim, drab book in his hand, wonder on his face. Evar lying in darkness, his pale skin the only source of light, eyes closed, deathly still.

Her vision cleared slowly, other images of places and times she had known trying to claim a place, though none as vivid as those of Arpix, Yute, and Evar. Livira found herself lying on the steps, partly intersecting the stonework. She levered herself up wincing. "That really hurt!"

A white-faced Leetar got to her knees beside Livira. "I thought we couldn't be harmed. Not here. Not like we are."

"We can't." Yolanda corrected herself. "It shouldn't be able to happen." She got to her feet and directed her puzzled gaze at Livira. "It . . . it's almost like the damage your book does. But it can't be reaching us here. Not already?"

Livira found it hard to be guilty about her book. She didn't feel that anything she'd done by writing it or by following her curiosity into the Exchange had been deserving of such an outcome or overmuch censure. "I'm pretty sure of one thing. We won't find the answer out here on the steps."

Leetar took the hint. She glanced around at the guards, sharing Livira's sense of amazement at their indifference, then hurried on up the stairs. She stopped short at the great doors, glancing back for instruction. Livira simply took her arm and dragged her through.

"Oh, I didn't like that at all!" Leetar stood shivering in her stained finery, looking back at the door, and flinching away as Yolanda walked through it as though it were a trick of the light rather than tons of bronze and timber.

Leetar pulled herself together and led on. Livira trusted the girl's instinct to navigate the corridors of power even in a different nation and era. Leetar might be guessing, but those guesses would be more informed than any Livira or Yolanda might make.

The path to the king's court proved to be a straightforward one, following the broad corridor—that in any other circumstances Livira would have called a grand hall—from the imposing exterior doors to a pair of similarly huge but far more lavishly decorated doors at the far end. In the process they passed a dozen chambers, all of grand design and indulgently furnished, but of unknown purpose.

The far set of doors stood open, though guards in elaborate armour waited to interrogate anyone that approached. Beyond them a capacious throne room, with walls of white and gold, held nearly a hundred of what must be the citadel's most important people. Livira couldn't tell if they were aristocrats, part of the royal family, or merchants, but she could tell that all of them were eye-wateringly rich.

The size of the room meant that it wasn't crowded. The glittering courtiers mingled in groups. Musicians at the far end of the chamber entertained without their playing filling the space. And before a dais that supported two great thrones, one silver and one gold, a more favoured group of five spoke directly to the man on whose brow the crown rested.

Livira recognised the king from his statue. The sculptor had captured his features with rare skill, and little time seemed to have passed since completing the work, as the man appeared unchanged. The curling hair was brown and thick, the eyes sharp, intense, a light colour. The king was still young, closer to thirty than to twenty, but fresh-faced, not yet corrupted by the excess to which his station gave access.

"It's him!" Leetar said.

"It is," Yolanda agreed.

None of them needed to have seen the statue, nor for the man to be wearing a crown. Their eyes would have converged on his if he had been the pauper in the crowd, or the least remarkable of men, an average of his fellows, with no single feature to latch upon. Livira tried to understand it. The man was lit by a different light. As if the sun found him and him alone on a dull day. He seemed like a figure added to a painting at a later date, by a different artist, somehow at odds with everything around him, edged by a border that didn't quite match the larger scene.

Livira wove her way towards the dais, avoiding the courtiers. Her gaze kept returning to the empty throne beside the king's. Shouldn't Carlotte be sitting beside her husband, just as her statue stood beside his?

Yolanda and Leetar followed, Leetar exclaiming in alarm when she inadvertently discovered the unsettling effects of having someone walk through you. As she stood shaking off the thoughts and memories of the old aristocrat, and the man walked on with a shiver of his own, the king's head turned in their direction.

He raised a hand, and then, slowly, a finger on that hand. The lord addressing him faltered and fell silent. The king stood from his throne, looking from Yolanda to Livira to Leetar with a puzzled expression.

"We should go," Leetar hissed.

"Why?" Livira asked. "What's he going to do? Have the guards arrest us?"

"We *should* go," Yolanda said. "He shouldn't be able to see us. Such things are dangerous. Do not, under any circumstances, speak to him."

"You three!" The king approached the edge of his dais. He pointed at Yolanda. "Am I the only one seeing this?"

A silence rippled out across the room, snuffing conversations. The courtiers closest to the king exchanged glances and stiffened their faces against expression. The woman most directly in the line indicated by the royal digit dropped into a deep curtsey amid a billowing sea of plush blue taffeta. "Me, sire?"

"No! Not . . . you." The king shook his head, stepped from the dais, and advanced on Livira and her companions at a brisk walk.

Yolanda led off for the nearest exit at similar speed, her shorter legs necessitating a jog. Livira followed, unconvinced that an escape was necessary. The king was clearly the quickest path to Carlotte.

"Stop!" The sound of more rapid footfalls behind them prompted Yolanda into a run. Leetar gave chase, skirts flapping. All around the room courtiers stood immobile, faces paling, breath withheld, watching the king.

Livira gave a sigh and made to run after Yolanda, but a hand burst from her chest before she could. "Burst" was how it felt. "Emerged" would be more accurate as there was no broken skin, no blood, no shards of bone. She pulled free and raced after Yolanda.

"The wall!" Livira's shout was enough to steer Yolanda into the wall. A moment later darkness swallowed Livira too, and in the next pace she joined the other two on the far side in a different chamber.

Livira stood, panting, not from exertion but from the flood of images that the king's touch had nearly drowned her in. Carlotte's face was front and centre of many of them. And not just her face.

"Ewwww." Livira shook herself.

Yolanda looked up at her expectantly.

"You don't want to know. But she's definitely here."

The ballroom they'd found themselves in was almost as echoingly empty as it was echoingly large. A single servant on his knees had polished around a tenth of the inlaid wooden floor and worked diligently to enlarge the gleaming portion.

"We need to find your friend." Yolanda surveyed the chamber's exits.

Livira gestured for Leetar to lead them. "Where would a queen live?"

Leetar headed towards the main entrance, and with less confidence, took a series of left and right turns, leading them along a galleried corridor that looked out over the lush gardens of an internal courtyard. She paused midway beside an imposing oak door flanked by two guards.

Yolanda gave the door a speculative look. "Here?"

Leetar pushed through. The room beyond lay sumptuously decorated, with statuettes in silver and gold set in niches along the walls. A servant stood in front of a lectern, reading aloud from a large book. It sounded like a romantic tale of star-crossed lovers, though Livira didn't have much time to make her assessment.

"Down there." Leetar led along a door-lined passage towards the distant strains of music.

"Why didn't they invite the invisible queen to the ball?"

A loud, theatrical question reached out just as Livira passed the corridor's only open door. She paused to look.

"They knew she wouldn't show up!" The speaker, an extremely short man in the motley of a court jester glanced around the empty room then smiled as if acknowledging applause. He continued with admirable gusto, "Why did the invisible man run away?" A quizzical glance around the chamber. "He was *a fade*!"

"Ugh." Livira shook herself and hurried after the others. The musicians in the beautifully appointed chamber at the corridor's end were likewise playing to nobody in particular, though with great skill.

The melody followed them as Leetar led to an ornate doorway, and through it into a bedchamber, where, atop a perfectly made four-poster bed, a woman lay sprawled face down in her slumbers, the hard-used folds of an expensive blue dress spreading around her.

Leetar turned towards Livira. "Is that her?"

The woman on the bed lifted her head from the sumptuous pillows that had nearly smothered her. Eyes bleary with sleep fixed on Livira and a heartbeat later a screaming ball of angry silk launched itself at her.

Reunions come in many shapes and sizes. The questions vary: Who got fat? Who went bald? I thought that shark ate you? But a common thread is the sensible wariness we exhibit around those who know who we were *but may no longer see that person before them.*
                    Invitation to the Class of '84, 40th Reunion—From Tony Brennan

---

CHAPTER 9

Livira

Livira found herself pinned to the floor even though she should be able to fall right through it. Her assailant's fingers knotted into Livira's robe, their grip deathly tight. Wordless shrieks evolved into a shouted repetition of her name.

"Livira! Livira! Livira!" Carlotte, now straddling Livira, paused to haul in a breath. "How are you here?" And without giving Livira a moment to answer: "Don't leave! You can't leave! I won't let you leave!" Jolting her with each demand.

"I'm." Livira fought to get the words out. "Not. Going—"

"Serra Leetar?" Carlotte seemed to notice the others for the first time. "Is that you?" She focused on Yolanda. "Someone's shrunk Deputy Yute!"

"Can I get up?" Livira asked.

Begrudgingly Carlotte got off Livira's midsection and let her find her feet. Though Livira noted that the girl kept one hand clutching her librarian's robe.

"So." Livira brushed herself down. "You have questions."

"Do I smell awful?"

It wasn't the question Livira had been expecting.

"I do, don't I? Gods, I must stink." Carlotte buried her nose in her shoulder ruff and inhaled. "I'm a ghost. I can't touch anything. Not even water. I haven't washed in years!" She looked at her hand in sudden shock.

"Wait! I can touch you!" She yanked on the material to prove her point, making Livira stagger. "I'm cured?" Without releasing her hold, she lashed out at the bed with one leg. Her foot passed effortlessly through the nearest of the four ornately carved posts. "I'm *not* cured! What's going on?"

Livira eyed Carlotte dubiously, waiting to see if another torrent of questions would follow, but it seemed she was being given leave to answer this time.

"We're all ghosts. You came here through a pool that took you into the past. None of us truly exist here—"

"Though some of us have fifty-foot-tall statues in the main square." Leetar found her voice at last, still raw with grief, her eyes red. Carlotte seemed too overwhelmed by their arrival to notice such details.

A shout rang out in the corridor they'd just come down. "Carlotte? Carlotte!"

"Speaking of your husband . . ." Livira shot Carlotte a speculative look.

"We should leave," Yolanda said. "If we speak to him it will just make the damage worse!"

"Damage?" Carlotte looked at her bedroom door. The faint strains of the orchestra beyond stopped mid-flow.

"Come on!" Livira led off towards the bedchamber's rear wall, trusting Carlotte's death-grip on her robe to bring the queen with her.

All four of them passed through nearly a yard of stone and found themselves standing in an empty dining hall with great displays of swords and pikes on the walls, empty suits of plate armour standing sentinel in the corners and midpoints.

"Can anyone else see you?" Yolanda asked urgently.

"What? No." Carlotte seemed surprised at the child taking over the conversation.

"How long have you been here?" Yolanda asked.

"In the palace?"

"With the man who can see you," Yolanda clarified.

"Uh . . ." Carlotte counted on her fingers. "Plague, palace, good year, this year. Four. Four! You left me here four years, Livira!" She tugged accusingly on Livira's robe. "Four!"

"How are you queen?" Livira looked around the room. She couldn't imagine that this palace was any less grand than the one King Oanold had been burned out of.

Carlotte released Livira, folding her arms. She mixed outrage, accusation, and pride into one stare that she swept across all of them. "I had to do something when you left me here. That was you. I know it was. Somehow that assistant was you."

"In a way," Livira admitted. "But the pool you escaped the canith by didn't lead here. You must have gone to the Exchange. The forest with the doorways."

"I did go to an orchard." Carlotte nodded. "But it was very boring, and there are only so many apples you can eat. They're terrible for the digestion. I mean if that's all you eat. And then where do you go when you need to . . . I mean . . . Behind a tree? I did see a guinea pig once but—"

"How much have you interacted with this man?" Yolanda interrupted.

Carlotte peered down at her. "Who *is* this child? And why doesn't she behave like one? Is something wrong with her?"

Livira stepped between them before Yolanda said anything that might start a fight. Carlotte had always enjoyed a good shouting match, and four years with only one person to talk to might have worn away at her self-restraint.

"How are you queen, Carlotte?"

Carlotte sniffed. "It turns out that I'm not as useless as Master Logaris used to say I was. I found Chertal could see me and hear me, and some of the things I know were not known here. They proved to be quite lucrative."

Yolanda covered her eyes with a white hand.

"I remembered the basics of making black powder. Gods know I was never very interested in alchemy lessons, but that recipe stuck for some reason. It was rather gruesome after all. You know you need to fill a big barrel halfway with wee and then fill the rest with dung and ferment—"

"What else?" Yolanda demanded. "What else did you tell him?"

"Uh . . . how to make steel. Just the basics. It was enough to get him very rich. After that I did a lot of spying for him. Secrets turn out to be worth far more than new inventions. You can cash them in quickly too."

"So, you . . . married . . . him?" Livira enquired, frowning deeply. "How does that work? I mean, they must call him the mad king? And the other stuff . . ." Her eyes strayed to the wall that now separated them from the bedroom.

Carlotte slumped. "Well, to answer the child's question about how much interaction the king and I have had: not nearly as much as either of us would like. Imagine being able to see everything and touch nothing! So frustrating. So yes, both of us have itches the other can't scratch. And the rest of them do laugh at Chertal behind their hands. But whenever I catch any of them at it, they get posted to some border town, which always makes everyone mind their tongue for a bit." She brightened up suddenly and grabbed Livira's arm in both hands. "I can touch you! You can't imagine how that feels. Just put me in front of Arpix and I'll show him a whole new area of study. The boy won't know what's hit him. I'll—"

"He's got a sweetheart now," Livira said. "Kind of. At least I think—"

"Nooo!" Carlotte released Livira and spun around, looking for a target for her ire. Her gaze settled on Leetar. "I bet she's pretty, and well read, and tall. Very tall. I hate her already."

"Taller than he is . . ." It pained Livira to talk about Arpix given what he'd said to her less than an hour ago. But she had been both amazed and glad and slightly jealous to see how he and Clovis had moved around each other, and she had been desperate to share it with someone, Carlotte most of all since Carlotte lived for such gossip and all its attendant drama. "Anyway, you're married. To a king."

"I'd rather be married to a peasant if I could touch them. Even a fat one that didn't bathe." Carlotte frowned, belatedly registering what Livira had said. "Taller than him?"

Yolanda interrupted. "This is very bad. Very dangerous. It might be as bad as what the canith brothers did with the ganar siblings. Not as bad as what Livira and Evar did with the book, of course."

"Who's Evar?" Carlotte looked pointedly at Livira. "You never mentioned any Evar before!"

Leetar, seeming to decide that the catching-up had gone on long enough, lifted her red-eyed gaze from the ground and answered for Livira. "Evar is Livira's sabber lover." She delivered the blunt truth of the matter without giving Livira a chance to wrestle it into something Carlotte might find easier to swallow. "And I think this Arpix of yours is the target for the sabber's sister. And"—Leetar's voice dried up and she forced the next words out wrapped around a painful sob—"Meelan is dead."

It should have been the first news Livira delivered. She flinched beneath it as if slapped. That was what it felt like each time the fact of it was given space in her mind: a blow.

Carlotte closed her open mouth with a snapping sound. A stricken look took possession of her face, and she staggered back as if injured. Yolanda used the moment of hurt silence as an opportunity to seize control of the conversation again.

"We need to leave here, now. Then I need to find a way to get us back to when we should be. We can only hope that the wound you've opened in reality's fabric is still of a size that can heal itself!" She turned to Livira. "You bring your friend. I'll take Leetar." And with that, she reached out for Leetar's wrist then shot skyward, dragging her aristocratic cargo with her. The vaulted ceiling swallowed the pair from sight as they passed through it.

Carlotte, overwhelmed by a series of what Livira had to admit were pretty huge revelations, could only stare as the pair left. She didn't even manage to protest about the flying part.

Livira held her hand out towards Carlotte, a question in her eyes.

"I can't leave Chertal," Carlotte said, a tear for Meelan running down her cheek. "Not just like that. He's been my only friend all this time, and this citadel is on the edge. I mean, there's cliffs on every side, but the entire kingdom is poised to fall. He needs me."

Livira hadn't forgotten the village in the forest or the ballistae on every roof of the citadel. Yolanda was right though, they had to go. "He needs you to watch him die?" Livira regretted the words immediately but what could a ghost do?

"If that's what has to happen, yes." Carlotte looked grim. "I owe him that much."

Livira sighed and tried to put herself in Carlotte's place. "Who's attacking?"

"The ganar." Carlotte shuddered.

Livira frowned, puzzled. She'd been chased by a giant mechanical killing machine created by one ganar's misguided hatred. But her reading had led her to believe that the ganar were a non-violent species barely half the height of men. A species that had been enslaved both by humans and by canith many times across millennia of recorded history. "Are they sending their engines against you?"

"Worse," Carlotte said. "They've managed to breed a slave-species up on the moon. A monstrous variant on some native Attamast creature. And now they've come down in their night-ships to multiply their soldiers and take the world for their own." She shuddered again. "Our armies can't stand against these creatures, Livira. They're some kind of insect. We call them the skeer."

When in danger of being dispensed with, the trick is to make yourself indispensable. Those with foresight will have mastered some small but vital skill. In order to maintain this edge one should habitually refuse to share information.
The Danger of Education, by P. Floyd

CHAPTER 10

Arpix

A rpix had been there, speaking with Livira! It had all been so real, even the bits that should have been wholly unreal—like wearing the white child's body. He hadn't managed to hold on to it, though. Like a fever dream the whole city had fallen apart around him. And with a sudden start, Arpix had found himself back in the library amid the foulness that King Oanold had made of it. Livira's book—the work of magic that had somehow transported him to her, inside a story that was true— fell from fingers numb with shock.

He was back in the library aisle. It was choked with resting soldiers. Behind him, the trio who had been beating him. In front of him, his unlikely saviour, Lord Algar, who had come bearing Livira's book.

Lord Algar scrutinized Arpix and the recognition in his eye told Arpix that the man before him had also been transported by the text. Arpix bent to pick up the book without asking for permission—a librarian's instinct. As he lifted the volume, Arpix saw, in the place where it had fallen, the faintest crazing of cracks. On any other surface he wouldn't have noticed, but the walls and floor of the library never showed even the slightest defect. Scholars had alleged that even if the sun were to consume the world, the stuff of the library would somehow endure, being made of something sterner than mere matter.

Arpix offered the book to Lord Algar. Arpix had no schooling in such matters, but Livira was given to sharing on many subjects and had spent considerable time researching the topics of espionage, subterfuge, and—though few would believe it having talked to her—diplomacy: Algar's own related area of expertise.

Arpix had picked up a few pointers, albeit unwillingly. Consequently, he now knew that if he tried to hold on to the book, it was unlikely he would ever hold it again. Offering it back to Algar improved his odds at a second chance with it. "It's a powerful piece of work. Somehow, it's become entangled with the library at a fundamental level."

Algar spread his hands, declining to take the volume back. "And how might such a power be exercised?" He tilted his head in question. "Any *useful* ideas, young Arpix?"

The slight stress on "useful" did not pass Arpix by unnoticed. If he ceased to be useful, the soldiers who had been beating him were ready and waiting, already warmed to their task. Livira had been trying to tell him something—in the story—something she'd known for sure? Or just a desperate guess? The Mechanism. She'd been saying something about the Mechanism.

"I might have an idea, but I should really take a closer look—"

Something was happening at the far end of the soldier-choked aisle. Men and women were scrambling to their feet and pressing themselves hard against the shelves.

A shortish, overweight figure in a purple robe was approaching, with guards crowding at his back. "The king . . ." Arpix based the claim on the robe and the grey wig balanced on the old man's head. He looked nothing like the man on the currency. "The king's coming."

"We'll speak of this later," Algar snapped.

"My friends, Neera and Salamonda, the other prisoners. They can help with this," Arpix lied, raising the book. "I need them both." He hoped the stare with which he met the lord's gaze was as meaningful as the one it was replying to. If the man wanted to hide this from his king, Arpix had his own demands, conveyed in a diplomacy of exchanged stares and slantwise allusions. Designed in Arpix's case to wring concessions from the man with the upper hand without bruising his pride.

Algar gave the faintest of nods, then turned to greet King Oanold. "Sire! I've been interrogating the new prisoners."

Arpix slipped the book into the pocket within his robe. The king waved aside Algar's words with a flexing of his fingers and peered past him. "A librarian." He sniffed. "They must use this one for reaching the top shelf." He laughed, triggering a wave of false amusement. "Touch of canith in him, do you think?"

"I think, sire"—Algar inclined his head—"that in a library we should make best use of any librarian we find."

The king scowled. His dull eyes, their colour dark and indeterminate, roamed over Arpix critically.

"He came out of the same door the sabbers did. Proof of collusion if any were needed!"

"They were chasing us, sire!" Arpix hated himself for the lie, for reinforcing the man's prejudice, and for honouring him with a title. "We were running for our lives!"

The king sniffed, unconvinced. "We have the head librarian. Do we really need any others?"

The head librarian? Arpix nearly said the words out loud.

"Master Acconite's insights are useful to us, sire." Lord Algar inclined his head again. "But a youth with considerably more recent experience of exploring deep among the chambers would also be an asset."

"Perhaps. Perhaps not." King Oanold narrowed his pouchy eyes once more and studied Arpix with an air of distaste. "Yute has clearly allied himself with the dogmen. I'm sure he was working against us in secret for years. Striking deals with the sabbers behind our backs, manoeuvring to place dusters in the librarians' ranks. A plot of epic proportions. It's how the sabbers took the walls. There's no other way we could have lost to them. Cheating, treachery, subterfuge, all the tools of the sabber and the duster. How do we know this librarian isn't one of Yute's protégés, up to his overlong neck in treason?" Flecks of spittle caught the library light as they fled his lips. "Treachery and treason! Crath City was stolen from me. Everyone's saying it."

"You make fine points as always, sire." Clearly not willing to tie his colours to any mast in imminent danger of sinking, Lord Algar merely gestured to Arpix. "Well? Answer His Majesty!"

"When the library caught fire, Master Yute left me to burn," Arpix said.

"I didn't escape to the enchanted forest like the rest of you. I was saved along with a few others by an assistant. The library saved me, not any of the librarians. I'm a citizen of the empire, and I owe my allegiance to you, sire." Arpix made an awkward bow. As he straightened, he could see that the king's open hostility had mellowed to something less readable.

"The only librarian I have any time for is the one that leads us safely out," Oanold said with surprising candour.

Arpix took it as a mark of the man's desperation. When his soldiers ran out of prisoners their hunger would turn to anger and there'd be no ruling over them. The king was asking him if he knew the way out.

"Are you that man? The one who knows the way out?" Oanold cut to the chase. Power rarely bred patience.

"I . . ." What had Livira been trying to tell him? Something about the Mechanism. She wouldn't want him to take the soldiers there unless all the others had already left the place. Arpix couldn't lead the king out of the library without a canith to open doors, and he wasn't about to suggest they needed one. The king would just try to capture Clovis or one of her brothers, and then torture what he wanted out of them. And it wouldn't work. "I can do something almost as good," Arpix said with a conviction he didn't feel. "Or even better. But we need to go back to the place you found us in, the reading room off the next chamber."

"The chamber with the sabbers, and the insects, and the mechanical giant that tears through steel bars with its bare hands? The place we just made a strategic retreat from?" King Oanold motioned two of his men towards Arpix. They came forward with expressions that promised nothing good.

"The door I was coming out of when you captured me leads to many worlds," Arpix spoke fast, trying not to sound panicked.

"Lies!" barked the king. "Why did you come back out of it to this misery?"

"It works only for one person at a time. If there's more than one, it pushes you out." Desperation pushed Arpix to invention. "But one person can go to a paradise. They can claim a palace, a city, a whole world! Fill their belly with the finest foods: roast pork, spiced chicken, pomegranates, grapes, wine, sweetmeats—"

"Stop!" Oanold held a hand up, one arm hugging his belly.

Whether he was talking to his personal guard or not, they stopped. Every person in the aisle within hearing distance had their eyes on Arpix as if instead of seeing a lanky librarian they could picture only a towering pile of the foodstuffs he'd been listing. He'd even made his own belly rumble and his mouth water.

Oanold elbowed his way past the two guards and came to look up at Arpix. "You understand that when you awaken such appetites they must be satisfied?"

Arpix nodded unwillingly, not wanting to acknowledge the contract he was entering into. "Yes, sire."

"And how do you propose to deal with the many threats I enumerated?"

Arpix hesitated. Livira had told him the Mechanism was what he needed. Or at least he thought she had. So, either she had forces marshalled there that she believed would save him. Or she thought it was safe there now, and that the Mechanism would save him. Or he had misheard her in the chaos of being ejected from her story. Or this was the best choice out of many bad ones, and all those threats remained. Whichever of those conjectures might be correct hardly mattered if Arpix couldn't convince the king to take him back to the reading room.

Arpix knuckled his forehead, trying to press his brain into the necessary invention. "I believe that the mechanoid will have killed or dispersed the skeer at the western door so that no reinforcement can reach the main chamber. And that the sabbers will have fled, with the mechanoid in pursuit. And the last skeer, if it didn't attack you when you crossed the chamber twice, must be hiding with the hope it can send a report about what has happened back to the nest. In short, the way should be clear."

To Arpix's surprise, the king believed him. It seemed that in desperate times people were ready to follow anyone with an idea. The drawback being that if the idea proved to be wrong, the consequences promised to be harsh.

Arpix found himself in grand company, walking behind the king and Lord Algar, who in turn walked behind a vanguard of what were presumably six of their most capable soldiers.

It wasn't until they reached the corridor to re-enter the chamber where the soldiers had battled Clovis and her brothers among the book columns that there was enough space to see the whole of the king's diminished following. Arpix estimated that eighty soldiers hemmed in a group of maybe two dozen civilians, some of whom were prisoners. He spotted first Salamonda and then Neera among their number.

"Eyes forward." A soldier slapped him around the head.

With a ringing in his ears, Arpix followed the king towards the great white door.

THE BOOK-COLUMN CHAMBER had a faintly acrid smell to it that undercut the rankness of the unwashed bodies crowding around Arpix. Whatever had caused the odour to pervade such a large space must have been a significant event. Arpix's thoughts turned immediately towards fire—but there was no evidence of one, not the haze of smoke or the flicker of flame glimpsed through the shifting corridors between the columns. It was, in any event, a smell more reminiscent of the alchemists' laboratory in Crath City than of the blaze that had so nearly consumed him four years ago in the library.

The soldiers advanced cautiously through the book columns, their numbers hidden once more, a cordon around the king and those following him. Many glances strayed to the heights, and on several occasions gleaming metal 'sticks were levelled at suspiciously dark patches, ready to spit their deadly projectiles at the first sign of motion.

Others watched the corridors of sight coming into vision then fading as they advanced through the orchard of columns. Arpix held scant regard for the soldiers but given that the monstrous skeer could charge them at any moment, he was, for the first time, glad to have them around him. The rapidly changing lines of sight made for a strange kind of claustrophobia, and Arpix's time on the plateau had taught him to fear the skeer. The only thing worse would be to be stalked by a cratalac.

Many times, Arpix saw the dark spatter of drying blood left on the library floor from the fighting retreat. He hoped none of it belonged to Clovis or her brothers. Twice, they passed the bodies of soldiers left behind on that retreat. None of the living soldiers made any effort to drag the cooling remains with them. None of them talked of their next meal. It seemed to Arpix that their hunger would lead them to kill and eat someone they could consider "other" than themselves before they would take advantage of a fellow soldier's death in such a manner. He wondered how long that fine distinction would survive the last mouthful of the innocent victims they'd murdered.

After about half an hour of walking through the seemingly endless forest of columns, they reached the path that the huge mechanical ganar had torn for itself. Despite the extra space, the going slowed: the ground lay littered with books, heaped in places, and twisted metal columns lay at intervals across the path. Many of the disk-shaped shelves had been left torn or bent, presenting the hazard of razored edges and sharp corners.

The acrid smell grew stronger as they followed the mechanoid's path towards the reading room entrance. A powdery white residue began to appear on the book heaps and reached a dozen yards up along the books on the surviving book columns. It began to rise around the soldiers' feet, a low, stinking fog, some kind of heavy alchemical smoke.

"Sire." A soldier stopped and gestured with his 'stick. At first neither the king nor Arpix saw what had caught the man's attention. The soldier went forward and reached up to touch the offending object with the end of his weapon. A steel cogwheel about eighteen inches across had embedded itself to its midpoint in the books, cutting through their spines.

"The mechanoid . . ." Arpix said, "it must have exploded." Even as he said it, he saw more debris lying ahead of them.

"Let's hope it killed those damn sabbers first," Lord Algar muttered. "I had that one we shot. Had it in my hands." He stared into his empty palm as he spoke.

A cold horror crept across Arpix's skin. Had the sabber been Clovis? Was it Evar? Fortified by anger, Arpix followed down the corridor into the reading room. A white cloud rose behind them, swallowing the view of the way they'd come.

The wreckage of the huge mechanoid lay sprawled across the floor, dwarfing the Mechanism that sat like a grey loaf at the centre of the chamber. The metal ganar appeared to have exploded from within, its chest an open bloom with jagged metal petals, and jettisoning the majority of its inner workings at high speed. Pieces of it could be seen everywhere, random chunks of torn metal in some places, cogwheels of all sizes from smaller than a fingernail to larger than a man, battered metal boxes leaking fluid and trailing wires, and other fragments stranger still.

Of Clovis, Livira, and the others there was no sign.

As Arpix entered the chamber he became aware of a buzzing. Not the frantic directionless energy of a housefly, nor a mosquito's high whine, but the low menace of a hornet hive waiting to take offence. At first, he thought it must be coming from the wreckage of the automaton but moving in behind the soldiers he was forced to revise his opinion. It was the Mechanism that was humming, seemingly with increasing urgency. And in his inner pocket an answering vibration set his teeth on edge.

Livira's book! The Mechanism could sense it coming, and they *really* did not seem to agree with each other.

Arpix might have said something there and then, but ahead of him a soldier vanished with a desperate cry and trailing arms, looking as if the library floor had grown a mouth and swallowed him whole.

CHAPTER 11

Evar

Evar remembered being shot. It hadn't hurt. It had been a punch that had somehow stolen his strength and left him kneeling at the mercy of the human soldiers. He remembered the one who had not been uniformed. The one-eyed man who had been about to gouge out one of Evar's own eyes.

"Clovis!" Clovis had saved him.

Clovis had dragged him back to the reading room, back to Livira. He remembered Livira holding him, and how he had tried to stop her tears. But in the end his arms had been too heavy to lift.

Falling. That was the last thing he remembered. Falling!

Evar opened his eyes. Or thought he did, because at first it seemed that there was no difference. He saw a vast black sky. It took a moment for him to wonder how he knew it was a sky.

Because I'm on my back. He wanted to say the words, but they sounded only in his head. *Because something is falling from the sky.* "Rain?" It wasn't rain, though. Even without ever having seen rain, Evar knew that was not what he was seeing. *Snow perhaps?* One of the white flecks appeared to be dropping towards him. As it came closer, following an erratic path, he understood it to be something far more familiar than snow. A page. It was a falling page. It veered away to land somewhere to his left.

"Evar?" His sister's voice. "He's waking up!"

Clovis's face moved into Evar's field of vision, softened by concern.

"Clo," he croaked her name, and tried to move.

Starval crowded in from the other side, obscuring his view of the black heavens and the scattered fall of pages. "Take it easy. Mayland said you're going to need time."

"Can't . . . move." Evar frowned, straining to lift anything that could be lifted. He realised then that not only didn't he hurt, he couldn't feel anything at all. Not heat, or cold, or the ground beneath him, or his own hands as he tried to make fists.

"Mayland said you'd find it strange to start with." Clovis echoed Evar's frown.

"Had a big hole in you, brother. Too much blood in your lung. Not enough in the rest of you." Starval's gaze kept darting from here to there, alert for ambush.

"What . . ." Evar swallowed to wet his throat. "What did he do?"

"We should sit him up," Clovis said.

Starval's mouth made a flat line. He nodded and bent in. Together they started to lever Evar up.

"Livira?" He couldn't even turn his head to look for her.

The look Clovis gave Starval was enough answer.

"Alive?" He couldn't feel his body, but he could still feel pain.

"Yes . . ." Clovis said, trailing uncertainty.

"Kerrol?" Evar wanted Kerrol. Of all of them Kerrol really felt like an older sibling, combining authority with competence in an annoying but non-threatening way.

"Gone." Starval looked grim.

"Not dead," Clovis hastened to add. "He went with the white human. The older one."

Sitting up did little to help Evar make sense of his surroundings. They seemed to be on a gently rolling landscape of loose pages and dust, everything around them black despite a directionless illumination bleeding from the air to paint all of them in a kind of half-light.

In the distance their surroundings became less certain, taking on a hazy aspect with almost surreal shapes suggested here and there. Evar blinked, wondering if the behemoth-sized creature, barely visible where it lumbered at the limits of his vision, were some after-effect of his ordeal.

His top half was bare, and his lolling head offered him a view of his own chest, along with the hole that had been punched through him. The wound looked too black, even if the blood had had time to dry and crust, and the hole had a curious liquid quality to it. The veins around that area seemed darker too. In fact, he'd never seen any veins crossing his ribs before. An image came to him, of a tiny black horse galloping around the perimeter of a white hand.

"Ah . . ." He understood it and, in that moment, raised his head. "Mayland did this. He used . . . the library's blood." The black stuff from which the Escapes shaped themselves in response to fear, and from which Yute had fashioned horses, flowers, butterflies, and fire. That same blackness now ran in Evar's veins.

"It was the only way to save you." Clovis removed the uncertainty from her voice but not her eyes.

"You were going to die." Starval seemed sure of that at least.

Evar raised a trembling arm. He was talking to his body in a new language. With his muscles deaf to his normal instructions, he found himself having to learn Yute's control over the unformed creation that leaked from the library's wounds and now filled his own. The Escapes had been monstrous because he had expected them to be. With Livira he had flown because she had taught him to believe that he could. Now he managed to stand through a combination of belief that he should be able to and his body's ability to meet those demands. He found it to be a strange experience. Very similar to what he had known before, but also not the same.

Feeling a hundred feet tall, but also, to judge by Clovis and Starval, the same height he had always been, he turned to see the full extent of his surroundings. Paper drifts, lakes of dust, a gentle fall of loose pages from infinitely black heavens, distant mysteries that might be anything from mountains to monsters. The only sensible question was: *Where are we?*

"Where's Livira?"

"She didn't come through," Clovis said.

"Through?"

"The assistant was destroyed. His blood made a portal. Three portals—or pools." Starval waved the detail away. "We came through one of them. She didn't follow. The automaton was going to explode or burn. Either way, she'll have left by one of the other pools."

"Where's the door?" Evar glanced around in case he'd missed a sparkling door of light somewhere in the twilit paper wasteland.

Starval made a brief upward gesture. "We fell. Only . . . slowly . . . like the pages."

Evar looked up, already knowing that there was nothing to see. "She would have followed if she'd been able to. Where's Mayland?"

"Scouting. He says he knows this place," Clovis said.

"And where are we?"

"At last." Starval grinned. "That would have been my first question."

Clovis glanced around doubtfully. "He says we're in the vaults. Below the library. An infinitely deep shaft below each chamber, the same width and breadth as the chamber."

"But how—"

"Don't ask." Starval shrugged. "All he's saying is it doesn't matter how far you climbed up or how far you dug down, you're not finding a ceiling or a floor. And the pages—anything that's destroyed up above, consumed by fire, eaten by hungry readers, devoured by book-mites . . . it all comes fluttering down here. It's like an underworld for books."

"And we just wait here, do we?" Evar turned, moving with slowly growing confidence.

"We were watching over *you*!" Clovis said, her face unreadable.

"I'm going to find Livira." Evar chose a direction and started walking, keeping things slow on the unfamiliar footing.

"I'd like to find Arpix," Clovis said. "But just wandering off and getting lost isn't going to help. Mayland says—"

"Mayland murdered Yute's wife in front of us!" Evar spun round. "He wants to destroy the library!"

"And?" Clovis shrugged. "I liked it outside better. The library stole our lives. It's a wonder we survived without murdering each other."

"The library didn't do this to us. Our own people did. And the humans, and probably the ganar and the skeer and other creatures we don't even know the names for yet. The library caught fire when canith were attacking humans. And yes, they probably had their reasons. But the fact is that the library didn't do anything to us. It was just there. And it was misused." Evar looked at his brother for backup.

Starval echoed Clovis's shrug. "One of the many ways I know to kill people is to take something that you know will attract them, make it lethal, and leave it where they will find it. For example, a juicy red apple, into which poison has been injected. You might say that neither the apple nor the poison meant you any harm. You just misused them both when you took that bite. But still, you would wish that someone had found it first and destroyed it. And you would agree that leaving it for you to find was in no way an act of kindness."

It seemed to Evar that Mayland's voice was coming out of Starval's mouth. Even so, the points he made were hard to argue with. Evar knew in his gut that the library was not an act of violence. He knew it was well intentioned and a force for good. But the words to make that clear, to persuade others of the choice his heart had already made . . . they were proving hard to find.

"We need to find Livira. And Arpix. And the others." Evar realised that the circle of people he cared for had been steadily growing. He felt a duty to Salamonda whom he had come to like despite the language barrier. He was concerned for Livira's friend Neera, and not entirely because of the hurt it would do to Livira if she were to come to harm. "We don't need to be . . . wherever here is."

"We still need Mayland to get us out." Clovis didn't sound as if she was disagreeing with the rescuing-Arpix bit. "So, we'd better stay put. How are you feeling? That wound looks . . . odd."

"It feels odd." Evar glanced down at it again. "But it beats bleeding. I feel . . ." He certainly didn't feel like he'd been knocking at death's door. "Ready."

A glimmer caught his eye. The gleam of something that wasn't endless pages. A ring? A gold ring. Evar bent to pick it up. The metal felt cold in his hand, heavier than it should have been.

"Mayland told us not to pick anything up," Starval said.

Evar looked at the ring in his palm. "I think you've spent too much time listening to what Mayland tells you." Even so, the whisper that ran around the back of his head, just beyond hearing, felt as if it came from the object in his hand, and Evar did wonder whether in this case Mayland's advice might be worth heeding.

Evar was about to drop the ring when Clovis spun around and, following her line of sight, he made out an approaching figure.

"Escape . . ." Evar's first thought left his unguarded mouth. He was both right and wrong. The thing was made of the library's blood. Coming out of the darkness its blackness had hidden it until it was almost upon them. But it was in the shape of a person, not some ravening monster.

"You found the ring!" The voice emanating from a face too black for features was deep and grave with undercurrents of wonder, perhaps even awe, and a suppressed excitement. "You touched it and yet you are not consumed."

Evar closed his hand around the ring, even though his first instinct was to drop it. "Who are you?"

As he spoke, the figure paled from midnight to evening, with hints of a face emerging, hints of a cloak, a broad-brimmed hat. A tall canith, though bent with age, eyes like the last stars in a predawn sky.

"The ring has chosen you, my son. You, of all your generation." The visitor touched his hat. "And I am Gamdot, come to guide you."

Shades slowly began to appear across the man, like plumes of coloured oil rising from the deep to spread across the surface. His cloak took on a brownish hue, the weave of the cloth visible, his mane a majestic grey beneath the indeterminate weather-beaten green of his shapeless hat. The eyes that had been stars became piercing blue, nested in the wrinkles of advancing age.

"Why me? Why has it chosen me?" Evar had many other questions and concerns, but destiny's hand pressed upon his shoulder. He had been called to greatness. A purpose awaited.

"Why indeed?" The old man came closer, leaning on his staff to study Evar. A mage perhaps. It seemed impossible that just moments before he'd lacked detail or colour. Compared to Clovis or . . . the other one . . . he seemed sunlit where they walked in shadow.

"I wish it had not come to me . . ." Evar felt the ring's weight on his heart rather than in his hand. It held a tangible power, at once both fierce and frightening.

"So do all who live in such times, but that—"

The point of a sword jutted bloodily from Gamdot's forehead. It withdrew with the same sudden violence with which it had appeared, and the mage fell gracelessly, spattering blood across the pages beneath him.

Gamdot's fall revealed Mayland, shaking the gore from a short sword.

"What? What in all the hells—"

"The Chosen One trope." Mayland snatched up some loose pages and used them to clean his blade. "Easy to get caught up in. You need to be careful down here. There's a lot of dead fiction and it's still looking for an audience. If you're not paying attention, it'll suck you down faster than quicksand."

Already Gamdot's body was leaking a tar-like substance that on contact with the pages beneath him ate its way through, sinking deeper.

"That particular variant was new and easily dealt with." Mayland nodded to the dissolving corpse. "Others are well established and very old. Those can be a problem, or a solution if you handle the situation well. But the main danger down here, the reason we can't stay very long, is—"

"You stopped Livira following me!" Evar advanced on his brother, ignoring the still-drawn blade. Mayland wasn't going to run him through. And even if he was, Clovis and Starval would never let it happen.

Mayland's glance took Evar in from head to toe. He didn't try to lie. "She would have got in my way. Better to leave her to take another path than bring her here and have to kill her. I didn't think you'd like that."

"But *you* don't mind?" Evar accused. "You murdered one librarian. You'd happily break another one's neck?"

"Look, we have to get on. This is the best place to find what we need but we don't have long." He glanced over his shoulder as if something might have followed him out of the distant dreamscape.

"I'm not going anywhere with a murderer!" Evar started to cross his arms over his chest, felt ridiculous, and let them fall. "I watched you kill that woman . . ."

"They're sabbers, Evar. They killed our people." Mayland looked to Clovis for support. Clovis frowned and studied her feet, the nails of her left hand digging into her right arm.

"And who says I'm not going to get in your way?" Evar's growing anger coloured his voice. "I don't want to take your path. Kerrol didn't either, or he'd be here too. And what about you, Clovis? You want to collapse the library that Arpix has worked in since he was a child? Bringing books to people who wanted them, *needed* them? You let one experience make you think the only good human was a dead one. Are you going to let another convince you that the whole library needs destroying? Yes, we were trapped in it—"

"It was our whole lives, Evar. And generations before us!"

"But it was still an accident. Not something the library did to us. Call it Livira's fault. If the Assistant hadn't cared—if she hadn't had Livira's humanity in her—she would have left our ancestors to burn and none of us would have ever existed, much less been trapped. It was bad, yes! But we have to stop looking for somewhere to put the blame. It's like hating the rock you stubbed your toe on."

Mayland stepped between Evar and Clovis. All around them the drifting pages rustled in an invisible wind. "Words are fine things, and pretty arguments can be made from them, but one thing I've learned in my travels is that they almost never change anyone's mind, certainly not in the time they take to speak, or even in a day. Sometimes, over years, they might change a person's course . . ." The sporadic fall of loose pages from the black vault overhead seemed to be freshening into a steady drizzle. A low and distant rumble shuddered through the darkening half-light. Evar had never heard thunder before but felt that perhaps this might be it.

"So, the historian advocates what when it comes to changing minds?" Evar demanded. "A punch to the face? Internecine war?"

"Time generally does the trick. It does heal all wounds, after all. I will acknowledge that words work better in the business of changing minds when they're on the page of a book rather than on the tongue of someone with a contrary opinion. They need to be consumed in private and in the reader's own time. But face to face? In the moment? No. Changing your mind feels like being defeated. It wounds the ego. And our opinions were never founded on words—they're just the garnish added on for show. A display of plumage to attract those of a similar mind."

Mayland filled Evar's vision, but even so he became aware of something odd happening all around them. The pages underfoot were variously crumpling and folding themselves into strange shapes, some reminiscent of parchment flowers. The rustling competed with the fluttering fall of pages, now thick enough to limit vision to ten yards or so. The thunder came again, louder, nearer, angrier. A sourceless rage began to bubble deep inside Evar. Mayland's lies, Mayland's machinations had led them to this. His brother had abandoned them. Left them trapped when he could so easily have shown them the way out.

The anger winding its way up from Evar's guts found its echo on Mayland's face. A mocking sneer, a poorly disguised hatred staring out of what had become a stranger's eyes.

Mayland shook his golden mane. "Words have had their chance. So, forgive me if I cut to the chase. I *am* going to destroy the library. And I *won't* allow you to stop me, Evar."

Another boom from above as if a raging god were trying to break the sky. Pages fell in off-white curtains, a tumbling confusion adding to the drifts on which they already stood.

Reflexive anger drove Evar's hand towards his brother's throat. At no point did he mean to harm him. Simply to show Mayland that he wasn't in a position to deliver ultimatums. In a fight Mayland had no hope against Clovis, Starval, or Evar, and it was time to remind him of the fact. Whether it was a lesson that Evar would enjoy teaching wasn't the point.

It was possible that Clovis or Starval could have stopped him, but neither of them tried. Both stood statue-still, almost lost in the page-fall. Instead, Evar's hand simply slowed as if he had thrust it into mud that thickened as he pushed through it.

"How?" Evar snarled, trying first to press forward and reach his target, and then to pull back the imprisoned arm.

"I'm impressed by the speed with which you learned to control what's running in your veins, brother." Mayland's eyes flitted to the hole in Evar's chest. "But I've been studying the library's blood for years. I've been gone longer than you think I have."

"I—" A wave of Mayland's hand cut off Evar's hot reply by taking command of both his jaw and his tongue. The casual gesture of power didn't seem to be for Evar's benefit though. Mayland stared past him into the page-fall, eyes narrow. "Well, this complicates things."

And in that moment a new strength filled Evar, redoubling his rage. His hand found Mayland's throat, and within a blinding maelstrom of falling paper he lifted his brother from the ground with a single arm and began to squeeze.

Those who believe that we are nothing more than survival machines—the end product of a billion-year evolutionary war—are incorrect. We are less than that since we have added conscious cruelty into the already vicious mix. And we are not the end product.

The Genetic Handbook, *by Fiona Bayzelon*

CHAPTER 12

Anne

In the rainswept streets of Amberg a virulent hatred ran free, communicated from friend to friend, neighbour to neighbour. In the gutters, water gurgled its way to the drains, trickled through gratings, and was swallowed into a dark underground sea. In the alleys, in the beer houses, across the factory floor, ran a darker muttering. A long-brewed anger had begun to crest. A fire banked across years, fed on lies, devouring the tail of its own prejudice. If it were a volcano, this would be the stage just before the eruption, the time when the ground began to bulge and mound, smoke escaping the cracks, tremors running through the bedrock.

Even in the parlours, the knitting circles, and the creches the talk was of justice, of payback, of it being time. The insult could stand no longer. The list of imagined crimes had grown too long and crossed too many lines. The Jews had to pay. The Jews, and any who stood in the path of the nation's greatness, any who threatened the purity of their blood, any who challenged the efficiency of the machine into which Herr Hitler was forging the nation.

Anne had not been privy to any of the conversations in which hatred fed off suspicion. She hadn't seen suspicion devour the newspapers' lies only to vomit out ten times more, their falsehoods both deeper and more fantastic. She had felt only the edge of the thing, and deduced the existence of the whole, just as a fossil hunter whose diligent chipping has revealed a single bone might know in their heart that the entire monster waits for them, entombed in the stone of the cliff that towers above them.

And yet, in Madame Orlova's parlour an unexpected strangeness eclipsed the brewing violence outside. If not for their host's own example of the many forms into which humanity might be cast, Anne would, to her own shame, have come to doubt that either man before her was in fact a man. As they took tea and talked of books, Yute seemed steadily more unusual, his whiteness beyond even that which might be credited to albinism. While Kerrol appeared to grow by the minute, shedding some cloak that had baffled Anne's eyes. Even the enormity of seven feet in height wouldn't encompass him. Perhaps eight might just do it. He might even threaten Goliath's inhuman record and top three yards. Moreover, in the light of Madame Orlova's old-fashioned oil lamp, his mane seemed closer to that of a lion than a man's hair. His lips thinned almost to nothing, the planes of his face taking on a more canine shape. His body too threw new shadows, his legs not even jointed in the same way Anne's were.

Stranger still, as the conversation continued and the tea cooled, Kerrol's speech became harder and harder to understand, until at last it sounded to Anne's ear like the growls and rumbles of a large, highly educated dog.

"I'm sorry." At last Anne had to speak. "What language is it that you're speaking now, Mr. Kerrol? I can't follow it at all."

Yute and Kerrol exchanged a look, the tall man raising a quizzical brow. Kerrol growled out something else, an interrogation of some sort.

"She says she can't understand you either," Yute said.

Kerrol nodded.

"Wait," Anne protested. "How can he understand you but not me?"

"Everyone understands when I talk." Yute frowned. "The words at least. It's a talent left over from when I served the library in a more formal capacity."

"More formal than a librarian?" Anne asked. "What were you? A shelf?"

Yute acknowledged her attempt at a joke with a small smile. "Something like that."

"Would you be a dear, Anne, and fetch some little cakes from the kitchen?" Madame Orlova tilted her misshapen skull towards Anne. "I feel today is a day for cakes. Who knows what tomorrow will bring?" A sigh lifted her shoulders. "They're under the china dome on the sideboard, and there's a silver stand in the high cupboard by the back door."

Anne got to her feet rather faster than she had intended. Even with the fascinating company, an offer of cake was something to be leapt at. She hurried through the indicated door and found herself in a narrow kitchen lined by cupboards with many small doors and drawers. A smaller window, divided into four little panes, afforded a view of a brick wall, the edge of a roof, and a sky already shading into night. Anne's grandfather always maintained that whatever the clever Dr. Einstein might have to say about speed and time, the swiftness with which it passed was really more about the quality of the conversation. A good discussion would, he maintained, devour the hours and leave you staring at midnight before you knew it.

She found the cakes quickly enough beneath a flower-patterned dome. Smallish cubes of three-layer sponge with white icing and a pink icing flower on top of that. Finding the silver holder required rather more exploration, and Anne had all manner of questions concerning the odd mechanical devices, curious jars, spice pots, and newspaper-wrapped parcels she uncovered before finding the three-tiered cake stand.

Finally, equipped with a loaded stand, a collection of small plates decorated with poppies, and four little forks, Anne made to return to the others. She paused at the doorway, listening to the conversation.

"—don't seem overly surprised, Madame Orlova?" Yute's voice.

"It appears that the whole world is starting to come apart at the seams." Anne couldn't see the shrug, but she could sense it in the old woman's voice. "When the world breaks, should we not expect new things to come through the cracks?"

"Kerrol says that when he spoke with the policeman and the others, they expressed a hatred for difference, the belief that anything which is in their eyes 'imperfect' should be destroyed. He feels it is only a matter of time before this society turns on its sick and disabled."

"For someone who has only just arrived, he sees with a clear eye. Amberg, this whole country, is tinder waiting for the flame. I worry for Anne—"

Anne pushed in, cake stand in hand, feeling guilty for eavesdropping, even though in her experience it was often the only way to truly know what was going on in the world. The people who loved her were, by and large, unwilling to weigh her down with harsh truths, and those who didn't seemed to feel that lies and insults would do her more harm.

"Have you seen our library yet?" Madame Orlova changed the subject.

"Not yet." Yute straightened in his chair. "When was it founded?"

"We've had the provincial library for well over a hundred years." Madame Orlova inclined her misshapen head. "Since my grandmother's childhood. It's not as grand as some, of course, but I like it."

Anne offered the cakes around. Only Madame Orlova declined. Kerrol's looked comically small, almost lost in the expanse of his hand. He studied it with interest, sniffing deeply, then consuming it in a single mouthful. The growl that followed was nearly as unsettling as the length of the tongue that searched his muzzle of a mouth for crumbs.

"Kerrol says your cakes are delicious, Madame," Yute interpreted, though in truth it had sounded like a combat challenge.

"We should visit this library of yours, Anne, as soon as we've finished our tea," Yute said. "I'm thinking that must be the place that called us here."

Anne laughed, nervous in case they meant to break in. "It will be shut now, of course. Tomorrow is Thursday. I think it opens to the public at nine."

Yute's white eyebrows elevated. "The library . . . closes?"

"Yes." Anne didn't know what else he was expecting.

"Still, we must go there, and I don't think we can wait. Better to take our chance now before word of our presence circulates."

"I'll come with you," Anne said.

"You won't. We will escort you back to your home." Yute didn't seem the type given to firmness but on this he sounded firm.

Kerrol growled his agreement.

Having finished their tea and cakes, and like visitors to an island of calmness amid the raging storm, they took their leave of Madame Orlova. The old woman pressed something from her knob-knuckled hands into Anne's palm as they paused at the shop's front door.

"I can't take this." Anne tried to give back the silver charm on its silver chain.

"I insist, child." Madame Orlova closed her hands. "It's from the old country, back when we Orlovs wandered from town to town entertaining everyone from serfs to princes. A ward against evil, for evil times."

Anne saw the futility of refusing, and instead offered her thanks.

It had grown dark outside. Pools of light dotted the high street around infrequent gas lamps, and shadows twitched to the dance of flames.

There were too many people around, crowding the corner by the butcher's shop, others smoking and talking in front of Fischer's hardware store. "Follow me." She let some urgency colour her voice. "Don't run. Don't look at anything."

She angled across the street, threading between the lamps' spheres of influence, aiming at the dark alley between the shoe shop and the milliner's. Kerrol's great height would be hard to miss, but perhaps she and Yute looked like children beside him, and perhaps all people would glimpse in the gloom was a father with his youngsters.

An exclamation of surprise followed them into the alley but no sounds of running feet came after it.

"Quickly now." Anne sped up. She led Yute and Kerrol by a much longer route, through unlit streets, squelching down alleys that were scarcely more than slots where buildings failed to quite reach each other. They passed people in twos and threes, groups of men mostly but not just younger ones. Even in trios though, none of them seemed foolish enough to take exception to a giant looming out of the thickening night.

By this method, combined with a degree of luck, Anne led her two guardians back to the street their journey around Amberg seemed to have begun in. The pair's mysterious appearance at the back of Anne's grandfather's bookshop still troubled Anne, and she resolved to question Yute about it before letting them take their leave of her. Had they broken in through the back door? It seemed to be the only possibility.

"Nearly there." Anne glanced back at the others.

Kerrol growled and Yute translated, "It seems you have company."

Squinting down the unlit street with the last streetlamp to her rear Anne could barely make out the Hoffman sign, but now that Kerrol mentioned it, the clump of shadows beneath the sign could very well be a tight knot of people gathered at the door.

Even as she slowed to a halt, a match struck ahead of them, the glow momentarily illuminating a bowed head, someone else's arm, a third person's coat. And then, with almost surreal slowness, instead of dying away, the flame wrapped itself around something the size of a fist. A torch like the ones the soldiers carried in the night parade. In the pool of its glow maybe nine or ten men . . . no, at least one of them was a woman. A jeer went up, all of them focused on something beyond the bookshop's windows.

"Grandfather!" Anne started forward, terrified, but not for herself. "They must have seen my grandfather!"

A huge hand closed over her shoulder, arresting her progress with a low accompanying growl. Anne opened her mouth in protest but the blast that followed was nothing of hers. The sound of falling glass filled the aftermath, tumbling into the street from the window beside the one broken the week before.

"Grandfather! They've shot him!" She fought to free herself, and failed.

"No," Yute said. "That came from inside."

And as he spoke, one of the men outside staggered backwards and fell into the road.

CHAPTER 13

Anne

"G randfather!"

Anne's scream was lost in the general outcry that filled the void as the gunshot faded. Some members of the crowd went to their knees beside the fallen man, tending him in the road. Many others took to their heels, while newcomers came from both ends of the road at a run. Lights went on in nearby flats above the offices that lined the street. Even as she drew breath Anne couldn't help wondering at how violence close up made people back away, but at a distance they rushed towards it.

Those ignorant of the danger were saved from a rapid re-evaluation of their courage by one of the women in the thinning crowd shrieking, "He's reloading!"

At which point the most emboldened of the mob began to climb in through the broken window, whilst another man kicked out the board from the neighbouring window, creating a less hazardous entrance.

The ten or so people rapidly swelled to a couple of dozen, and still Kerrol's implacable strength kept Anne from rushing to her grandfather's aid.

Anne turned to demand that Kerrol release her, resolving to bite his hand if he refused. Even in her distress, with no room for thoughts other than those surrounding her grandfather's well-being, she was shocked to notice that the hand that so easily engulfed her upper arm had only three fingers—seemingly by design rather than through some amputation.

"That's one of Oanold's men." Yute blinked in surprise.

Anne looked back towards the shop. The people had dragged someone out. A soldier, but not in a uniform she recognised. One of the men following him out was carrying an odd-looking rifle. The word "spy" rang out. A Jewish spy! It made no sense whatsoever. Who would come spying in army uniform, carrying a rifle? But the crowd devoured the suggestion and multiplied it.

"We should leave." Yute turned towards the side street they'd arrived by.

"Let me go!" Anne tried once more to free herself. "My grandfather's in there!"

Yute paused to stare at her. "What makes you say so?"

"I . . ." Shouts from the crowd distracted her. Angry cries, jeering, shouts of "hang him!"

"If he had arrived and found you missing, and you had not yet returned, would he sit and wait for you, or believe you might be in trouble and go to search for you?"

"He . . ." The thought of her grandfather out in the febrile town, looking for her, asking questions of the very sort of group that had gathered outside the shop, filled her with horror.

"Where would he think you might go?" Yute asked.

"To Nana Hoffman's." If Anne were in trouble she would go to her great-grandmother's house. Her great-uncle, two uncles, an aunt, and four cousins all shared the matriarch's roof.

More shouting echoed down the road. Kerrol drew her into the shadows of the side street. "Take us there then, and perhaps we will catch him."

Anne nodded, though why these strangers should risk themselves further on her behalf she wasn't sure. She didn't want to abandon the shop either, but a glance that way showed the foreign soldier being beaten to the ground and kicked.

"Let's go," she said.

To reach her nana's house Anne didn't have to cross the town centre but even so the night echoed with cries, and ran to the tempo of racing feet, and above all of this the sound of breaking glass shattered every lull.

Anne reasoned that if she could hear the mobs even here among the residential streets, far away from the high street, it must be mayhem where the Jewish-owned businesses clustered. And there was no doubt in her mind that this attack—this madness that had turned neighbours into enemies—was directed at the Jews.

Somehow over the course of this one night a tipping point had been passed. The single stones had become many. The hostility on the street that had started as slights, and had progressed into name-calling and threats, was now violence: a wilful open violence that would chase you into your home and beat you to death.

Twice, Anne saw crowds outside the homes of people she knew from the synagogue. The windows of the Lucas family's house had been broken and the curtains had become caught on lingering shards of glass. As a child, Anne had been there to play with their daughter, Miriam.

She pulled back in the alley by the furniture factory, and with a nearly synchronized tramp, tramp, tramp of boots a dozen brownshirts hurried past. Anne had no expectation that they were in town to keep the peace. They were here to incite the chaos.

Anne led the way across Neustift Strasse in the militia's wake, pulling a growling Kerrol into the shadows as a truck rattled by, headlights blazing.

"He's intrigued by the manner of its locomotion," Yute explained. "I myself am—"

"It doesn't matter," Anne snapped, fear displacing her manners. "We can't be seen."

She advanced at greater speed now, wanting to minimize the time they were exposed. So many people were hurrying towards the riot or whatever it was that three more breaking into a run wouldn't draw too much interest.

They crossed Maltsergarten by starlight, slowing so that Anne could catch her breath. Yute too was puffing and blowing—worse than she was, if anything. Kerrol seemed utterly unaffected, though he did keep pressing a hand to his left shoulder as if it troubled him.

"That's the library." Anne waved an arm at the large, two-storey building.

Yute and Kerrol showed no signs of abandoning her to the night, though whatever strange book-related interests had brought them to Amberg, it seemed they were now on hold until Anne was delivered into her family's keeping.

They threaded through the backstreets until at last Anne turned onto the road on which Nana Hoffman's house stood, a well-heeled neighbourhood, not the finest the town had to offer but close.

Anne's growing confidence became in an instant an empty hole inside her, devouring her strength and making her feet falter. The quiet residential street on which one might expect to see at most a handful of people after dark, and more likely none, tonight held a crowd.

Many of Nana Hoffman's neighbours had left their homes to stand at their gates and jeer like jackals as Cousin Daniel was brought out through the front door by a pair of brownshirts. Other stormtroopers stood in the street with the lit torches of a military parade, the flames delineating a path to a waiting lorry.

Uncle Walter followed, similarly manhandled. When he turned as if he'd forgotten something, one of the men shoved him roughly and he fell to the ground. They hauled him up like a sack of grain and, even at this distance, Anne could see he'd lost his glasses.

Somehow the torchlight felt appropriate. As if the world she knew, a world of electricity and radio waves and modern medicines, had given way to something from a previous century, enlightenment abandoned in favour of the basest desire to persecute, to wound, and to burn.

It wasn't until Kerrol's hand closed around her arm that she realised she was walking towards the scene. "I have to—"

Kerrol's rumble cut across her.

As the stormtroopers pushed Anne's uncle into the back of the lorry, the torchlight afforded her a glimpse of men crowded inside, and briefly—so briefly that she might persuade part of her mind she had imagined it—she saw her grandfather's grey head.

KERROL'S HAND, WHICH had sealed away her scream almost as it emerged, remained in place until well after he had carried her, at remarkable pace, several streets away.

Yute came puffing up behind them, favouring one leg noticeably.

He held up a white hand in the darkness as Anne struggled to free herself from Kerrol's grip.

"I must apologize." Yute hauled in a breath. "It was never our intention to deprive you of your liberty." Another deep breath, calming now. "But, for the kindness you've shown us, it was necessary to give you a moment to think." He nodded to Kerrol, who released Anne. "I've lived many more years than you might imagine from my appearance. And although I am a stranger here, I know about mankind. Like many other species, in the grip of the moment, absolved of responsibility by society, they will commit horrors."

"I'm going back," Anne said.

Yute inclined his head regretfully. "They appear to have taken males from your family. I assume the females remain within the house. I advise you to seek shelter with your matriarch."

Kerrol turned his dark eyes on her, just gleams in the moonlight, and rumbled out something, a full sentence.

"Kerrol says that your intervention will not stop your grandfather and the others being taken." More growls. A narrowing of those non-human eyes. "But in such times, on such nights, the unfortunate truth is often that those most at risk are young females. If you put yourself in danger, you will achieve nothing, hurt yourself, and hurt your family. This is the harsh reality, no matter how honourable your intentions."

"And what," asked Anne, making no effort to keep the anger from her voice, "would Kerrol do in my position?" She was enraged that he'd laid hands on her, furious with the mob outside her nana's house, and perhaps angriest of all that he was right, and that the world held nothing even close to justice in it.

Yute translated for Kerrol and translated his reply. "Kerrol says he *is* in your position. His family are in danger and beyond his reach, and he is surrounded on all sides by those that mean him harm with no means to defend himself against such numbers. He says that what he plans to do is follow the little librarian and hope that something more than just survival will result. Because he agrees with you, that without the prospect of anything more than simply enduring in such a world, it would be better to die fighting, however hopeless the odds."

Kerrol showed his teeth, which proved to be considerably sharper and more numerous than Anne had imagined when they first met.

"Oh." Anne hadn't thought beyond running to the lorry and trying to pull her grandfather out. But Kerrol had the truth of it. She could fight, and lose, or try to endure into whatever grey existence was allowed her. And whilst she wasn't about to abandon her family, neither of those unappealing options was denied her by exploring this utterly strange and unexpected third option. "This is magic." It sounded stupid when she said it out loud, but also true. The world had gone mad, broken like a pane of glass. Why should the madness end with ordinary people becoming monsters? She gestured at the length of Kerrol's body. He wasn't a human twisted by failures within the womb like Madame Orlova. He wasn't a human. His strangeness was by design. And it had been hidden from her. His appearance, his body, his clothes, even his language, had all been disguised when they first met, not by artifice of paint, not by smoke and mirrors, but by something that could only be named enchantment. "This . . . is . . . magic." Anne shook her head. "I don't understand." And to her dismay, she began to cry uncontrollably.

Yute led them back the way they'd come, showing no hesitation despite the unfamiliar streets and the darkness. Once three men shouted and ran towards them, only to come to a faltering halt as they fully understood Kerrol's size. Without hesitation, Kerrol grabbed the first two and heaved them over a high wall. The third man stood frozen until Kerrol unleashed a snarl more blood-curdling than anything Anne had ever heard, part wolf, part what she imagined must be tiger. The man ran, not looking back, and all down the street the lights that had flickered on behind lace curtains snapped off.

Yute hurried them on. Around the next corner the library loomed into sight, blotting out stars.

Anne came to a halt. "What are you going to do in there?"

"I'm not sure yet." Yute frowned up at the walls.

"But you can do something?" Anne persisted. "You can use your . . . magic. You can repair what's happening here!"

Yute walked back to her. "I'm so sorry, Anne, but no. The library has never been about taking charge. It's a memory. It's ideas. It might have hoped to stop what's happening here, but it's too late. There will be blood, and horror, and probably all the worst things that humanity is capable of. The library can make sure that nobody has a good excuse for forgetting what happens and striving to prevent repetition. But it cannot stop even that. People have to want to know. I wish I could tell you that free and easy access to information solves these problems—it doesn't. People find their own wells of poison to drink from."

Anne wasn't really sure what Yute was saying. The library was just the library, and apart from scholars and children, only a minority ever visited it. Yet Yute spoke about the building as if it were a sleeping god. Even so, the conversation felt important. It felt like so much more than logic said it was.

"You could give them only truth," she said.

"Who judges? Who decides what truth is and which truths to hand out?" Yute shook his head, slow with sorrow. "We take to ourselves the power of the almighty when we control it. So, not intending to rule, the library just gives access. The truth is there on the shelf. You just have to reach out and take it. Information is like water—without it you won't live long, too much and you'll drown. And there's a difference between truth and information. Even correct information is not the same as truth—truth does not mislead—correct information bereft of context can be more dangerous than a lie."

Anne turned to go, yet again. Yute's talking had nothing to do with her life. She had to get back to her family, to her grandfather, secure the shop, repair the windows . . . She faltered.

"The library can't prevent tonight's terrors." Yute spoke the words to her back. "But it is important to note that those preparing to carry out such horror, those who want to lead humanity down the darkest paths it can walk—their first instinct is to burn books, ban books, close the gates of information, allow no voices of dissent."

Kerrol growled in affirmation, the sound rumbling through him.

"Provision of information might not cure these ills, but it is an impediment to their formation. The wind can't stop the advance of armies, but eventually it wins. In the end mountains become dust, and the wind still blows. It is my faith that the library will save us in the end. Not you, not me, maybe not even humanity, but it will save life itself, and because of it, someone will climb the heights and know the divine."

"I don't care about that," Anne said, wiping at her nose as she turned to face him once more. "But tell me what happens here, what happens to my family, tell me that won't be forgotten."

"If the library survives, then this shame, this stain, this lesson will be preserved. And though people may still forget it, they will at least have no excuse for doing so."

Anne glanced at the building behind him. She still couldn't understand what Yute thought he'd find in there, but somehow, she believed it to matter, even on this night. After all, the people who had taken her grandfather had also burned books.

"Let's go."

The promise that the meek will inherit the Earth is oft repeated. What is less known is that, in almost all of the instances where this sort of thing has happened, they rapidly cease to be meek.

Power Corrupts, *by Ming the Merciful*

———

CHAPTER 14

Livira

Ganar leading skeer armies?" Livira stared at Carlotte. "That's *all* we have to deal with? We—as ghosts—just need to lay waste to armies of skeer, and then you'll come with us?"

Carlotte nodded.

Yolanda and Leetar had come back through the ceiling of the great dining hall when it had become apparent that Livira and Carlotte weren't following. They stood side by side now, the white child in her white wrappings as if ready to play the part of a ghost to its fullest, and the bedraggled princess, her finery stained and none too fragrant.

Livira shook her head slowly. "We can't interfere. Yolanda just said you've already done too much damage. You've altered the course of this nation!"

"I mean . . . she doesn't have to come with us." Leetar eyed Carlotte from on high, as if she were still a lowly house-reader rather than queen of a nation with a huge statue of herself in the main square of the citadel. "If she's happy being queen—"

"I'm not happy being queen!" Carlotte stamped her foot noiselessly and came forward, taking both Livira's hands in her own. There had been a lot of touching, but Livira understood that her friend hadn't been able to touch anything save her own flesh for years—and that was a lonely place to be. "I want to go back. More than anything—wait, there's something to go back to, right? Not just a burned city and those damned sabbers?"

"Well—"

"It doesn't matter." Carlotte cut Livira off. "I want out. But I can't just leave Chertal." She squeezed Livira's hands until the bones almost creaked. "He's the only person I've spoken to the whole time I've been here. He's nice. Nice-ish anyway. I mean, you don't stay king for long if you're Arpix-nice. Actually, he's pretty cut-throat. But he's been good to me."

"But what can we do?" Leetar asked. "I mean, even if we could touch anything, a single skeer would chop all of us into pieces in no time at all."

Livira had to agree. She didn't like Leetar's defeatism, but she was right. Livira lifted her gaze to Yolanda. The girl had been silent since passing her earlier judgement.

"We can't leave her." Yolanda's pink gaze wandered Carlotte's tattered dress disapprovingly. "It's possible that the harm she's done will be self-limiting. But if we leave her to continue disrupting things it will pass the limit and start a chain reaction. If it hasn't already done so."

"So, you'll help me!" Carlotte flashed her old winning smile.

"Or force you to come," Leetar said darkly.

"How are you expecting us to help?" Livira wanted to, but their options seemed limited . . . to . . . zero.

Carlotte nodded at Yolanda. "She's got magic. I just saw her fly."

"You can fly too," Livira said. "There's nothing to it. It's just a matter of not falling."

Carlotte gave her a doubting look. "And you've got magic too, Livira. Don't say you haven't. That assistant, the one who told me to jump into the pool that . . . took me to the wood between the worlds. You made that happen, somehow, I know you did."

"I really don't. And certainly nothing that will work here . . ." Livira faltered, seeing the hurt in her friend's eyes. "Let's go and look. Let's watch these ganar and these skeer. We can do that. We're made for that."

"You think I haven't tried?" Carlotte shook her head helplessly. "I've spent weeks trudging around in those damn woods. Got so lost! I'd have starved to death if I needed to eat. Oh, gods, you don't have something to eat, do you? You wouldn't believe how many cakes I've looked at!"

"You forget . . ." Livira looked down meaningfully and Carlotte followed her gaze, eyes widening at the empty space below their feet. ". . . we can fly!" And with that, Livira drew Carlotte further towards the ceiling, keeping tight hold of her hands.

They'd just reached Yolanda and Leetar among the rafters when the far door crashed open, and an out-of-breath king rushed in, shouting for Carlotte. Yolanda pulled Leetar on, vanishing through the plaster overhead.

"Come on," Livira said quietly.

Carlotte resisted without seeming to know that she was, gazing down at the unsuspecting man as his guards followed him into the chamber. "It's hard."

Livira nodded, unwilling to just drag her friend away.

"It was chance that put us together," Carlotte said. "I'd have been stuck with whoever could see me. Or gone slowly mad if nobody could."

Livira had always suspected that, in matters of romance, destiny's role was overstated. Most of the magic was in how any two vaguely suited people could discover the wonder of each other if given space and time. Would she have fallen for a different canith if they had been there in Evar's place? One of his brothers perhaps? She would never know. Accepting that truth both took away some of the enchantment in love, the romance-book type of magic, and added a different kind of wonder in its place, one that perhaps made you a better person.

"I can't just abandon him," Carlotte said.

"I know."

Carlotte met her gaze. "How could you? You've never been in love. You said it wasn't like that with Meelan . . ." Carlotte had always been a little cruel, or more careless perhaps than cruel, but the results were the same. Now she caught herself, as if years of semi-solitude had made her listen more carefully to her own words. "Sorry . . . I didn't mean—" She broke off, staring into Livira's eyes. "Do you know? You seem different . . . How long has it been for you?"

Livira managed a half-smile. "Not so long. But I really did meet someone in the library. I'll tell you later. But now we really do have to . . ." Below them King Chertal, who had been marching to the opposite door, paused and lifted his face to examine the shadow-haunted rafters. ". . . go!"

A moment later they were through the roof and speeding towards a cloudless sky.

———

CARLOTTE'S SHRIEKS MIXED delight and terror as Livira hauled her higher and higher. The citadel dwindled beneath their heels, rapidly becoming a patchwork of rooftops which in turn shrunk into some incomprehensible toy. The ground over which they flew started to look more like a map than an actual place. It would, Livira thought, be very easy to lose one's humanity making decisions from such an altitude. She wondered if the gods felt the same way as they pushed their pieces across the playing board. Did they forget the blood and suffering way down there, too small to see? Or was that what made them gods in the first place? The ability to see both the biggest and smallest picture at the same time?

Livira pulled up level with Yolanda. Leetar remained unwilling to fly by herself, but the contact she maintained with Yolanda was light compared to the death grip Carlotte had on Livira, both arms wrapped about her neck so tight that she was almost choking.

"This is great," Carlotte said breathlessly after a final shriek. "But I can't even see my house . . . and it's a palace! How can we spot skeer from up here?"

"We saw what might be their tracks in the forest. We can follow those and see what we find. The trail looked fresh."

"When did you become a tracker, Livira Page?" Carlotte asked, still hanging on for grim death.

"It's a corridor of destruction wide enough for an army," Livira said. "They just break or push down any tree that gets in their way."

"That does sound like skeer . . ."

FINDING THEIR WAY back to their point of arrival proved too great a task of navigation: one patch of a great forest looked very much like another. Instead, they flew low enough to see any likely signs of passage, whilst retaining sufficient height and speed to inspect many square miles each hour.

On discovering one of the trails, it was Carlotte who divined the direction of skeer travel by noting the lie of the trampled vegetation. They followed it, immune to the heat and humidity, untroubled by the legions of midges or by mosquitoes that were sized more like small birds than insects and looked capable of draining a whole armful of blood. A smaller track joined theirs and later their track joined a bigger one, like tributaries converging to form an ever-larger river. It also put Livira in mind of the near-invisible paths that spread from any bone-ant nest, along which the ants would drag victims as large as a rat and as heavy as a human femur.

"It doesn't quite feel real, does it?" Carlotte asked, back at ground level, having insisted on walking.

"It's a bit like what the Mechanism does," Livira said. "As if the whole world were a book and we were just turning the page to reach the part we want. If it weren't for people like Chertal and Celcha I'd think that's all it was. An illustrated history—painted with such vivid colours that it fools the eye."

"Celcha?"

"A ganar who saw me dancing with Evar over the city. But not our city. I mean, it's in the same place, but this was a thousand—"

"Evar?" Carlotte stopped walking. "Dancing!"

"The point is that she could see me too." Livira continued to glide forward, her toes inches above the flattened vegetation.

"WHO IS EVAR?"

Livira turned to face Carlotte, while still moving forward with Yolanda and Leetar flanking her. "He's . . ." It felt strange to say it out loud. Especially in the depths of a huge forest that would be ancient dust by the time she was born. She and Carlotte had been close, bound tighter still by their love of gossip. It felt like only yesterday Livira had ushered her into the pool to escape the canith. But also like two centuries ago. Time stretched between them in all manner of ways as Carlotte began to dwindle into the distance, still refusing to follow.

"I love him," Livira said simply, suddenly unsure if she'd ever said that before, especially to Evar.

"I need *all* the details!" Carlotte was at her elbow in an eye-blink.

"I think we're getting there." Leetar raised her arm to point ahead.

Something could be seen above the treetops, an irregular black-and-green something, like a mountain, but not a mountain.

"No guards," Yolanda observed. "Their confidence is alarming."

The way ahead did appear to have no eyes on it. But from what Livira knew about the skeer, only the suicidal would seek them out for violence. She still had trouble fitting into her head the idea that it was the ganar who bred the skeer. The small, inoffensive ganar—who had lived as slaves beneath the cities of men and canith alike—had first come down to invade the world, throwing their slave-bred skeer armies at unsuspecting towns and cities . . . Or was it first? Were they in turn answering some older insult? It didn't matter. As Yute had said: it was a cycle. A cycle that ground lives into dust and sucked worlds dry.

As they drew closer, the track they had been following widened from a river to a delta and ahead of them lay square miles deforested not by the axe or saw but by bludgeoning force. The mountain revealed itself as a misshapen pyramid of some black substance—perhaps metal—smooth but complex. It had been there for a long time, judging by the vines hanging from its projections in waterfalls, and the full-grown trees that had managed to find footing in some of the larger hollows.

"A ganar night-ship?" Livira wondered. It seemed impossible that it had travelled from Attamast, sailing the black space above the sky, but equally impossible that it could have been constructed so deep in the forest without the knowledge of the surrounding kingdoms.

Yolanda seemed unimpressed, though the child rarely showed emotion of any kind. She led the way out into the cleared space without pausing to gawp at the great structure in its midst. The others had to hurry after her to catch up.

Livira swallowed the words of caution her tongue had tried to give voice to. Nobody would see them. They were in no danger. That was the point of the exercise. They could be reading a book about this place for all the harm it could do them or they might do it.

As they crossed the rutted soil and pulverised, long-dead remains of perhaps a million trees, the distance to the night-ship closed far more slowly than Livira had anticipated.

"It's bigger than the citadel," Carlotte breathed. She looked at Livira despairingly. "There's no hope for Chertal . . ."

Livira stretched her mouth into what she hoped was a sympathetic line.

From what she remembered, there weren't even ruins visible on the Ar-thran Plateau in their day. She knew it was more important to Carlotte whether the city fell to ruin within months or centuries than it was to her. Even so, a brief wander through the streets, and a short time within the palace, had made the place far more real to her than just some dead empire noted in the histories. If she could, Livira would help Carlotte's king, though she couldn't see how that was possible.

"Over there!" Carlotte pointed.

A skeer column was emerging from the forest to the west, along an es-tablished trail. Dozens, scores, hundreds. A river of the insectoid warriors, marching so close to each other that they resembled a single vast multi-legged organism.

Yolanda led the way towards the newcomers. Livira found herself in reluctant second place, filled with sudden doubts concerning her invisibil-ity. Even if she hadn't seen the destruction the skeer were capable of, some primal instinct warned her to keep her distance, telling her that any dis-tance where she could still see the things was too small and should be en-larged by sprinting away.

"You're sure they can't see us?" Leetar gave voice to Livira's concern. Even Carlotte, who had been seen by nobody but her king for years now, looked worried.

Closer up, the dull thunder of heavy feet spearing the earth and driving on made conversation impossible. Livira tried to imagine the mass of skeer coming at an army of men. Their momentum seemed unstoppable.

"HOW CA—" Livira's shout fell away as within the space of two heart-beats the entire column came to a halt. ". . . can . . ."

The question went unfinished. Two hundred skeer heads turned her way. The half a dozen black eyes each insectoid possessed seemed to sweep across her. Three skeer at the front broke from the pack, their lustrous white armour plates gleaming, the dark edging and the veins, that looked black even in the library light, showing a deep, rich blue in the fierceness of the sun.

Slowly, tilting their heads in an almost human gesture, the three be-gan to advance towards Livira and her companions, as if searching for something they couldn't quite focus on. Without warning, they broke into a flat charge, and with a single scream shared between them, Carlotte and Leetar fled.

Livira, frozen in the moment, discovered with predictably poor timing the sudden inability to move which so often afflicts prey beneath the claws of predators. She had died to such creatures before. Her near-indestructible assistant body had been bludgeoned into pieces. And standing there, paralysed by primal terror, she knew with utter conviction that ghost or no ghost, the creatures were mere moments from reducing her to bloody ribbons.

One hallmark of intelligence is a propensity for doing stupid things.
                                        Pull the Pin, *by Frank Oltmanns-Mack*

CHAPTER 15

Arpix

The soldier had fallen through a portal that appeared to have been drawn on the floor by the splattering of a large quantity of assistant blood, then concealed beneath the dust. Whether the assistant had been destroyed by the huge metal automaton or by the explosion that ripped the automaton apart, Arpix couldn't say. Either way, it seemed impossible that any assistant could have lost so much blood and survived.

All around him, soldiers were probing the ground with their weapons, alert to the new threat. Several of the lost man's comrades stood around the edge of the revealed portal, but none had made any move to follow him even after the muffled sound of a stick-shot had reached them from the other side.

Some of the soldiers spreading out across the dust-laden chamber were pushing civilians ahead of them. An older woman, a painfully thin young man, and, looking as frightened and helpless as the rest, the head librarian, Master Acconite. Arpix stood for a moment, skewered by sudden amazement, though the scene contained nothing he hadn't seen before. These soldiers, these men and women, weren't the sabbers who had at such cost swarmed over the walls of Crath City. They were fellow humans who had sworn to defend the city and everyone in it. They had lived among the citizenry, neighbours in the same districts, elbow to elbow in the markets, listened to the same songs, danced in the same taverns. And yet here they were, a month or two after the fall of that city, carrying out all the evils they had ascribed to their enemy, on their own people, literally eating the very citizens they'd vowed to protect—and that had been the worst of the accusations they could find to level at the canith, an unfounded accusation as far as Arpix knew. And even as they did it, they delighted in their victims' pain, perhaps to distance themselves from it, or perhaps something had broken in their minds. Kerrol would know, Arpix thought. Kerrol would offer some dispassionate and horribly truthful analysis that concluded all mankind carried the seeds of such monstrous behaviour in the marrow of their bones from the moment of birth.

And now the soldiers were using the weakest of their captives as an expendable property to test dangerous ground. In this vast temple to learning, populated by works of intellect stacked higher than houses, the city's head librarian was being goaded ahead of murdering cannibals to test for danger. Cannibals who just months before had seen their duty as being to protect him and all their fellow citizens. Murderers who had loved their children, helped their friends, and seen their lives as everyone else did, reaching from one small hope to the next, wanting to be good, wanting to be seen, wanting to be valued.

A shout alerted everyone to the fact that another portal had been found. Arpix hoped fervently that Livira, Clovis, and the others had all managed to escape the automaton. The lack of corpses gave him hope. But given the ferocity of the explosion, which had torn inches-thick metal plate like paper, he wasn't sure any bodies would have survived in large enough pieces to be noticed, let alone recognised.

The buzzing from the Mechanism had grown louder, a grating rumble now as if stones were being dragged across rough ground. Of all of them, only Arpix seemed to notice it. The others had little idea that it should be silent, like the rest of the library.

The answering call from Livira's book had become a trembling whine that rose and fell in time with the pulses of sound from the Mechanism. Arpix was already worried both that someone would see the thing trembling in his pocket, and that it would shake itself apart into a collection of loose pages, and lose its power.

Livira had said to take the book to the Mechanism, and while the soldiers hunted for more magical pits into which they might fall, Arpix edged closer to the grey structure at the centre of the reading room.

"You, librarian!" Lord Algar fixed Arpix with his single eye. "Come here!"

Two soldiers turned from their search and angled towards Arpix, still probing the white dust ahead of them.

The king raised his grey head from a fascinated study of the portal that had swallowed one of his men. "Shoot anything that comes out of there," he directed. "And you, boy, you promised me a banquet." Oanold swatted down the 'stick barrel one of his personal guards was raising towards Arpix. "He'll *wish* he'd been shot if that was all lies. Don't any of you dare kill him!"

Arpix felt the weight of the king's authority settle on him, adding to Lord Algar's command. He'd obeyed the rules his whole life. And those were only rules, not law. Laws were a whole other level, and the king's word was law. Dry-mouthed, he looked from Oanold, the king not just of Crath City but an entire nation beyond, to the Mechanism. Part of him was desperate to sprint for the grey block just twenty yards away. If the salvation Livira had offered didn't reveal itself, perhaps he could hide inside until his captors left.

Arpix spotted Salamonda and Neera surrounded by soldiers, their wrists bound. The moment passed and the breath he'd been holding hissed out of him. He wanted to think that it was the other captives that kept him from running, rather than an inability to defy authority. He wanted to be more like Clovis and less like himself. He hung his head. "I wasn't lying." Arpix lifted the book he'd plucked from the shelves almost at random. *A History of Western Aphasia, 2nd century to 4th century*, by R. Lethe, written in a little-used dialect of Juntran. As long as Western Aphasia had restaurants, or feasts, or poorly guarded kitchens, and at least one peaceful month, it should be possible to find some food. The illusionary fare wouldn't sustain any who consumed it, but they'd get the full benefit of the taste and perhaps some sense of fullness. Arpix wasn't particularly confident about the details, but Livira had told him plenty of stories. "I can show you how to reach the food. You just need to take this book into the Mechanism and then—"

"Bring me the book!" Oanold waved at his guards. "And watch our spare librarian. I don't want him slipping off anywhere." He snorted as if he'd made a joke.

Bony hands gripped him painfully while the history was pulled from his fingers and taken to the king. Oanold squinted at the title then turned the volume this way and that as one might inspect a puzzle box. Then, with a dissatisfied grunt, the king pushed through his guards and approached Arpix. The white powder from the floor coated the bottom eighteen inches of his stained robes and a low white cloud rose in his wake. He still walked like an overweight man, waddling even though the fat had melted from his bones.

The soldiers around Arpix backed away as Oanold approached with four of his personal guards. The king trailed a sour look up the length of Arpix's body, his gaze dark with suspicion. Arpix realised just how old and unhealthy the man was. His paints and powders were cracking, and the skin beneath showed its age, his eyes looking as if black stones had been thrown into a half-set pudding.

"Tell me . . ." The king looked around at the soldiers around him. "Hmmm. Over there I think." He gestured to the Mechanism, clearly not ready to share the secret key to this promised feast with those that served him. "You, Jons." He indicated the hard-eyed veteran. "Keep your weapon trained on the spare. If I say I want him shot, I don't expect to be kept waiting."

The man nodded and raised his 'stick until its single dark eye pointed directly at Arpix.

"Come on then," Oanold urged, unable to keep from licking his lips. "Lead the way."

Hunger was, Arpix had observed during his long stranding on the Arthran Plateau, a powerful motivator. He took the lead as instructed. Lacking anything but his own feet to probe the ground with, he scuffed away the dust, and it filled the air with a whitish fog.

No word of reprimand came from Lord Algar. It occurred to Arpix that the lord, whilst goaded by the same pangs of hunger that afflicted them all, was exercising more caution than King Oanold. The king was Algar's own probe, testing the threat of the Mechanism in the same way that Arpix was testing the ground for Oanold.

Arpix walked on. In his pocket the book's vibration became something wild, as if it were mere moments from exploding into shredded pages and broken bindings. The Mechanism's rumbling slid so deeply down the registers that he could feel it through his feet, almost like the wheels of some great wagon shaking the ground, an avalanche rotating into being from some place beyond the senses.

The fear had left him. If he fell through a hidden doorway, it was unlikely to place him in worse hands. If the Mechanism tore itself apart and killed him in a storm of shrapnel, it would be a quicker and cleaner death than his imminent demise in Oanold's keeping.

"Stop!" Oanold could feel it now.

All around them the ground's vibration was turning the dust back into the smoke it had once been, a slowly rising cloud already calf-deep. Arpix pulled out Livira's book. The moment his fingers found it, the book ceased to vibrate and instead it was Arpix who shook—not in a teeth-rattling way but in a manner that blurred his boundaries, so that he seemed to see himself from the outside, an overlapping collection of half-seen Arpixes, all of them holding the same book, as if it were the only real thing about him.

"Stop, damn you!" Oanold barked. "Stop him!"

Stick-shot rang out—one or many, Arpix couldn't tell—he felt no pain. Perhaps with so many images of him, none was the right target.

Ten yards lay between him and the Mechanism. Some instinct told him that he wouldn't make it. That if he tried to advance, then the many Arpixes would each go a different route and he would lose himself, and his purpose. Instead, though it hurt his librarian soul, he drew back his arm to throw the book at the Mechanism.

To Arpix's great surprise, King Oanold came charging through the rising smoke and seized his arm. Arpix had painted too tempting an image of the feast that waited within the Mechanism. Oanold had seldom been accused of being clever but even his worst critics rarely denied that he was cunning. Some instinct had told the king that the book was the key to his promised meal. Despite having more than sixty summers behind him, the old man threw himself upon the young librarian, reaching for the book.

Perhaps it was the shock of being clawed at by the screeching monarch of the nation in which he'd lived his whole life, or weakness from four years of eating little but beans—either way, it was not a contest that Arpix won. Both of them stumbled closer to the rumbling Mechanism before Oanold's sharp elbow struck Arpix in the neck and with a cry of triumph he jerked Livira's book from Arpix's grasp.

Oanold's victory shout became a startled yelp as one of his feet tangled in some stray piece of the fallen ganar's internal workings. The king staggered backwards, arms pinwheeling, almost losing hold of his prize. His outstretched hand struck the grey wall behind him.

The impact of book against Mechanism should have made no noise. Instead, it was as if a clapper larger than an ocean-going ship had struck the mother of all bells, the sound so deep that it wrapped up the echoes of the 'sticks' roar into it and rolled through the room setting everyone in tumbling motion.

From where he landed, through dazed eyes, Arpix could see that both Oanold and the book had slid down the Mechanism's wall to rest at the base, the book falling open as it landed. Even as Arpix convinced himself he must be dreaming, Livira's book began to vomit pages into the air, enough pages for a dozen books, scores, hundreds. The stream continued, filling the space above with a maelstrom of loose leaves rising even more swiftly than the dust rose.

Arpix saw the library floor fracture, black chasms spreading like the fingers of a dark hand, the cracks more real than anything that lay between them and Arpix's eyes, showing through as if they were the only truth and the rest of the world mere suggestion.

The first and largest of these fissures opened beneath King Oanold and, still clutching the page-spewing volume, he fell into darkness, wailing all the way.

The king was the first of scores to topple and be swallowed. Even as the victims fell, the sound grew. The rolling thunder of great wheels, and the sure and certain knowledge that something was coming.

The curative power of time is often overstated. However, old arguments do some-times become dust beneath the march of years. Feuds often survive all recollection of their cause but are on rare occasions outlived by some of the participants.
Life's Too Short, *by Methuselah Adamspawn*

CHAPTER 16

Evar

T he act of being throttled drew Mayland's attention back to Evar, and once more Mayland's will imposed itself on the library's blood running through his brother's veins. Evar's grip loosened and Mayland pulled free.

The weight of the presence at Evar's back, combined with his siblings' focus in that direction, turned him around. The matter of Mayland's crimes, and the control he held over Evar's body, would have to wait.

Another round of thunder, the loudest yet, shattered the air, and for a time no speech was possible. It seemed, in the ringing aftermath, that perhaps the blast had been the crescendo. Certainly, the torrents of falling pages began to slow.

Somehow a lone figure, robed, cowled, and bearing a staff, had crossed the undulating surface of loose paper, advancing through the thickening page-fall to get within twenty yards of the canith without even Starval noticing. And Starval noticed *everything*. Only now as the paper downfall thinned was the newcomer's presence obvious.

Evar eyed the stranger speculatively. The wizard who had earlier emerged from the rain of falling pages had turned out to be some piece of rogue fiction, trying to snare him into an archetypal story. This new arrival looked more obviously false, and also rather short. "It's another story, right?" Evar muttered to nobody in particular.

The stranger proved to have remarkable hearing. "If I am, I'm a caution-ary tale."

Mayland took a step back, worry, perhaps even fear, taking possession of his face. Evar realised that he couldn't remember ever seeing Mayland look worried.

"You took quite a risk returning to the vaults, Mayland." It wasn't a canith voice, or a human one, but something more guttural.

"Shit . . ." Starval drew his blades. Clovis kept her hands at her sides, still undecided in the matter of friend or foe.

Mayland managed to affect nonchalance and shrugged. "We fell." He looked up, far above the newcomer's head. "Besides, the view is better from down here."

Evar followed his brother's gaze and there, in the black heavens where there had been nothing before, was a red star. Beneath it, picked out in flecks of crimson by ten thousand falling pages, a pillar of light, as if the star were pouring almost all of its brightness into gravity's arms.

"And lo, the star in the east which has led me hence," the cowled stranger said, as if reciting a line.

"It's only just appeared," Evar protested. "It hasn't led anyone any-where."

"And yet here you are." The stranger lifted their head and offered a narrow slice of a smile.

Evar saw the big square teeth, the golden fur touched with grey cover-ing cheeks and chin. "Ganar," he breathed. Then more loudly, "Who are you?" And in the moment's silence that followed, he turned to face his brothers. "Who is this? Both of you know."

The ganar pulled back its cowl. To Evar it looked much like the au-tomata that had plagued their travels through the library, but it felt pre-sumptuous to accuse the first ganar he'd met of being the author of that misfortune.

"My name is Celcha. You've met my brother, Hellet. These two"—she gestured at Starval and Mayland—"ruined my life. But they also gave me a life by engineering my transfer from the Arthran mines to the library." She looked from each sibling to the next, dark eyes giving nothing away. "What I can't forgive"—the pagescape surged around them as if the graveyard of books had become a rolling sea—"is that they made me kill an entire city, from babies born to slavery to the queen born to her crown."

"Made?" Mayland struggled to keep his feet as the ground rose and fell beneath him. The fear that had been in his face didn't make it to his voice.

"Tricked me. Tricked us." Celcha's growl, very different to a canith's, reverberated through the air as though she were the size of her largest avatar. The page-storm's intensity picked up again, swirling around them.

"You knew you were going to poison them! That was always going to be a dangerous business," Mayland shouted over the flutter and flap. "The stain on my hands doesn't clean yours!"

Starval had one arm raised, ready to throw his knife. Evar caught his wrist. "Don't."

Evar knew the ganar before him had spent a lifetime trying to engineer her misplaced revenge on him and Livira. A revenge properly aimed at Mayland and to a lesser extent, Starval. And whilst he didn't want to see his brothers die for that crime, the ganar deserved a better answer than a dagger in the throat.

The ganar advanced on them along a path that stayed level and untroubled by the storm. A final spasm of the page-quake threw Mayland to his hands and knees. The rest of them staggered but kept their feet. Clovis's hand found the hilt of her white sword.

"I can't forgive." Celcha levelled her driftwood staff at Mayland, a gnarled thing, polished by age. "But I've watched the bitter harvest of revenge and the years since have tempered that old anger. Even exacted upon the correct targets, revenge . . . however tempting"—and here she looked meaningfully from Mayland to Starval and let her gaze linger on each—"is no longer my goal. I continue my journey to my own centre, and of necessity to the centre of the library."

"There's a centre?" Evar blinked.

"Of course there's not a centre," Mayland snapped. "It's a quest to distract the gullible. It's exactly what happened to you with that story trope just now. The old wizard comes to tell you you're special, and that you need to save the world. It's just like that, only on a grander scale. This ganar"—he waved a hand towards Celcha without sparing her a glance—"thinks she's drained the library dry of every secret but the last. Instead, she's been duped by a fiction that's escaped the vaults. She thinks she's some sort of mystic, and all that's happened is she's fallen for the simplest—"

"She knows more than you do?" Clovis asked. "It sounds like that's what you're saying."

Evar couldn't help snorting. Celcha barked something that might have been a laugh.

"I'm looking for a way to destroy the library," Mayland said, ignoring his sister. "And that doesn't start with finding the centre. It starts here. Or, more precisely"—he pointed to the red star—"up there!"

"On that we're agreed." Celcha raised her staff towards the star. "That's why I'm here and where I'm heading." She started to walk off across the paper dunes. "You may accompany me."

Mayland stood, watching her go with a sour expression, as if few things might displease him more than being forgiven.

"Well?" Starval prompted. Starval had never had a problem with being forgiven. It was his standard operating procedure: to do what he wanted and then ask forgiveness afterwards. "What now?"

Mayland released a long sigh and, without comment, set off after the ganar.

"Wait!" Evar hurried after Celcha too. "I don't care about stars and centres. I just want to get back to the library. Or wherever Livira is. The rest of it can go hang."

"Oh, we're going back to the library all right." Celcha, who seemed ridiculously short now that Evar had drawn level with her, leaned on her staff as they climbed a rise. Despite her height, and the fact that she'd spent a large chunk of her life planning his and Livira's demise, Evar's sense of her was one of gravitas: she reminded him of Yute. Both of them wise and at the same time sad, as if the former bred the latter. "That's the biggest chink I've seen, and I've been around awhile." She nodded ahead to the star and the column of light beneath it. "Once we get close it'll suck us all up, whether we want it to or not. It's the mess on the other side you should be worrying about. Something bad happened to put that hole there. Something very bad."

Evar resigned himself to following. His questions had multiplied beyond hope of answers. And when it came down to it, what he wanted most were results rather than answers. He wanted to find Livira and know she was safe. He wanted to apologise for leaving her behind when he went after Arpix, without saying that he wouldn't do it again. Whether he had that right or not, he would always take the bullet in her place.

Evar and Clovis kept pace with Celcha, flanking the ganar. Clovis had her sword out now, and her eyes to the crests of each rise. It seemed Evar's sister's desire to get back matched his own. She'd been prepared to go to war for Arpix, but that wasn't setting the bar particularly high for Clovis. The fact that she'd retreated to save Evar spoke volumes though, and he would not forget that particular testimonial to the depth of the bond between them.

Clovis looked serious now, focused, nervous even. Not the eager, fierce anticipation of combat he would have expected if it were simply a second chance to wage war on those who had slaughtered her people. Clovis saw Evar glancing at her and bared her teeth, but he knew her too well to miss the true feelings behind the bravado. Clovis was worried. Worried for Arpix. Worried they would be too late. And if he was honest, Evar was too. He'd never had a friend before, save Livira who was both that and more. But Arpix, he realised, was his first male friend, and as soon as he was sure of Livira's safety, Evar would be turning all his thoughts towards aiding Clovis in rescuing him.

Celcha led on, circumventing the largest page-dunes, and steering clear of dust lakes in which she said a cart and horses could sink from sight even as the ropes to haul them out were being unslung. Evar noticed that the hazy, half-seen backgrounds that had seemed to shift when studied and to change when his attention wandered from them, were now closer though no less strange. To their left marched a grey jungle, its papery leaves slowly taking on a dark greenish-grey if he stared at them. A quick diversion would see him in among those trees, chasing whatever it was that could be glimpsed flitting between thick trunks. To his right the narrow streets and tiled roofs of some town where shadowy figures haunted the alleys—humans maybe, to judge from their walk.

"Hey . . ."

"What?" Clovis turned his way.

"I don't . . . know." For a moment he could almost have sworn he saw

Kerrol vanish down one of those alleyways, following a pale human man and a human girl, towering over the pair.

"Don't look," Mayland instructed. "It's very easy to be led astray here. And those who do, don't come back."

As the column of light beneath the star drew ever closer, so did the dreamlike surroundings, and the terrain became harder to navigate, as if the crimson ray had struck down with physical force that had created larger and larger page-dunes, like the ripples in a pond where a stone has fallen.

A strange vibration began to fill the air, a buzzing that made Evar lick his teeth. The beam seemed to touch down just over the next, and largest yet, page-dune, the light spreading to paint the ground blood-red and drench every member of their small group in crimson.

Celcha turned, seeking a path over the last obstacle, and as she did, something made Evar look up, squinting into the glare of the distant star.

"That can't be good." Beside him Starval looked too, shading his eyes.

The light flickered then faltered and was swallowed away. The descending page cloud looked like a heavy fluid poured into a lighter one, billowing, pluming, plunging down, spreading out, plunging again, spreading and spreading.

A descending ceiling of seething paper promised to engulf them within moments.

"Grab hold of each other," Celcha instructed, her voice urgent.

And then, with a rustling *whoof*, everything was falling pages.

"Clovis?" The endless fall of paper swallowed Evar's shout. "Starval?"

They'd been right beside him. Clovis to his left, Starval just behind. Yet now as he waded forward, climbing to keep from being buried, he felt utterly alone.

The vaults' twilight, as sourceless as the library's illumination, could not be cut off by the page-fall as the star's red glare had been, and even amid the downpour Evar could see. His gaze caught for a moment on the most recent page to fill his reaching hand. Amazed, he snatched another from the air, then another.

"Livira?" It was her handwriting that sprawled across the paper. He scooped up a handful and flicked them away, one by one, spitting out an errant page that tried to enter his open mouth. "It's not possible." But surely a single book couldn't account for the heaps around him, let alone the greater storm still descending. He reached for another as it fell.

Livira's carelessly graceful hand occupied the page from one side to the other, devouring space with loops and curls. Brushing aside more page-fall, he started to read. *"You're sure they can't see us?"* As he read them the words sounded in his head, not in his voice but in one that carried a familiar edge.

Evar looked up. The storm had gone. Everything had gone. A startlingly blue sky reached across a wide expanse of churned earth spotted with the shattered stumps of trees. He turned in the direction the voice had seemed to come from. At first, he saw nothing but more wasteland. His eyes felt strange, his vision split into overlapping fields that offered confusing multiples of everything. But . . . there! Shimmering like a heat haze . . . there was something. He tilted his head, tried to squint. Faint, ghostly, but there. Not more than a hundred yards away, coming into sharper view as he focused. Four human females: Livira in her librarian's robe, flanked by two women of similar age in tattered dresses, and at the fore, a child, Yute's daughter, white as her father.

"You! Stop!" Someone behind him, barking the words like orders.

Evar started forward, trying to shout Livira's name. He felt strange, barely in control of his body, but he kept his fractured vision focused on Livira. *It's me!* he wanted to shout but somehow couldn't. Livira should be running to his arms, not just standing there, watching with what seemed like a mixture of trepidation and distaste. Her two friends, one he recognised from Yute's group, looked terrified, barely able to keep from sprinting away. The girl from Yute's group—Meelan's sister—looked as scared as when they'd first met and he'd been the first canith she'd ever seen up close, certainly the first not trying to kill her.

Evar readied himself to run. The four humans might be ghosts, just as he and Livira had been. If they flew away, he'd never catch them.

"Stop!" That voice again. Evar ignored it, only to find his whole body locked tight, utterly paralysed.

"Back in line!" the unseen master called, and Evar's body answered. He turned and found himself unable even to flinch at the shock discovery that he was bracketed on either side by a full-grown skeer. Worse, he was marching back towards a column of hundreds of the things.

At the edge of his sight, he spotted the small figure that seemed to be the source of the commands. A ganar, a tiny, harmless ganar in charge of maybe two hundred skeer. It made no sense. What made even less sense was the growing realisation that not only was he not in command of his body, his body wasn't his at all. With shuddering disgust Evar understood that some of the white limbs churning the dirt around him were in fact . . . his.

In desperation, Evar screamed Livira's name. The cry emerged as nothing but message-scent, but it was enough to draw the scrutiny of the skeer to either side of him.

The skeer marched on. Evar couldn't even turn his head to see Livira.

"This is a dream, a nightmare." Understanding arrived late. "I'm in her story." It should have been obvious but the sight of Livira just yards away had bound him to the narrative and the horror of finding himself a skeer had taken over, keeping his mind too occupied to ask the important questions instead of the immediate ones. "It's just a story."

But how had Livira written a tale about skeer? When had she written it? How could he escape it? He ignored the many-legged advance that surrounded him and tried to remember where he'd come from. *The star! The page-fall!*

Evar focused on the memory of the descending page-storm that had engulfed him and his siblings. He remembered the blackness as it had tried to smother him. And in that blind memory a sucking blackness drew him down a well of its own making.

Evar had hoped to escape, but when the darkness let him go, it wasn't back into the page-storm.

Where? Where am I? What am I? He was no longer a skeer. He was something else, somewhere else, something worse. He lay on a table in a chamber lit by a pulsing crimson light, a chamber that looked more grown than made. Ganar moved around him, their pelts bloody in the light.

Evar had been drawn into Livira's stories before, but they had never been like this. They had been charming, sometimes sad, but always a place to be with her, to explore together and to deepen his understanding of this being who had taken hold of his heart. But this was something else. Some dark and tainted fever-dream. He couldn't move, not even to turn his head.

At least when he had been the skeer he had been alone in the shell of that great beast, slave to the limitations of its body but at the helm in all other regards. Here he felt as though he were adrift in a small open boat on a vast black sea, heaved high and laid low by the swell, and that he was far from alone, for the sea was a mind much larger than his, and the huge waves were only the outer ripples of its pain and of its anger.

The contemplation of any single object will eventually draw in every other, and with them all wisdom. But a swifter path to understanding our kind is to consider a child stamping upon ants.

One Good Deed Burns Another, *by Charity Jones*

CHAPTER 17

Livira

For no obvious reason three of the skeer had broken from their column. Whether the trio's route would lead them directly to Livira's group wasn't clear, but they would certainly come far too close for comfort.

"We should go . . . up?" The returning Carlotte took a firm hold on Livira's arm.

"They can't see us." Yolanda, always so certain, allowed a measure of uncertainty to enter her voice, mixed with amazement.

"You! Stop!" From the back of the column a small figure emerged from the forest of armoured legs.

Livira had never seen a ganar in the flesh, but she was sure that she was due many years of nightmares about the huge metal versions that had hounded her within the library. This one was less than four feet tall, almost as broad, and covered with a long coat of golden hair that fell in slightly curling sheets.

"Stop!" the ganar repeated and held up a plain iron ball indistinguishable from the one that Evar and Arpix had brought with them into the library.

The three skeer froze as if every joint of their armour had seized at once.

"Back in line!" the ganar barked, running his fingers across the sphere's surface in complicated patterns.

The trio returned to their places, the middle one seeming to fight the command, its body stuttering with effort. The ganar stood for a moment, looking first towards Livira and the others, his gaze not quite settling on them, and at the ball in his hands, as if perplexed. Then, with a brief hunch of his shoulders, the ganar headed back into the column.

"That's the ball Arpix found. He used it to push the skeer away. They couldn't come within a hundred yards of it," Livira said. She wished she'd had more time to talk to Evar and the others about their experiences outside the library prior to intercepting her escape from King Oanold's evils, but everything had happened so quickly. She wished a lot of things about what happened after their reunion had been different . . .

"Arpix?" Carlotte looked amazed. "Fighting skeer?"

"Not fighting, no!" Livira laughed off the notion.

"He killed a cratalac," Leetar said, quietly. "Meelan told me."

"Arpix?" Livira and Carlotte said it together in matching tones of disbelief. "Killed a cratalac?" Carlotte finished for them both.

"With quicksilver." Leetar nodded as if she could hardly believe it herself. "Meelan told me." The way she said her brother's name hurt Livira's heart.

"Wait, how do you know about cratalacs?" Livira turned to Carlotte.

"They're the worst thing in this forest. I saw one once, and I do not want to see another!" Carlotte shivered. "The stories they have for scaring children here, they're about cratalacs. They scare the grown-ups too."

Yolanda remained silent, watching the skeer column draw away towards the fallen night-ship. Livira went to stand beside her. "Maybe we could get one of those metal balls for King Chertal. Then he could defend the citadel."

"Absolutely not." Yolanda shook her head absently.

"Why not?" Livira wouldn't care about seeking the girl's permission, but she had no idea how they could steal an item they couldn't touch, and her hope was that Yolanda might come up with a solution.

"Haven't you been listening?" Yolanda looked up at her and blinked. "Every interaction with the past damages reality. Nobody knows quite how much it can take before . . ." She moved her hands apart while fluttering her fingers.

"Well, leaving Carlotte here is going to do more damage. So, let's do this and take her back to our time."

"There are other ways to deal with that situation," Yolanda said darkly. She steered her gaze towards the night-ship. "What I'm interested in right now—no, 'terrified of' would be a better way of putting it—is that the skeer could see us. Your friend and her king are a danger. Your ill-advised book is a terrible threat. But a whole species that can look through time . . . I can't understand how any of us still exist!"

"Maybe we could guide the king and his army to ambush—"

"I'm going in." And, without giving Livira any chance to object, the girl took off, flying directly at the night-ship's central mass.

Livira steeled herself against a sense of growing dread and reached out a hand to both Leetar and Carlotte. "We're following. If we lose her, I don't give much for our chances of ever getting back."

Livira's words proved sufficient motivation and moments later she was hauling the other two through the air. Despite Livira's best efforts the white child was streaking away. Leetar's and Carlotte's doubts were anchors holding Livira back, and she had doubts of her own to do that.

The black expanse of the ship's side grew to encompass their vision, and as Livira's eyes adjusted she saw it resolve into an alien landscape, half architecture, half biology, all black. Yolanda, tiny in the distance, vanished through the wall beneath a vast protrusion that resembled a knobbled dome and served no purpose that Livira could guess at.

"She's worried the awful monsters can see us, right?" Carlotte shouted as if the wind were whistling in their ears—which, since they were ghosts, it wasn't.

"Yes."

"So worried that she's going into their lair to find more?"

"Yes."

"I hope they can't . . ." The wall of the ship loomed, then leapt at them like blindness, and with a slight shudder they were through. ". . . touch us too . . ." Carlotte trailed off.

"I felt that," Leetar murmured beside Livira. They were standing in a softly lit corridor. To the left a featureless door sealed the way. About fifty yards off to the right was a strange dislocation, as if a giant had grabbed the structure and shoved one part out of alignment.

"I did too." Livira rubbed her arms, trying to rid them of the odd sensation. The light shuddered around them, then restabilized. It had a pervading, sourceless feel to it, but whether it cast shadows or not she couldn't tell.

For her part, Carlotte was pushing her arm in and out of the wall. "It's like spiderwebs! How can I be feeling it? Everywhere else even the ground doesn't feel like it's really there . . ."

Livira remembered the huge ganar automaton that had chased Evar and had also seemed to be chasing her. At the end of the pursuit it had, with a sweep of its leg, sent Malar flying, making some form of contact with him even though they had been ghosts, unable to interact with Evar in any way at all.

"The assistants can see ghosts, move them about, do what they like." Livira touched the wall, feeling that tingling resistance as her hand slipped into it. "Maybe these ganar are so clever that they've unlocked some of the library's secrets and used them in their creations. Maybe this ship could twist time around it?"

Leetar peered dubiously down the corridor. "If they can do that sort of thing why fight with legions of skeer?"

Livira shrugged. "This place looks pretty broken. Did they leave their moon by choice? Were they running from something? Did they build this, or find it? Did—"

"Questions, questions!" Carlotte snorted. "I'd forgotten what you were like." She shook her head. "The one that matters is where did that little girl run off to?"

Livira considered. "She's not the sort who stops until she's given a good reason to. That way." She pointed at the opposite wall in the direction they'd been travelling. "Hang on tight." And they plunged deeper.

Walls, corridors, chambers, pulsing flows of light, tight-packed crates, the throb of sound—all of it flashed past, and every hundred yards or so a new hull would oppose them, a box inside a box inside a box. Each hull added new resistance to their passage, until at last, Livira strained to pull her two companions through a wall of black steel or something equally durable.

In the dark heart of the night-ship a deep red light throbbed through the corridors, too dim to illuminate anything save corners and angles. Yolanda stood some distance off before a great valve that sealed the end of the passageway they had stopped in. The whiteness of her skin and wrappings caught the crimson in the unsourced light and returned it, leaving her blood-clad.

Livira swept along the corridor to join her.

"It's in here." Yolanda sounded doubtful—not doubtful that what she'd sought lay behind the door, but doubtful that she wanted to go through.

Livira opened her mouth to suggest going in, but then she felt it too. The closest thing she could liken it to was a smell, the reek of Oanold's camp in the centre circle of the chamber where Livira had returned to her body. It wasn't a smell, but it held that same corruption, the absence of hope, a surfeit of horror, a pain that was more terrible because nobody cared about it than for the detailed manner of its infliction, though that too was an obscenity. She opened her mouth again, this time to say that they should go—but those words wouldn't leave her tongue either.

"We should go in." As Yolanda spoke, the door opened noiselessly and a ganar, its pelt crimson in the ambient light, bustled out.

Livira and her companions stepped aside, letting the creature pass without intersecting with them. It reached no higher than Livira's lower ribs and like its fellows didn't bother with clothes, though this one wore a pair of goggles such as she had seen at the alchemists' laboratory. It went past briskly, occupied with the illegible scrawl on a notepad in its hand.

A chemical stink wafted into the corridor before the door resealed itself. The odour, at once both cloying and clawing, made Livira gag, even though she knew no poison could touch her and that she needed no air to breathe.

With a muttered something that sounded rather like an oath, Yolanda pushed through the closed door. Steeling herself, Livira followed.

The chamber beyond was large, circular, domed, and lit by the same light that seemed to slide through the reds into blackness. At least a dozen ganar moved around the periphery, some monitoring dials and panels on which glowing characters flowed in cascades of text. Others looked to be alchemists at work with tubes and potions and radiant heat sources to set the liquids in their flasks bubbling.

Four great standing circles of patterned metal walled off the centre of the chamber, though imperfectly due to their shape. In the space each circle encompassed lay a mirrored surface some three yards across and stopping a hand's breadth before the metal so that no means for supporting it could be discerned.

Gritting her teeth against what felt like an inevitable shock, Livira followed Yolanda towards one of the gaps that would afford entrance to the space between the four mirrors. She noted with mild surprise that she could see her reflection and Yolanda's in the nearest mirror. It reminded her that Leetar and Carlotte remained outside, probably listening to their instincts, which felt by far the more sensible course of action.

She ducked through the gap, not wanting to touch the rings or their mirrors. On a low table whose span dwarfed the ganar, and that marched away to the four points of the compass in mirrored infinities, lay something that exercised all parts of the word "nightmare."

Livira recognised the cratalac only from descriptions given to her as a child, from a claw she had once found in the Dust before swapping it with Acmar for sweetmeats from the markets, and from diagrams in an obscure book on the biology of cata class insectoids. It was this latter source that proved most useful since it had focused mainly on partly dissected pieces of the creatures. At the time, Livira had wondered how exactly the authors, A E Weebling and E A Webly, had come by their specimen, and had assumed that some still larger creature, like a roc, had helpfully killed one and scattered parts.

The other animal used to construct the patchwork hybrid before them was not one that Livira recognised. Shortly before she doubled up to vomit, she reached the conclusion that the brilliantly white, heavily muscled beast must be native to Attamast, brought down from the moon by the ganar for this purpose. She backed away, retching, tears filling her eyes.

Few of the pieces joined each other directly. Silver pipes, tubes of flexible glass, and bundled wires connected one twitching chunk of cratalac anatomy to a white-fleshed upper arm. Another black piece of cratalac thorax, carefully dissected and weeping ichor that the many pores on the table swallowed away, lay beside a beating organ whose pale meat pumped milk-white blood into yet more tubes. It seemed a half-completed jigsaw monstrosity, marrying flesh that was never intended to fit together.

"Why would they do this?" Livira wiped her mouth and tried to control her rebelling stomach. She kept her distance, physically repelled, the strongest emotion in the roiling sea within her: sadness. Something was looking out at her from those nightmare eyes, something in pain, something somehow almost familiar. "What is it?" She found herself whispering and was not sure why.

"A template of some kind," Yolanda answered in a hollow voice.

There were enough pieces of the two—at least two—creatures on the table to form a new monster, but even if the parts could be welded together through some ganar magic, the resultant creation would be an awkward patchwork that surely couldn't function even if the same fluid could run through its veins and sustain it.

"The mirrors," Livira said, "they have to be important." She forced herself to stare along the endless lines of reflected tables, each with an ever-decreasing image of herself and Yolanda beside it. "Something . . . changes . . ." The overlap and rapidly diminishing scale made it impossible to be sure, but the thing on the table seemed to evolve into the distance.

"A melding. It's a projection and a melding." Yolanda shifted her position. "The skeer—all of them—they're copies of this." She waved a hand at the carnage on the table. "But blended somehow."

"If we destroyed it then maybe—"

On the table, something moved. The head was three slices, the outer pair from the white monster, the central one cratalac, offering the weeping walls of its cranial contents to either side. If pushed together the resulting horror would have six eyes, the outer two winter blue and the inner four black. All six were watching Livira. She knew it even though none of them held a pupil to indicate direction. Cratalac claws tapped gently on the metal tabletop—not gently enough to evade the ganars' attention though, all of them hurrying unspeaking to their stations to read the dials and adjust numbers on screens.

A broken sound filled Livira's head without bothering with her ears. If it was a voice then the translation normally afforded to ghosts by the library was failing—it sounded like pain and anger and dreadful wordless promises of revenge, all mixed into one nerve-shredding mind howl.

The aftermath of any explosion is an opportunity, both for picking up the pieces, and for moving on.

Maintenance of Munitions, *by Sergeant Tyler Dickerson*

CHAPTER 18

Arpix

A rpix lay amid the rumbling and the dust and the page-fall, unsure of whether he'd been hurt in the detonation that had thrown him across the chamber, and if so, how hurt. He tried not to breathe, not wishing to fill his lungs with the sour smoke. At first that had been easy, what with the wonder of it all stilling his breath. And then, when the wonder had worn thin, it had still been easy, since his lungs, evacuated of breath by the initial impact with the floor, refused to fill themselves. Now though, starved of air beyond the point at which complaining chest muscles and bruised ribs held sway, Arpix sat up sharply, shedding drifts of loose pages, and inhaled with the ferocity of a drowning man.

The act might have drawn attention to him, but for the fact that dozens of similar figures were also in the act of sitting up, or rolling from side to back, or struggling to their knees, anonymous in their powdered whiteness.

One person, turning onto their side, promptly vanished with a scream, having rolled into one of many broad fissures spreading across the floor. Arpix would have paid this distressing occurrence more attention but for the fact that he suddenly understood himself also to be sitting beside a chasm large enough to swallow him.

He shuffled away and got unsteadily to his feet, his mind still dazed. The old smoke, reinvigorated by a new explosion, hung in the air, sour on the lungs and reducing vision to ten yards or so. Where Arpix stood, the floor was largely intact, though divided by cracks. Towards where the Mechanism had been, the cracks became chasms.

Dust-clad as the survivors were, it was hard to tell friend from foe, but as his focus returned Arpix could identify the soldiers by the shape of their uniform, and of course those who had found and picked up their 'sticks declared themselves immediately. Glancing around, it seemed that more than half of the company had fallen through the cracks into— Arpix peered into the nearest one and found this did little to answer the question. The darkness onto which the fissure opened was populated by shifting shapes and distant islands of light. He thought he even glimpsed the Exchange for a moment before a grey cloud of what might be leathery wings obscured the view.

"Salamonda!" Arpix called out her name in the instant memory returned her existence to him. He felt immediately guilty. "Salamonda? Neera?" He spun, trying to find them in the crowd of dazed and dusty figures. In three strides he had a hand on the shoulder of the nearest non-soldier, turning them to face him. A stranger.

"Arpix?" A voice turned him back towards the Mechanism.

The thinning smoke revealed a yawning pit where the structure had been. Around the jagged perimeter, with their heels at the very edge of the bottomless drop, stood Clovis, Evar, Starval, and Mayland. A fifth figure swayed there with them, far shorter, holding a staff out for balance.

"Arpix!" Clovis began to run, slamming into him a moment later, lifting him from the ground, swirling him in a tight embrace alarmingly close to the edge of another chasm. And although her face was pressed against his neck and shoulder, breathing him in despite the dust, he found that he didn't mind at all.

"You're alive!" They said it together as she set him down. They grinned at each other and then, looking about them and realising both where they were and who they were among, their smiles slipped, Arpix's into a worried frown, Clovis's into a snarl. The white sword flashed into view, and around them a dozen soldiers either bent for their 'sticks or began to raise the ones already in their hands.

"Don't!" Arpix held his palms out. "We don't—" But it had been too late even before he started. The time for reason and negotiation had long since passed.

Clovis spun away, snarling. She'd let her heart lead her into a situation that her warrior mind would never have allowed. Weapons levelled at her on all sides, ones that could sidestep both her quickness and her blade skills. Arpix found himself stepping towards her. Not wanting either of them to die alone.

"Stop!" A barked command, spoken in canith.

The soldiers might not have understood the word, but the tone made their eyes flicker to the source. Brows rose and the soldiers stared at the dust-white apparition now holding a blade to Lord Algar's overlong neck.

Somehow during Arpix and Clovis's brief reunion Starval had found a circuitous route that must have involved considerable leaps, camouflaged himself in the dust, identified the enemy's leader, and come through their number to take him unawares. The shortest of Clovis's brothers, he was barely taller than the man he had hold of but looked infinitely more deadly.

"Lower your weapons!" Evar arrived through the thinning dust clouds. He snarled the words in the soldiers' own language.

Even with the dark eyes of several 'sticks pointed his way, Arpix's heart lifted a fraction at seeing Evar alive. He reached for Clovis's sword arm and held it below her wrist, her almost invisible fur bristling against his palm.

Behind Evar the fifth figure, the staff-bearer, drew near, plotting a more cautious path along the broadening strip of floor. A ganar!

"I'm sure these differences can be settled without violence." The ganar spoke no louder than Arpix had, but all eyes turned her way. "My name is Celcha. I am on my own journey and where I travel, all stand under my peace."

One of the soldiers swivelled to direct her aim at Celcha, and Arpix recognised her to be the woman from the trio that had beaten him back in the other chamber. She'd revelled in her power then, but now seemed close to broken by her lack of it, clinging to the 'stick as if it were all that kept her afloat in a sea of confusion.

Evar began to say something, and in that instant someone fired. The booming detonation set off several more before the first echo of the shot had time to return, a deafening cacophony of explosions, each pushing death before it.

"As I was saying. You stand under my peace."

A dull metal ball rolled from the end of the first soldier's 'stick, dropping to land noiselessly in the white powder at her feet. The same thing happened to half a dozen others, though the woman was the only one of them to throw her weapon aside as if it had become a serpent that might suddenly strike her.

Evar took several strides towards Lord Algar, the man still held by the blade at his throat. He seemed to be wrestling with some strong emotion, for his fist holding the dagger trembled.

"He was going to take your eye," Clovis growled. "He doesn't deserve to live."

For a moment Evar hung in the grip of the dilemma that tore at him, his knife ready for the thrust, easily close enough to plunge into Algar's chest. In the next moment he freed himself with a shudder and turned away, calling, "Livira?"

"She's not here," Arpix said, and Evar swung his way. "I don't know where she is." The intensity of the canith's stare drew more from him. "A city somewhere. I saw her in a city. With Yolanda and Leetar." It dawned on him only now, though it had been obvious from the start. "The city. The statue. She's on the plateau. Or was there. She's a ghost in the city that stood there."

In Arpix's moment of epiphany Clovis had pulled herself away from his grasp and stood now with the tip of her white sword touching the soiled finery that wrapped Lord Algar's chest. The man's single eye showed only bitter contempt where fear should lie.

"Clovis . . ." Arpix pushed past Evar's half-hearted attempt to stop him reaching her.

Clovis glanced at him, quickly returning her gaze to Algar. "He deserves to die."

Arpix wasn't sure he had an argument against that, only that it felt wrong. "You're a warrior, Clovis! I've seen you fight. It took my breath from me. This"—he waved a hand at Algar—"this isn't war."

Clovis's lips rode up, exposing a worryingly sharp array of teeth. A growl rose through her, so deep that the air throbbed with it. With a snarl she spat at Algar's feet and turned away.

"And this is why we have Starval." Starval drew his knife through Algar's throat and let him fall, gasping and clutching at his neck with both hands. "What?" Starval spread his arms. "We live in a library for gods' sake. Have you never read a book? You let the bad guy go and he comes back to make you regret it." Starval stepped over Algar's twisting form. "If anyone deserved to die it was that one. Right?"

Behind him, Algar was making quite a production of his death scene. Starval made to wipe his knife before returning it to its scabbard. He frowned at the gleaming metal. Algar meanwhile was shuffling backwards, raising a cloud of dust as he headed into a clump of his men, the veteran Jons among them. He took the other hand from his neck, choking on his own dust. The wound that should have been there wasn't.

"As I said—" Celcha spoke again, "there is a peace."

"Dammit." Starval started back towards his victim. "I was going to break his neck. I should have. But no, I didn't want to copy Mayland."

Evar caught his arm. "Wait."

Celcha nodded her thanks. "I'm moving on. In normal times I would offer to escort you to an exit, but time is no longer normal, and my search for the centre must take precedence. You're welcome to follow, of course, as long as you respect the peace." And with that she turned away.

Clovis began to follow, snatching hold of Arpix's wrist. "Wait." Arpix resisted. "I can't . . ." He turned back towards the soldiers and the civilians dotted through their number, anonymous in their dusty whiteness. "I have to check . . ." He couldn't say the words. He had to check to see if he'd killed Salamonda. If the explosion he'd made happen had sent her tumbling into blackness along with Oanold and so many of his troops. Livira's childhood friend Neera too! Where was Neera?

"I . . ." Arpix spotted Salamonda first, her dark eyes seeking his. Then Neera, limping along behind a large soldier. The relief he felt drew a gasp from him, almost a whimper.

"Arpix. Are you unwell?" Clovis moved closer.

"I'm better now." Arpix nodded ahead to Celcha. "We're going with her?"

"Of course," Clovis said. "Where else is there to go?"

And Arpix allowed himself to be towed.

Despite the fact that many of the worst things to ever happen happened in base-ments, people keep digging them.

                                    Domestic Architecture, *Vol. 6, by Atle Norstad*

———————

CHAPTER 19

Evar

A mid the page-storm in the blackness of the vaults, Evar had been drawn into a story that Livira could surely never have written. A nightmarish tale where he lay in the broken body of a horror, tended or tortured by a dozen or more ganar, most of them too afraid to let their eyes stray to the dismembered ruin that seemed to be his flesh. When they did look his way, he could sense the effort with which they pushed down any tendril of self-awareness, before it reached up to throttle them with the knowledge of what they'd become.

Evar would have convinced himself that some other person, unknown to him, was the author of this tainted tale. He saw, between the mirrors that surrounded him, a white figure, short as the ganar but slight. The white-child. And then he saw Livira, her ghostly form fighting its way through the wall as if escaping a tangle of hook briar. They locked eyes in a moment of frozen discovery, before an awful pain and a voice much stronger than his own drove him out of both the body and the dream.

He'd regained his senses perched on a fragment of solid ground with a void yawning on almost every side. Finding Arpix alive had been a great relief. Discovering Livira's absence had reinstated his anxiety almost im-mediately.

Now, as Celcha led the way on short legs down the corridor joining the reading room to the main chamber, Evar walked with his siblings at the head of a long, dusty vanguard, comprised mainly of the soldiers he had so recently been at war with.

Arpix and Clovis were between Evar and Starval. Starval had his knife out and was testing the blade against his thumb, distrust haunting his face. No assassin wants to be let down by their tools, and yet somehow the edge he had so often honed had left no mark on the human lord.

Clovis had Arpix's hand in a firm, almost triumphant, grip and she met any glance from her brothers with challenging eyes. The librarian seemed confused, looking alternately apologetic and relieved, unable to keep a foolish smile from straying across his lips. Evar understood that last part at least. When he was reunited with Livira he had no intention of leaving her side again for quite some time.

He could feel Lord Algar's stare boring into the back of his neck, as if the man's hate had been made into something physical that reached out for him. It hurt to endure his presence. Even so, Evar would not kill him if the peace were lifted. Starval's pragmatism might be the most sensible route to take, but Evar didn't want to live in a world where such paths defined him. It was hard to deserve something as good as Livira whilst being so flawed, and he wasn't going to do anything to deepen that inequality. Livira, Evar guessed, would have kicked Lord Algar between the legs and left him to it. Killing and revenge didn't seem to be part of any of the many languages she had learned.

Mayland walked behind them, head down, deep in thought.

As they pressed on, moving out among the never-ending book columns, lines of sight narrowed to rapidly changing corridors. The scores of soldiers and dozen or more civilians had ample opportunity to slip away from their non-human leader and her company of canith, but it seemed the numbers flickering into view behind them remained constant.

Evar found that his siblings had moved up to join him. Arpix had detached himself from Clovis and was walking in conversation with Salamonda and a girl from Yute's group, and Evar raised a hand to acknowledge the older woman.

"Are we really just going to follow this ganar?" Starval asked. "Whose side is she on anyway?"

"I can hear you, you know," Celcha said without looking back at them. "And I'm on my side, mostly."

"Irad or Jaspeth," Starval said, defiantly. "Burn the library or unchain it?"

"There's always a third way."

"You're on Yute's side?" Starval asked, surprised.

"I'm not even sure Yute's on Yute's side." Celcha shook her greying head. "Maybe there's a fourth and a fifth way. A whole spectrum! Analogue over binary . . ."

Starval frowned, impatient. "Are we really just going to follow this ganar?" he repeated himself, more loudly this time.

"No." Mayland spoke for the first time. "She's more lost than we ever were. She's grown old chasing a will-o'-the-wisp. There's no centre to the library and even if there were, it's of no more significance than the edge. We're going to find that book."

For once Evar found himself in agreement with his oldest brother. "We need the book." It was his gateway to Livira. He had to have faith that somehow it would reunite them, because nobody else seemed to be trying to. The library seemed in no hurry to bring him to her, and perhaps it might not last long enough for chance reunions. A faint shudder ran through the ground beneath his feet, ground that had never once in his life shuddered before.

"The king took it." Arpix spoke up behind them. "King Oanold. He had it with him when he fell."

"We need to find him then. If we can get to the Exchange—"

"Excuse me, ma'am." Salamonda had come around the other side of Arpix with Neera in tow. She caught Celcha's attention. "I'm so sorry to ask, but how is it that you don't starve in this place? We have desperate people, and I was . . ."

The ganar turned her dark eyes to Salamonda, peering at her out of the silver-furred caves of her brows. Salamonda's question immediately woke Evar's appetite, which had been strangely absent since the library's blood had replaced his own. In an instant he felt every part of his own starvation.

For a long moment Celcha stood, looking up at Salamonda as if wrestling with some decision, perhaps old memories of when different humans had held complete power over her and had abused it. Behind Salamonda and the canith, the soldiers shuffled to a halt, starting to crowd, those at the back muttering, not understanding the reason for the hold-up.

The ganar shook herself slightly, as if throwing off an unworthy thought. "I'm sorry. That was thoughtless of me." She reached into her robe and brought out an ornate flask of enamelled copper with a narrow top that she unstoppered. "What is it that humans like to eat? Apples, is it?"

"C-cake," Salamonda stammered. "We like cake." Her whole body shivered.

"Hmmm. I don't know about cake." Celcha thrust her staff at Neera. "Hold this." Then she reached for Salamonda's hand, taking it in her smaller, furry grasp. "You'll have to help me. Hold out your other hand . . . Lower, where I can reach it. Flat, as if you were holding one of these cakes."

Salamonda did so, the tremble in her arms now. Celcha raised the flask and began to tip it very slowly. "Think of the cake. Picture it. Taste it."

"I am. I really am. It's one of the ones I used to make, honey almond—"

"You don't need to tell us. Tell your hand." Celcha continued to tip the flask and a black drop formed at its lip.

Evar recognised the stuff immediately. The library's blood. He'd seen Yute make it into a tiny horse that ran around his palm. It hadn't lasted, though. The same stuff now ran in his veins, bonding him with the library in a way that a life lived entirely within its walls hadn't managed.

The drop swelled, pregnant with possibilities, glistening, swirling with dark reflections . . . and fell.

"Oh!" Salamonda cried out and nearly dropped the cake in her hand. Evar had never seen one, but he'd seen illustrations. This looked far more tempting. So large that it started to sag over the sides of Salamonda's hands, beginning to teeter until Celcha released her grip and gave Salamonda two hands to wrestle with her creation.

"Is it real?" Neera gasped.

"It smells real!" Evar's nose was full of the wonderful aroma.

"Mnnghhn!!" Salamonda's mouth was too full to form comprehensible words.

"Is it real, or a trick?" Evar demanded. The Mechanism wouldn't feed you, he knew that. Or rather it would feed you, but it wouldn't sustain you.

"Both." Celcha eyed him with sudden interest. "It's real and it's a trick."

The ganar stepped towards him and Evar stepped smartly back, worried in that moment that the little creature might turn his blood to cake with a wave of her hand. Celcha halted her advance, turned, and caught her staff as Neera let it fall. The young woman joined Salamonda, uninvited, in devouring the cake. The thing fell apart between their two sets of hands, crumbling chunks dropping to the floor. The canith resisted following those pieces to the ground, mouths twitching into snarls of self-control. The soldiers, wary of the canith, hesitated, but an older woman, a citizen of Crath City, in a simple shawl and skirt, broke from the lines, scrabbling after the crumbs.

That single act of casting aside caution in favour of food started a flood. The soldiers surged forward.

"Stop!" Celcha raised her staff and her voice boomed like rolling thunder from every direction. Everyone stopped, even the soldiers on their knees, though those with something in their mouths continued chewing. "Nobody who fights will be fed. Everyone who doesn't fight will be."

And with the combination of threat and promise, Celcha turned aside what could easily have been a riot, one that might have tested whatever peace magics she'd woven. Instead, under the direction of officers indistinguishable from the rank and file, the remnants of Oanold's army formed an orderly queue.

"Those Escapes could have been anything we wanted?" Starval asked Evar's question. "We could have been eating them instead of being hunted by them?"

"We could have turned them into this . . . cake?" Evar joined in.

Mayland shook his head. "To make something real, like she's done, that's rare skill."

Evar realised in that moment that the hunger he saw on his brother's face had little to do with cake. What Celcha had done, Mayland couldn't do. Time's variable currents and the unpredictable twists of fate had somehow reversed Mayland's and Celcha's places. The ganar was the master now. And possibly what hurt Mayland most was that she wasn't taking advantage of the upper hand.

"To do that here," Mayland continued, "I didn't know it was possible. In the Exchange I might—"

"The Exchange!" Evar couldn't believe he'd been discussing cake when he still had to find Livira. "How do we get there? You know a way, right?"

"I know a way." Mayland didn't look very enthusiastic about the prospect.

"Let's go, then." Evar glanced around as if Mayland might open one of the magic doors.

"We will." Mayland nodded.

"Yes." Clovis elbowed her way between her brothers, headed towards Celcha. "But first, we eat."

Some take the librarian's "Shhhh!" to mean that the library is a place for peace. It was never thus. On every shelf ideas make war. The silence is so that we may hear their screams.

Long Overdue, *by Gertrude Steel*

————————

CHAPTER 20

Anne

Anne stood looking up at the black silhouette of the library on a night of breaking glass. Beside her, the two strangers who had proved much stranger than they had first appeared, and they had been far from ordinary to start with.

It seemed that from the moment of Yute and Kerrol's arrival her life had crumbled, and yet she knew that this day would have happened regardless of them. It was almost as if the nightmare had somehow summoned them to it, as witnesses from afar.

A small part of her wondered if perhaps her mind hadn't broken at some point, and she had simply failed to notice. Maybe delusions were what enabled people to keep going when their world fell apart. Or worse still, perhaps each person walked around in the shroud of their own delusion all the time. The people of Amberg were certainly running around wearing versions of a world sewn for them by those hungry for power, a world in which the Jews were devils feasting off their flesh. Perhaps her version of events was just as false, and some more concrete reality dwelt in the overlap of many minds. Or worse, maybe there was none, no underlying reality at all, just competing sets of lies, all screaming to be heard, fighting to walk the stage alone behind the mask of unsullied truth.

Kerrol growled out a question.

"Window or door?" Yute supplied, before answering, "Doors seem far more civilised."

"We should look around the back," Anne said. Climbing the broad steps to the large front doors felt far too public. "But there won't be anyone there. And the windows are all closed." She huddled in her coat. It wasn't cold for November, but it was still cold, and a mist was rising, the first of its tendrils questing among the bushes. Anne shivered. Amberg should welcome the fog. It was a night that needed something to hide its sins behind.

Yute led the way around the side of the building and, sure enough, there was a single door facing a gravelled area, a door of more modest size than those at the front entrance. Yute crunched his way up to it.

"Kerrol should try it," Anne suggested. "He's the strongest."

Yute translated both ways. "He says that he spent his whole life until just a couple of weeks ago trapped in a library chamber, and never managed to open any of the doors that would have let him out. In the end it took a young woman very much like yourself to open the door he escaped by."

Anne found this claim too strange to refute and wondered if it were perhaps some clever way of saying something she lacked the wit to recognise. Rather than argue, Anne went forward, and tugged on the letterbox. "Locked." She stepped away.

Yute pursed his lips, then set a white fingertip to the keyhole. A moment later he gave a gentle push and the door swung inwards.

"It was locked," Anne protested.

"You pulled. I pushed."

"I . . ." Maybe she should have pushed, but it must have been locked. Late at night with all the lights off. Of course it was.

Yute went through. "The library still tends to let me go where I want to, even now."

Anne followed on in. Kerrol came behind her, dipping his head beneath the doorjamb and growling something.

"It is dark, yes," Yute agreed. "This is not *the* library. Though parts of that lie in darkness too."

"It *is* the library." Anne patted around for the switch. A click, and the hallway filled with electric light. The doors to either side must lead into administrative rooms, the public area lay ahead.

"Ingenious." Yute looked up at the nearest light then raised a hand to shield his eyes before looking away. "There don't seem to be many books for a library . . ."

Anne edged past him. "This way."

She was going to lead on but paused instead, finding herself emboldened by events, ready to ask more questions. "I almost understand why you're here, Yute. Though I couldn't properly put it into words. You fit with the library somehow. But Kerrol?"

"She's asking why you're here, Kerrol."

Kerrol regarded her from his great height, eyes dark and assessing.

Yute translated the soft snarling. "He's hoping to keep his brothers from killing each other. He says that he's very good at changing their minds, but he's even better at knowing when he can't." More rumbles, so deep that the sorrow bled from them, requiring no interpretation. "And perhaps, if he's honest, he's here so that he doesn't have to watch them do it." Yute looked up at his companion with compassion as if all of this might be news to him too.

Anne nodded and, unsure how to reply to such an admission, she led them along the corridor. The door at the far end was unlocked and brought them out behind the librarians' desk. At first the rows of shelving were just suggestions in shadow, but after a little hunting she found the switches she wanted and turned on half the lights.

Yute lifted the hatch in the wraparound desk and went out among the shelves. "There don't seem to be many books for a library . . ."

Kerrol strolled after him, making an unimpressed kind of snort. Yute began to wander, much as he had in Madame Orlova's shop. Running his fingers across the spines of books as he went, as if the briefest of touches were sufficient to know each from prologue to epilogue. Kerrol, who could almost look over the tops of the shelves, prowled, the tension outside not forgotten. For her part, Anne watched the strangers that she had led to a place that had, long ago, seemed as holy and perhaps more mysterious than even the synagogue with its giant scrolls and ancient songs. Her father had often brought Anne to the library as a young girl, even though they lived above a bookshop. The bookshop, he said, was a beach where the currents of chance washed up this book or that book, and beachcombing through such wonders had a charm all its own. The library, though, was a cultivated collection. The selection was, admittedly, only as broad as the minds of its librarians, and only as deep as the pockets of the city council. However, where the librarians saw a gap, they tried to fill it, acting with deliberation to ensure a full spread of answers to every question a curious mind might conjure. Or, failing that, perhaps at least to equip that person with the tools to discover their own answer.

The library, Anne had come to think, was an imperfect reflection of something divine, a shadow of the impossible. It was shaped by bias, prejudice, and held within its pages every human failing. And yet, in its conception and in its ideals there ran an echo of some great song that if it could only be heard would wrap every listener in its beauty and lift them to some higher, unattainable ground.

The violence of the night outside, the horror of seeing her loved ones taken away to uncertain futures, hadn't left Anne. A large part of her still wanted to rage against it all, to demand that Yute and Kerrol use whatever magics they had to make things right. To scream at them for their aimless patience, for their wasting of time among the sleeping shelves whilst outside the book-burners spewed their vitriol, broke glass, and shattered lives. But she stood in silence and when Yute's path took him from her view, she followed.

"This book"—Yute plucked a slim volume from the shelves, seemingly at random—"was written a century ago, by a man of your faith. Heinrich Heine. A poet. He says on page forty-seven, '*Where they burn books, they will ultimately burn people also.*' This I have seen recently with my own eyes. The wisdom sits here, waiting quietly to be found again." He returned the book to the shelf and moved on.

Yute's wanderings brought him to the foyer where wide steps led from the double doors up to an open, tiled space. Two grand statues in the classic style faced each other across the expanse of floor, and midway between them stood a wooden lectern where the librarians always left an open book as if welcoming visitors with an immediate offer of the printed page.

"Do you know who they are?" Yute nodded towards the statues.

"Plato and Aristotle," Anne said from memory. "Though I don't know which is which." The two men stood in togas, one staring at the other over an open book, both with curling hair, fine beards, and marble musculature that seemed unlikely given that both were scholars rather than famed athletes. But then again, the library was a temple to fiction. The statues were almost certainly not marble either, but plaster reproductions.

"Ah, Aristotle. *'Memory is the scribe of the soul.'* That's one of his, and he was not wrong. Where I come from," Yute said, "we call that one Irad." He indicated the man with the book. "And his brother is Jaspeth." He turned towards the second figure. "But we all have our own traditions."

Kerrol appeared from the aisles. Yute waved a hand at the statues. "Irad and Jaspeth's grandfather, Cain, killed his brother. He invented murder. The third brother, Seth, failed to stop them. Let us hope you are more successful at finding a peace between your siblings."

Anne had never had a brother or sister. Her mother had died before Anne could properly fix the woman's face into her mind, taken by tuberculosis on a sea of coughing and red-stained handkerchiefs. Anne looked down at her fingers. She had touched Kerrol's hand before she had known that she was going to, finding it warm and slightly bristly, much as she remembered her father's chin. "Where are they now? Your brothers?"

"He doesn't know," Yute replied for him. "But Mayland will have taken them to the vaults. It's the easiest place from which to locate the book he's looking for. Something that powerful, that dangerous, would shine through the divide. It would be a star in those dark heavens."

Kerrol cocked his head, absorbing the news.

"The vaults?" Anne asked.

"The graveyard." Yute tried to wave an explanation into being. "Where books go to die."

"Like the genizah," Anne said. "In the synagogue there's a room, the genizah, where we put damaged Torah. Anything with the name of God on it, really. It's forbidden to destroy them. So, we keep them."

"Like the genizah," Yute agreed. "I can see you come from a cultured people. And what are *any* letters but the name of the divine waiting to be assembled? All alphabets are the bones of something holy. The most powerful tools ever placed in any hand. The library keeps its books: damaged, beyond use, even burned. It keeps them."

Yute turned to the open book on the lectern. He reached out, touched it, and recoiled as if he had stuck his fingers into some foulness on the street. "This however—" He shuddered. "This was not well done."

Anne came to stand beside him. "*My Struggle*, it's the chancellor's book. I think everyone's supposed to have a copy these days to show their loyalty to the Fatherland."

"When I was a servant of the library I would have said—if asked—that there were no evil books. Just books. Some which might turn weak men evil. Some written by weak evil men." He shook his head. "But I am both less and more than I was. More frail. Stronger." He glanced left then right, then pointed at the lectern. "And here it sits, a book that many might say is begging to be burned. Jaspeth looks down on us and he says we should burn the library down with it, so that there is no place for poison to linger. Irad gazes at us and says that the shelf cannot choose which book sits upon it. He tells us that the option to read this book should be there, for good or ill, that memory is our right and our duty. Surround it with sanity, context, and judgement, but don't deny it a place."

"And what does Yute say?" Anne asked mainly to avoid the question being turned her way. In her mind's eye creamy pages crinkled beneath the fire's hunger. The covers blackened, the swastika becoming smoke. Justice. Cleansing. And yet . . . and yet . . . however vile the crime, she couldn't be one of the wild-eyed crowd, face lit by the conflagration's glow, smoke and ashes all around as words burned.

"Yute says that worlds fall to ruin when those who dwell there take into their hands the gates of truth and seek to usher through only what they feel is true or right or proper." The librarian shook his head. "And worlds burn when Irad has his way. And with Jaspeth's forgetting also: the path is longer, slower, mired in more primitive killing, but no less awful, and the destination is the same fire."

Kerrol, who had been silent since Yute had mentioned his brothers, stepped up and directed a growl at the man.

"I know you followed me for a third path. And you have every right to ask where it's leading us. But I don't know." Yute hung his head, the thin veil of his snow-white hair falling around his equally pale face. "I simply don't know."

From back among the shelves, hidden from view, something struck the ground with extraordinary force. As if a church bell had fallen from a great height. Anne felt the floor tremble beneath her feet.

"A bomb?" It made no sense. Were they bombing now? Out in the streets? But this had not been outside. It was here. With them.

"I don't—" A second blow cut Yute off.

"We should—" A third buried Kerrol's opinion.

Something like oil spread out from beneath the nearest shelves, a thin, perfectly black sheet, liquid and flowing.

"What is it?" Anne stepped back.

"The library's blood," Yute breathed. "It runs here . . . I was wrong . . . this place is more important than I thought."

"Why is it bleeding?" Anne took another step back and, as she did, the black flow began to withdraw, as if the floor had developed a gradient in the other direction.

"It's under attack." Yute shook his head. "Something has happened. Somewhere, some-when the library is dying."

The black "blood" withdrew beneath the shelves, leaving no stain on the floor tiles.

Slowly, unwillingly, Yute began to follow. Anne couldn't see anything different about the library, but even so, she sensed it. They were no longer alone. Among the aisles something was moving.

Kerrol growled, a long rumbling growl. For once Yute didn't translate.

"What did he say?" Anne could hear footsteps now, heavy, unhurried footsteps. Ahead of them among the aisles. Oddly, she almost knew what Kerrol had said. Almost but not quite. And she was almost sure that he'd said something just now that she *did* understand.

"He said that I'd told him the blood was harmless, a tool to be shaped to a purpose. That I'd said it was only a danger to those who were afraid of it, because then it becomes an Escape. It takes the shape of their fear and hunts them."

"So," said Anne, trying to sound braver and less out of her depth than she felt, "why do you still sound as if there's a problem?"

Yute stopped advancing. "Because I'm terrified."

Kerrol growled again, a more muted sound with something of a yelp in it. Anne didn't ask what he'd said, because she imagined it was the same question as her own. "What have you made?"

A crashing, the source unseen. The splintering fall of one shelf into another, spilling books in a thudding rain. "A demon. My fear's made a demon." Yute started to turn, clutching his umbrella. "I think we should run."

Kerrol placed himself between the shelves and Anne, snarling out a challenge that would send a pack of wolves running with their tails between their legs.

"Yes, you've fought them before." Yute hesitated, seeing that Kerrol was making a stand. "But this is different. In the library, the blood's only source for inspiration is you. Oh, it can take some form from books too, but the raw power behind it is all you."

Kerrol growled out another comment. Anne was starting to feel the shape of the words inside these utterances where first she'd heard only an animal's complaints.

"We're out in the world," Yute replied. "And not a good one. The Escape's drinking it all in. All the poison of a sick city. The wilful ignorance of a people who know in their secret hearts that they're being lied to and listen anyway because to them the lies are sweet." His hands moved through the air as if he could feel the emotions he described, flowing around his bloodless fingers, drawn in by the unseen gyre that was the demon being built from the black blood of the library.

The nearest shelf fell towards them, spilling books, and the monster stood behind it, revealed in silhouette, sucking down the electric light and returning nothing. If it had been drawn from Anne's nightmares it would have worn a uniform and borne a swastika. Yute's fear had crafted something blind and shambling. It swayed towards them, reaching with strangling hands, bleeding anger. Its presence deadened Anne's internal voice, pushing back her intelligence to expose primitive emotion of the sort immune to reason, driven by primal hungers, the logic of selfishness, the justice of the mob.

It brought with it a blindness, not of the eyes but of the mind. A blindness and a darkness more profound than the one from which Helen Keller so marvellously escaped, and one that was not inflicted as a wound on the innocent, as hers had been, but required a degree of complicity to enter. Anne could feel Yute's fear of it, and in that moment knew her own.

Kerrol moved with inhuman swiftness, wrenching up an entire reading bench and wielding the weight of wood as Anne would swing a stick. He brought his impromptu weapon down on the Escape's head with such force that it splintered into two halves.

Incredibly, the monster barely flinched. Instead, it surged past Kerrol as though he were unworthy of its attention. Even with this turn of speed added to the Escape's formerly sluggish approach, there should have been enough time to run. Somehow there wasn't. Anne remained mired in the horror of its advance, and a moment later found herself swept up in a hand the colour of midnight and larger than the paws of the stuffed bear in the burgermeister's hall.

Yute saw her plight and turned from his retreat towards the main doors. With the desperate expression of a man braving his own worst fears for someone else, the librarian seemed to draw on the books scattered all around his feet. Even as Anne was hoisted aloft and felt the awful pressure of the Escape's fingers close around her throat, she tried to scream at the others to run.

Yute stood amidst a whirlwind that touched the visible only briefly here and there. It seemed as if the books were smoking and that smoke, pulled into the invisible gyre, wrapped around him, weaving an ethereal armour. And thus armoured, he flung himself at the Escape.

Anne hung, choking, while for a moment the two combatants came together with a sizzling like meat hitting a hot skillet. Yute didn't fight, but hung on to his foe, while the aura around him seared the dark flesh, smoking it away to dissipate in the air. Even as Anne's vision filled with black spots, she thought she could see lines of text orbiting Yute's limbs, as if the words had risen from the fallen books and joined his service, trying to burn their way through the thick layers of ignorance that protected the Escape from the self-awareness that would surely tear it apart.

With an angry shrug, the Escape sent Yute staggering back. A swing of its arm launched him into the air on an arc leading towards the foyer. The sort of blow that shatters ribs and breaks spines.

The Escape strode after Yute like a dog pursuing a toy. Anne found herself dangling, an afterthought, still cut off from the next breath as her heels trailed the ground. Kerrol had found another weapon, a plank that had been a shelf, but his strength proved useful only in producing splinters. The Escape hardly noticed his efforts. Its stomping advance on Yute's sprawled form placed the lectern squarely between them. As it drew near the book set in that place of honour, the monster seemed to draw strength from it, pulling barely seen threads of power towards itself in much the same way as Yute had gathered his own from the wider library.

Kerrol threw himself forward, seizing the arm that had hold of Anne, trying to free her without breaking her in the process. A heavy backhander sent him to the floor with sickening force.

Anne drew in a long-denied breath in a gasp. "Stop it!"

The Escape tossed her down as if stung. She scrambled to her feet, coughing, and—mostly on purpose—knocked the chancellor's book to the floor as she did so. Quite how she had managed to steal a lungful of air past the Escape's grip she couldn't say, but, as it loomed above her fallen companions, the mismatch between her strength and its mattered less and less to her.

Out in the harshness of the night a different calculus was at work. There were monsters there too and interposing herself between them and her grandfather would have earned her a jackboot in the face, achieving nothing, but Anne refused to believe the same rules held sway here in the library. This was magic—she couldn't deny that any longer—and if magic danced to the same tune as the rest of the world, then the library, and her grandfather's own bookshop, had lied to her for her whole life.

The Escape's huge hands descended towards her, and Anne raised her own to intercept them.

"I know you." She caught its wrists. The monster that had so haunted Yute, the one that had defeated his enchantments, was one Anne had grown up with. Nothing scared the librarian more than a wilful refusal to acknowledge facts, the elevation of ignorance to a virtue, the casting of curiosity and intellect as defects of character. But Anne had swum from childhood to the shores of her majority through such toxic waters. She had read the book that lay behind her on the floor. Not out of any appetite for its contents but out of an honest desire to understand the mind and motivation behind its crudely written screed. And although she knew that anger and hate were valid responses to its message, she had felt pity for those poisoned by it.

"I know you." She knew why they hated her kind. They hated because humans are tinder waiting for the flame. The chancellor had given them an excuse to hate, the relief of having someone to blame. It was a selfish, rambling, poorly worded excuse, but they had taken it. Not because this country, this people, were inherently evil, but because they were weak, like all men. Their morality a fragile thing, a flower to be cherished and grown, too easily corrupted.

The strain nearly buckled her. But where Kerrol's strength had been knocked aside with contempt, Anne's frailty somehow endured. Midnight flesh bubbled and ran and smoked beneath her grip with a ferocity Yute's attack had been unable to match.

"I know you," Anne repeated.

The Escape started to lose form.

"You're clay." She released its arms and stepped forward to place her palms upon its torso. "I'm the potter."

And, like falling water, the blood of the library was all around her, once more merely a puddle.

CHAPTER 21

Livira

H ow could it see us?" Leetar shuddered convulsively as if spiderwebs might be clinging to her, still thick with many-legged occupants.

They were back in the brilliance of the sun, out by the margins of the great clearing that surrounded the ganar night-ship. The horror of what they had discovered within had driven them out again almost immediately.

"Chertal can see us. A ganar saw me and Evar da—" Livira glanced at Carlotte and decided not to repeat what she and Evar had been up to above a freshly minted necropolis.

"Some few are cracked," Yolanda said, sounding like an elderly mage rather than a young girl. "Cracked by blows they sustained in life. Some are even born that way. And they glimpse us. But that thing in there . . . broken as it was . . . could even see us through its minions. And maybe . . ." She paused as if the idea made her uncomfortable. "The immortal can often see what belongs to the future. Immortality is a step out of time. And wounded as it was, I fear that creature—that made-thing—might bear immortality as just another of the burdens thrust upon it. Endless pain and endless horror. The price of birthing a nation of slave-soldiers for the ganar."

"But the ganar were slaves themselves!" Livira protested. Arpix had told her that they had been kept in chains, labouring to dig out the very ruins of the city that Chertal was even now building. Kept beneath the palaces and temples of the mighty in Crath City or its predecessors.

"This is the wheel we're bound to," Yolanda said. "And the library is our best chance of getting free of it. Oppressors become the oppressed. Opportunity makes tyrants. Write these truths large enough, populate so many shelves with them that no fire could ever consume them all, and pray that they'll be heard. Jaspeth would have us stumble blindly into these crimes over and over, not remembering the last time, free of shame that we have failed yet again to learn from the record of our mistakes."

Livira looked at her hand, still stained with the ink she had written her story in. An indelible accusation, like the blood-spatter guilt of the murderer. "My book couldn't threaten the library. It makes no sense." The place had stood for millennia. Possibly for geological ages. The scrawlings of a girl barely out of her teens could no more scratch the impervious floor of that place than could an ant.

Yolanda levelled a cold pink stare at her. Livira could see a lot of Yute in the girl, but his gentle sense of humour seemed to have fallen out of the mix in favour of some trait from her mother. "It's harder to believe it in this time, and easier to imagine in the land of your birth, but this entire world, and its moons with it, were made from nothing more than accumulations of dust. The great ruin of one star, or many, falling back into itself after the most violent of deaths.

"The accumulation of things as small as dust can build worlds, and the gathering of things as insubstantial as letters can build vast libraries . . . the mounting weight of the minuscule can break them too. Your contribution may have been small on the grand scale, tiny, but it was the last of many straws. We have assuredly passed the tipping point, and the ruin that ensues may be without limit."

Carlotte had been rubbing at the tatters of her once-fine gown, as if physical traces of the nightmare inside the night-ship might be lingering on her. She looked up now and shook her head. "What matters to me is helping Chertal. Yute's daughter is probably right about the being-cracked business. The childhood that man had—well, I don't want to talk about it. And he kept me going when I was all alone. For years. So, do I have to bang those too-clever heads of yours together?" She looked pointedly from

Yolanda to Livira. "Or is there a better way to get an idea to drop out of one of them?"

"Oh," Livira said. "I thought that was obvious."

Carlotte took a threatening step towards her.

"Balls!"

"Livira . . ." Carlotte raised a hand.

"Get one of those iron balls! The ones the ganar use to control skeer. You bring your king and most of his army out here. We track the smallest ganar-led patrol we can find. We guide the king and his soldiers to them. And if they get their hands on the ganar, don't all die in the process, *and* can work the ball, they'll have protection."

Carlotte frowned. "Won't the ganar know how to . . . undo . . . the magics if someone else gets hold of one of their toys?"

"It's a weapon," Livira said. "If you steal a sword or a bow, the previous owner can't stop it working just because it was theirs once or they made it. Also . . ." She closed her eyes, dredging through memories. "I think the ganar left their moon because they were escaping other ganar in some huge war. There are lots of factions, different races, they don't trust each other. They're not going to make weapons and defences that other ganar can simply turn off."

Carlotte shrugged and then nodded. "We'll do it."

"How many soldiers can your husband muster?" Yolanda asked.

"He's not my— Well, he is. But we never . . . so it doesn't really count." Carlotte looked rapidly from Livira to Leetar before fixing her slightly flustered gaze on Yolanda. "Five thousand?"

"And how many skeer could they trap and kill?" Livira asked.

Carlotte's frown returned. She bit her lip, thinking. "Well, you've seen those things. They're monsters!"

"How many?" Livira persisted.

"Like . . . five?"

"No, really! How many?"

"I have no idea," Carlotte admitted. "I don't think Chertal or his generals do either. I mean . . . if the soldiers don't just wet themselves and run away like I would. Fifty?"

"We'll see what we can do," Yolanda said. "We need to leave this place, soon. Dead husband or protected husband, both are the same as far as leaving goes, yes?"

Carlotte scowled, her mouth moving to form a "no," but the word that eventually emerged was "Yes."

And Livira understood. Life as a ghost, an untouched, unseen, unheard observer, was barely life. It was a form of the same starvation that the library's healing circle offered. A type of death that walked the line but didn't cross it. One of the horrors of Irad and Jaspeth's compromise, pleasing no one.

Even for an introvert at ease with their own company, such isolation would build into an unbearable burden. For Carlotte who lived for company and needed to gossip in the same way she needed to draw breath, it must have been so much worse. She needed to leave. And even with unknown odds, a gamble like this was worth taking.

IN THE END an army from the city of Arthran followed the mad king out of the doors of his palace to do battle with the skeer. It was suicide. All of them knew that much. But Chertal's visions had brought him to the throne against impossible odds. They knew him to be ruthless, often capricious, subject to dark moods, long silences, and longer manias, but they also knew that he spoke to spirits, saw things that mortals were not meant to see, and knew secrets that no one could know.

Six thousand foot-soldiers followed their king down the narrow stair to the city below the citadel and together they issued from the western gate to cross the plain beyond the walls. Ahead, the forest waited, vast, unknown, and full of death.

The process of bringing the army and a suitably sized skeer patrol together, whilst avoiding the chance of meeting a larger force or having the insectoids reinforced during the ensuing battle, took considerable organizing. The skeer had to be tracked from above in order to prevent detection through their connection with the template-skeer in the night-ship. At Yolanda's insistence, King Chertal had to be kept updated by Carlotte alone, to prevent extra damage to reality, over and above that already being caused. And the king, not being an idiot, knew that he was being given a goodbye present, making these interactions protracted and emotional. None of which did any favours to the morale of his troops who, bound for a seemingly suicidal encounter, heard rumours of their red-eyed leader shouting his heartbreak at thin air in the dubious privacy of his royal tent.

"They have to win, right?" Carlotte hung high above the forest with Livira, her voice tight with tension. "I mean, it's nearly sixty soldiers to each skeer."

The smallest skeer patrol to venture out far enough to be attacked without fear of interference during the course of a short battle numbered one hundred and four insectoids and two ganar.

"I hope so." Livira had seen the beasts in action. It was hard to imagine a man killing one on the battlefield. If sixty human warriors had the same fearless dedication the skeer demonstrated she would have more confidence, but she had read enough accounts of war to know that armies are made of individuals, and their courage was a fragile mix of both the collective and the individual. Chertal's soldiers wouldn't keep attacking until the last of their number was killed. As the bodies mounted without success, their resolve would falter and fracture, and they would flee. The deaths of their foes would help to keep them on the field. But where the balance lay and what could be expected of them, she really didn't know.

King Chertal had been given every advantage. His forces had had the time to hide themselves in the treeline beside the skeer-broken trail by which the patrol approached. They had the wind in the right direction to hide their scent. They had approached without detection. They'd dug traps further along the trail. They had ample supplies of arrows, two thousand archers, even five ballistae primed with iron-shod spears longer than a man and as thick as Livira's arm. Carlotte's gift of the secret of black powder was too recent for arrow-sticks of the sort in Crath City to have been developed, but six hundred of the king's force were armed with devices they called "guns," which would fire a lead ball at lethal velocity over short ranges. Sadly, they took almost a minute to reload and were prone to various failures. Even so, Livira imagined a volley of six hundred shots would be devastating.

Livira's memories of her own violent encounter with skeer were thankfully and uncharacteristically vague. Her mind still held glimpses of the

Soldier performing martial miracles in his near-indestructible body before even his limits were exceeded. Suddenly, she missed Malar, in that raw, emotional way that hollows out a chest and fills the rest of a person with an aching absence.

"Stay here." Livira caught Carlotte's hand as she made to descend, having now grasped the rudiments of flight. "You don't want to see this up close."

The white column of skeer tromped along the trail, churning the earth and raising a small haze of dust behind them. In another ten miles they would reach areas of the forest less denuded of game and spread out to hunt. The patrol's speed showed no variation as it moved into the killing ground.

From on high, Livira didn't hear the command, the thrum of bowstrings, the hiss of arrows in flight, nor the deeper thuds of ballistae launching their missiles. Livira couldn't imagine how many arrows it would take to put down a skeer warrior. Maybe there was no number that would achieve that goal. Even the insectoids struck by ballista bolts continued to move, though Livira couldn't imagine that they could refuse death for long after such grievous perforation.

In short order the bulk of the skeer force charged into the treeline where the Arthran soldiers waited with spears, swords, and axes. And of course, with six hundred guns. As the skeer vanished among the trees, the guns began to boom, so many that it made a near continuous roar for what seemed an age. White smoke filtered up through the canopy, and Livira wondered if any of the insectoids had survived.

Five skeer remained to shield the pair of ganar. Neither of these two seemed inclined to show its face, relying instead on the skeer's natural violence rather than seeking to guide the battle.

Here, Chertal had followed Livira's advice, delivered by Carlotte. The king had been unwilling to split his force, wanting instead to overwhelm the foe by weight of numbers, and hoping that those numbers would also instil the necessary courage. He had, however, on Livira's instruction—Livira being painted by Carlotte as a famous general from a great warrior nation, rather than a young librarian—set five hundred soldiers among the trees on the opposite side of the trail, with instructions not to loose so much as a single arrow during the initial engagement.

Now as screams rose from the woods to the left of the ganar, arrows and spears began to rain in from the right, peppering the five remaining skeer with sharp iron. The skeer hunched around their masters, refusing to fall or to run. Torrents of arrows fell upon them while the carnage continued among the trees on the far side of the trail. Nothing could be seen of that battle, only the swaying of the foliage in the still air. But for the screams, audible even at Livira's height, and the splintering of wood, she might have been able to imagine there was merely a fierce squall passing.

The first of the skeer engaged on the far side began to emerge from the trees, red and dripping, seemingly alert to the new danger to their masters. There were far more of them than Livira had thought could possibly have survived this long.

Taking their cue, Chertal's second force charged at the five pincushioned skeer. Hundreds of men in the first wave, more following. All determined to get to the ganar and somehow break their control over their slaves before those slaves broke every soldier under the king's command.

Livira watched the human deluge and it reminded her of watching bone-ants swarm a ram beetle out on the Dust when she was a child. The skeer scattered half a dozen men with each sweep of their blade arms but anchored to guarding the ganar they couldn't rampage through the attackers. Even at the height Livira maintained with Carlotte and the others, the carnage looked red and awful, underscored by the screaming of the wounded and the war cries of those seeking their courage.

"That's him!" Carlotte clutched Livira's arm and pointed. A small knot of heavily armoured knights was emerging from the treeline on the side from which the second force had attacked. Two bore vibrant banners, and at their centre, the king.

Chertal's personal guard pushed into the fray. One crumpled, impaled on the spiked limb of a skeer, and was flung into the air on a glittering arc of metal and spraying blood that carried them back to the trees.

"Chertal!" Carlotte released Livira and began to drop like a person who couldn't fly.

Against her better instincts, Livira gave chase. Yolanda and Leetar made to follow.

The sheer violence of the scene seemed to double every time the distance to it halved. The skeer's brutal strength when applied to flesh made a ruin of even the most skilled fighters. Armour, be it iron-studded leathers, chainmail, or plated steel, made little difference. The mere sound of it—splintering bone, chopped meat, joints wrenched from sockets—turned Livira's stomach. The mass of corpses and the injured mixed among them stole her breath.

"This has happened," Livira muttered to herself. "This happened. Everyone who died here, everyone who survived, all the people in the city. They died already. They're all dead. They're the dust." She repeated it, faster, with more intensity. It didn't help. History or not, she was in the page, not outside it, and the battle she was dropping into was written in blood, not ink.

"This already happened." Livira landed beside Carlotte, outside the main knot of figures locked in combat. "It's over." And suddenly, almost as Livira said that it was over . . . it was.

Not one of the five skeer had fallen, but as one, they stopped moving, as did the half dozen that had ploughed into the king's second force from behind, and the two score still returning from the increasingly shattered forest on the left flank.

For what seemed an age, but might have been moments, the skeer stood without motion, allowing the soldiers to hew at them. Two of the five fell during these moments, finally damaged beyond their mechanical ability to stand.

The din of battle died as soldiers began to understand that something had changed. Without warning, the remaining skeer turned and fled to all points of the compass, some trampling more of Chertal's troops as they ran, others hitting trees, some of which toppled. The two fallen skeer began to haul themselves brokenly away, crushing wounded men and women as they went. Soldiers finally stopped those two by driving spears into the most obvious of their eye sockets.

Chertal emerged, unsteady on his feet, armour running crimson. In one gauntleted hand he held an iron ball. He reached clear ground and thrust his prize aloft.

The cheering that followed was loud enough to drown out whatever he had to say but a pale shadow of what six thousand voices would sound like.

Livira hoped the ganars' weapon would serve Chertal and his people well. Looking around at the few hundred still on their feet and the scattered survivors stumbling from the trees, it was clear that the cost had been ruinous.

"Come on." Yolanda interposed herself between them and the king, stepping through the fallen. "We need to go."

Livira had expected Carlotte to protest, or at the very least to drag out a dramatic leave-taking, but she hung her head and allowed herself to be led away.

The horror of hunger is not how completely it strips away humanity—one pain will do that as well as another. The horror is that it happens slowly enough for us to see it go, a strand at a time, until that ugly, mewling appetite lies naked for all to see.

Intermediate Cookery—Cajun Style, *by Gordon Bennett*

CHAPTER 22

Arpix

A rpix managed to restrain himself and not run to join the queue for the fruits of Celcha's magics. He told himself that waiting was the civilised thing to do, that he had waited this long to eat and could easily wait a little longer. Even so, had the ganar's flask been even a touch smaller, Arpix suspected he would have been amongst the crowd of half-starved soldiers, scrabbling for his own bite.

The first of the soldiers, though they might have requested roast beef, fresh bread, or anything else their imagination could summon, asked instead for water. Celcha dripped the library's blood and where each drop fell, a brimming bucket stood. The sight of soldiers quenching their long thirst and wiping the grime from their faces with wet hands was nearly enough to break Arpix's reserve. He could somehow smell the water—though he'd been sure that water held no scent—and it was enough to wake the awful thirst that had been building ever since his return to the library.

Clovis held back too, saying that she wouldn't lower herself by standing in line with the troops. Arpix suspected that she would actually have relished fighting for food, but to stand behind the soldiers who had slaughtered her people was more than she could stomach. Violence would be only a sneer away.

In time, the queue shrank to just two of the civilians who had until recently been the soldiers' prisoners and prey, just as Arpix had. He stood behind the last of them, and after helping himself to water he asked Celcha if he might have a plate of butter cookies, the ones he remembered from Salamonda's kitchen and that had haunted his dreams across five hungry years on the Arthran Plateau. The ganar took his hand and let another drop of the blood fall, tilting the flask further than she had at the start. And there, in his open hand, on a glazed earthenware plate, were eight golden, buttery cookies, as perfect as he had ever imagined.

Arpix was so astonished, despite seeing the miracle dozens of times already, that he promptly dropped the plate with a despairing cry.

Clovis caught it. So fast. So fluid. So sure, that she took his breath away. She raised the plate, its precious burden still in place. "Yours."

"Do you— Would you like one? Some?" He received the plate in hands that trembled just as much as Salamonda's had, his mouth full of saliva, his stomach a hard and demanding knot.

Clovis sniffed the plate, inhaling so deeply that Arpix half expected the topmost cookies to start lifting towards her nose.

"You keep them. I'll have mine." She stepped forward, towering above Celcha. "Steak. Please."

For far too short a time Arpix lost himself in an ecstasy of eating. He filled his mouth, shuddered with pleasure, remembered to chew, swallowed, filled his mouth. His resolution to pace himself joined the one about keeping some for later, in the graveyard of good intentions.

At last he looked up, wiping crumbs from his mouth with one hand while holding his belly with the other. Clovis had already devoured her steak, whose merits she had either read about or picked up from her brothers and was licking her teeth with enormous satisfaction. The gaze she turned on him was accompanied by a half-smile. A smile that suggested she still had appetites to be met.

With their hunger dented, the canith and Arpix grouped together while Celcha led on, bound for the door by which the ganar automaton had entered. Salamonda and Neera came to join them, Salamonda walking boldly up among the towering canith and giving Arpix a rib-creaking hug, while Neera hung back, still nervous.

"You saved us all," Salamonda said, her face pressed into Arpix's chest. "I don't know how, and I'm happy keeping it that way. But it *was* you."

Arpix didn't try to deny it, although the result had been somewhat cataclysmic, and only luck had prevented Salamonda from tumbling into the cracks that spread from the destruction of the Mechanism. Slowly, he freed himself from the old woman's embrace. Over the course of their years on the Arthran Plateau, Salamonda had provided Arpix with more mothering than his own loving but undemonstrative mother had managed in the twenty years prior to their stranding. In consequence, he bore the current attentions without complaint until the soldiers coming up behind encouraged them both to move.

Clovis eyed Salamonda's hugging without comment, showing her teeth to Neera, who fell back three more paces. Arpix threw Clovis an admonishing glance and beckoned Neera to join them. His gaze lingered on the shabby line of Oanold's troops following the ganar, the gift-giver, source of their food. None of them that he had noticed had asked for meat of any kind. It seemed impossible that these men and women, now exchanging grins of relief at being fed and watered, and perhaps at having the burden of the king's authority removed from their shoulders, were the same who had literally been eating their fellow citizens alive not much more than a day previously. How long after the dust and blood were washed from their hands and faces would their crimes continue to stain them? Would they forgive themselves, forget, move on with their lives, settle, marry, produce children? As if they had not been monsters. As if the horrors behind them belonged to strangers. Perhaps, having taken on the skins of ogres all together rather than singularly would make it easier to shed them and walk away. A shared offence, owned by nobody.

Arpix found it hard to imagine that he would forgive them. But also, that he might live among them for years to come and somehow maintain this level of . . . was it hate he felt? Arpix didn't think he had ever hated before. It felt like sorrow, but with the knives turned in every direction, not merely inwards. He didn't like it. He should, he thought, find a way to leave the soldiers behind, though they constituted the bulk of the survivors. Without the uniforms only their relative youth would mark them out among the others who escaped the city.

"You think too much." Clovis took his hand and pulled him along, keeping pace with the others.

"Perhaps I do."

"You hate them too." Clovis motioned with her head to indicate those behind them, not looking back.

"Everything about what happened makes me sad." Arpix couldn't deny what she'd said. "At least you can tell yourself they're a different species. To me, they're a mirror. They're telling me that something's rotten at the core. This cycle Jaspeth says the library binds us to. The reason Mayland wants to destroy it . . . It's not the library, it's us. It's humans." He looked at the hand Clovis hadn't taken control of. "It's me." Their eyes met, hers large and grey, his feeling like small, hot beads, prickling in their sockets, insufficient windows onto an insufficient soul.

Clovis didn't answer, but her grip tightened on his hand, and she chewed at something, as if finding every answer she had unsuited to the task. "Not *just* humans."

It was all she had to say. And perhaps it was all there was to say. No species came to the fore without having emerged through an epic struggle of tooth and claw. Nature put its creations through a constant meat grinder, and nothing survived that was not prepared to do *anything* to cling to its existence. Anything at all. Every hand that ever wrote out words was driven by an intelligence born of war, and instincts shaped to win at all costs. The hope that they could rise above such things was only that, a hope, fragile and apt to tear apart in the winds of any challenge.

"How are we going to find her?" Evar's voice, up ahead, pulled Arpix from his gloomy philosophizing.

"We're going to find the book," Mayland replied. "It would be better if we didn't find your human with it."

Starval, an unlikely peacemaker, interjected over Evar's hot reply, "Nobody is going to harm Livira, and finding her book might be a big step towards finding her." The assassin pushed between his brothers, both a head taller than him. "So how do we take that step, Mayland?"

"Well, that's obvious enough, isn't it?" Mayland ran a three-fingered hand up across his face and into his mane. Arpix still found canith expressions hard to read, but it seemed to him that Mayland looked tired, the confidence in his words not mirrored in his face.

"Indulge me." Starval reached up to sling an arm around Mayland's shoulders.

"We go into the cracks the book fell into."

"What?" Evar turned back. "The cracks we've been walking away from ever since we got here?"

Mayland shrugged. "I was hungry."

Evar stepped threateningly towards him.

"And you *do* know how time works here, brother?" Mayland shook off Starval's arm. "If we get there we'll arrive when we need to."

"If?" Evar asked.

"If," Mayland confirmed. "We'll be heading into a wound that the library is trying to heal. It will be . . . dangerous."

Evar turned and started to stride back in the direction they'd come. The soldiers fell quiet as he approached and parted before him, falling away to either side, revealing Lord Algar seemingly stranded by his pride with no one save two of his personal guards to back him up. It seemed that Evar would pass him by without a word. And he almost did. But at the last moment, and quicker than the eye, he sent the lord reeling away with a back-handed slap.

"Ha!" Clovis barked a laugh.

Algar's retainers prevented him from falling, and he covered his bloody mouth with both hands. Clearly Evar had exercised restraint. A full-grown canith could easily break a man's neck with such a blow. But even Evar's good nature had its limits, it seemed. And Arpix couldn't find it in his heart to blame him.

Starval followed, nodding to himself. "Seems like we know how far Celcha's peace extends. Slapping's allowed."

Whether it was just his snarls or that they caught some of his meaning, the soldiers moved back rapidly from Starval's approach. Mayland strode after him.

"Come on." Clovis pulled Arpix's hand.

Arpix glanced from Salamonda to Neera. "You have to stay with Celcha and the others. She'll look after you."

"We're coming!" Salamonda bristled.

"Really, no." Arpix used every ounce of the authority his companions had slowly heaped on his shoulders during the Arthran years, despite his protests. "I'll bring Livira and the others back. We'll find you. I promise I'll do everything in my power to make that happen. But you can't follow."

And as Clovis followed her family with Arpix in tow, Salamonda and Neera stayed.

THE CANITH AND Arpix moved swiftly back along the route they'd taken.

"What is it?" Clovis asked when Arpix glanced back for the third time. "You saw those cowards. They won't follow us."

"Not that," Arpix growled back. He hadn't been thinking any soldiers might come seeking revenge. "It's Algar. The man Evar hit. I feel as if we've left a poison seed in Celcha's charge. I worry what's going to have grown by the time we come back." He had more to say but didn't say it. What really worried him was not the idea that Lord Algar might somehow overpower Celcha, an individual with magics that seemed nearly equal to those of Irad and Jaspeth themselves. His concerns remained wider and more ephemeral. It helped him to believe that Algar was in truth a poison seed— a corruptor who through special talent and unique evil had pulled others under his sway and led them into the horrors that had followed. What truly worried Arpix was the possibility that Algar was nothing special, and that if it hadn't been him, someone else would have stepped up to lead the mob to the same destination.

"You're doing it again," Clovis said.

"What?"

"You know."

"I promise to stop thinking too much," Arpix lied.

"Liar."

"STOP!" EVAR HELD up a hand.

Arpix and the others backed in the direction he next indicated.

"What is it?" Starval held a blade in each hand.

The library answered him. A crack advanced across the floor, accompanied by a deep, barely audible creaking. The leading edge moved in short bursts, its progress slower than a man walking. Behind the front edge, the sides of the crack continued to retreat from one another, much more slowly but still fast enough that before Arpix lost sight of it among the book columns, the fissure was wide enough to accept his fingers if he cared to offer them.

"It's spreading," Starval said, rather redundantly.

"That's what you want, isn't it?" Evar turned to Mayland. "Isn't your job done? You should just leave."

"This is a wound. It might yet heal. We have to get to the book and ensure that it continues the destruction. If we just leave it, the damage might be limited and localized." Mayland led on, tracking the crack back towards its source.

"You don't want to destroy the library," Arpix hissed at Clovis as they followed. "Do you?"

"I haven't decided." Clovis kept her gaze forward. "It's complicated. I think I have a brother in each camp now. Evar's sided with his Livira and the strange little girl, trying to save the place. Mayland's trying to tear it down. Kerrol went with Yute to find another way." A long pause. Arpix could feel Evar and Starval listening hard whilst trying to look as if they weren't. "And what about Arpix?" she asked casually.

Arpix would have bet on himself to be on the side of the library every time. Now though it seemed that Clovis was right. It *was* complicated. He was on the side of books, of writing, of stories and histories, the recording of wisdom and discoveries. But the manner of its distribution . . . the bricks and mortar of it . . . the library? "I'm with you," he said at last.

By the time they reached the entrance to the reading room, the crack had grown large enough to accommodate a canith with a little elbow room to spare. Arpix couldn't resist looking into the fissure periodically. The thing drew his attention, holding the same fascination as a long drop, though there were no depths to be seen, only blackness and the occasional ghostly image, as if his imagination was patterning itself into the dark that dwelt there.

The crack didn't follow the corridor but forged its own way through the wall, a tear that reached up at least five yards. However, other cracks had spread along the corridor from the reading room, crossing it in several places, intersecting, and emerging to finger their way through the book columns, some of which hung at angles, their footing removed.

"Do we really need to go down there?" Arpix eyed the corridor dubiously.

"What we really need to go down is one of these." Mayland pointed to the crack they'd been following. "We just needed it to get wider. This will do." Again, despite the confident depth of the canith's growling, there was a twitchiness about him that did nothing to set Arpix at ease. Not that there was much that could set him at ease about dropping into a bottomless chasm filled with midnight and ghosts.

"How do we do it?" Evar was already at the edge of the crack, peering into it, eager, or at least determined, to begin his hunt for Livira.

Mayland's shoulders slumped. He sat on the library floor. "We need to go in together. Holding hands."

All five of them sat in a line, Arpix at one end, holding Clovis's hand. Their advance towards the crack was undignified. If not for the plunge ahead of them, Arpix would have found it comical. One human and four canith shuffling forward on their backsides. Clovis's grip on his hand tightened to the point where it hurt. Arpix didn't complain. He'd rather end up with broken fingers than lost in the dark on his own.

"Don't put your feet in yet," Mayland cautioned as they closed the last yard. "Something might grab them. We go together. On my count. Five. Four."

"Are we going on one or zero?" Arpix had no more desire to stick his legs into the crack than into an open fire.

"Three. Two."

"Are we—"

"One."

"Now?"

"Go!"

Arpix pushed his legs over the side, ready to wriggle forward for the drop. He didn't need to. The drop seized him, and he was gone.

Studies indicate much lower rates of rollercoaster riding in countries where people frequently experience mortal fear involuntarily.

Compulsory Carnival, *by Evie Wong*

CHAPTER 23

Evar

Falling, Evar discovered, was every bit as terrifying as he had imagined it would be when Livira had taught him to fly. Instinct tensed his everything as he dropped through the far-too-penetrable dark. Aeons had constructed the canith body to expect the sensation of falling to end swiftly and painfully. When, after the first scream had emptied his lungs, Evar found himself still plummeting, further acceleration opposed by the great rushing wind of his already fatally fast descent, he started, ever so slowly, to unclench.

He still had hold of Starval's hand, but the roar of air passing around and between them made any communication impossible. Slowly, it began to be the unaccustomed darkness that most unnerved Evar. Until his recent escape from the library, he had never experienced a night, and only in the tunnels beneath the plateau had the darkness thickened to something like what now wrapped him.

It seemed bizarre that it was possible to get bored of falling, but Evar found his fear of a sudden end to what had felt like a short trip was being replaced by the worry that there wasn't going to be an end to it at all.

"I—"

A sudden jolt cut off his first attempt to complain. A jolt, a twist, flashes of light, and he ended up sprawled across something more forgiving than the library floor, with a mouthful of grass.

Evar rolled to all fours, spitting, ready to fight. The Exchange lay all around him. Clovis had fetched up against a tree and had some sharp complaints about the situation. Arpix lay dazed, his legs still in the pool they all appeared to have been spat from. Mayland was getting to his feet.

". . . what in the hel—" Starval dropped from a nearby tree, followed by a shower of leaves.

Evar went to help Arpix up.

"Something's different."

Now that Arpix mentioned it, Evar saw that he was right. The sky, that had always been a timeless blue, had turned an ominous shade of grey. And a chill breeze had insinuated itself among the trees, twitching at the leaves. To Evar it seemed a wound more grievous than cracks in the library floor, like the one they'd dropped into. The Exchange had always filled him with a kind of peace, a muted joy, the sort of contentment that had made him want to sink roots too and remain a part of the place. Now, it felt wrong, like a song sung off-key.

"I didn't think we'd end up here." Starval brushed leaves off his leathers.

"I brought us here." Mayland wasn't looking at any of them, but staring up at the branches, turning slowly as if he might be hunting for the sun.

"This pool should take us back to where we came from," Arpix was explaining to Clovis, whose ventures into the Exchange had been limited to two brief excursions, on one of which she'd made a spirited effort to kill Livira. "Though, since we came from a crack in the ground . . . I'm not really sure." He pointed along the row. "If I've got my bearings right, that's the future, and the past is back there." He indicated the pools marching off to his left. "And each of the parallel rows is another world, I believe. Each with their own past and future pools." He glanced towards Mayland. Evar guessed that the human had a list of questions as long as his arm, but was naturally hesitant to engage with the canith who had murdered the head of the librarians' order in this very place.

"So, where has this damn book gone?" Clovis asked the question of nobody in particular while removing a piece of bark from her mane.

"There are lots of pools to choose from . . ." Evar rolled his neck. As much as he hated to be dependent on Mayland, it seemed that without his brother their chances of finding either the book or Livira were essentially zero.

"It's not in any of these." Mayland continued his study of the branches as if Oanold and the stolen book might be hiding in a tree.

Arpix couldn't restrain himself any longer. "You appear to have ruled out all of space and time. Where else do you suggest we look?"

By way of reply, Mayland waved a hand and somehow the action divided Evar's vision. Every tree became two overlapping images of a tree, pulling slowly apart from one another. As the distance between them grew, each image doubled again and the speed with which they were parting company increased. The gaps widened, the doubling happened again, the speed increased.

Within the span of a few heartbeats a great stack of identical Exchanges layered the space above them, ghostly and translucent, and with some sense unconnected to his eyes, Evar knew that the layers repeated below them too.

"Time and space." Mayland encompassed their surroundings with a sweep of his arm. "Possibility." He pointed upwards. "May have beens, might have beens, must have beens. In short: alternatives. That's where the book fell."

"How do we get up there?" Evar didn't care about the wriggling of time. He cared about how he felt, and he felt that each hour he wasted was an hour in which Livira faced dangers without him. To his mind and body, the conviction was as real as the falling had been once he'd dropped into the crack, but unlike the plunge, the shock of it wasn't wearing off the longer it went on.

"It's more a question of where we want to get to." Mayland began to climb steps that weren't there, rising towards the first of the perhaps infinite layers.

"Wait!" Evar tried to follow. "How are you doing that? Wait!"

Mayland glanced back, irritated. "I doubt any of you who can't work out how to follow me are going to be much use."

"I wasn't aware that being useful was a necessary qualification for being part of our family," Evar found himself scolding. "Go on then, you've walked away from us all before."

Mayland continued his ascent, without looking back. "We're not a family, we're a chance alignment."

"That's all any family is!" Evar shouted.

Mayland stopped. Dark and curiously grim eyes found Evar's. He drew a deep breath, and said, "Brother, you really would be better off walking away from this. Staying here. Doing anything else. But if you really must come, then just climb the stairs."

"What stairs?"

But Arpix, stepping into thin air and elevating himself to Evar's height, answered the question. "It's a state of mind. I think it's a visual metaphor for ascent of some kind."

"Huh?" Clovis tested the air around Arpix with her foot, finding nothing.

"Up here." Arpix turned slowly and touched between his eyes. "Look at me." He took both Clovis's hands in his. "You need to want to follow me."

"I guess hunting is a type of following." Clovis grinned.

As Arpix climbed the invisible stairway backwards, leading Clovis up, it seemed to Evar not dissimilar to the way that Livira had taught him to fly. Arpix appeared most confident as a teacher, and Clovis, eager to learn, rose from the ground, her steps mirroring his.

With an effort, Evar calmed himself, focused only on the next layer of the Exchange, until it seemed almost solid, and without looking at his feet, began to climb the stairs that weren't there.

"Well, this isn't right," Starval complained behind them. "I'm the one who's great at climbing. Never met anything I can't climb, except the library walls. And I still haven't. There's not a damn thing here *to* climb."

"Just pretend there is," Evar said. "If growing up in a library doesn't equip you for pretending then I don't know what would."

Starval raised a foot and with great deliberation set it back down, passing through any invisible step that might be there on the way. "Damn it!"

Mayland looked back. "You know why you're still down there, brother. It's a matter of commitment. You know what I've asked of you and why it must be done. If you have the courage of your convictions, step up."

Starval locked eyes with Mayland, a bleak stare. It had in it something of the look his eyes used to hold on emerging from the Mechanism after a long day of imaginary death dealing, plying the trade for which he'd trained so long. "Damn you, Mayland." Once more he took the step, and this time, he rose.

———————

THEY CLIMBED THROUGH several dozen layers before Mayland halted, jumped down, and set his feet squarely on grass which in that moment became as real as the grass they'd left behind. The trees, the pools—it was the Exchange as Evar had always known it, but with a greyer sky and a cool whisper of a breeze. The malady that had changed the Exchange they left behind was present in this alternative but to a lesser extent.

"So, all we need to do is find this king and take the book off him?" Clovis looked around her. "And everything can go back to how it was?"

"It's easier to poison a well than purify it." Starval patted the nearest tree as if uncertain whether it could be trusted.

"I don't intend for anything to go back to how it was, sister." Mayland narrowed his eyes. "We're here because I don't trust that venal human to finish the job Evar and Livira started and Arpix helped along recently in grand style."

"How do you even know about Oanold?" Arpix asked, still wincing at the praise he'd received for unwittingly destroying the Mechanism.

Mayland started a slow walk along the nearest timeline, pausing by each pool. "Starval and I have done quite a bit of spying. Once I realised what Evar and his human were making, I needed to understand all the factors at play so I could manipulate events should they go off course."

"I don't understand why you even needed us," Evar growled. "Couldn't you just write your own book or whatever?"

"It's a complicated knot you two tied through time. It's written into our lives. Fated, if you like. Something I could take advantage of once I became aware of its existence, but not a thing I could craft myself. In any event, completing a work like this needs vision. And Arpix's little king can't see past his own greed. Besides, given the manner of his arrival and the level of his ignorance, he may well have spread himself across dozens of alternatives. This one is just my best bet. And in each alternative he will, most likely, have fallen into himself. We're not looking for Arpix's Oanold. We're looking for whatever he was in this alternative." Mayland pointed at the pool just ahead of them. "Let's just hope he didn't land hard enough to scatter, or if he did, that at least the book will be here."

And then, as if what he'd said made sense or was in any way enough to equip them for what lay ahead, Mayland reached out an open hand to Starval and to Clovis. Evar took Starval's hand and Arpix Clovis's.

"Ready?"

Evar swallowed his "no." Livira was out there, and her book was the key he needed to unlock whatever doors stood between them.

"How do we stop ourselves from doing the same thing as Oanold?" Arpix asked. "The fragmenting thing, and the falling-into-ourselves thing. We're not going to be any use if we forget who we are and why we're there."

"Focus on who you are and why you're going," Mayland said. "If you smear out across possibilities, that's not such a problem. You can search them too. Staying yourself is the key. Using the Exchange should ensure that, but these are strange days. Any other questions?" He looked left then right.

Receiving no answer from any of them, Mayland stepped forward, and the waters took them.

"WHERE ARE WE?" A twisting jolting rush had filled Evar's eyes and mind with unimaginable colour, only to leave him stumbling into a dimly lit somewhere, blinking to clear his vision of shades he would never be able to remember.

"It looks like a rather poor copy of the library." Starval's whisper reminded Evar that stealth might be a sensible precaution.

They were in a chamber whose ceiling was almost low enough to touch and whose walls were scarcely more than ten yards apart. The bookshelves that filled the place were so short that simply by lifting up on his toes Evar could peer across their tops. Large windows at the front of the chamber should have filled the place with light, but the space beyond them was grey and featureless.

Evar seemed to have emerged from a portal rather than a pool, a shimmering circle of light drawn on the chamber's rear wall. "Where's Arpix?" Evar spun around. "Where's Clovis? Where in all the hells is Mayland, come to that?"

"I lost hold of them." Starval moved out slowly among the shelves. "Hopefully Mayland's nearby."

"Hopefully they *all* are." Evar reached for Starval's arm. "We could go back. Look for them."

Starval shook his head. "They came through. We'll find them here. And it's not like Clovis and Mayland can't look after themselves. We're the ones that need saving now they're gone."

Evar frowned, looked back at the portal, shrugged, and branched off into a different aisle to Starval's.

Evar's path brought him to the front of the chamber ahead of his brother. His surprise at finding a counter there with a balding human behind it, reading a book, was matched only by the man's at seeing Evar emerging from the aisles.

The man blinked several times, glanced down at his book, rubbed his eyes, and set the volume on the polished surface before him. "I could have sworn the shop was empty." He rubbed his eyes again, wrinkling the pouchy skin of his face, before smiling. "Did you find what you were looking for?"

Evar inspected his empty hands. "Not yet, I'm searching for a very rare book, by Livira Page."

"Never tell a shopkeeper that what you're looking for is rare, my friend." The man stood from his stool. "Maybe Inistren has it. He specialises in rarities. Five doors down on the left."

"This is a shop?" Evar asked.

"Of course it is." Starval came up behind him, setting a hand on his shoulder. "A bookshop." He turned to the bemused shopkeeper. "Thank you for finding him. My apologies, sir, sometimes our brother wanders." And Starval steered Evar to the street door.

"Are there any more of you back there?" The man peered towards the shelves.

"Just us." Starval reached for the door handle.

"Careful." Evar pulled back. "Looks like a dust storm out there." He had encountered two dust storms whilst on the Arthran Plateau, and both had been deeply unpleasant.

"Wasn't it foggy when you came in?" The man looked puzzled. "Rolled in from Lake Cantoo before dawn, I thought." His frown deepened.

Starval laughed and tapped the side of his head. "Dust storm! My brother's imagination sometimes carries him away."

A moment later they were out in the cold, grey damp with the shop bell tinkling behind them. Evar shook his brother off. "I'm not an idiot."

"You should stop acting like one then."

"It looked like a dust storm!"

"To someone who hasn't seen any other type of weather." Starval hunched against the chill, tiny droplets of water already gathering on his dark fur.

"Should we try this other shop?" Evar looked both ways down the street. He couldn't see much, just the grey shapes of people walking before the fog swallowed them, and a few hanging signs above what he assumed were other shops. Bookshops possibly.

"We need to get a better understanding of the place," Starval said. "I doubt we'll find what we need in a bookshop. Better to look for trouble. Wherever it is, the book is going to be making waves of some sort."

"Won't that man back there end up wandering into the Exchange and causing more problems? We left a big sparkly door in his shop." Evar could already see the shopkeeper through the windows, advancing into the ordered ranks of his own shelves with the caution of a man expecting to discover something entirely new. "And why did he seem more surprised that we'd got into his shop without him noticing than by the fact we're canith? Most humans I've met either want to run away screaming or to kill me."

"It's that thing the Exchange does," Starval answered, still eyeing the unyielding greyness for threats. "The effect carries over when you come through a door, even when you've not gone back to the past. Only lasts a few hours. Anyone that looks at us will see something close to what they expect to see. Also, they'll understand us, and we'll understand them. Once it wears off, things can get tricky." With that, he headed off into the fog, and with a last glance back, trying to fix the shop front into his memory, Evar followed.

"You sound like an old hand at this sort of thing."

Starval shrugged. "I may have been away longer than you think. Not as long as Mayland, though. He's very definitely the elder brother now."

"How long?" Evar hadn't really considered the possibility. Since Mayland and Starval vanished in the Exchange after Mayland killed Yute's wife it seemed that a couple of weeks might have passed. Certainly not more than a month. A lot of things had happened, but somewhere between a week and two weeks felt right.

"It's hard to tell when you're on the move. Maybe a year. More perhaps. Mayland's plans have a lot of moving parts. We spent a lot of time oiling the wheels. Not everything paid off but—"

"You seem pretty committed to it then." Evar lowered his voice as if someone—Mayland maybe, even if he wasn't there—might overhear them. He returned to his normal tone, feeling foolish. "Committed to destroying the library? You've put a lot of effort into it."

Starval shrugged. "What's an assassin if not an agent of change? Besides, it's been nice to be needed for once."

"I . . ." Evar was going to say he needed Starval but opted not to insult his intelligence. Starval and Clovis had both, by a combination of chance and inclination, made weapons of themselves. Evar, though he'd dedicated himself to getting them out of that chamber, had at the same time hoped that neither would ever have cause or opportunity to put their skills to use. Things had not worked out as he hoped. "Is every shop on this street a bookshop?"

"Seems that way." Starval reached up and set the nearest sign swinging. *Manenoth's Grimoires.* "This, however . . ." He slowed in front of the next set of windows, whose panes were smaller, squares of puddle glass that distorted the warm glow from within and muted the faint refrain of a song. ". . . seems to be a tavern." He advanced to the door, a heavy slab of oak with iron studs across its length.

"A tavern?" Evar hesitated. "Isn't that where people break barstools over each other's heads?"

"Only in books." Starval wiped the wetness from his mane. "Besides, we're on a street full of bookshops. It's going to be full of readers. How bad could it be?"

Anyone undertaking extensive travels should, like the nomad, carry the essential core of their existence with them. Be it a shrine, portrait, or simply a favoured stone. Without a centre the soul becomes unmoored and immune to the wonders of change.

The Eternal Tourist, *by Halley Combit*

CHAPTER 24

Livira

I don't feel good." Livira's stomach had already threatened rebellion over the carnage that unfolded after King Chertal's army ambushed the skeer patrol. Now though, something else added itself to her discomfort. They had flown a few miles over the forest to put additional space between themselves, the battlefield, and the night-ship. Without warning, the act of flying, which had been effortless, had become a burden.

"Livira?" Carlotte descended beside her.

"You're crying." Livira tried to distract herself from her own problems by focusing on Carlotte's. "It was horrific. The fighting. We should all be crying after what we've seen . . ."

Carlotte wiped at red eyes. "We should. I should. But it wasn't that. It's Meelan. We've been busy the whole time since you got here. Now we're leaving, it's hit me. He won't be there."

Yolanda had dropped lower in Carlotte's wake, bringing Leetar with her.

Carlotte noticed her. "Sorry." Deferential, as if a friend's grief should bow before that of a sister.

Leetar managed a weak smile, hair whipping around her face as if she weren't a ghost and the wind of their passage could touch her. Belief, Livira noted, was a force of nature too.

"Brothers are strange things. We fought a lot, not all of it as children. And when we weren't fighting, we really weren't that interested in each other's lives. But you can't believe how much it hurt losing him." She paused, momentary doubt on her pretty face. "For a trained diplomat I can say some stupid things."

"Tell me about brothers." Livira, still struggling to keep flying, needed something to think about other than the pull of the forest beneath them. "I never had one . . ." Leetar had been there, seen the canith family split between all three of the choices that Irad, Jaspeth, and Yute had laid before them. Evar would have come with her to save the library, she knew that. Kerrol went chasing Yute's endless compromises. Mayland had stolen Evar away with Starval and Clovis to seek the library's destruction. "And now we're getting to the sharp end of things." It wouldn't be long before the bonds of Evar's family were put to the test, set in the balance with ideals, conviction, ambition—every corrosive product of an intelligent mind and a wounded childhood. It was Livira's family too, almost more real than the one that she'd been born into out on the Dust. Livira and Malar had raised Evar and his siblings, albeit behind masks the library had imposed on them. "Tell me about brothers."

Leetar brushed a hand across her face, dragging aside the auburn spray of her hair, her expression that of someone grappling with too large a question. Just as Livira thought she wasn't going to answer, Leetar shook her head and said, "They'll always surprise you."

Instead of asking further questions, Livira found herself on a downward trajectory, like an overambitious hawk that had taken off with prey clearly too large for its wingspan. "I . . . I need to rest."

The treetops threatened, close enough to see individual branches, the flutter of leaves.

"Catch her!" Yolanda's call from higher up.

Carlotte tried, but a moment later everything became a green blur, a rushing thicket of tree limbs, and then a sudden, jolting reunion with the ground, almost hard enough to convince Livira that she'd become something solid. She lay, cradled by the forest floor, groaning.

"What's happened to her?" Carlotte demanded as Yolanda alighted with Leetar.

"I'm fine." Livira forced herself into a sitting position.

"Something's happening." Yolanda offered Livira a small white hand to help her up.

Livira forced the sarcastic reply to stay on her tongue and let the surprisingly strong child heave her to her feet.

"There." Yolanda nodded to where Livira had landed. To what Livira would have to admit was more of an impact site than any ghost had a right to make.

"What are those . . ." Livira peered at black lines that almost seemed like . . .

"Fissures," Yolanda said. "Something is happening. Your book and the hole it keeps cutting through time has started to break the world."

Livira dusted herself off, feeling heavy, slow, and rather bruised. "Well, get me back to it then, and maybe we can do something about it. I think—"

Carlotte's shriek cut her off.

"What? What is it?" Leetar tried to stop Carlotte's hopping dance of pain or distress.

"Something bit me!"

Yolanda went to where Carlotte had been standing. "There's nothing here. Just this bush." She waved a hand through its leaves and jerked it back with a yelp.

"Told you." Carlotte shook Leetar off and hobbled back.

Livira turned away, distracted by the glimpse of a reflecting surface between the tree trunks. "Is that a . . . pool?"

"They moved!" Leetar said. "When you touched them. The leaves."

Carlotte reached out gingerly, squealed, and snatched her hand back. "I can touch them!" She did it again. "I really can." She buried both hands in the leaves. "I haven't touched anything in years. I mean except me. And you three, just recently." She moved her hands. "This is *so* weird."

"There's another one." Livira pointed to a second pool. Then a third. The others ignored her, still discussing how they could all touch the bush that had "bitten" Carlotte.

Livira turned around, taking in their surroundings. Fragments of sky fingered in through the foliage, the sun absent now, hidden behind slate-grey clouds.

"We're in the Exchange. Somehow."

That got Yolanda's attention. Pink eyes widened in recognition. "It shouldn't be possible."

"It wasn't like this?" Carlotte turned from the bush and looked around too. She slapped a tree and examined its bark with fascination. "It wasn't so wild?"

"It's changed," Livira agreed. And the Exchange was not a place that was given to change. She was sure of that. Change was a time-thing. And yet somehow, though it was different, it was also the same. She had been to this place before, she was sure of it. "What does it mean? Can anyone just wander in here now? What if the skeer find it?"

"It means that things are falling apart quicker than I thought possible," Yolanda said. "I think the book is calling you back to it."

"That's a good thing?" Livira edged closer to the nearest pool, pushing the undergrowth aside with her feet. Brambles grappled at the hem of her robe.

"The closer you get the more you'll accelerate the damage," Yolanda said. "But also, it's probably the only way to ensure that it stops. Though, if you make a mistake, that would be the end of everything."

"A mistake? What exactly is it that I have to do?" Livira asked.

"I've no idea."

"ARE YOU SURE this is the right pool?" Carlotte's grip tightened. Already Livira's bloodless fingers were heading towards the whiteness of Yolanda's.

"There's only one pool," Livira murmured, seeing in her mind a faint, timeless recollection of a wild wood, a stream, a glowing sphere larger than she was. "There's no pool . . . only the nexus."

The water before them began to glow, lit from within by its own light.

"The nexus," Yolanda agreed. "You've seen it?" A sharp look, her face made sinister by the shadows painted across it from below.

Livira nodded. "It doesn't matter which pool. The book's part of me. I'm part of it. It's calling."

The pool that wasn't a pool flowed and rose and in the space of three moments became that same ball of radiance Livira had seen in the memories of her years as the Assistant.

"Touch it." She reached out with the hand knotted with Carlotte's and with the one knotted with Yolanda's.

They touched it and were gone.

LIVIRA STUMBLED INTO a cool white mist. For a moment she stood, blinking, her robe pulled tight around her. She wondered if she might be in some strange sort of in-between domain. An insubstantial, interstitial place.

"Where's the girl gone? Yolo? I want to say she's called Yolo."

"Yolanda." Livira turned to find Carlotte standing behind her, looking even colder than she felt. Behind Carlotte, the portal through which they'd come decorated a stone-block wall, the shimmer of its light lending a glow to the nearest fog.

"Where's Leetar?" Carlotte started off into the mist.

Livira caught her arm. She could see the ground beneath their feet, brick-paved, and literally nothing else save the wall behind them. "Maybe we should wait."

Carlotte stamped on the floor. "It's solid! Let's go and see what else we can touch! Maybe they'll have food . . ."

"We can't just lose ourselves in all this." Livira waved her free hand at the dampness. "Yolanda and Leetar will never find us."

Carlotte shrugged. "That creepy girl can take care of herself. She'll be invisible in this stuff in any case. And Leetar . . . I'm sorry, I know you like her, and she's Meelan's sister and everything, but yawn. Even her family weren't rich enough to buy her a personality. I mean—" She broke off, noticing how Livira was looking at her. "They're standing right behind me, aren't they?"

Livira was sorely tempted to say yes. "Yes."

Carlotte spun round to face the empty mist. "Oh, you bitch!"

"Even if I didn't like her, and I do a bit, and even if she was boring, which she might be, we can't just aband— Stop it. They aren't standing behind me."

Carlotte continued to stare wide-eyed at the mist over Livira's shoulder for a few more moments, then gave it up. "All right, we can wait a little while. But not long. I haven't eaten in years, and I'm hungry!"

Livira retreated to the portal, wondering if she should go back and where it might take her. A sudden thought hit her. "You didn't let go of Leetar's hand, did you?"

"No!" Carlotte looked shocked. Livira couldn't tell if it was fake shock or the real thing. "It did get kind of rough in there though!"

"It did?" Livira had been stepping into the light one instant, stumbling from the portal the next.

"It did."

The sound of people approaching forestalled any further discussion. Male voices, raised in heated debate, both loud and strangely muffled.

"We should move," Carlotte said. "Quickly."

"Why?" Livira had come to find her book, which might prove difficult without speaking to anyone or even being seen.

"Do you know what the local punishment for witchcraft is?" Carlotte asked. "In my city they just threw them off the plateau, and I always said that was stupid because if they really were witches, they might be able to fly."

"I don't see—"

Carlotte thrust a pointing finger towards the glowing portal.

"We should move."

Ten yards proved sufficient, even with her vision extending not much further than the reach of her arm, to tell Livira she was in a city. She stumbled over a kerb, stepped in a wet gutter, and slipped in something nameless. They passed a doorway then a window holding a span of remarkably flat glass, and then another doorway between windows of a more familiar sort through which warm light spilled. She smelled ale, and the chant of a rowdy song challenged the fog.

"In here!" Carlotte reached for the door. "Maybe they have food!"

Much as she shared Carlotte's desire to plunge into some warm place and be fed, they had no money, no idea where they were, and no plan. "Not here. Somewhere quiet."

Carlotte looked ready to argue, but behind them the approaching men seemed to have missed the existence of the portal entirely and were still at their heels. Two tall figures loomed through the glowing mist.

"Quickly!" Livira pushed Carlotte onwards.

They passed two more shops. From one hanging sign Livira read, *Markam Makram's Fine Folios.* "Bookshops?" She glimpsed the answer through the window of the next: well-stacked shelves inviting inspection.

"This way?" Carlotte paused at a corner and turned to face the side street. "We might find a meal more easily somewhere less educational."

Livira glanced back. The pursuit, if it had been a pursuit, seemed to have ended. The men might have been diverted into the tavern. She peered down the street Carlotte had chosen, and after a moment of indecision, nodded. "This way."

If you love someone, let them go. Except when that would be really stupid, like in a crowd and they're two and you're their mother.

Uncommon Sense, *by Margery Taylor*

———————

CHAPTER 25

Arpix

A rpix had no memory of losing his grip on Clovis's hand or on Evar's but as he staggered out from the seething light of a library portal into a cold mist it seemed that neither of the canith were with him.

A spiky bush immediately interposed itself into his path and tried to trip him up. Given Arpix's disorientation it proved an unequal contest. He would have hit the ground hard but for the presence of a wet shrub that cushioned his fall, engulfing him in glossy leaves whilst a hundred twigs tried to stab him through his tattered robes.

For some time Arpix lay on his side in the damp undergrowth. The diffuse light pervading the fog told him it was daytime. The wall just beyond suggested that he was in a garden. The fact that the glowing portal in that wall hadn't attracted any attention made him pretty sure that there was nobody close by.

The mist muffled sound almost as effectively as it shuttered sight, but enough noise still penetrated for Arpix to believe himself somewhere populated. Had that been a distant cry? And that the slam of a door?

He levered himself up, shivering. Going back to the Exchange was tempting, but the others had come with him. They would not be in the Exchange, and visits to that place carried the danger that years would slide between him and the others. Years that couldn't be undone, and that he would not want to have missed.

With a degree of rustling and snapping that would have hurt Starval's assassin-soul, Arpix began to follow the wall, stumbling over well-manicured bushes, picking his way around flower beds.

The others must have emerged from their own portals. Arpix's fingers trailed the damp stonework. Hopefully Clovis wasn't on the far side of the town. Or in another town altogether. He reached a corner and found a window, gracefully curving ironwork defending large panes of glass. The curtains disclosed the faintest suggestion of a glow behind them, a lamp perhaps, lit in defiance of the dreary day outside.

A sound drew Arpix's attention, a sniff piercing the grey veil, a rumbled growl.

"Clovis?" He whispered her name.

Someone approached, crunching along a gravelled path that Arpix had yet to discover. He resisted the urge to run. Even if it wasn't Clovis he was hardly going to hide amongst the dripping vegetation indefinitely. A sudden fear seized him. What if the Exchange's intrinsic desire to join loose ends had delivered him into Oanold's hands? What if it were one of his soldiers approaching?

Too late to run. A figure loomed through the mist. Tall. Too tall for a human. "Clovis?"

A heavy hand reached out, grabbed his arm, jerked him forward, and the face of a canith looked down at him. A stranger.

"Wait!" Arpix tried to forestall violence.

Instead, the canith glanced back the way it came. "Got an intruder. A human." The canith drew Arpix forward, pulling him onto the path. "A rather ragged one. Another beggar. 'Lost' in the mist, are we?"

Arpix opened his mouth to deny it but didn't get as far as speaking before two new pieces of information commandeered his attention. Firstly, that the canith was wearing what seemed to be a military uniform. And secondly, that the uniform bore an unsettling resemblance to those worn by King Oanold's soldiers. Not the ones that went out to patrol the Dust or that marched up and down on the city walls, but the more decorated variety that guarded his palaces.

Struggling was going to be pointless, and Arpix had neither magic nor weapons to aid him, not that he believed in violent solutions in any case. He considered shouting for help but pressed his lips together, unwilling to provoke Clovis into premature action if she were close enough to hear his cries. Instead, he settled for doing what he had always done: gathering information. "Where are we going?"

"To the gate before the captain finds out about you. You don't want that." The canith sniffed again. "You don't smell the same as the last vagrant we picked out of the bushes."

"Thank you?"

"Don't get me wrong. You stink, it's just the wrong sort of stink. How long have you been in the city?"

"Ah. That depends which city this is, and how you measure these things."

Another canith loomed in the mist. Behind him the fog revealed a building and a door. "Got another one." The first guard shoved Arpix forward. "Talks like he's drunk. Smells like he's sober."

"You know how it is. The streets take 'em 'cos they're cracked. Or the streets crack 'em." The new soldier ran a dark eye up and down Arpix's length. "Skinny one. Still, can't have 'em trespassing. Going to rob the stores, was you?"

"I assure you I didn't—"

"Climbed the wall by accident, did we? Thought you lived here? Came to apply for the potentate's army?" The first soldier laid a heavy hand on his shoulder from behind.

"Really . . . I . . ." Arpix looked around. The canith couldn't be working for Oanold no matter what uniform they were wearing, or what tricks the currents of time had played in delivering the king to this place. Arpix had voluntarily jumped into the chasm in the library less than an hour after Oanold had fallen in with Livira's book. The king couldn't have fashioned himself a replacement empire already. Especially not with canith. "This isn't Crath City? Is it?"

The second soldier shook his head. "He's not all here, Hadd. You can see it by looking at him. Give him a smack and shove him out before the captain gets wind. You know what'll happen otherwise. That business with the quartermaster this morning left her in a foul mood."

The first soldier growled in his throat. "That's what I was doing before you shoved your nose in. Come on then, twig. I'll send you on your way

with a farewell tap. Might lose a tooth or two, but we can't have you thinking you can just come and go." He started to drag Arpix along a path that
led directly away from the building, out through the garden.

They got perhaps three yards before the sound of the door opening behind them brought Hadd to a crunching halt. "Shit." Muttered under his
breath.

"What've you got there, Private Hadd?" Another couple of yards and
the mist would have swallowed them.

Arpix looked back to see a stern-faced woman in the doorway, dwarfed
by the soldier still standing there, but wearing the same uniform. Where
the two canith had short swords at their hips and some design of 'stick
slung across their backs, the captain had a proportionately longer blade, no
'stick, and three crimson stripes on her upper right arm.

"Intruder, Captain. Was going to eject him with a physical reprimand."

"Intruder? I see a thief, caught in the act." The woman stalked closer.
She looked to be in her fifties, sturdy, grizzled, hair iron-grey and short,
coiled across a blunt skull. The eyes she fixed on Arpix were the same colour as the mist and held about as much warmth. "Looks like an Amacar to
me. You an Amacar, boy?"

"I don't know what an Amacar is. I'm not—"

The words "from around here" were slapped out of Arpix's mouth. The
woman's blow left his face a strange combination of numb but stinging and
deafened his ear.

"Amacar for sure," she said. "Lies like one. Stinks like one."

Arpix, still developing the bruises from the beating he'd been given by
a different military, kept his mouth closed. He tasted blood.

The captain sneered. "It's hanging day down at the Alarg. He can be
strung up with whatever else they have for the gallows when the fog breaks.
Make sure everyone knows where he came from. We'll see how many we
have to drop before that wall starts doing its job."

"Yes, Captain," Hadd said without enthusiasm.

"Damn straight, yes, Captain!" the woman shouted. "And get your
backside back here as soon as it's done. I know how long it takes to walk to
the Alarg and back."

———————

ARPIX FOUND HIMSELF being frogmarched through an impressive set of gates and out into what he assumed was a square but felt limitless in the enfolding mist.

"You're really going to hang me?" It didn't feel real. And yet the first sliver of fear had worked its way close to his heart.

"Not me. But yes." The guard pushed him to keep up the brisk pace. "What did you expect? Robbing the potentate's barracks was always going to be a short trip to a long drop, no?"

"But I wasn't . . ." Too late Arpix thought of taking them to the portal. It would have prompted a lot more questions, but execution would have been avoided or at least substantially delayed. He opened his mouth to say they should go back, then closed it. Hadd already thought he was mad. The guard wasn't about to face his captain's wrath on the strength of the least likely tale he'd ever heard: *I didn't climb the wall—I came out of it . . .*

They reached a street between two sets of tall buildings. Arpix had never been anywhere other than Crath City, and, two hundred years later, to the barren plateau out on the edge of the Dust. The city around him could be the one in which he'd lived. Except for the mix of canith and humans cohabiting within its walls. They passed dozens, most just shapes in the mist, some canith tall, some human short.

Arpix wanted to know what an Amacar was. It had almost seemed that the idea he might be one was more of a crime than his trespassing. Livira would have found out already. She didn't appear to have ever met a question she didn't ask. Arpix wasn't sure he'd like the answer though, especially if it was another blow.

The streets they followed had a general upward trend, and the altitude combined with a developing breeze began to extend the range of Arpix's vision. He saw town houses, stables, a tavern. They arrived at a crossroads at the same time as the head of a column of troops, complete with limp banners and a drummer thudding out the beat for their slow march. Somewhere further down the line pipes wailed.

"I think we can make it . . . just." Hadd hesitated, then decided. "Quick!" He dragged Arpix across, drawing a glare from the two officers

just behind the drummer and the banner bearers. The double row of soldiers behind them snaked away beyond sight.

Hadd slowed down once he'd got Arpix past them. "We could have
been there forever. I swear some of those parades are a mile long."

"I'd have been happy to wait."

"I bet. But Captain Biggie will be handing out latrine duties, the mood
she's in. Damned if I'm giving her an excuse."

Arpix resisted sarcasm and couldn't muster any sympathy without it.
"You're really going to let them kill me?"

"I really am." Hadd nodded, though without enthusiasm.

"You could let me go."

"And spend a year in the box if the captain finds out. Or, if she's still in
a mood, get my neck stretched instead of yours."

"She wouldn't find out. I'd—"

"Get caught again within a week doing something else stupid. You're
three-quarters starved. A sniff of food and you'll be climbing over the next
wall you meet."

"I'll leave the city. I'll—"

"Hadd? Is that Hadd?" An exceptionally broad canith at the head of a
patrol of half a dozen soldiers came to a halt in their path.

"It is." Hadd agreed in a weary voice. "Hello, Janks."

"Corporal Janks." The canith tapped the single stripe on an upper arm
as thick around as Arpix's chest. "And who's your friend?" The canith,
taller than Hadd, as tall as Kerrol maybe, and quite possibly as heavy as
any two of Clovis's brothers, stepped closer, well into Hadd's personal
space if Arpix was any judge.

Hadd's shoulders slumped a fraction. "Gallows meat." He glanced at
Arpix with a frown. "And we're in danger of missing the drop. So, if you'll
excuse us . . ."

"Don't let's rush off on my account," Arpix ventured. "I mean it's bad
manners—"

Janks's hand closed around Arpix's throat and sealed away his words.

"Let him go," Hadd said without heat.

"You're taking him to be hanged. No harm in a little foretaste, is there?"
Janks shook Arpix in a playful manner whilst lifting him, with just one

arm, to a point at which his toes barely made contact with the flagstones. "Hanging's so quick after all. A hardened criminal like this one deserves to linger. Give him a chance to rue the day he crossed paths with Private Hadd of the Potentate's Outer Guard!"

"You break him, you keep him." Hadd stepped around Janks and made to continue on his way.

Janks dropped Arpix on his heels where he somehow stayed standing, gasping air in through a still-constricted throat. "Don't be like that. We'll come along and help you, Hadd. Don't want to risk this dangerous criminal overpowering you and escaping." His patrol, four canith and two men, lined up behind him.

Hadd shook his head and motioned Arpix forward.

They crossed another square, a large one where Arpix could see the buildings rising to left and right, albeit hazily. Stallholders had already set up shop around the margins but were only now starting to see much business, some rising from their chairs to deal with customers come to buy pans, pots, strings of garlic, beadwork, rugs, small cakes. Arpix's eyes lingered on the cakes, remembering the recent glory of the butter cookies Celcha had created from her flask. He wished the ganar would come along now, spreading her peace out across this strange but familiar city he'd fallen into.

"Oh." He saw the gallows now, their shapes resolving through the evaporating mist, the nooses hanging empty, waiting. He wanted to protest further, no matter how faint his chance of salvation. And he would have if Hadd had been his only audience. It felt ridiculous to hold on to pride or shame so close to being murdered in such a cold and functional manner, but Arpix couldn't bring himself to plead with a bully like Janks looking on. Hadd contained a better nature, that much was obvious.

The patrol and guard escorted Arpix to the gallows. There were three nooses, each depending from its own timber frame. The whole structure of raw timbers crudely bolted together seemed to be temporary, designed to be assembled at speed and taken away just as fast. Eight prisoners stood roped together in a sorry line behind the gallows, two canith, six humans. Four of them had a broad red stripe across their faces, as if someone had carelessly trailed a paint brush from one ear to the other. These four stood at the far end of the line, an old man in an expensive frock coat, a young man and woman in simple garb who held hands like a married couple, and the shorter of the two canith. Fresh paint by the look of it . . . or blood . . . drips running down across their cheeks like crimson tears.

The crowd that had gathered before the platform showed a similar demographic to that of the prisoners. Young, old, humans, canith, rich and poor. Perhaps a hundred citizens distracted from their bargain hunting. Enough to acknowledge the hangings as a spectacle, but not so many that it might be considered a rarity. Arpix had seen more people assemble to hear one of the more popular singers on Trandor Corner. His death was to be a minor entertainment, with a crowd-pulling level that ranked somewhere between a skilled juggler and the sort of magician who snatched coins out of people's ears while an accomplice tried to filch additional ones out of their pockets.

As Hadd brought Arpix towards the end of the line, two more canith guards, these in a dark and shabby uniform, came forward to take charge of him. A wiry man with wiry greying hair and narrow eyes came forward with a small bucket of what might be pig's blood, and a dripping brush. "Amacar?" He raised the brush.

"Says he isn't." Hadd waved the brush away.

"Well, he would, wouldn't he?" The man made to go around Hadd's half-hearted defence.

"Of course he is," Janks called with jovial malice from somewhere further back.

"Does it matter?" Arpix found himself saying. "Are they going to hang me twice if I am?" It was something Livira would say. Arpix wondered if staring death in the face had finally uncovered some courage in him.

The man with the brush slapped at Arpix, and, partly deflected by Hadd, ended up scoring a wet red line across Arpix's chest. The blood—it smelled like blood—looked black on Arpix's faded robes rather than red.

"Enough," growled the nearest of the executioner canith, and jerked Arpix forward by one arm. With practised ease, he secured Arpix's wrists behind him using a short length of rope which he proceeded to tie to the much longer rope joining the prisoners.

Arpix resisted pointing out that they would just have to untie them all soon unless it were some kind of joint hanging. It all seemed suddenly absurd to him, funny in the bitterest of ways. To die here, impossibly far from all he'd known, killed for no reason by people who didn't particularly care. When Hadd turned away Arpix called after him, "You're not staying to watch?"

The canith looked back with a frown. "You've got a bigger audience than most of us get."

"But I don't know any of them." Arpix realised he was babbling. Already his prediction was coming true. The three prisoners at the front of the rope were being untied and the crowd's chatter had stilled to an expectant hush.

"You don't know *me*." Hadd turned and shouldered his way past Janks, who apparently had no better place to be.

Arpix stood, shivering despite the midday sun now tearing through the remnants of the mist. One of the executioners read the crimes of the first three condemned. The words washed over Arpix. He scanned the crowd, hoping to see Clovis or Evar there. Starval would do. Even Mayland. But there were no familiar faces, no friendly eyes. It seemed no time ago that he had been watching a different sea of faces without compassion. There had been no kindness among Oanold's soldiers. United in their togetherness, they had become something other than human, substituting a mob's instincts for those of a person. And here again, the simple mathematics of us and them had given a crowd licence to chew pasties and joke among themselves while they watched the living become the dead.

The creak of a lever shook Arpix from his reverie. Three bodies dropped through trapdoors and came to a juddering, devastating halt beneath them. Arpix nearly vomited. His breath came in short, horrified gasps.

Voices in the crowd expressed their disappointment. All three necks had broken. None of the criminals had danced for their audience. Someone pointed at Arpix. "Skinny's gonna kick. Ain't got the weight to snap 'is spine."

The next three went up. Boos from the crowd, abuse hurled, stones too, aimed at the couple with the bloody stripes. The executioner announced that the criminal to the left, a heavy-browed man sneering at any who met his eye, was a street robber, and that the couple had been caught poisoning a well. The young man's protests of innocence were drowned out by the audience's rising anger. "Amacar filth!" "Conspirators!" "Child stealers!"

Under a barrage of insults, the last adjustments were made and the trio dropped. The couple, Arpix noted with horrified detachment, had shorter ropes, but whatever the executioner's intention, both died almost instantly. The citizens of the still-nameless city shouted their disappointment, cursing the executioners, a stone bouncing off one of the canith's broad shoulders.

Arpix looked around for an escape route, only to find Janks grinning at him good-humouredly, almost inviting him to try to run. And before he knew it, rough hands were guiding him, the well-dressed old man, and the last canith up the steps.

"It can't end like this." Arpix had been thinking the words, but it was the old man who said them out loud. He looked younger close up, perhaps not even sixty. Both his hands were shaking to a degree he'd empty any cup before it reached his lips.

This is where they save me. Arpix's lips muttered the words without sound. *This is where they save me.* It had to be. Where Clovis and her brothers emerged from a side street, swords in hand. But that wasn't how it worked. It wasn't how real life worked. People didn't turn up in the split second you needed them most: they were a week early or a day late. Even now, under the shadow of the gallows arm, Arpix couldn't shake off the shackles of his rationality. Statistics didn't lie, they were just misunderstood. A million-to-one shot might not even happen if you took a million tries.

Impatiently but without malice, one of the executioners positioned Arpix on the trapdoor where an "X" had been helpfully scorched into the planks to mark the spot. The noose descended around his neck, prickly, rough. Arpix fought to keep a ridiculous complaint about it being too tight from his lips. *This is it. They have to save me now.*

It had to be now. Once they dropped him, he was dead whether his neck broke or not. His throat would be crushed. Undoing the rope wouldn't save him. It had to be now.

"And this one . . ." The executioner paused, looking at his list. "What's his name?"

"Skinny," Janks called out.

"And Skinny, of no fixed abode, guilty of trespass and attempted theft."

"A filthy stealing Amacar!" a woman shouted.

"Hang them all." It sounded like a child.

"Wait!" Arpix said.

The executioner walked to the lever, a length of wood over a yard long, hinged to the platform. Throwing it would release all three trapdoors together.

"Don't . . ." the old man whispered.

But he did.

The drop was more like misstepping off a curb than a proper fall. But Arpix heard his neck break.

Time is an illusion. Lifetimes doubly so.
Collapsing the Wavefunction: A Compendium of Maybes, *by Boris*

———————

CHAPTER 26

Clovis

S omething tugged at Clovis. She yawned hugely, batting a lazy hand at the irritation, still wrapped in sleep. She had been dreaming that she was falling, but the nightmare had given over to dreams of sunshine, blue skies, and smooth fingers interlocked with her own.

Something tugged at her. A faint, sourceless ripple of worry ran through her. She hunched in on herself.

Fear, like other weaknesses, was something Clovis admitted to herself, but not to others. To deny such things would be to omit them from strategy and tactics, leaving oneself vulnerable. To share them would be to put those weaknesses in the hands of potential enemies, and everyone she had ever met was a potential enemy.

Heights frightened her. The library, as she'd experienced it for the first twenty years of her life, was flat. Spilled water did not run. Falling from any elevation more than that of a reading desk was a rarity. She had faced her fear in the Mechanism, but somehow the heights and drops of the real world had still had surprises to offer her. Surprises that had remained undiscovered until very recently, when she'd reached her second chamber. She'd had her revelation when standing up for the first time on top of a bookcase many times taller than she was. The unfamiliar quantity of "down" on either side pulled at her with a worrying, sick-making urgency. There had been some new ingredient in the mix. Perhaps the slight wobble of the shelves beneath her feet. Perhaps the anxiety drifting up from her brothers. Or maybe just the cold hard knowledge that a fall in the real had so much more bad stuff to offer than the forgiveness of the Mechanism did.

There had been little time to investigate the fear, however. The huge mechanical killing machine pursuing her had required her to jump endlessly from shelf top to shelf top, and her fear of falling had been pushed aside by a fear of being ripped into pieces. It hadn't been until she and her brothers escaped the library entirely and met the mountains that Clovis's abstract fear of dropping had been augmented by actual experience, at which point her vertigo had solidified.

She'd found that in the heat of battle, such as when chasing down the human king's army in an attempt to save Arpix, she could shoulder the feeling aside, focusing on her prey while her body obeyed her orders. But when she'd jumped into the pool in the Exchange, an unexpected fall had seized her. No water reached up to take her weight, just an endless plummeting that had drawn a howl from her mouth and made her forget all about the hands she had been supposed to hold on to.

She'd fallen, tumbling, expecting at any moment a crushing impact. Instead, the softness of a dream had received her, and she lay now, still enfolded in the remnants of it, not wanting to open her eyes.

Something tugged at her.

"What?" Clovis sat up sharply, her fingers now encircling the wrist behind the intruding hand.

Half a dozen small figures scattered shrieking into the mist. The human child whose wrist Clovis held bent its head of dirty blonde hair and sank small teeth into the meat of one of Clovis's fingers.

Clovis snarled and with her other hand dragged the head back by the hair, revealing the grime-streaked face of a young girl. A skinny one.

The girl snarled back, and one of her accomplices ran out of the mist, swinging a length of timber at Clovis's head. Clovis rose so that the blow landed across her shoulders. The shock of the impact shook the weapon from her assailant's hands, and the young boy had retreated into the mist by the time Clovis reached her full height.

"What were you doing?" Clovis lifted the young female by her arm until they were face to face.

"Robbin' you." The child winced and reached up to try to share the load with both arms. "Thought you were drunk."

It took Clovis a few moments to understand what that meant. "I've never been drunk."

She looked around. The mist concealed everything save the glow of the portal. She lowered the child to the ground, then pulled her in the direction of the shimmering circle. "Have you touched this?"

"Have I touched the wall?" The human girl eyed her with less fear than a canith three times her height and nine times her weight should inspire. "You sure you're not drunk? You were asleep in the gutter. And you've got no money."

Clovis's hand went to the hilt of her sword in sudden panic and relaxed a little on finding she still had it. "You can't see this?" She set her fingers to the middle of the circle of shimmering light set into the wall.

"I can see it," the girl said.

"You don't find it odd?"

"Why would I find a brick odd?" The girl frowned, tried to pull free, then stared up at Clovis. "Maybe you ate fligar mushrooms? 'Cos you're acting really weird."

"What city is this?"

"Like that."

"What city?" Clovis shook the girl.

"New Kraff! New Kraff!" the girl shouted. "Stop hurting me!"

Clovis released her grip and the ragged child scampered away to be lost with the others in the mist. Clovis stood, considering the portal. It seemed that just as the Exchange and its doorways often played games with perception, going so far as to translate both languages and appearances to meet expectations, it also disguised its exits, at least to those in the places they led to. Children were inquisitive in the same way that locusts were hungry. The only way a band of street urchins would not have investigated the portal was if they had been unable to see it.

Muffled sounds reached her. Knowing herself to be in a human city, Clovis resisted the impulse to draw her sword. Cutting a child in half would likely not recommend her to the locals. And it would disappoint

Arpix too. She inspected the bitemark in her finger and snorted. The girl had spirit.

She moved cautiously along the paved street, sniffing the damp air. A great number of scents laced the mist. Many of them made her stomach rumble, others variously intrigued or repelled. None were familiar. As a whole, the city smelled neither good nor bad. It was something complex and new. Therefore dangerous.

She sniffed for traces of the others. Her brothers would be fine, but Arpix . . . despite his wisdom Arpix was an innocent in many ways. She felt that their ignorance complemented each other, his expertise lying where she lacked the most, and hers where his was absent.

The road sloped. Clovis chose "up." She passed several doors and shuttered windows. Thirty yards on, an adult human passed her in the street, little more than a darker blot in the enfolding grey, paying no heed to her height. Twenty more yards took her to a crossroads. Another long inhale brought more confusion, and the faintest rumour of something known. She twisted her head this way and that, sniffing.

"Hey!" A figure swerved to avoid her. "Watch where you're going."

Clovis stared at the retreating shape until the fog swallowed it, too shocked to take offence, and in truth the near collision had been her fault. "A canith . . ."

The humans' indifference to her hadn't been due to the Exchange's illusions. The small girl and the passing adult shared the city with canith. Clovis put her surprise aside for later and sniffed again. "Arpix?" It was possible. It was also possible that the intensity of her desire to find him was playing tricks on her.

With nothing else to suggest a direction, Clovis followed her nose. The sniff of Arpix was probably a figment of imagination, but that made it no more likely to be the wrong choice.

The path she took led her higher. The mist thinned. Sunlight set the remnants glowing. The city, built of stone and brick, rose around her, impressing her with its architecture. The streets began to fill, or perhaps the citizens had been there all along, concealed under a grey blanket.

". . . mercenary . . ."

"A striking one!"

Clovis turned towards the speaker who had raised his voice for her benefit. He was one of three canith in a doorway, all male, all of them in uniform, all with the projectile weapons Arpix called 'sticks slung across their backs, and sabres at their hips.

"Come to join the potentate's liberation?"

"No feast's complete without rats waiting in the wings."

"She'll get her crumbs, that one. Look at the evil eye she's giving us!"

All three of them smirked and elbowed each other, as if the idea that Clovis might be a danger had never occurred to them.

Clovis walked on. Another sniff confirmed her suspicion. Arpix had been this way. For the first time Clovis found herself grateful that he'd been unable to have a decent wash for five years. She picked up her pace, weaving her way up a more crowded street.

In the distance she could hear a drumbeat, and at a crossroad she glimpsed a seemingly endless column of soldiers marching down an adjoining road. She pressed on into the outskirts of a market whose stalls spread down either side of the street.

"You. Stop." A tall canith sought to cut her off, head and shoulders above the humans thronging around streetside stalls. He wore a dark uniform of black leather different to that of the three soldiers, and on his head a black cap with a brim at the front. People got out of his way as he approached Clovis, their attention suddenly drawn to random things as if they were striving not to catch his eye. An officer of some sort then, set to policing the populace.

"Me?" Clovis tented her fingers over her breastbone.

"You." The canith's mane was braided and drawn back behind his head. A silver death's head glimmered on his chest, and a similar but smaller badge adorned his cap. "Show me your papers."

"Papers?" Clovis kept her hand away from her sword hilt.

"Papers."

"I'm in a hurry—" Clovis began.

The officer swung a backhanded blow intended to strike Clovis's cheek and snap her head around. Clovis caught his wrist and frowned at him.

"I really am in a hurry. Let's not make a big fuss—"

As the man opened his mouth to shout, Clovis jerked him forward into a savage headbutt, caught his limp form against her, and wrapped the arm she held over her shoulders. Supporting the unconscious officer as best she could, Clovis steered for the nearest alleyway, squeezing between a stall selling an array of cheeses and a stall selling a . . . different array of cheeses.

One fortuitous aspect of the aura of fear the man generated was that everyone turned away from the pair of them, except for one small canith boy tugging his mother's hand on the far side of the street. Clovis dumped the man on a refuse heap a few yards behind the cheese stalls. She took a moment to rub her forehead before hurrying on down the narrow passageway. The canith had a thick skull.

A short while later Clovis had looped around and re-entered the street where she'd scented Arpix. Now though, however hard she tried, his trail eluded her, submerged beneath the aroma of cooking pots, ripe cheeses, cold sausage, and a hundred other things demanding that she put them in her stomach immediately.

Ahead of her the market spread into a large square fronted by grander buildings, though by no means palaces. On the far side, over the heads of humans and canith alike, Clovis could see a curious wooden platform with a trio of timber uprights that might be used to load market supplies onto carts, though it seemed like over-engineering. Surely, a few strong canith could heft anything the market needed on and off carts and wagons.

Clovis advanced, frustrated by the crowd, but also pleased by the anonymity. The market stalls drew New Kraff's citizens to the sides of the square, allowing her more space as she crossed towards the centre. It seemed there had been a sizeable crowd before the curious wooden platform but that it was now dispersing. Clovis made her way towards it. A canith heading in the opposite direction shook his head as he passed her.

"You missed it. No more hangings till tomorrow."

Something cold knotted itself in Clovis's stomach. She suddenly understood what she was looking at. Three gallows. "More tomorrow? Where do they come from?"

The man paused and stared at her. He was richly dressed in dark velvets, older than her though she found it hard to judge by how much. A heavy silver chain hung over his shoulders and down to his large belly, the first belly Clovis had ever seen on a canith. "You're not from around here, are you?" He didn't wait for an answer. "Mercenary?" His gaze dipped to the white hilt of her sword.

"I'm not." The answer served for both questions.

"They always find more." The man snorted. "I think the potentate sets a quota. If they can't find enough rebels, they'll hang thieves, and if they can't find enough thieves, they'll just smoke out some Amacars and call them thieves." He shrugged. "Can't say they don't deserve it." And with that he moved on, casting "Glory to the potentate" over his shoulder without great enthusiasm.

Clovis thought back to when she'd scented Arpix on her approach up the hill. Just the faintest detection, a half-recalled memory that might have been a dream. Her eyes found the gallows arms again, one, two, three. She started to walk towards them. A heavyset man stumbled into her path, and she deflected him to the flagstones without a glance. *One. Two. Three.*

It wasn't possible. A cold, tingling sensation spread from her upper arms, across her back, down into her fingertips. A sense of detachment, of floating above her body, watching as some sixth sense concerned with self-preservation, and possessed collectively by crowds, cleared a path ahead of her more effectively than even the black-clad officer's aura of bad news had managed.

It wasn't possible that while she had lain, sleeping in a gutter, enfolded in the mist, Arpix had wandered into trouble. It wasn't possible that these people had found him. It wasn't— And yet, there by the base of the platform, still watched by a scattering of ghoulish elders and mesmerized children, was a pile of bodies poorly concealed beneath a stained tarpaulin. A canith in executioner black stood beside the dead, beckoning to a cart that looked just about large enough to carry all the corpses away.

Clovis found herself shaking, remembering Arpix's scent so strongly that she could no longer tell if it was there around her or in just her memory, remembering his unfathomable combination of fragility and strength, the reserve that armoured him, and the smiles which sometimes cracked that armour.

"No." It wasn't possible that the longest pair of legs escaping the cover were his. Those were not his rag-bound feet, his tattered clothes. It would not be his face, distorted in death, that she saw if she had the strength to snatch the tarp away. "No." She could smell him though. The growl that escaped through her bared teeth proved sufficient to clear the last onlookers without further prompting. The man closest to her flat-out ran away as if knowing that his life depended upon it.

"No!" She found herself on her knees, nails scoring the flagstone beneath her hands. ". . . no . . ."

"Clovis?"

Her eyes fixed on the corpse pile. She'd read about madness visiting at such moments but hadn't expected it to call on her.

"Clovis!" Coming from behind her.

She turned and rose in the same motion.

Arpix started to run towards her, only to be brought to a halt as the canith behind him, a soldier in a fancy uniform, caught hold of his shoulder. Behind Arpix and his captor came a huge canith at the head of a six-strong patrol, four canith and two humans, all in less showy uniforms than the first.

Clovis drew her sword. A muted gasp ran through the closest fringes of the thinning crowd. She walked towards Arpix. "Did they bring you here to kill you?"

Arpix hesitated. He looked as if his mind were furiously hunting for some answer that might avoid what was going to follow. He nodded, pale-faced.

"Who the fuck are you?" the huge canith demanded.

The closest of the two executioners unhitched the iron-bound club from his belt.

Clovis closed most of the gap between her and Arpix in four unhurried strides, ignoring the barked command to stop. Her body still trembled, but that had nothing to do with the threat in front of her, just the one that had now passed.

Before coming close enough to swing, Clovis thrust her sword tip between two flagstones so that it remained standing when she withdrew her hand.

"Is she mad?" the big canith asked, coming to the shoulder of the fancy soldier holding Arpix.

Both executioners were approaching from behind with their clubs at the ready. The rest of the big canith's patrol were standing a few yards away, confused.

"This is Private Hadd," Arpix said, still pale, eyes wide. "He's having a bad day. Don't kill him."

Both Hadd and the big canith burst out laughing at that. Clovis launched herself forward and upward, setting her hands to the big canith's shoulders, and driving her knee into his face as she vaulted. She rode him down when he fell, stretching out an arm to catch hold of Hadd's forehead and topple him backwards, driving his head down onto the flagstones.

She was among the six-strong patrol before they knew it, her body scything the legs from beneath the two leading canith, surging up to drive stiff fingers into the eyes of the second pair, and lunging between them as they staggered. Her lunge brought her to the two human soldiers, whose hands were only now closing around the hilts of their sabres. She slammed their heads together.

Clovis stood, kicking the back of one of the blinded canith's knees. The joint crunched and he collapsed to the ground clutching it. She straightened, rolled her neck, and eyed the approaching executioners over the front pair now starting to stand.

A side kick to the stomach folded the other blinded canith in half. She caught the muzzle of the first canith's 'stick as he tried to point it at her. The thing roared, spitting its projectile over their heads with a cloud of smoke. Clovis twisted it from his grasp, breaking at least one finger, and slammed the stock into the face of his companion.

The executioners came in swinging. Clovis ducked beneath one blow, blocked the other on the 'stick, then felled both opponents with a flurry of punches and kicks targeting face, throat, groin, and knees.

Leaving them groaning on the ground, she walked back over the big canith's motionless body and kicked teeth from Hadd's mouth as he struggled to rise. She met Arpix's eyes as she passed him. "Keep low."

She pulled her sword free and turned to face her opponents. One of the humans had a thicker skull than she'd imagined and stood, dazed, blood sheeting down her face from a scalp wound, 'stick wandering but pointed generally in Clovis's direction.

"Take your shot," Clovis called, her gaze narrowing to the finger the woman had on the weapon's trigger. "But I will kill *everyone* if you do. Or, I can just walk off with this man, and you can go on with your lives."

Clovis waited. She should have killed them all already. She knew that. It had been a strange combination of anger, relief, hubris, and the desire not to disappoint Arpix that had made her leave her sword behind.

The woman's aim swayed, and for a moment she started to lower her weapon. But as the broken-fingered canith gained his feet, and another, with one eye screwed shut and the other weeping crimson tears, drew his sabre, her resolve strengthened, and she steadied her aim.

More soldiers were approaching through the crowd that had drawn back to form a perimeter at what consensus deemed a safe distance. Three human troopers broke clear and started running towards Clovis, presumably so bold because they'd not seen her in action.

"You win." Clovis shrugged and stabbed her sword back into its place. Arpix's wide eyes widened further.

Clovis spread her arms, turning towards the first soldier as he reached her.

None of us truly know our limits. The point where we surrender hope and the point where we cease to fight may lie further apart than we imagine. Indeed, it's often those you least suspect of endurance that will die with their teeth still locked in the enemy's flesh.

Hockey for Girls, *by Mrs. Elsa Primrose*

CHAPTER 27

Arpix

Clovis had done magnificently, turning the tide against eight canith and two human soldiers. Arpix's heart had been in his mouth when she'd confronted the massive Corporal Janks, who was a head taller than her and at least half as heavy again, but she'd put him down almost too swiftly to see, and even now he was barely stirring.

It couldn't last though. The canith were professional soldiers, with strength in numbers and with 'sticks at their disposal. No amount of personal skill could dodge a bullet. Technology spelled the end of the warrior's way.

And now, a woman barely able to stand had command over Clovis, aiming the black eye of her weapon at her. The hope that had sprung up in Arpix's breast on seeing Clovis there, kneeling before the gallows, now came crashing down so hard that it burrowed into new depths of despair. They would be hanged together. Or die here in battle. Perhaps that was better.

As fresh soldiers from the square converged on Clovis, Arpix looked around briefly for a weapon of his own. He considered drawing Hadd's blade but stayed his hand. It wasn't—as Livira would say—his style. He'd look pretty stupid waving it around in any case.

Instead, he raised his empty hands and stepped into the line joining the muzzle of the soldier's 'stick to Clovis's heart. He turned away from the soldier, preferring instead to be looking at Clovis when he died.

Contrary to Arpix's expectations, he wasn't greeted with a despairing gaze. Instead, Clovis gave a roar that might have emptied his bladder if he were just a little better hydrated. In the same moment Clovis grabbed the first soldier to reach her, lifted him like a shield before her, and charged, snatching up her blade as she went. The soldier with the levelled 'stick fired her shot and a red wound blossomed between the shoulder blades of the man Clovis carried before her.

Arpix blinked and missed seeing three of the soldiers receive the wounds that would kill them. Clovis pirouetted through four more, carving deep furrows through flesh and bone, leaving the ruins to fall behind her, pumping blood until their hearts failed. The big canith managed to reach his knees before his head fell to the side and bounced on the flagstones beside his decapitated corpse. Three more soldiers and a black-clad officer broke from the crowd, one managing to get off a shot that hammered the flagstones where Clovis had been standing an instant before. All of them fell within moments, one canith tumbling in a different direction to his sword arm.

Clovis shook some of the crimson from her blade and sped back to Arpix's side. "We have to go." She took his arm between shoulder and elbow and propelled him into a run.

"Where are we going?"

"Anywhere but here." Clovis roared a challenge at the thinning crowd ahead of them and everyone started to run, humans and canith alike, some of them screaming. The entrance to a street beckoned, and Clovis took it, with Arpix running for all he was worth to keep up with her jog.

"WE— CAN—" ARPIX struggled for breath. "Put the sword away!"

Clovis shot him a challenging look, then complied with a snarl, sheathing it.

They turned left at the next corner, down the hill. In this street fewer people looked alarmed. Confused maybe—why was an angry canith running from an exhausted beggar? But not scared. There was no bloody sword being brandished at them.

Clovis took a right turn, following the gradient. Arpix stumbled to an almost halt, limping along, trying to answer his lungs' clamour for air. "Wait!"

"We need to run!" Clovis returned for him.

"I— I know cities," Arpix panted. He straightened up. "These people don't know us. They didn't see what happened. They don't care who we are or where we're going, except if we're running or looking guilty."

Clovis looked around, ready to fight.

"They don't care. Nobody's chasing us. Not yet." Arpix glanced back along the street, then looked her up and down. "We need to wash that blood off you . . ." There was a lot of blood, thankfully the stuff on her leathers wasn't immediately obvious.

"Off you too." Clovis reached over to wipe at his cheek.

Looking down, Arpix discovered that the remnants of his librarian's robes were now decorated by arcs of blood spatter. If the robes were still as white as when they'd been awarded to him then all eyes would be turned his way, but five years in the wilds had left them a grimy grey on which the blood seemed almost black.

"We need a place to hide." Clovis scanned the street.

"We could try an inn." Arpix nodded to a sign hanging above a large door further down the street.

Clovis raised an eyebrow. "Beg them to take pity on us? Why would they let us in?"

"Money?" Arpix suggested.

Clovis narrowed her eyes, nodding. "Yes, that's how it's done. Where would we find money?" She took hold of her chin, pulling down as if trying to draw the answers out. "Work! People work, don't they? And money is exchanged?"

Arpix nodded, remembering that Clovis had never lived anywhere but the library. He reached inside his robe and rummaged in his coin pouch. "Luckily . . ." He drew out a handful of silvers. There were even a few gold crowns gleaming in the mix. A decade of trainee allowance and a year of librarian's salary, minus what he'd given to his parents, to charity, and spent on rare almond honey cakes.

Clovis peered at the handful. "Is that enough? Will it work here?"

"Well, even if they have a currency without intrinsic value, as long as gold and silver hold a good value . . . yes to both."

And with that, Arpix took the lead, walking briskly but unobtrusively down the road, pausing at the inn sign only long enough for both of them to clean the other as best they could with water from the horse trough.

Arpix wound his way towards the east, aiming downhill all the time. The mist had all but dissipated, revealing encircling mountains with very familiar peaks. "This is where Crath City stood. My city. It's a different version, but close enough that mountains are the same even if the people might have changed. The gods rolled their dice here and came up with a different tally but at least they were the same dice."

Clovis grunted, more interested in watching the street ahead for danger. The housing grew cheaper, less well maintained, the people's clothing more drab, their language more colourful. The mountains hadn't changed, nor had the distribution of poverty and palaces.

At last, not far from the city walls, Arpix picked an inn, the sort he would never have dared to enter in his old life, the sort he imagined to be full of bandits, adventurers, thieves, and vagabonds. In fact, he'd only been into a small handful of inns, three to be exact, all well-heeled establishments near the grand square. On all three occasions it had been at Livira's insistence. She'd practically frogmarched him into the first one with one arm twisted behind his back.

The reality of the cheapest end of the hostelry trade was less exciting, sadder, and almost exactly as pungent as Arpix's expectations. The clientele in the tavern front were labourers and tradesmen, their dull garb stained with evidence of a variety of professions. Most nursed a tankard that they leaned over protectively, showing little interest in anyone else, and evidencing no obvious threat. A few heads turned to track Clovis, striking, young, out of place. The only other canith in the room looked ancient, her mane in ratty grey braids, a foul-smelling pipe hanging from a withered mouth.

Arpix presented himself at the bar, self-consciously, banging his forehead painfully on a ceiling beam as he closed the last yard. Someone sniggered, stopping immediately when Clovis ducked in behind Arpix with a growl.

"We're looking for a room." Arpix addressed the barkeep, a beefy man with a face so red you'd assume he was furious but for the placidity of his expression. "I mean, we want to hire one. To stay in." Arpix forced himself to stop talking.

The man had been rubbing the inside of an empty tankard with a grimy cloth. He stopped and ran a speculative eye up Arpix before looking over his shoulder at Clovis, who had turned away to watch the entrance. "Day use?"

"I beg your pardon?" Arpix frowned.

"Day use?" the barman enunciated.

"I'm sorry, I don't under—"

A tired-faced labourer in muddy overalls looked up from his ale. "He means are you going up there to fuck, and then pissing off, or will you only need it come night-time?"

"I uh . . . We. I mean." Arpix had wanted the room immediately, so they could regroup and rest without risking being spotted. Somehow it had already gone terribly wrong. "What I mean to say is—"

"Now. For fucking." Clovis leaned around Arpix and set both hands to the bar, staring down the barkeep. "Give him the silver, Arpix."

Arpix found his hands shaking as he fumbled three silver coins onto the counter. He felt himself blushing furiously and imagined that he looked as red as the barkeep now. He slid the first coin forward, hoping for some sort of cue as to when he should stop. Clovis pushed a second one forward. "And tonight."

The barkeep's face took on a hitherto unseen animation as he claimed the coins. Arpix suspected they'd paid considerably over the odds. "And a meal," he added. "Later."

"Right you are, yer worship." The man didn't look up from his study of King Oanold's head, stamped on the florins in his palm. He pursed his lips, frowning in puzzlement, then dropped them into his apron. "Room's up the stairs. Third door."

Arpix hesitated, still blushing and flustered. Finding the barkeep turning away, he ventured, "We'll need a key?"

"No key. Encourages thieves to break the doors."

"Ah." And with nothing else to say, Arpix turned towards the rickety flight of stairs that headed up at the end of the bar. Clovis was already half-way up them.

Arpix followed, sure that every eye in the tavern was watching him follow his flame-haired companion towards the bedroom. *Day use . . .* He banged his head a second time negotiating the stairs, which were at an angle most often found on ships.

The corridor at the top of the stairs smelled of spilled ale. Clovis had already gone in through the third door.

For fucking. That's what she told the barman. Arpix shook his head. It had been their cover story. *Fucking.* Even Livira didn't use that word. At least, not often.

The room proved larger than he had anticipated, though with less furniture. He had expected some. In addition to floorboards, the room boasted a thin, grey, straw-filled mattress, a small, shuttered window, and . . . Clovis. She closed the door behind him and went to peer out at the street.

Arpix rubbed his head and looked around as if he might have missed something. "You saved my life."

"You saved mine first." Clovis turned from the window, the brightness outside turning her mane to fire.

"But it was so"—Arpix had been going to say *violent*—"random." He shook his head. "I mean. You turning up there, just when I needed you. What were the odds?" The more he thought about it the more unlikely it seemed. "Me and Hadd got stuck waiting for a big column of soldiers to march past. A returning army. We almost didn't. The vanguard arrived at the crossroads just as we did, and Hadd thought we could get past, started pulling me across. But someone shouted. Maybe an officer. And he stopped and we waited."

Clovis had moved closer as he spoke and stood just in front of him now, watching his face. "Uh-huh."

"But my point is that we could so easily have made it. And if we did, then we'd have got there well ahead of you. They might have hanged me before you got there."

Clovis put a hand on his upper arm.

"Mayland showed us all those might have beens. This whole world is a might have been, just like ours is. And he said if Oanold landed badly he might have spread himself over a bunch of layers, each one a little bit different."

Clovis put her other hand on Arpix's hip. Close enough now that just inches stood between them, her chest nearly brushing his. "Uh-huh."

"What if we landed badly? What if there were dozens of Arpixes all in nearly identical versions of this city, and dozens of Clovises, and in all of them but this one Hadd rushed over that crossing, and I got hanged before you ever knew I was in danger?"

"You think too much." Clovis leaned closer, her face filling his vision, her eyes huge and grey, her mouth covering his next question. Her arms closed around him, drawing them tight together, her tongue invading as he tried to speak.

She pulled back after their first kiss.

"Oh," Arpix said, realising that he'd been too tied up in his theory to see any of the signs. "That was . . . nice." It had been more than nice. Strangely not at all like he had imagined kissing would be. More licky. But better. "We really should be making plans."

"I have been," Clovis said, glancing down at the mattress.

"They'll be hunting us in the streets," Arpix said, suddenly very conscious of every inch of Clovis. "Circulating our descriptions . . ." His mind might have missed all the cues, but his body seemed to know exactly what was going on, and although it hadn't bothered to tell him, it had risen to the occasion. The mattress, grey and thin as it was, seemed far more inviting than it had a few moments earlier. "We really should find the others . . ."

"We will," Clovis said in a low, throaty growl. "Afterwards. First, there's the canith code to consider."

"The what?"

"The canith code. Rule one." She went to her knees, pulling him down with her.

"Rule one?"

"Never lie to barkeepers."

The question "Is it wrong to punch a Nazi?" raises a range of ethical dilemmas over the use of violence in a good cause. For many people however, the true question is simply how hard should one punch them?

Deplorable, *by Helen Clintoff*

———————

CHAPTER 28

Anne

Anne stood trembling. The thing had been some sort of unholy alliance of bear and ape, fashioned by the city's hate out of the tarry blood that now pooled before her. In the face of her defiance, the monster had lost cohesion and fallen apart. The black puddle at her feet seemed too small to have contained such horror.

The library's neatly arrayed shelves lay toppled and broken, books scattered everywhere. Out in the foyer, Kerrol levered himself up, groaning. He got to his knees and inspected Yute, who lay beside him.

"Is he . . ." Anne had been going to say "hurt?" but of course he was hurt—the monster's blow had thrown him through the air and Yute had never struck her as sturdy.

"I don't think he's broken any bones." Kerrol sounded as if he might have a few broken ribs himself, speaking with the wheezy delicacy of someone unwilling to test the limits of their own ability to inhale. "Can't see any blood . . . except . . ." He wiped at the trickles from the librarian's nose and mouth. The man's blood wasn't even red but something closer to a mix of crimson and silver with both colours trying to separate at every opportunity.

Anne picked her way through the wreckage and knelt beside Yute. "He's breathing." She looked up at Kerrol, tall as a man even when kneeling, his chestnut mane, the muscle and the bone of his chest and shoulders not those of a human. The face, that she had first seen as nothing out of the ordinary, shared similarities with that of a lion and that of a dog, his mouth and nose closer to a muzzle, whiskered, almost without lips. He looked at times regal, adorable, and scary, though now he was none of those, merely concerned, the face of a friend worried about another friend. "We just fought a monster made out of oil." The strangeness of it crowded her vision. She felt faint, breathless, as if she were the one whose chest had nearly been staved in.

"Breathe," Kerrol advised. "Deep breaths." He waited while she took a few. "And yes. Well, you fought it. Yute and I mainly got thrown around."

At the mention of his name, Yute inhaled sharply and began to stir.

"Wait . . . how am I understanding you?" Anne realised she'd been talking to Kerrol for a while without Yute translating. "It's like it was before . . ."

Kerrol looked puzzled. "Yute would know. But we're connected to the library here—the *real* library. It's bleeding into this place. Literally. So, that must be it. Somehow."

"But what—" Lights moving in the blackness out beyond the foyer doors seized Anne's attention. "People are coming!"

"That's not good." Kerrol stood up, wincing.

"What should we do?"

"My first instincts would be to talk my way out of the problem, or failing that, ask Yute, even though I really haven't known him that long." With a deep groan Kerrol lifted Yute in both arms. "But something about this place has set me knocking heads together and trying to punch monsters." He started to retreat into the library as outside flaming torches drew closer. "And even if I can suddenly speak the language again, I'm not sure I can talk down an angry mob. So . . . I suppose we hide?"

Anne could hear voices outside now, muted by the intervening glass and wood but still carrying an angry edge. Glass broke. Shouts. Shoving. Splintering. The first of the torchbearers pushed in through the front doors, alien in the light of flames, as monstrous as the creature Anne had just defeated, though they were neighbours, people who lived in the same streets as her family, worked in the same places. Some of them might have held cards to this very library, and come here in the daylight, respectable citizens, looking to be enlightened or entertained or even educated. Now they bayed like hounds.

"Quick!" Anne beckoned. "We'll take the back door. Lose them in the night."

Her plan lasted only as long as it took to open the door to the corridor. The rear exit had already been opened. The first men through it brushed her aside and brought Kerrol down, tackling his legs while Yute encumbered his arms. More people poured in from behind, piling on top of Kerrol as he struggled to rise.

A woman carrying an electric flashlight took painful hold of Anne's arm, nails digging in. "This one's a Jew!"

"Whore!" someone shouted from the back without even seeing her.

The main lights went on, suddenly painting the scene in full detail. The burning torches looked pale now, the people holding them more ordinary, the destruction more shocking.

"Oil!" someone shouted, discovering the remains of the Escape. "The Jews were going to burn the library!"

Anne tore herself free of the woman, but two new people seized her, one a large man with an unbreakable grip.

The crowd at the front parted, shouts falling silent, as someone new arrived. A tall man in a black leather coat and military cap strode in. Four other men in black uniform followed, all of them bearing the swastika in black and white on a red armband. "Secret police," he announced unnecessarily.

Anne fought a hysterical urge to ask how they could be secret if they marched in and told everyone who they were.

The officer hooked leather-gloved fingers into the collar of a beefy fellow with an old-fashioned lantern who was leaning curiously over the "oil" pool. "Do not." He hauled the man back roughly and strode past. He glanced Anne's way but walked past her to come to a halt in front of the pile of people beneath which Kerrol had disappeared. "Get them up!"

People had already been disentangling themselves from the heap. Now, with the secret police looking on, they leapt clear, not wanting to be confused for one of the suspects.

Gasps went up as the last few men removed themselves and Kerrol was exposed. A few of the more stupid among the crowd muttered "Russian," a few of the more imaginative muttered "werewolf," most just took a couple of steps backwards and looked shocked. The lead officer drew his pistol and levelled it at Kerrol, who lay where he was, teeth bloody, watching with his overlarge, liquid-dark eyes. Two of the man's subordinates also drew their pistols and trained them on the canith. Yute, seemingly not worthy of a weapon pointing his way, sat up, rubbing his forehead with both hands.

"Secure this one." The officer flicked the muzzle of his handgun towards Yute. "Commissar Jung will wish to interrogate him at headquarters. Turn the Jew out into the streets. Let her take her chances there. This one"—he returned his aim to Kerrol—"is an abomination, and I am torn between shooting him between the eyes, or letting the German people exact their own justice." He looked around. "If they can find a streetlamp tall enough to hang him from!"

A cheer went up at that, as if the officer had suddenly handed them back their right to be a mob rather than a collection of scared individuals.

Yute stood as the first of the crowd moved in to take hold of the battered canith. Something in his strangeness gave the men pause. Perhaps they thought his paleness a contagion that might spread by touch. None made to lay hands on him. A new hush spread.

"I appeal for calm," Yute said in perfectly accented German, not raising his voice but somehow being heard. He turned his pink eyes on the pistol-carrying officer. "You serve the laws of this land? What crime are we accused of? To whom will we be given an opportunity to state our case?"

The captain—Anne could see he was a captain now—manufactured an ugly smile, showing small white teeth behind bloodless lips. He leaned in as if about to share a confidence but didn't lower his voice. "Commissar Jung employs men who will enjoy breaking you. Communist, Jew, spy, all of them break, and broken men are so much more agreeable."

"I'm sure we don't need to—"

The captain's fist landed in Yute's stomach, doubling him over. Laughter spread through the crowd. The woman who had first grabbed Anne sneered and called out to ask how "Whitey" liked that?

Among the jeering, the larger of the two men holding Anne leaned forward and hissed into her ear, "I don't think you're even going to make it to the streets, little Jew-rat." His breath smelled of sour beer and he twisted her arm behind her, making her cry out.

Somehow Kerrol seemed to hear her amid the laughing and catcalls. But when he tried to get up, ignoring the guns trained on him, the men around him started to kick him on all sides, heavy work-boots thudding in. Already injured, he seemed unable to rise.

The captain, warming to his audience, folded his arms and waited for Yute to finish retching. When Yute straightened, wiping his oddly pearlescent blood from his mouth, his eyes held a dazed look. His wandering gaze fixed on one of the few sets of shelves that remained standing. His eyes widened and a look of resignation entered them that was so profound that Anne followed the line of his stare.

Incongruously, a large cat had somehow found its way onto the top of the unit and was busy washing itself, licking a paw then rubbing behind its ear with the paw. Anne had never seen a cat so big. More than twice the size of Mrs. Schreiber's tom. Almost three times.

In the rowdy throng within the now-smoky library, not one other person had seen the animal, though now with both Yute and Anne staring, several other people exclaimed above the thuds of the kicking being delivered to Kerrol and the jeering.

At last, the captain glanced back.

Anne couldn't give a proper account of the events that followed. Not even a few minutes later when Kerrol was back on his feet, hunched around his injuries, and the cat was sitting peaceably at Yute's feet licking blood from its paws. The key moment. The moment that would stay with her for the whole of her life, however much was left to her, was that the cat had bitten off a man's head. And not just any man—the captain who had struck Yute. She could see it in her mind's eye: the captain's head, complete with his black captain's hat, framed by many sharp teeth, almost seeming to look back at her with those pale blue eyes in the instant it was swallowed away. But ask her how a cat, even one almost as big as three normal cats, could bite the head off a grown man, and she had no answer.

Similarly, she had no idea how the animal had clawed officers of the secret police from face to foot with single swipes of its paws, or pursued half a hundred previously bloodthirsty citizens from the library while yowling like all the souls of the damned. The cat hadn't simply grown bigger. It had somehow been all manner of different sizes at once, even in different places at once, before somehow collapsing back into one single, big cat.

"That was unfortunate." Yute looked out across the fallen shelves, now blood-spattered, with three corpses and an unclaimed arm strewn across them. An injured officer was dragging himself slowly away, focused on nothing but the distant exit.

"They'll come back." Kerrol spat crimson onto the headless body by his feet.

"They will," Anne said, aware that her voice was an octave higher than normal and quavering. Several shots had gone off during the chaos and her ears still rang with them.

"You'll have to come with us," Yute said.

"Come where?" Anne looked around again in case some other miracle had presented itself.

"I thought if we followed the library's currents it might wash us up on the shores of an answer." Yute bowed his head.

"I don't think this place is an answer." Kerrol wiggled one of his teeth. "Or at least not an answer either of us wanted to hear."

"I thought . . ." Yute looked at the blood on his hands. "I thought there was something. The corner of something." He slumped. "We'd better go."

Rather than repeat her question, Anne stood silently and waited, trying not to see the dead, or track the agonizing progress of the young officer as he painted a broad blood-trail towards the main doors.

Yute went to the black pool that had been the Escape. "I don't suppose either of you have a needle?"

Anne shook her head. Kerrol snorted.

With a shudder, Yute picked up a shard of splintered wood and, trembling, jabbed it into the pad of his index finger. He held his hand out over the pool and let a drop of his curious blood fall into it. Another followed, and another.

The pool, so black as to have resembled a well filled with darkness, shimmered into life, glowing from within.

"It's a doorway," Yute said. "I think perhaps we should be talking to those who disagree with us rather than hunting for some solution to them and their ideas. Coming here was a mistake."

Kerrol grunted and limped across to join him. "I rather liked the place while I could speak to people. The bookshops and their owners . . ." He looked towards the windows. A fire glow lit the sky to the east. "I wish we could save them."

"I'm surprised we saved ourselves," Yute said. "Well, we didn't, did we?" He reached down to ruffle the fur of the cat-monster currently butting its head against his legs. "Wentworth did that. And it's not the first time I've owed my life to his intervention."

Kerrol beckoned Anne. "You need to come with us."

Anne backed away. "They said I could go."

"That was before"—Yute swept an arm at the carnage—"this."

"This whole town, and who knows how far beyond, was on a knife's edge, and tonight was the cut. A night of broken glass," Kerrol said seriously. "There's something burrowing into the minds of these people. They've tasted blood now. It will get worse, not better."

Anne knew he was right. Both of them understood her world in a way that she did not, despite seeming to have arrived around lunchtime. But she also understood it in ways that they didn't. Parts of it at least. She wanted to leave. A year earlier she might have knocked her own brother down to get to the exit that Yute appeared to have made. To see new worlds, filled with different possibilities, to share the wonders that had brought Yute and Kerrol to her doorstep.

"Come with us." Yute reached out a hand, an urgency in his voice she'd not heard before, a pleading almost.

"I belong here."

"What would your father—"

"Don't." Yute cut across Kerrol. "It should be her choice. Don't manipulate her."

"What are rational arguments if not manipulation?" Kerrol growled.

"Playing her emotions is not the same, and you know it."

Part of Anne wanted to ask what it was that Kerrol knew about her father. She took another two steps back. "I have to go. This is my place. I can't run away." She turned and hurried to the corridor at the rear before pausing and looking back. Both Yute and Kerrol were watching her from the edge of the glowing pool. "Thank you. Thank you both. Whatever happens, I'll never see the world the same again." And without giving them a chance to reply, she ran.

To gain the full measure of any city in a single day simply start with one of its libraries, move on to a market or cathedral, either works equally well, and let the evening find you a tavern, public house, or speakeasy. By the second day the streets will hold little that surprises you.

The Traveller's Guide to Krathe, *by Mallory Schultz*

CHAPTER 29

Evar

Starval pushed through the tavern doorway. Evar hesitated for a moment, eyeing the street. It felt as if every shadow looming in the mist might be someone he knew, Mayland, Arpix, Clovis . . . even Livira. The damp air muffled smells as readily as sounds, but for a moment it almost seemed he'd caught her scent.

"Come on!" Starval leaned back out and dragged him in. "They have food!"

The tavern's interior was warm, lantern lit, and crowded. To Evar's surprise, the place was mixed. Canith drank and ate alongside humans. Even some of the groups at the tables were mixed, canith dwarfing their fellow drinkers.

"This is like the poisoned city." Evar shuddered at the memory. "The city you and Mayland— Tell me you didn't know they were going to die."

Starval frowned and twisted his mouth. "I have . . . regrets."

Evar had expected a denial. One that he wouldn't be able to identify as a lie. "Brother! A city . . . a whole city."

"Do the numbers matter? Is there an arithmetic of murder? Are five innocents less of a crime than five hundred or fifty thousand?"

Evar became aware that two men close by were giving them alarmed looks. "We'll talk about your book later. I'm hungry," he said quickly, reframing the subject. And he was. Famished. Celcha's generosity had hardly touched the sides. "How do we . . . ?"

Starval laughed. "You have to kill your darlings, Evar. Fiction's a bloody business." Deploying his elbows with an assassin's precision he began to forge a path to the bar.

Evar followed in his wake. "Don't you need money?" He felt quite proud of himself for remembering the concept. He'd only spent a day ghosting through a city, but money, or at least talk of money, had been everywhere.

Starval held up a fat leather purse. "It grows on trees, brother."

Two young human women were serving behind the bar, but as Starval and Evar arrived an older man rose into view from some task lower down and greeted them with a cheerful smile.

"Evening, gentlemen. You can call me King Oldo, or just Oldo if we're friends, and if you're buying then we're friends!" He patted the sides of his large stomach which even a generous leather apron had no chance of hiding. "What can I get you? You look hungry. I do a wicked plate of ribs. More like a shield than a plate, if I'm honest. Covered in secret sauce." He pressed his fingertips together, kissed them, and spread them as if to indicate some explosion of flavour. "My own recipe. Tangy, sweet, a touch of bitter spice out of the east. You'll think angels are holding a party in your belly. And then there's—"

"Sold! All of it." Starval slapped the jingling purse on the counter. "Drinks too. The big ones! And that stuff as well!" He pointed to one of the steaming bowls a server was carrying past him to the tables.

Oldo's grin broadened. He looked out across the crowded room, fixed his gaze on a group near the kitchen door, and bellowed, "Give that table up, Abra! And you, Gothon! Got some decent, paying customers here who need it." Then, turning back to Starval, "Take a seat, young sirs. I'll be over with your meals presently."

"I hope 'presently' means 'almost immediately,'" Starval muttered, heading over to the table being vacated by the two older canith, both clutching their ale tankards to their chests as if reliant on them to keep afloat.

Evar nodded apologetically to one of the canith, who swayed drunkenly out of his way. "We can't stay long. Livira might be out there. That's what Mayland said. We find her book and if she's not with it already, it'll draw her to us."

"You'll learn a lot more here in the warm than wandering around in the fog, trust me." Starval had somehow acquired a wooden goblet, complete with wine, leaning back against the wall, sipping contentedly as he watched the patrons.

"I'll learn how long it takes for you to get arrested." Evar shook his head. "Someone's going to miss that . . ." He lowered his voice. "What you took."

"I don't think Oldo will care, as long as I empty it faster than the previous owner. That man's a rogue. Takes one to know one."

WHEN CELCHA HAD deployed her flask of library blood to create food for her half-starved followers, Evar hadn't known what to ask for. In the end he'd requested sugar-cake, remembering a child badgering his mother for one in the market of another Krath. The little boy's shriek of delight when the woman purchased one from a street vendor, and the look of bliss on his face when he consumed it in a shower of crumbs, had stayed with him. Sadness tempered the memory—the city had been ransacked by a human army that same night, the boy had probably died in one of the great fires. But Evar had few memories not laced with sorrow. The sugar-cake had been more delicious than anything he'd ever tasted, something that nothing produced by the Assistant's pool-garden had ever prepared him for or even let him dream of. His bliss had not, perhaps, matched that of the small, doomed child, but it had been considerable.

If the situation were revisited though, Evar would now ask for beef stew with root vegetables and a hunk of black bread.

"Ribs'll come along in a bit." Oldo set two platters before them and laughed as Evar bent to scoop the steaming mess into his mouth, careless of the heat.

"One of these might help?" He reached into his apron, producing two large wooden spoons.

"I apologize for my brother, sir." Starval slapped at Evar's arm. "He was raised by wolves."

Embarrassed, but still chewing and suffused in an ecstasy of flavour, Evar fumbled for the offered spoon.

"Chef'll take it as a compliment. Both you boys look like you need a few good meals inside you. Thin as rakes. I'll send Kella out with more bread when she brings the ales." Oldo paused. "You're not from around here." It wasn't a question.

"No sir." Starval licked his teeth but resisted diving into the food. Evar continued to shovel stew into his mouth, using the spoon and finding it a fine invention if a little awkward at first.

"From the west, are you?" Oldo ventured. "Kelso way, or maybe the Cronnin shore? I can normally place an accent but you fellows sound like you were born around the corner and raised next door."

"We've come a long way." Starval kept a smile in place and popped a chunk of bread into his mouth. "But yes, from the west of late. Through the passes."

"Bad over there now, is it?" The landlord frowned, rubbing a hand absently through his thinning grey curls.

"Bad." Starval nodded and looked down as if it might be too bad to speak of.

Oldo took the hint. "Enjoy your meal. Bread and ale coming soon. And those ribs. Kella! Where are you, Kella? Thirsty travellers over here!" And off he went.

Starval, with enormous restraint, merely tapped his spoon on the table rather than joining Evar in the race to clean his plate.

"Gothon, was it?" He hailed one of the elderly canith they'd displaced. "Apologies for stealing your table. Join us? I'll stand you a beer."

Mention of beer had both canith drawing up stools and squeezing alongside Evar at the small table. Gothon's greying mane was braided into thick, matted cords through which carved wooden pegs had been pushed, giving them a spiky appearance. The other one, Abra, wasn't quite so old and his mane was as dark as soot, his skin too, and his eyes, the whites bloodshot. He twitched from time to time, and when he spoke it was in short bursts so rapid that the listener had to divide the string of sound into words on their own time.

Starval, good as his word, supplied both old-timers with ale, and in return extracted far more information about the city than Evar could have discovered in a week of wandering the streets. After cleaning his plate and devouring the bread, Evar sat back with one of the newly arrived ribs.

He let Starval do the talking, interjecting only once to announce, "I've got a new favourite now. Spicy ribs." The ale was rather foul stuff and he wondered at its appeal. Even so, he drank it down, and by the second flagon it didn't seem as bad. He was gnawing on his seventh rib and quite content with the world. Taverns, Evar decided, were an excellent invention. To his great surprise, he found himself unable to manage even one more bite and discovered that his jaw was aching from overuse. Admitting defeat, he rocked his chair back against the wall and watched Starval work, admiring the way in which he got the answers to flow without ever seeming to ask a question.

New Kraff City was, it seemed, contrary to the good food and convivial atmosphere in the Stained Page tavern, between a rock and a hard place and under a heel. The potentate had come from humble beginnings, borne to power through the bloody end of the royal line of Hosten. Under the Hostens' benevolent but largely ineffectual rule the empire had been reduced to a shadow of its former glory, nibbled at by insurrection, humbled by wars, rotted by corruption.

The potentate's masterstroke had been to point out that the empire's misfortune, at each and every level, both on the battlefield and off it, was the fault of the Amacar. These demons in human and canith flesh formed a small minority who still followed an older religion, one from which the current, state-approved, faith sprang centuries before the Hostens came to power.

"So, you all worship the same god?" Evar had managed between mouthfuls as his stomach began to protest.

Gothon who, although drunk, had seemed until that point a reasonable enough person, with both a sense of humour and of fair play, now spat on the floorboards. "The Amacar exiled the prophet. I don't care what god they pretend to worship, they're all in the grand demon's pockets."

"So, you're a religious man?" Starval asked gently.

Abra spluttered out his beer, artfully recapturing most of it in his tankard. "Gothon? He's not been to temple since the priest sealed his name onto him. You'll hear the Lord's name in his mouth when he stubs his toe, or if a woman ever takes pity on him, that's it."

"Doesn't change a thing." Gothon's own tankard muffled the rest of his muttering, but Evar caught snippets: ". . . damn thieving Amacars . . . giving babies to the . . ."

It seemed to Evar that these Amacars, less than one-twentieth of the population, must be working very hard to have managed all the evildoing laid at their feet. But whatever the truth of it, hate had proved to be sufficient glue to weld New Kraff and the wider population into a weapon of war for the potentate. Thus armed, he had set off variously reconquering territories the Hostens had lost or conquering new ones wherever a monarch looked unsteady on their throne.

For the best part of a decade everything had been going swimmingly, provided you liked swimming in blood. The Amacar were being rooted out of society and sent to camps on an island in Lake Cantoo or executed for their crimes. The borders of empire were being pushed outwards, welcoming "liberated" populations into the potentate's care. New Kraff had never seen so much wealth or glory.

"Then they came." Gothon shook his head. "Everyone says they're in league with the Amacar."

"I can't see it." Abra rubbed his forehead furiously, glancing around before continuing in a lower voice, "I mean, maybe the Amacar were sucking the blood out of us, maybe they did pull the Hostens' strings. But the insects? They'll turn an Amacar into blood and guts quick as they will anyone else."

"Skeer?" Evar asked.

Gothon shot him a suspicious look. "Not an Iccrah are you?"

"Does he look like a fucking Iccrah?" Abra smacked his tankard down on the table. He continued in a hushed voice, "The Iccrahs are all that's standing between us and the insects. 'Skeer' is what the Iccrah call them. Iccrah has better guns than we do. Famed for them. And forts. So many forts and castles." He jabbed a finger here and there as if pointing them out. "Our armies never went there, no sir. But the insects are on their east border and the stories . . . well . . . if I hadn't been a drinkin' man to start with, the shit I've heard about what's happening in Iccrah would have been enough to push me into the barrel." He swilled his ale around, staring into his tankard. "I'm planning to drown in this stuff before the bugs get here. That's my plan."

No insurrection will ever succeed without angry people. Fortunately, nobody ever seizes power without angering anyone.

The Unicycle of Violence, *by Maximus Macrinus*

CHAPTER 30

Livira

"What was that?"

Before Livira could answer, it came again, a blow struck from beneath, as if some buried leviathan were testing its bonds. A blow that made the bedrock shudder, throwing Livira to the ground and setting every rooftile rattling.

"Earthquake?" suggested Carlotte, who had already reached for the support of the wall. Her answer was one that few who hadn't trained at the library would think of. Their homeland had never evidenced such tremors. "Earthquake" wasn't part of the local vocabulary.

A third shock, like the tolling of some great bell far beneath the sea, and then nothing.

"Well, that was odd." Carlotte released the wall, somewhat self-consciously despite the enfolding mist.

Livira, frowning, picked herself off the ground. She seemed to have been treated more roughly than Carlotte, who in turn had been more shaken than the buildings. "It was familiar."

"Tell me about it over lunch." Carlotte moved on down the street. "Or dinner, or breakfast, whatever damned time of day it is. I—just—want—to—eat!"

Livira followed her. "I felt it in the library. That same sensation. When my book hit the floor and cracked it."

That made Carlotte pause and turn. "Cracked it? The library floor? Your little book?"

"Yes."

"You think Oanold's dropped it?" Carlotte looked doubtful.

"I don't know." Livira felt suddenly uneasy, not wanting to talk about her book and the damage it seemed to be wreaking. "Let's keep going."

THEY PRESSED ON through the streets, Carlotte and her hunger leading the way. Her appetite appeared to be too lazy to climb the slope on which the city had been built, instead following the gradient at each opportunity like spilled milk. Rather than thinning, the mist thickened about them, something Livira hadn't thought possible. People who passed close by were never more than shadows in the surrounding greyness.

"We could ask someone where we are," Livira suggested. They were definitely in a city.

"They might toss us in jail." Carlotte led the way down a flight of worn stairs between two tall, grimy buildings. "As foreign spies or some such. I want to eat . . . Godsdammit, does this murky piece-of-shit city only have one damn tavern for the entire populace? I've half a mind to turn round and go back to . . . what was it? The Stained Page?"

Reaching the last step, she followed the nearest wall, sniffing as though by relying on her nose she might hunt out the meal she was so desperate for.

"We should be looking for Yolanda and Leetar," Livira complained.

"We're as likely to find them at a table eating a good meal as wandering blind in this stuff." Livira picked up the pace. "More likely, if they've any sense."

Without warning, a full-grown canith loomed at them out of the fog. Livira let out a yelp of surprise, but that was as nothing compared to Carlotte's reaction. She took to her heels, shrieking as loudly as she would if she'd been grabbed and bitten.

Livira set off after her, not wanting to lose her in the mist.

"I do beg your pardon . . ." The canith's parting words, at once apologetic and somewhat startled, chased her as she ran.

Livira followed the sound of running feet and shouted for Carlotte to stop. After about a hundred yards she did, though Livira couldn't say whether it was her shouts that had brought her to a halt, or the hanging sign and the warm light spilling through puddle-glass windows challenging the weather.

"Heaven's Gate." Livira read from the greying board above them. The faded illustration might have been a fist clutching a tankard, or two frogs fighting. "It doesn't look very heavenly." One of the windowpanes had been replaced with a piece of wood, and the drinkers hunched over the tables inside did not look to be in paradise. "Maybe it's called that because people say they'd die before they ate here."

"If I don't eat something immediately, I'll die right now." Carlotte shoved the door open and went in.

Livira followed her, muttering, "Out-of-towners coming through, please rob us . . ."

THE TAVERN RESEMBLED a cave, being low-ceilinged and dimly lit. The patrons seemed mainly to be labourers, perhaps a market stall keeper or two, ruffians who hustled a mean existence out on the streets, and by the stink of a shabby hulk near the door, a night-soil man. There were canith too, sharing the squalor: by the empty fireplace an older female, bone-thin, sucking on a pipe whose smoke competed with the fellow by the entrance for the title of stinkiest thing in the place.

Carlotte, who on any of the non-ghost days that Livira had known her, would have turned on a heel and walked back into the street retching, ploughed on, making for the bar. Livira followed. It was the sort of place her people would have come to, exhausted after a day of whatever Crath City had demanded of them. She could imagine Acmar and Benth here, bent over a table, nursing an ale, Acmar smeared with the dirt from whatever road he'd been digging, Benth's leathers scorched from the blazing iron in the foundry that had claimed his life so long ago.

"Two bowls of something hot. And bread. And butter." Carlotte had reached the bar and slapped down several coins that she must have kept through the years since she'd fled her burning city. "And then two more bowls of the same stuff and some more bread. And more butter. And if it gets to my table really fast, I'll pay double." She lifted a silver crown. "How many beers will one of these pay for?"

The red-faced barman took the coin and squinted at it, eyes widening. Livira would have been surprised if the man hadn't been surprised. However far away he imagined the silver piece to have come from, its true journey was much much longer and stranger. "About fifty." He paused then added, "Ma'am."

Some of Chertal's imperial ways had rubbed off on Carlotte. "Free drinks for everyone until it runs out!"

The resulting rush solved the problem of securing a table. The meal arrived at breakneck speed, and although basic, the magic of an empty stomach worked its culinary wonders. For quite some time Carlotte and Livira ignored everything around them, including each other, and concentrated on eating. When Livira did eventually surface from her second bowl of stew, it wasn't any of the more animated chatter around her that caught her attention. Instead, as the sounds of her own slurping began to diminish, a rhythmic banging drew her eyes towards the low ceiling. "What's that?"

"Mmmm?" Carlotte did not look up from the task of cleaning her bowl with the last of the bread.

"It sounds like . . ."

"They don't call it a knocking shop for nothing, dear." A hefty woman in a shapeless, colourless dress grinned from the next table.

"Oh." Livira had realised, too late to shut her mouth, that the sound was probably that of a bed's headboard smacking against a wall. Or, if beds were too fancy for such an inn, perhaps just the thump of flesh on floorboards. Whichever it was, the participants seemed to have plenty of stamina.

Carlotte finally looked up, wiped her mouth, and pushed her bowl away. She patted her belly and gave a loud, satisfied belch. "Excuse me."

Their neighbour in the tentlike dress laughed at that. "And here I was thinking you were a princess who was down on her luck."

"A queen actually." Carlotte frowned at the faded blue tatters of her gown. "And I've a feeling my luck's turned for the better. Where would I get some decent clothes? Something warm?"

The woman drained her tankard and wiped the foam from her upper lip. She looked about forty but could be in her thirties or fifties. She had passed into that zone where Livira lost the ability to make good guesses.

"I'm Carlotte, by the way."

"Lady Amma of Iccrah," the woman replied, plucking at her skirts.

"Really?"

"Of course not." Amma snorted. "I can't tell if you're the worst spies the Gates have ever seen, or if this is genius."

"Spies?" Livira thought it would take a world-class spy to fake the surprise now owning her face. "What's there to spy on in this dive? No offence, Amma."

"See, there you go. I'm almost tempted to tell you! Genius!"

One of her companions, an older woman, almost as much underweight as Amma was overweight, jabbed a sharp elbow into Amma's gut and turned to gossip with another neighbour.

"Oh shush." Amma shook her head. "There's no crime in knowing that our benevolent potentate sends his agents out to protect us all."

"From what?" Carlotte asked.

"People say the Saviour recruits in the places hope's abandoned." Amma glanced around at the room. "So, obviously they wouldn't come to our little paradise."

"The Saviour?" Livira asked. "It's some sort of religion? A cult?"

"Oh, you two. You're killing me." Amma reached for her second tankard, presumably one paid for with Carlotte's silver. She ran a tongue over yellow teeth stained with grey.

"Honestly—" Livira was interrupted by shrieking outside the tavern.

The door burst open and the shrieker, a robust young man whose voice had been driven by panic through more octaves than Livira thought possible, rushed in, knocking patrons out of his way. A wild-faced woman replaced him in the doorway and at first Livira was certain she'd been the one chasing him. Her conviction lasted only long enough for the woman to shout, "It's a bug!" and for a black shape to snatch her away leaving only a crimson splatter to prove she'd ever been there.

The room erupted, tables overturned in panic, one person trampling the next in a general rush for the back. The noise made communication impossible. Livira found herself being borne along on a tide of human fear, separated from Carlotte, her main concern not what was at the door but how to draw breath in the crush and how to keep from joining those unfortunates already on the floor.

Rotated by the crowd, Livira saw that the blackness that had snatched the woman had now returned to fill the doorway. A dull thud, then another, and the wall began to spill its blocks inwards, the doorframe splintering.

Livira found herself free, like driftwood cast upon the shore by a retreating tide. In front of her, the broken remnants of tables and chairs, behind her a press of humanity and canith, each trying not to be the one left showing their spine to whatever was coming.

The dust from the destructive nature of the monster's entry was what finally teased its shape from the unyielding blackness of its form. Livira realised several things in swift order. Firstly, that the thing before her looked a lot like a skeer from some child's nightmare, mixed with touches of extra cratalac for good measure. Secondly, that it had been shaped by the fear of the people running from it. And thirdly, that it was an Escape.

In a shower of broken timber and stone the horror charged at her. Livira stood, frozen in the moment, armed only with her empty hands and the conviction that she would not allow herself to die there.

"Mine." She had time only for a single word, but her mind ran faster than her mouth. Livira had learned a lot over two centuries within the Assistant's skin. The fearsome grip of her memory, a cage that hardly ever relinquished even the smallest recollection, had been unable to hold on to more than a tiny fraction of those years, but she'd kept the broadest strokes of it. Her time with Yolanda had been a tutorial in and of itself, a series of lessons in the power of belief within the unbelievable labyrinth of the library.

She knew that the blackness before her was the library's blood, the ultimate clay, given form by the undirected terror of the masses. Her task in the fraction of a heartbeat remaining to her was to imprint her own desire upon it, the focused determination of the individual overriding the unconscious will of the many.

She failed. The midnight spear of the skeer-blade took her in the stomach and sent her tumbling.

"Livira!" Carlotte broke free of the retreating mob, stumbling and tripping over the smashed furniture as she came for her friend.

Gasping and wheezing, Livira found her feet. She'd blunted both the edge of the weapon that hit her and the force behind it. Now with one hand extended, fingers splayed, as if to project her command, she advanced on the faltering Escape.

Rather than seek to change the skeer-thing into some other shape, Livira sought the shortest path to safety, attempting to return it to its natural form.

The horror matched her advance, stuttering towards her on four great legs whose points drove deep gouges in the ale-stained boards and shattered furniture. It came onwards, a hissing wail escaping from every vent in its armour. The thing dwarfed her. It scraped the ceiling, spraying limewash and splintering the boards above. Every inch of it bristled with the cratalac barbs and hooks that lay so deeply embedded in the racial memories of all that those creatures preyed upon. But as it came, darkness ran from it like wax from a candle thrown in the hearth. Its raw substance dripped from it, poured from it, pooling about its feet.

"Get back!" Carlotte came to stand with Livira, white-faced, wielding a broken chair.

The Escape surged, closing the last yard, its dripping jaw opening inches before Livira's face.

"Don't." Livira used her other arm to push the chair down as Carlotte tried to swing. "Stay calm. You're feeding it."

"I will be if you—" Carlotte gave up her struggle to disentangle the chair. "If you won't let me . . . fight it . . ." She trailed off, noticing the creature's increasingly rapid collapse. "You're doing that?"

"I'm trying to."

The Escape swung at Livira again. She made no attempt to block it. That would only add strength to the blow. The limb broke across her, splashing down, black drops rolling over her like water from a bird's feathers.

"Back!" Livira thrust her hands at the creature in a gesture of negation.

The black nightmare retreated several steps. "Out!" It turned unwillingly towards the wrecked doorway.

For a moment Livira stood, panting with effort, her whole body a knot of tension although her mind was doing the work. A shard of pain struck between her eyes, and rather than struggle for further mastery she simply spread her hands. The remainder of the Escape collapsed as if it had only ever been a liquid and the vessel holding it had suddenly vanished.

Livira stood, breathing hard. The tavern room lay in ruins, the majority of its patrons having fled out the back. The Escape was now an oil pool, reflecting nothing, rendered insensitive by Livira's will that it should be so.

Some of those felled in the exodus but not badly injured began to pick themselves up. The canith with the foul-smelling pipe emerged from the shadows of the furthest corner. She tilted her head, the grey straggles of her mane falling across her face but not obscuring the dark-eyed curiosity in her stare. Laying a hand on both Livira and Carlotte, she started to steer them towards the wreckage of the entrance and the thinning mists outside. "Come with me. Quickly." She kept her growl low. "There's someone you should meet. Unless you want to stay and explain this to the death's heads."

Good sex, like good comedy, is primarily a matter of timing and chemistry. The similarities end when considering the ideal size of the audience.

The Ping Pong Ball, *by Ansell Dam*

———————

CHAPTER 31

Arpix

rpix lay comfortably trapped between Clovis and the mattress, with enough of the canith draped across him to make escape a difficult business. His body felt wrung out, a wet cloth that had been twisted to squeeze out the last drop. A strange combination of sated and bruised. Clovis, now fast asleep and growling softly, had shown both the energy and strength of her species. And of course, her warrior training had accentuated both. She had also been unexpectedly tender though, and Arpix's fears that human anatomy would be incompatible with her needs or inadequate to meet them, appeared to have been unwarranted, at least to judge by her reaction at the time and her current state.

Quite how long his body would stand up to the punishment, he wasn't sure. He thought he'd probably need a week to recover. On the other hand, the message didn't seem to have reached all quarters, and certain parts of him seemed to be eager for round two.

Arpix relaxed, wishing only that the mattress was thicker and the boards beneath less hard. The sun had risen, and its light strained through the shutters. It had sounded like a wild night down in the tavern room below them, but they'd both had other things on their minds, and little short of actual fire would have diverted them from it—mere smoke would not have qualified.

"We've come a long way from the library." Arpix murmured the words to himself. He tried to imagine what the people from his past would have made of his present. It would have seemed as unbelievable to them as it did to him. And yet here he was, with a gently snoring, slightly furry canith, puffing stray strands of her crimson mane away from his mouth.

Of all of it: the growing excitement, the ecstasy of union, the satisfaction of consummation, it was this part, or more accurately the part before Clovis had fallen asleep, that he found himself loving the most. The gentle communion of lying together, wrapped in each other, each feeling the other's breathing, a whispered conversation of inconsequential words and vital emotion.

The sounds of the street reached in, wagons creaking by, the rattle of carts, voices raised in conversation. It felt much busier outside now than when they'd arrived. A man shouted a greeting. Someone dropped something, possibly an empty barrel.

Clovis stretched, yawning mightily to show an array of teeth that still surprised Arpix. She lifted up over him on all fours. The six breasts had been a surprise too, though with each pair considerably smaller than the one above it the lowest pair at the bottom of her ribcage were hardly there at all. "I'll never get used to this night-and-day stuff."

"It takes a while. I lived in the library long enough to forget darkness existed." Arpix wriggled clear and reached for his robes before the canith got any ideas. "We need to find Evar. And the others." Evar would be enough for Arpix. And then the book, and then Livira. Mayland and his plans could stay lost.

"Or we could go find this king who took the book. This *Oanold*." She spoke his name like a curse. "The others will be looking for him too, and I'll bet he's easier to find than they are. Kings live in castles, yes?"

"Palaces normally, at least when they're in their capitals. But Oanold fell here like we did. He's not going to be king."

Clovis stood, still naked, still stretching. "Mayland said he would fall into himself. Into whoever he was here." She looked around for the leathers she'd scattered the evening before. "And I'm ready to bet he's this shitty potentate whose guards were trying to have you hanged."

"He might not even exist here. I mean we don't. Or at least . . . do we?"

Clovis shrugged. "If there's another me, the bitch can't have you."

Arpix couldn't help but snort with laughter at that. He tied the cord around his waist. Clovis somehow made him a different person. Normal-Arpix wasn't a snorter. "We came here because we followed Oanold. But something brought Oanold here, it means something to him. Maybe because there was a version of him living out a life in this place. In a palace."

"We'll go after this potentate," Clovis said. "Even if I'm wrong, it sounds like I'd be doing everyone a favour if I twisted his head off. And I bet I'm not wrong. This Oanold, this human king, he had his soldiers kill my people without cause or mercy. That sort of evil doesn't change. That hunger doesn't go away. He'll claw his way to the top. And that's how I'll find him."

Arpix held his tongue. Nobody had said the potentate wasn't a canith. He let it slide. Oanold's deeds had inflicted wounds that ran through the whole of Clovis's life. She couldn't be argued out of them. And besides, Oanold *was* a monster, a devil wrapped in human skin. The terror Arpix had felt beneath the man's indifferent cruelty would return to him every day of his life.

He kept his counsel until Clovis had finished dressing. "He'll have soldiers. Hundreds of them. A literal army. I mean—I saw a whole army march past me yesterday. We can't just stroll into his palace and challenge him."

"Of course not." Clovis tightened her belt.

Arpix relaxed.

"We scout first. Then attack." She aimed for the door. "Come on. Let's see if there's a back way out of here."

THEY LEFT THE inn via a dirty yard at the rear where carts came to unload casks of ale into the cellar and drive off with empties. A patch of mud allowed Clovis to tone down the distinctive red of her mane with a handful of grime. At her suggestion Arpix led the way and she trailed him at a discreet distance. The authorities would be looking for the pair of them, and whilst humans and canith kept close quarters in the city, Arpix had yet to see any holding hands.

Their first task was to buy some less distinctive clothes. Arpix sold his gold and silver coins to a blacksmith for a fraction of their worth. Using the local currency, silver marks and bronze pennies, he replaced his library robe with a set of second-hand clothes, trousers that ended well above his ankles, a homespun shirt that billowed around his spare frame, and worn leather shoes. Clovis opted for a hooded cape.

They made their purchases separately, but Arpix still had the strong impression that the shopkeeper suspected him. He'd heard two men on a corner talking about the massacre in the square as he passed. In hindsight he was surprised and relieved that none of the inn's patrons had informed on them during the night. He could only guess that the enforcers of the potentate's laws were not popular in some areas of the city. Or perhaps the locals were just waiting for a reward to be posted. No point giving the authorities something for free now that they would pay for later.

In his new—or at least newer—attire, Arpix turned towards the heights where the rich would live and set off up the slope. He scanned the street, watching for patrols, or anyone in authority, making sure to keep his distance. His main hope was that Evar or one of the others would spot them and suggest a better plan than Clovis's. He'd suggest one himself if he had one, but all his years of study hadn't been of much avail of late. For the years since escaping the blazing library he'd felt distinctly undereducated in all of the things that his life had suddenly come to depend upon.

Ever since Clovis's arrival at the plateau, the life he'd been living, delicately balanced on the edge of survival, had become even less certain. He'd careened from one seemingly fatal scenario to the next, and the current one felt no less dangerous than when he'd been in Oanold and Algar's clutches. It was, however, infinitely preferable to face those perils in Clovis's company.

Arpix studied the city as they climbed through it. The similarities and differences to Crath City were both considerable. Mayland had called the place, the whole world, a *maybe*. A reality where the gods had rolled their dice and come up with a different result. The mountains held the same shapes as far as Arpix could tell, but the world around them was wetter, cooler, and greener. The mists had rolled in off a great lake in the distance. The waters lay in the place his people had called the Dust. The Arthran Plateau must be an island in that lake now.

The higher Arpix took them, the more patrols of soldiers there were, the more black-clad officers of the interior police. Arpix had to assume that the potentate enjoyed support from a sizeable proportion of the populace. The city looked prosperous, its people well-fed, but their leader clearly didn't trust them further than he could spit them.

Arpix realised with a shock that he'd reached the market square where they'd been about to hang him the previous day. He stopped dead in the street, unwilling to go on. The scaffold had gone, and the bloodstains had been washed away, but it felt as though there were a noose about his throat even now, tightening with each passing moment. A shadow loomed behind him, and he knew with conviction that a hand was about to land on his shoulder, and an officer in execution black would demand his papers.

"Follow me." Clovis swept past him.

Now it was Arpix's turn to follow. Clovis set a fair pace for a canith, and Arpix began to sweat as they started up a steep street after crossing the square. Although he had spent most of their trip through the city fighting the desire to run, he had kept to an amble, not wanting to draw the gaze of those in authority. Hurrying was always an admission of guilt, even if the crime was only that of being late, or merely overeager. Hastening after Clovis, he felt even more exposed. The previous day's mists had not returned, but Arpix would have welcomed them as he puffed his way after his self-appointed guide.

At last, having climbed nearly to where in Arpix's city the Lesser Palace had stood, Clovis ducked into a largely deserted side street where, between rows of grand four-storey town houses, she beckoned him forward. Arpix came, trying not to look suspicious, and failing by glancing over his shoulder.

"I don't want to jinx it, but I'm not even sure they're looking for us." Arpix wasn't sure how that could be. "I mean, we walked across the square where it happened, and nobody looked twice at us."

"A few of them looked twice at me," Clovis said, "but I am rather fine."

"We shouldn't be together like this, not in public."

"You're ashamed of me?" Clovis raised an eyebrow, her smile playful. She lifted a finger as he opened his mouth to protest. "You're forgetting the Exchange. Mayland said it would disguise us. Show people what they expected to see. Perhaps it's still working. And the people in the square clearly expected to see something different from the ones in the inn, or the ones who've looked our way today."

"Ah." Arpix felt like an idiot. "But why put mud in your mane? Why the hood?"

"Because it will wear off at some point. And I may want to change my appearance quickly." Her smile broadened. "I thought you were the clever one."

"I didn't get much sleep." Arpix met her gaze.

Clovis laughed at that.

"Why are we here?"

"Because I was walking behind two men who were discussing something very interesting. There's to be some kind of tourney in Blue Tower Square. A bug-fight, they called it. And from the number of people coming this way it looks as if there's going to be quite an audience. Who knows, maybe even the potentate will come to see."

"Bug-fight?" Arpix frowned.

"Could be skeer."

"How do you catch skeer?" Arpix tried to imagine it. You'd need to get one on its own first. Even then you'd have to be pretty clever to avoid casualties.

Clovis shrugged. "Maybe they'll tell us."

"And how," Arpix continued, "do you suddenly know where to find a particular square in a city you know nothing about?"

"You really do need your sleep." Clovis took his shoulders and steered him back down the street.

"I don't—"

She tilted his head until over the rooftops of the houses the tip of a tower came into view, its blue tiles glimmering in the early sun. "I can see I'll have to do the thinking from now on, because I don't plan to stop keeping you up at night any time soon."

Blue-on-blue transgressions are statistically the result of poor comms more often than poor targeting. Fratricide accounted for 11% of losses in the Desert Stork campaign.

Friendly Fire, *by Major Tom Thomas*

CHAPTER 32

Evar

E var had been surprised by the suddenness with which the need to urinate came over him. He'd been somewhat alarmed when realising that for the first time in his life there was no library corner to visit, not even a private spot in the loneliness of the Dust. The city people must obviously have a solution to the problem, but it wasn't one he remembered reading about in any of the vast number of books he'd consumed. If the fog was still thick enough outside, then maybe . . .

His alarm grew dramatically when he pushed his chair back and stood from the table. "I've been poisoned!" The world spun around him.

"Relax." Starval's hand clamped around Evar's wrist as he staggered back. "You're just drunk."

"Oh." Evar steadied himself against the wall.

"I mean, technically it *is* a form of poisoning."

"But it won't make me sick?"

"I wouldn't go that far, brother . . ."

Evar gazed out across the crowded tavern. "Where do I . . ."

"There'll be somewhere out the back. Little huts, or just a trench. You'll know," Starval said.

Evar nodded, gathered himself, and started to forge a path.

"Don't fall in!" Starval called after him.

Evar didn't dignify that with an answer. He resolved instead to drink no more ale. It was foul stuff. Or at least the first tankard had tasted pretty awful. The second had been all right. By the time he found the back door he decided that perhaps a third tankard would decide the matter.

Outside, the mists had thinned a little, but the sun was setting, dying a crimson death in a valley to the west, and overall the visibility had hardly improved. Someone stumbled out of the gloom, headed for the door Evar had just come out of.

"Excuse me . . ."

But the human male just grunted into his beard and bundled past.

". . . where do I . . ."

Evar followed the building's wall rather than forge out into the mist blind. Starval had mentioned the possibility of a trench, and with his balance knocked askew by the local poison of choice, Evar could see himself ending up in said trench, unless he exercised caution.

He came to a corner and continued his slow advance. The wall now had a top, low enough for Evar to stretch and grab, but studded with broken glass. He reached a door, paint peeling from greying wood as if diseased, pushed, and found it locked. "Privy." He finally remembered one of the names for the places where nature's call was answered. Was this the privy?

Evar knocked on the door. He could hear something on the other side, a kind of clattering, clomping noise, some heavy snorting. Not the sort of sounds he would have imagined issuing from a privy if he'd ever given the matter any thought. He looked up at the wall. Its poorly set blocks made it something Starval could scale in the blink of an eye, but Evar had never had the luxury of the Mechanism to teach him climbing skills. He spotted a missing block and dug his toes into the gap. Even with the stones wet and two ales in his belly he should be able to get far enough up the wall to check what was on the other side.

"Did you find it?" Starval raised a refilled tankard at Evar as he wove his way back through the crowded room to the table.

"I did." Evar wrinkled his nose and slid in beside his brother. "You go straight out across the yard, and there are four huts. Don't follow the wall. There's a door but it's locked. Don't climb up—"

"Climb?" Starval took the ale back. "I think you've had enough, Evar."

Evar lowered his voice to a whisper. "There's something strange going on here . . ."

"I know," Starval said.

"You know?"

"Secrets are my business. And that Oldo has at least one big one. You didn't notice how he looked at us? He thinks we're here for him. Spies. I'd put money on it. That, brother, is a guilty man. But it's hardly our concern."

"Does beer sneeze?" Evar hissed, scanning the tavern to see if anyone was trying to listen in.

"Only when you've had way way too much of it."

"Well, there's an unloading area round the back, separate, behind a wall. And I saw them unloading barrels . . ."

"That *is* pretty suspicious," Starval mocked.

"And one of them sneezed."

"Don't care," Starval said. "He can be making his own special brew out of humans, I don't give two hoots. We're here for the book. It's a *maybe* place anyway. Mayland said so. This whole world is a what-if."

"You think this place is a maybe and we're not? We're the one true world and those alternatives we climbed through are 'pretend'? I'm not even sure anymore if all the people you killed in the Mechanism were pretend. But I *am* pretty damn sure that we're just another maybe. So, don't go killing people here because they don't matter. Everyone matters. Everywhere."

"Or nobody does."

"Right." Evar faltered, unsure how his brother meant that last part. "King Oldo?"

"What?"

"King Oldo. That's what he said to call him, unless we're friends. Then Oldo's fine. I wonder what that's about."

"I'll find out using my assassin skills." Starval drained his tankard and wiped his whiskers. "Hey you, Gothon."

The old canith turned with the exaggerated caution of the very drunk.

"Why do people call him King Oldo?"

"Says he's a Hosten. Cousin of a cousin of a cousin probably." Gothon had started to slur his words. "Secret police would've strung him up long ago if it was any sort of decent claim."

Starval turned to Evar. "There you have it." He pushed Evar's beer at him. "Drink up, time to go."

"Go?" Evar eyed the suds slopping in the wooden tankard. "Where?"

"We'll find that out on the way. I'm sure this city has more to offer than the Stained Page's taproom. I'll grant you the ale's decent, the landlord mysterious, the food good, and it has a better class of drunk than most places. Still, I don't plan to wait here until our siblings find us, or until they do the job we came to do and head off, leaving our sorry arses here."

Evar frowned at his drink and set it down. "Let's go then. I've got a book and a girl to find."

Starval missed a quarter-beat then set off for the door.

THE SUN HAD set and been replaced with streetlights. The fog had thinned considerably but Evar's view of the city remained limited. Starval led off as if he knew where he was heading.

"Where are we going?"

Evar had kept his mouth closed while Starval had taken one turn after another, each narrower and darker than the next, as if he were trying to worm into the city's underbelly by force of instinct. He emerged now into a muddy square, narrower across than the height of the shabby buildings that hemmed it in to create a shaft showing a black sky and Attamast's disk, the moon a curious shade of purple in a sky laced with ribbons of cloud.

Evar shivered. It felt as if the surrounding tenements had turned their backs on the square, ashamed of it. The occasional shuttered windows released only whispers of light, and the place reeked worse than the privy huts behind Oldo's tavern.

Three lines of ragged washing hung out of reach, crisscrossing the space above them, the garments grey and listless. There didn't seem to be any exits.

"Where are we going?" Evar repeated his question.

By way of answer Starval posed a question. "Where did we come from?"

Evar spread his hands, not prepared to enter into one of Starval's games.

"A prison," Starval said. "A place we all expected to grow old and die in, within a mile of the spot we were born."

"I guess . . ."

"A place we'd all found our own escape from long before Mayland disappeared. And then you discovered that the pool led somewhere . . . and changed everything." Starval began to pace as he always did when agitated. "Clovis had lost herself in revenge fantasies years before that. And you'd fled into your own obsession: finding an exit. Forms of madness, that's what Kerrol called them behind your backs."

"To our faces too," Evar grunted. "Or at least to mine." Clovis might have punched him.

"Mayland hid himself in the past. And me . . . I signed up to a code, not a code of honour *per se*, but one that was rigid enough to hold me up, keep me standing when nothing else would. Kerrol said I'd detached myself from emotion and fabricated disposable replacements. Also a form of madness according to him. But he's the most lost of all of us, so what does he know?"

"It's an odd conversation to be having here, and now." Evar looked around. "But I suppose this *is* a dead end, so maybe it's appropriate after all." He paused and looked at his brother, small and dark and deadly, as if seeing him for the first time in a long while. "Why aren't you drunk too?"

"I was tipping mine on the floor when you weren't looking."

"But you let me drink . . ."

"Why didn't you have the last one?" Starval asked. "Didn't even so much as taste it."

"I don't know." But Evar did. At some level, down where the thoughts that never surfaced swam, he had seen a truth and acted on it, all without properly acknowledging even the action, let alone its source. "Because something was wrong."

"It's good to see that my training wasn't completely wasted on you. Who's easier to kill than a child who hates you?"

"A warrior that trusts you." Evar had given this answer many times before.

"And you thought that lesson was for the outside world that we would never reach, rather than for the four square miles that were our universe?"

"Yes."

"Why didn't you drink your third ale then? Why do I never turn my back on any of you?"

"I don't understand." Evar's hand understood, though, and it went hunting the hilt of his knife. The weapon had been taken.

"I escaped into a code, Evar." Starval magicked a large gold coin into his hand. "Mayland was the only one who understood that. Well, maybe Kerrol too. But Mayland was the one who used it."

"I don't understand." Evar repeated the words like a shield against the truth.

"I've been paid to kill you."

"But you don't have to."

"I've built myself around a transactional world view. It made my existence bearable. And now it's part of me." The hand without the coin held a knife.

Evar strangled a laugh. Starval was very far from joking. "You poisoned the last ale."

"I did."

"You could have stabbed me in the back before we even got to the tavern."

"I wanted you to have a nice time first. You'd never had a proper meal. You missed out on a lot of things."

"You could have stabbed me in the back when we entered this square." Evar found himself in a strangely bifurcated state of mind. He could both believe what was happening, and at the same time be shocked, horrified, and saddened by it. Starval had always worn a mask. He'd not even lied about it. But Evar's brain had always chosen to forget that fact as swiftly as it could. Starval was a nihilist to his bones, the sunny smile painted on.

Starval dropped the coin to the muddy cobbles. "The money means nothing. It's a challenge token. And this . . . this is like a true believer being martyred for the faith or offering up their firstborn to a demanding god. That piece of gold is a question. It's saying 'Do you really believe that nothing matters? Or are you going to give the world a stick to beat you with? Are you going to open your door to every deed you've done, every life you've taken, and let them march into your heart with their pale faces and their accusations?' Mayland wants you gone, brother. And he's paid me to do it."

"You could have stabbed me in the back," Evar repeated, and with a deep breath he turned away from the knife. "But you couldn't because we're brothers."

The knife hurt going in, but as the blood began to flood around the steel, betrayal was the deeper pain.

Life is full of moments where we get to choose the blue pill or the red pill. Only there's no pill. And no choice.

Matrix Multiplication, *by C. F. Gauss*

———————

CHAPTER 33

Livira

Livira and Carlotte followed the canith woman through the streets. Despite the earlier urgency in her voice, the canith led them at the calm and gentle pace of the innocent, as if they had no particular place to be.

"Why are we following her?" Carlotte asked.

"Because of the way the Exchange works," Livira answered in a low voice. "It doesn't just spit you out at random. It drops you into important days, important places. This canith didn't find us—we found her. We were meant to."

Carlotte scowled. "That sounds like a bunch of mystic hoo-hah you just made up."

Livira shrugged. "I found you, didn't I?"

Carlotte's frown deepened. "But we didn't even appear at the tavern. We were on some street with bookshops. And there was a tavern there too. A much nicer one. Maybe we were supposed to go in there, not wander randomly to the Gates of Misery."

"Heaven's Gate," Livira corrected.

"I call it as I see it."

Ahead of them, their guide took a swift glance around then veered into a side street. She picked up the pace immediately they were clear of the main road. Despite the canith's grey mane and emaciation, her lengthened stride forced Livira to jog in order to keep up. A few more lefts and rights took them from broad, well-lit streets into grimy alleys. The setting sun didn't reach far into the slums, but above them the last strands of the earlier fog lit with crimson. The canith led them between tall rows of tenements, black with the smoke of whatever local industry tainted the air between one blocked sewer and the next. Clotheslines spanned the street, connecting random rooms. Overalls and aprons hung sullenly in the damp air.

"A dead end." Carlotte stated the obvious. The canith hadn't spoken since leaving the wrecked tavern and the vanquished Escape behind them. She glanced around at them now.

The square they'd arrived in was little more than five yards across, walled in by buildings. Livira could see no doors. The few windows were all shuttered.

"Come." The canith approached a wall, pushed, and ducked through the opening that appeared.

Livira followed Carlotte in, fighting against the strength of the spring that wanted to return the centrally hinged section of wall back to its original position. A flight of steps led down. The place smelled earthy and was utterly dark.

"Don't trip," the canith advised.

Livira edged down the stairs, a hand on the wall to either side, not convinced she could find enough traction on the slimy stone to prevent her tumbling should she miss her footing.

None of them fell. Livira saved injury for the final step, jolting as she expected another drop, and biting her tongue. "Damnation!"

A door opened and lantern light blinded her. Blinking, she advanced into a chamber about the same size as the square above. Two men with crossbows stood against the far wall, one aiming at Carlotte, the other still cranking his cable back. Between Livira and the men some chairs and a table bearing the remnants of a meal offered little opportunity for cover.

The younger man finished loading his weapon and pointed it at Livira.

"Relax, everyone," the stooping canith growled. "Don't shoot them—but stay ready to."

"Thanks," Carlotte said with total insincerity.

"We need to consider the possibility that you're the potentate's agents," the canith explained. "If the potentate got his hands on someone who seems able to work magic, I don't think he'd risk sending them to a shithole like the Gates in the hopes of rooting out the Saviour. But I'm going to keep that possibility in mind."

"Magic?" The older of the crossbow men snorted.

Livira took a step forward and both crossbows pointed her way. She reached for the nearest chair and sat down. "This would be easier if you assumed we've both dropped off one of the moons and landed today. I don't know who the Saviour is or what your king's called or what wars you're fighting. I don't even know what this city looks like in daylight without the fog. We"—she flickered a finger from herself to Carlotte and back again—"are not from around here. I'm looking for a book. A particular book. And if I help you, I'll expect some help in return."

"Who says we need anything from you?" sneered the older man.

"You'd like us to go then?" Carlotte turned for the exit.

"Enough!" the canith snapped with surprising authority. "Sit." She pointed the former queen to a chair beside Livira. "I'll get Tremon. She can decide what to do with you." She stalked across the room to a door behind the men. Before opening it, she paused to address both men with a degree of menace. "Do *not* shoot them." She held her hand out and the older man gave her a heavy key. She used it, went through, and locked the door behind her. "Unless you have to," she called back through the thickness of the wood.

Livira and Carlotte sat in silence for a minute until the younger man lowered his weapon and said, "We don't have a king. The potentate had him killed."

"What's the difference between a king and a potentate?" Livira asked.

The older man snorted. He seemed prone to snorting. "Don't humour them."

"About this much." His companion used a hand to measure the distance from his shoulder to his full height. He grinned. "The potentate had the king decapitated and took his throne."

Livira grinned back, despite the grim topic. The companion was a sandy-haired fellow of about Livira's age, his pleasant face marred by a livid scar running from chin to cheek, carving through his lips on the way. She gestured to the chair opposite. "Sit down. Your friend can shoot anyone who misbehaves. You can tell me about this Saviour of yours . . ."

The man obliged. He wouldn't give his name, but he proved eager to talk about the Saviour, his zeal almost religious, although despite expectations, the Saviour turned out to be promising salvation from New Kraff's current woes rather than for anyone's immortal soul.

Livira dubbed her new friend "Scar," admitting a lack of imagination as she did so. Scar might not have believed the level of Livira's professed ignorance, but in charting the deeds and ambitions of his leader, he provided a quick tutorial in the state of play within the city and beyond its walls, so by the time the canith returned, Livira's education in local matters had improved considerably. She knew the potentate to be an upstart rabble-rouser who had ridden to power on the back of a witch hunt against the Amacar, a religious minority found across the continent in many countries. The Saviour—whose true identity was a well-kept secret—was leading an insurrection. The movement, while mildly sympathetic to the Amacar and the terrors being heaped upon their dwindling numbers, had been founded on a very different source of malcontent. The Saviour and his followers objected to not just the potentate, but monarchy in general. Carlotte had raised an eyebrow at this revelation. The Saviour planned to put votes in the hands of all adults in the city and have them set a leader of their own choosing in the potentate's place and allow them a chance to change their minds every five years. Democracy, they called it. Livira had read about the concept but knew of nowhere in her old life that put it into practice.

"Won't this Saviour just take the throne for himself while the last occupant's corpse is still cooling?" Carlotte asked.

"Or just get all the votes because it's his idea and everyone knows him," Livira said.

"No! Because nobody knows who he is. None of us have ever seen his face. He wears a mask. And when the potentate is cast down, the Saviour is going to vanish. He'll be one of us, but we won't know him. He might ask for votes, but never as the Saviour. Everyone will have the same chance." Scar's eyes almost glowed with belief. Behind him even his friend's snort lacked its usual derision.

"And why does he need me?" Livira asked.

"Nar— Our friend said something about magic?" Scar shook his head. "I mean, I doubt it, but we could use a miracle. There's not much time left now."

"You're losing?" Carlotte glanced towards the exit as if considering an escape bid. "I'm not surprised if this is how you recruit members for your little rebellion."

"Because the bugs are coming." The big man levelled his crossbow at Carlotte, and under the pointed stare of its steel eye, she swallowed her retort.

Scar explained, "The Saviour wants us to ally with Iccrah before it's too late. They have the weapons and the defensible position. We have the numbers. But there's not long left to do everything that needs doing. But the potentate just wants to conquer Iccrah. He's not even taking the bug threat seriously. They've got some sort of games going on in Tower Square. Men and canith against bugs, to calm the public. What he's not telling them though is there's an ocean of the things, and the tide's rising."

Livira frowned. "Why would a king . . . potentate, whatever, ignore a threat like that? It's his cities, his land, and in the end, his life, that are going to be lost."

"He's found advisors that tell him what he wants to hear. That the bugs will turn north before they reach us. Take a hundred experts and you'll always find a handful to dissent on any subject. The potentate's chosen to listen to those ones. Thinks the idea that the bugs won't turn is put about by his enemies, by the Saviour, to force him into decisions he doesn't want to make."

The door behind them banged open. The canith came back into the room, followed by a large woman, perhaps the largest Livira had seen.

"You can call me Tremon." She stood as tall as Arpix and twice as wide, packed solid, her face one that looked to have been punched a lot and to still be angry about it.

"Livira," Livira said. "And that's Carlotte."

"Show me this magic." She shot a sharp look in the canith's direction.

"Why should I?" Livira asked.

Tremon sighed. "I could say, because there are two crossbows pointed your way. But I hear you're after a particular book?"

"Do you have it?"

"Does it make holes in things?"

Livira thought of the cracks spreading across the library floor from where she'd dropped it that last time it left her possession. "Probably."

"Then I know where it is."

Gladiatorial combat has been a central pillar of many civilisations' entertainment—the method by which their minds are diverted from the issues that truly impact their lives. The balance between emotional and physical suffering in such contests swings with the prevailing societal winds.

Big Brother: Season 8—A Companion Guide, *by David Macaw*

CHAPTER 34

Arpix

B lue Tower Square boasted five paved acres starting to bake beneath an increasingly hot sun. Bleachers offered seating along three of the four sides, tiered eight rows high, the timbers so fresh as to still be bleeding sap around the bolt heads securing one piece to the next.

A crowd of thousands had largely assembled itself and proved every bit as ready for entertainment as the smaller one that had gathered to watch Arpix hang the day before in a different square further down the slope. Hawkers moved up and down, calling out their wares to the packed stands. Beer, salted bread, sausages, flags, even highly inaccurate models of skeer fashioned from clay or wood.

Along the most distant side of the square, black cloths, large as sails, obscured what might be half a dozen large crates—the breeze exposed a glint of bars. The most important-looking members of the audience sat directly opposite these cages, high up, a splash of colour amid the more drably garbed populace. A line of orderlies to either side ensured that money didn't have to rub elbows with aspiration. Arpix considered the possibility that the potentate himself might be sitting amidst the nobility and persons of influence arrayed between those two lines. He concluded that it was unlikely such a man would leave himself so exposed.

Front and centre below the dignitaries stood a double line of armoured soldiers, each with a gloved hand on the barrel of a long gun that rested with its stock on the ground. And in front of the troopers, standing a little way out on the square itself, six or seven individuals, no one of them like the other. Arpix wasn't sure if he should call them soldiers or mercenaries, champions perhaps. All of them appeared well equipped in both the weapons and armour departments. All of them looked very intimidating. He counted four canith and three humans, carrying a variety of guns, some longer than a man, some short but with a barrel almost as wide as a cannon's, others with multiple barrels.

"Surely this is madness?" Arpix gazed at the stands where families watched on with eager faces, some unpacking food as they waited for the theatre to start. "These people are in danger!"

"If they've got skeer under those covers, then yes they are," Clovis agreed.

Arpix had meant from stray bullets, but Clovis was right too. He saw now that the heavy palisade of timber behind the covered cages must be to stop the insectoids escaping in that direction, and also to prevent the challengers' shots from peppering the buildings behind. That still meant that any free skeer could charge off over the stands, cutting a swathe of carnage through the seated audience before dropping off the back.

"This way!" A uniformed man approached Clovis, Arpix, and the stragglers still arriving behind them. "Get to your seats. They're nearly ready!"

Clovis ignored the orderly and set off along the inside perimeter in the opposite direction, towards the group with the weapons. One, the tallest canith Arpix had ever seen, dressed in a blue velvet waistcoat, and with a mane teased into a mass of curls, all set with gold rings like a storybook pirate, turned to watch her approach. Beside him a woman half his height and almost spherical, but muscly with it, said something that made him laugh. The woman shook her head and returned her attention to a blunderbuss taller than she was.

"Wait! Stop!" The orderly took the words from Arpix's mouth.

"Where's she going?" A woman in the same uniform joined the man in pursuit of Clovis.

"She's heading for the contestants!" The man gave chase.

Arpix bit back on his own objections and followed too.

Clovis shook off two attempts to intercept her and earned a few cheers along with scattered jeers from the crowd. Several more of the contestants turned her way as she drew closer.

"Who the hell are you?" The hulking canith with the cannon scowled at Clovis.

"She brought a sword." One of the two men smirked before looking back down the large sighting tube of the long, gleaming gun he had pointed downrange, supported on a slender tripod. "How quaint."

"I didn't know this was a free-for-all," the other man growled. Where his companion was tall, bald, and of middling years, this one was hairy, athletic, and sported a sizeable number and variety of handguns holstered about his person.

Arpix wasn't sure how the scene would end, but he fully expected it to start with Clovis breaking someone's face.

"Madam!" An orderly caught up with Clovis, another took hold of Arpix's arm. "You have to return to the stands."

A couple of soldiers moved forward to impose the peace.

"I know how to fight skeer," Clovis said, not backing down. "You should let me show you how it's done."

"An Iccrah without a rifle. How droll." The "pirate" peered down at her, then drew two heavy, double-barrelled guns, each nearly two feet long, from his silk waistband. "Sit yourself down, lass, and let the Kraffians show you how we do it."

Two soldiers converged on Clovis, each reaching for an arm. Arpix winced, anticipating the violence which neither man, confident in their uniform, seemed to know was coming their way.

"Find her a seat!" the pirate boomed. "Don't arrest the wench. Let's just get on with this, shall we?"

Whether through expediency or an unconscious instinct for self-preservation, the soldiers followed the pirate's command, and Clovis allowed herself to be turned towards the stands behind the combatants. Some lordling a couple of rows back waved wearily for space to be made for her.

Arpix, by contrast, was manhandled back to where they'd entered and given a shove towards the public seating. He found a place, and sat down, feeling the splinters through his newly acquired trousers. His hunger had returned after a night's sleep but somehow the pervasive aroma of the many foodstuffs on offer left him feeling slightly ill. He knew what was in those cages, and whatever happened once they were opened would not be pretty.

A hush fell as an announcer in colourful silks strode out. Arpix couldn't hear what he was shouting—it seemed to be primarily for the benefit of the aristocracy—but after a short while the herald retreated and two of the three human champions stepped forward, the tall bald man with the very long gun, and the hairy, younger one with all his handguns.

At the far side of the square, wranglers drew back the black cloth from one cage, and the audience gasped at the large white creature revealed within. The men retreated behind their barrier and pulled on ropes to raise the bars at the front.

The skeer emerged awkwardly and scanned the arena with multiple eye-pits. The midnight-blue trim on its armour plates drank in the sunlight. Arpix could see that one of its legs had been shattered, ichor spattering the broken chitin exoskeleton. As it made ungainly progress across the flagstones, Arpix realised that something was wrong with all of its legs. He sucked his breath in in distaste. Each limb had been foreshortened, the sharp points cut back by a foot or more, so that it walked on weeping stumps.

The first shot cracked out, striking the skeer in the middle of its eye clusters. Pieces of chitin flew out and the skeer's whole body flinched. The boom of the gun and sizeable cloud of smoke focused the skeer on the di-rection of the attack.

"How is it not dead?" a woman beside Arpix complained.

Arpix couldn't answer that one.

The skeer began an excruciating, broken advance towards the shooter. The bald man started to reload as the other, with his great dark mop of hair, strolled out to meet the creature, a gun in either hand.

The second man began firing with a quarter of the square's width still between him and the skeer. He shot rapidly with both weapons, smoke billowing in puffs, pieces spraying from the skeer where the bullets hit. The creature lurched on drunkenly, a shrill wail pulsing from it. Behind it, the half-dozen covered crates began to vibrate, one jolting left, another actu-ally lifting from the ground before crashing down.

With a hundred yards to go, the man discarded both handguns and pulled two more from his harness. With fifty yards to go, he began to fire again, aiming for the skeer's head. It seemed clear to Arpix that whilst some of the bullets were turned by the thick chitin armour, many were not, and white ichor leaked from the holes they made, blackish-grey where a shot found an eye.

"Lie down!" a man shouted behind Arpix.

"Why won't it die?" A child's voice.

Scattered shouts of outrage mixed with fear went up along the bleachers. And still the maimed skeer staggered towards its small tormentor.

With ten yards between them the gunman exhausted his ammunition and reached for what might be his final weapon. The skeer dwarfed him, drawing back the arm with the lance-like end to it.

BOOM. The long gun spoke again, and this time the pieces flew from the back of the skeer's head. With a shudder it slumped to ruin, its arm reaching for the man before it, and dropping to within a yard of his boot toes.

A shocked silence held long enough for the echo of the final gun to die away, only to be broken by the erupting cheers of the crowd. The people around Arpix surged to their feet and he stood too.

The man with the handguns turned and began to walk away, pausing to pick up discarded weapons. Arpix didn't fully trust the skeer not to launch itself after him in a broken scramble. But the insectoids were just very hard to kill, not supernatural, and it lay where it had fallen, still twitching.

A new hush spread as the one Arpix had mentally dubbed "the pirate" stepped forward with an appropriate degree of swagger. People began returning their backsides to the benches.

"This'll be good," the old woman to Arpix's left confided to a similarly antique friend.

The day dimmed slightly. High cloud in front of the sun, most likely.

At the far end, another black cloth whipped away from another cage.

The bars lifted and a second hobbled skeer skittered out, losing its footing on the flagstones. The mutilation of its "feet" was the only obvious measure taken with this one.

The pirate strode out to meet his opponent, heavy guns in hand. Something swift and glittering flicked by, momentarily eclipsing the pirate's flamboyance. In the wake of this interruption the canith stumbled, fell to his knees firing both guns at the ground, and toppled forward.

"Where's his head?" the old woman's friend asked.

Blood sheeted in front of the fallen pirate, and Arpix found the same question on his own lips. Where *was* his head?

More guns boomed. People started to scream. And the missing head bounced on the flagstones. Arpix saw the flier then. Lighter than the skeer soldier, or even the long-legged runners, the flier was all limbs and sharp edges, white and hard to see against the sky save for the iridescent shimmer of its wings. More swooped in, a dozen perhaps. Plumes of smoke rose in front of the privileged seating as a score of the potentate's troopers opened up, loosing bullets skywards.

The fliers dived in, spiralling as they came, hitting from multiple angles. One ploughed a furrow along the full length of the soldiers' rank, razored limbs shearing through flesh, leaving a wash of crimson ruin in its path as it took to the heights again.

The mercenaries—or whatever they were—in front of Clovis threw a thunderous barrage into the air and several fliers came tumbling down with shredded wings or shattered limbs. Moments later, the glittering cloud descended. More shots rattled out. Arpix saw a young woman in the stands lose half the back of her head as a stray bullet emerged from her long hair.

Screams and yells from the mercenaries were lost in the general uproar of the crowd. Something about the situation, the fact that it was still an arena, and they were still an audience, had kept the great majority of people where they were. Some sensible few were escaping from the rear of the stands, dropping down and making a run for the edges of the square. But most either sat or stood where they were, shouting their anger, or screaming it behind the shake of a fist, as if some invisible barrier protected them from the skeer's invasion.

The lone skeer soldier turned in place as if seeking some foe worthy of it.

As one the fliers lifted. A handful remained broken and twitching amongst the broken and twitching bodies of the humans and canith that had been chosen to show their superiority. An almost silence reigned beneath the fluttering buzz of skeer wings as the five remaining fliers gained height in a knot, each weaving around the others. Arpix had seen skeer intelligence at work before. They had brought cratalacs to defeat the forbidding that protected the Arthran Plateau. They had dropped rocks to pierce the barrier that held them at bay. But this, this was a different order. This was warfare of the mind. The people of New Kraff craned their necks and watched the blood drip like rain. In moments the skeer would break formation and *everyone* would run. Arpix imagined that more would die beneath the feet of their fellow citizens than to the skeer's predations. But either way, it would be slaughter.

Clovis's emergence onto the square went almost unnoticed. It wasn't until she was well clear and raised her white sword, with the transfixed head of a skeer flier impaled upon it, that the eyes of the crowd found her. The skeer soldier saw her too and started its hobbled advance.

Clovis had scooped up one of the fallen pirate's short guns, and demonstrated that he hadn't fully shot his load by firing it at the aerial display above her. The weapon's boom, and the peppering of small projectiles, focused all insectoid attention on her, along with that of the crowd. The challenge had to be met, and as if animated by a single mind, all five fliers ceased the vibration of their wings, falling towards Clovis in a tumbling confusion.

Arpix had seen this before, when Clovis had arrived at the plateau with Evar and Kerrol. Even so, both his heart and his breath seemed to stop. When she had danced amid the thrusting cloud of needled limbs that first time, Arpix hadn't even known her name. He had stood, amazed at her skill, but hadn't properly valued what could so easily be lost at the slightest misstep.

The fliers reached her before the soldier did. Clovis moved with the blinding speed of her kind, scything the white sword through limbs that would have entangled any lesser blade. She let her foes crowd each other, and used their flight against them, carving ruinous wounds every time an opening presented itself. Two of the skeer hit the ground as if they'd made no attempt to check their speed at the last moment. Another lost two legs, then two more. A fourth fell into unequal halves. And as the fifth flier lunged for the skies, Clovis acknowledged the soldier's arrival by climbing the thing.

She bounced from one leg to another and onto its back. Before the soldier could twist to lunge at her, Clovis had executed a huge leap, her lead foot powering off the soldier's shoulder. Against all possibility, she caught one of the escaping flier's trailing limbs, clamped a hand around the end of the leg, and forced the skeer to drag her into the sky with it.

She stabbed up into its thorax then dropped. Arpix's gasp became one with the thousands watching. Clovis had released her grip too high: the fall yawning beneath her was more than from the roof of a three-storey building, onto hard stone.

Clovis slammed into the ground, landing on her feet, then hands, then knees. Her side hit the slabs next as she rolled to absorb the impact. She lay motionless for a beat. Two beats. The crowd held its tongue. Already the soldier had turned to face her. Now it started to close the five yards between them.

As one, the whole audience flinched when the forgotten flier hammered down in an ungainly tangle of limbs, almost hitting Clovis. The impact cracked the skeer or the paving slabs, or both.

"No!" Arpix's shout joined hundreds of others protesting the unfairness as the soldier skeer loomed over Clovis's prone form. It raised its blade-arm like a chef preparing to chop vegetables for the pot, and the cries from the stands turned to screams.

Clovis rose an instant before the soldier could take its swing, pushing her sword ahead of her, driving the length of it up through the skeer's head. When she stood, she brought the crowd's roar up with her, victory and relief mixing in the many-throated cry.

She hadn't finished, though. Not trusting in a sword through the head to finish her opponent, she lunged and twisted, using the entire weight of her body to enlarge the wound then bring the blade out through the skeer's face, trailing white ichor.

The soldier collapsed behind her as she walked away.

CHAPTER 35

Evar

Evar pulled free of Starval's blade, turning to confront his brother as the blood ran from the wound in his lower back. The physical pain was bad, but less so than Evar might have guessed—less so than being shot. It was the emotional pain that rocked him on his heels.

"You stabbed me! You actually stabbed me!"

Starval stood there, his blade raised between them.

"That's not even how you do it." Evar couldn't believe he was complaining about how he'd been stabbed. Shock had hold of his tongue. But he was right. It wasn't how Starval had taught him, and the fact he was still standing showed it to be an inefficient method. Was Starval being cruel? That wasn't the assassin's way.

"No," Starval agreed woodenly.

"Did he pay you to hurt me first?" Evar would never have imagined Mayland putting a contract on his life, much less anything less than a clean, painless one.

"I have to." Starval continued to stare at his knife and the blood black upon it. "This truth is all I am."

Evar took a step back, one hand pressed to his wound, the other raised towards his brother. The closed square offered no retreat, its walls rising on all sides, the scarce windows all shuttered, as if the buildings themselves were looking away. Kerrol would know what to say to Starval. Evar could understand the knot his brother had tied himself in, or that Mayland had tied, but couldn't see how to undo it.

Starval's escape from a life sentence amid the book towers of their chamber had been to retreat from it. To distance himself from everything. To make a game of it. To say it didn't matter, that nothing mattered, and to repeat that mantra a million times until the boy that had emerged from the Mechanism lay buried beneath that rejection. He stood beyond emotion now, beyond appeal, armoured in so many layers of denial that nothing could reach him.

Or that had been the plan. Because if everything about sunny Starval had been a lie, Evar would be sprawled in the mud, his heart pierced by his brother's first blow. But the next blow, the final thrust of the dagger, was coming. Evar could sense it. Starval had built his life upon a particular contract with reality. He had been paid. He allowed himself no choices.

"This—" Evar bit back on the pain. "This is like Jaspeth and Irad. Brothers at war. Their grandfather invented fratricide. That's the story. And—"

"I have to do this." Starval advanced.

Evar saw it. The stack of crimes Mayland had piled upon Starval, using him as the weapon he'd shaped himself into. If Starval had refused this commission, the poisoning of a whole city would become a choice. If one thing mattered—everything did. In one moment, Evar saw the only way to undo the knot, and how it would be impossible to do so. He had to beat Starval. And despite the chance his brother had given him, he stood unarmed and wounded before the most skilled of assassins.

"Ready?" Starval jabbed and Evar skipped back despite his injury. The look in Starval's eyes promised there would be no more chances.

In a knife fight perhaps even Clovis would not have been Starval's equal. Evar had been trained by the master, but even on his best day he would stand no chance in a fair contest. And this wasn't fair. He had no knife.

There, in the dank shadow of the nameless square, inspiration struck.

Evar whipped his arm across the space between them, even though his brother was too far away to punch. Starval, ever cautious, lifted his dagger to block the non-existent blow, and tensed, ready for any projectile that might leave Evar's hand.

Evar had no throwing stars, no blade, no handful of sand to blind an unwary opponent. He had nothing in his hand save his blood, and even that was not his own. Mayland had, under the scrutiny of Kerrol and Clovis, healed Evar. The blood of the library ran in Evar's veins now. And Starval had set it free.

Evar didn't form the weapon until the swing of his arm had passed Starval's blocking manoeuvre. He made a black rod, as thick as the volume of blood allowed. Even Starval's breathtaking reflexes couldn't save him entirely. The cane struck him around the temple. He staggered back.

"Clever." Allowing Evar no time to think, Starval spun in, sweeping a leg, knife moving.

Evar jumped the leg sweep and, in mid-air, deflected the lunge of Starval's blade on a black buckler of his own blood. He tried to kick his brother in the chest, but the knife wound in his back robbed the attack of strength. He landed badly and Starval was on him. The blow to the head must have dazed and slowed the assassin: his knife struck sparks from the flagstones. Evar wrapped the blade in a thickness of black blood, taking away its sharpness. In the same moment he kneed Starval in the stomach, throwing him clear. Both of them rolled to their feet at the same time.

"Very clever." Starval spat blood and turned his now-useless blade this way then that. He tossed it aside and drew a new knife from a hidden scabbard on his chest, a thinner, sharper one.

"Stop this . . ." Evar could feel himself weakening.

"Stop me," Starval replied. A hint of helplessness ran through the words, faint but there for Evar to hear.

Suddenly he was angry. Angry with everything: Mayland, Starval, himself as well. "I've better things to do, godsdammit." Evar strode to the nearest wall, reached up, and with a snarl of effort ripped down one of the shutters. "I've got better things to do than fight my stupid brother in a dirty hole over some war I don't even care about." And with a roar he charged, holding the shutter before him like a shield.

Starval's acrobatics had no match among his family. Wherever Evar leapt, Starval would no longer be there. He would sidestep, and he would stab.

Evar threw himself at his brother anyway, both feet leaving the ground.

He could see his target through the slats of the shutter, already moving now that Evar had placed himself in the hands of gravity and momentum, slave to both. The assassin had made his calculation, as inflexible as his contract, and as deadly.

The fight ended here.

It would have ended with a knife thrust, but for the fact that Evar's blood moved to his will, outside his veins, and inside them too. By force of will he steered his whole body through the air on an impossible, unexpected curve. The shutter caught Starval's knife thrust. It caught Starval too, slamming him into the wall. Evar's weight followed. Then his fists. And in a flurry of angry blows, he set his brother senseless on the ground.

Groaning and limping, Evar hobbled away to recover the discarded knife and the much-needed blood around it.

"I KNOW YOU'RE awake."

"Only because I got bored and let you know." Starval's voice sounded thicker, a painful rasp.

"What happens now?" Evar asked. "Does the mission carry on until one of us is dead? Or now I've beaten you can I buy out the contract?"

"I don't know. I've never failed before."

Evar shook out the contents of the purse he'd taken from Starval. "This looks like enough." He flicked two of the coins at his brother, who lay propped against the wall of the alley Evar had dragged him to.

"Paying me with my own money?" Starval shook his head. "That's low."

"Lower than stabbing your brother in the back?" Evar shifted his stance and winced. "Besides, it's not your money. You stole it in Oldo's pub."

"I can't pick it up unless you untie me." Starval flexed his shoulders as if to prove it. His hands remained behind his back.

"You don't expect me to believe you're still tied up?"

Starval rolled his eyes and reached out for the coins.

Evar pinned his wrist to the ground with one foot. "This better be over. I need to find Livira. And I'm going to have to go through anyone who gets in my way." He hoped he sounded convincing. He felt convinced.

"Understood," Starval answered through gritted teeth.

"I've no idea if you're lying. Still." Evar released the hand. "None at all."

Starval took the coins. "I'm not sure either."

Evar helped him up. The wound in his back hurt, but it no longer bled. It seemed that all Evar had to do in order to stop bleeding was to will himself to stop bleeding. Whether he would bleed to death when he next slept remained to be seen.

"What now?" Starval asked, still unsteady from the beating that had taken him down.

"Sneezes," Evar said.

"Sneezes?"

"You said this was a maybe place. I said that it has to matter as much as where we came from. Everything matters, or nothing does. And we've seen where nothing mattering gets us." Evar still couldn't believe that Starval had stabbed him, or that they were standing together now almost as if it hadn't happened. "The barrel being loaded into Oldo's pub sneezed. I want to know why. It seems to me that there's no more reason to find Livira over there"—he pointed in a random direction—"than in Oldo's cellars. So, let's look there and satisfy my curiosity. After all, the Exchange spat us out there. And the Exchange has always put me somewhere significant."

"It put us in that bookshop to be specific."

"I'm checking out this damn barrel. Are you in or out?"

"In."

"You'd better lead the way then, because I have *no* idea where we are."

THE NIGHT DEEPENED and the mist grew shallower. The streets felt familiar, though whether his feet would lead him to the Stained Page if Starval stopped showing him the way, Evar couldn't say.

"What was that?" Starval spun, seeking the source.

Before Evar could answer, it came again, a blow struck from beneath, as if some giant were striking up from below with a great hammer. The impact made the bedrock shudder and set every rooftile rattling. But whatever the effect on the buildings around them might be, it was as nothing to the shock that ran through Evar. He lurched into the air and hung there as if on a butcher's hook, both his stab wound and the older stick-shot wound starting to pump black blood.

"Evar!" Starval ran for him.

A third shock came, like the tolling of some bell both far away and bigger than the world. And it took everything with it.

There are very few good reasons for someone putting a bag on your head. But in some cultures, that's just how they carry their bags.
                    Perspective and How to Change It, *by Jabari Abimbola*

CHAPTER 36

Livira

For the journey to the Saviour, Tremon insisted that Carlotte and Livira be blindfolded and hidden beneath sackcloth in the back of a cart. Since Tremon was head and shoulders taller than either of them, weighed more than both of them together, and had a canith and two crossbow men to back her up, there was no arguing.

"Scar," the younger of the two guards, drove the cart with seemingly nobody else to watch over them. He spent what felt like several hours clattering along city streets. Up the prevailing slope, down it, weaving in great figures of eight through built-up areas. Livira wondered who exactly the exercise was attempting to confuse.

Eventually the quality of the sound changed, and Livira understood that they had come inside some structure.

"Up you get, ladies."

The sacks were pulled away. Livira could see nothing in the gloom but heard large wooden doors being closed with the rickety banging of a stable rather than the portals to some great castle. The place smelled of hay and livestock too. Stiff, sore, and edging towards angry, she shuffled out of the cart.

"I've had enough of touching things now." Carlotte rubbed at her arms and side. "I'm ready to go back to being a ghost."

"This way." Their guide unhooded a lantern and led them past a series of stalls out of which the heads of incurious horses projected.

Rather than heading down, they aimed upwards this time, climbing a ladder into an attic as large as many churches. A second ladder led up to a trapdoor which opened after the man had knocked out a code. The secondary, much smaller, attic above had several shuttered windows offering potential escape routes over the roofs.

Tremon waited for them, crowding the place all by herself. Two well-armed guards squeezed in beside her, leaving space for a fourth person sitting in a plain wooden chair. This individual wore a white mask, curiously reminiscent of an assistant's face, and a black cape concealed the rest of their body.

Carlotte and Livira wedged themselves in with their guide coming up behind them to close the trapdoor. "Well, this is cosy." Carlotte beamed around at everyone, still enjoying the idea that so many people could see her.

Livira, more familiar with the consequences of being both visible and touchable, felt more apprehensive. The Saviour cut a sinister figure in his, or her, cape, dark eyes glittering behind the slits of their mask.

"The mysterious strangers." The Saviour's deep baritone settled Livira on "he." He sounded like an older man, not ancient, but far past the flush of youth. "Normally, I wouldn't entertain dealing with individuals who claim to have dropped into the city out of a clear blue sky. However, when you hear the nature of the matter in which you might be of aid to the cause, you will also understand my willingness to believe you."

"You've found a portal?" Livira guessed.

The Saviour raised his hand. "First, I want you to understand our struggle. I wouldn't ask you to risk yourselves in such a matter if it weren't for the stakes not just for this city but for the kingdom, and even our neighbours. The potentate has been carried to his throne on a river of blood. He has made demons of the Amacar, an ancient religious sect who have lived peacefully among us for centuries. Their suffering has been a thing of legend, and still, as I raise my hand to the one true god, that is far from the worst of his crimes. This kingdom he has stolen is nothing to him but a weapon with which he might cut himself a larger empire. There is no bottom to his greed, no limit to the lives he will spend to feed it.

"In short we exist to end the potentate's reign of terror and replace it with a lasting peace that is responsive to the will of the people and established on a foundation of fairness and tolerance."

Carlotte snorted, perhaps used to the ways of kings and would-be kings. "You want us to help you empty the throne so you can occupy it."

The Saviour tilted his head, and for a long moment of silence Carlotte was the focus of four disapproving stares, with only the Saviour's emotion hidden. "An ungenerous but not wholly inaccurate assessment. I wish someone better to lead us. Chosen by the people."

"I'm here for a book, not to kill anyone," Livira said.

"We just need you to get us in," Tremon said. "We'll do the rest. Just give us . . ."

The Saviour waved her to silence. "My spies tell me that the potentate has a book that opens doors. There is, in the mountain above us, a library of surpassing size and great antiquity. Many of its doors will admit neither man nor canith, and our ancestors have long believed that the secrets for true power lie behind them."

"It didn't feel like he was opening doors," Livira said. The blows she had felt had seemed to rock the city's foundations, but hardly anyone save her appeared to have noticed. The screaming hadn't started until the Escape had turned up at the tavern door. "Opening doors wouldn't make the library bleed."

"Bleeding? I suppose you could call it that." The Saviour inclined his head. "I hesitate to describe a book as a blunt weapon, but reports are that the potentate isn't using knowledge from inside the book to gain access to new chambers. Instead, he is—"

"Punching through walls?" That's what it had felt like.

"Correct." The mask hid any surprise. "The book is a source of great destructive power where the library is concerned. The potentate appears able to focus that destruction. His aim is far from perfect, however. Cracks are reported to be spreading from the passageways he has opened up, and those cracks are not confined to the library. Fissures are running beneath the city and one in particular looks to have connected the palace sewers to the main system. Allowing the possibility of sending a task force through to strike a blow for—"

"If you know about it, then they'll know about it too." Carlotte seemed unimpressed. "The fact you need this breach at all tells me the main access points are monitored."

"None of the sewer system is guarded anymore," Tremon growled, looking daggers at Carlotte for interrupting the Saviour. "It's too dangerous to go down there. Which also means they don't need guarding."

"Instead, they'll guard the exit points with three times the numbers," Carlotte said.

"The fissures are where the Escape came from." Livira understood why they wanted her now. "The blood monster," Livira clarified. "There are more of them down there?"

"Many," the Saviour agreed. "But you have a magic that works against them."

"It's not magic." Livira didn't want to explain further. Perhaps it was magic.

"And Narbla"—the Saviour mimed a pipe—"said you turned it away, ordered it to leave." He paused, as if expecting confirmation. "If you can not only clear the way for us but turn what had been impediments into allies, then you may be the salvation of this nation."

Livira waited for Carlotte to say, *So you mean she'll be the saviour and not you.* It felt too perfectly teed up, too completely Carlotte, for her not to say it. But she didn't.

"You'll help me secure the book?"

"If you promise to take it far away."

Livira eyed the mask. She wasn't sure she'd be able to read the truth on the man's face if it were exposed to the light, but the mask brought the fact home. Few of those who sought power would willingly pass up the chance of more. Perhaps the Saviour would have a change of heart when it came to letting the book go. On the other hand, were Livira to refuse to help, would he let her and Carlotte go? Or seek to compel them? Or simply discard their bodies in a ditch?

Livira exchanged a helpless glance with Carlotte. She hadn't expected or wanted to be hauled into the middle of a bloody intrigue, let alone intrigue on which the fate of a nation stood. She knew next to nothing about this potentate. The man might be a saint, painted as a devil by those who sought to overthrow him. "I . . ." She looked around the room, at the frowning faces of the four guards, at Tremon's blunt curiosity, at the Saviour's blank mask. "I need to be on the right side of this. Or at least, the least wrong. Make me believe this potentate of yours needs to die. Don't use words. I've heard enough words."

The Saviour nodded slowly. He turned to Tremon. "Let Narbla show them."

THE CART TRIP after leaving the stables hideout was shorter than the one that brought them to the Saviour, but no more comfortable.

"Bugger this. If he jolts us over one more pothole, I'm—"

"Ssssh!" Livira reached out under the sacking to cover Carlotte's mouth.

The cart slowed to another stop and someone clambered on to join or replace the driver. They rattled on around another couple of turns, through busier streets, then down a long incline. A low growl from the driver's seat. "This looks promising . . ."

Finally, they drew up somewhere quiet. Livira caught a whiff of pipe smoke.

"Out you get." The sacks were swept away to reveal a starry sky and the midnight silhouette of their original canith guide.

"Narbla, I assume." Livira edged off the cart, looking around.

The canith sniffed and took a pull on her pipe.

They were in a small loading area behind what seemed to be a smith's forge, closed for the night. Their original driver appeared to have abandoned them.

"I need somewhere to go," Carlotte complained.

Narbla shook her head. "Hold it." She puffed out a cloud of noxious smoke. "Come on." The glowing ember in her bowl led them through the dark. Behind Livira, Carlotte stumped her foot on something and hopped on, cursing.

Around the corner the light of scattered streetlamps replaced the starlight's efforts. The librarians of New Krath must have found different texts than those of Crath City, for their lamps had a different glow to those of Livira's youth, a whiter light but with a hint of blue and prone to sudden fluctuations. The street they illuminated wasn't crowded but a handful of citizens were in sight even at this late hour, all of them heading in the same direction. Narbla joined the flow. "Don't bring attention to yourselves." She cast an eye over Carlotte's tattered gown and shook her head. "If you can help it."

Livira and Carlotte followed, clutching themselves against the night cold. A strange urgency had taken hold of the citizens around them: they walked with the brisk determination of people not prepared to miss an appointment, a curious mix of seriousness and suppressed delight on their faces.

The numbers increased as they closed on a square where at least a dozen pitch torches held among the already gathered crowd competed with the street lighting. A woman's cries brought Livira's gaze to the open doorway of one of the tall, terraced houses that bordered the square. The place seemed to be the focus of the onlookers' attention. A black-clad canith emerged, military of some sort maybe, though his leathers didn't look like armour. He dragged the wailing human out behind him.

Carlotte tugged Livira's arm and nodded to where a man and two children stood in the custody of three human officers in the same ominous black uniforms.

The woman being dragged towards them, and the man, both looked too old to be the parents of such young children. Grandparents, Livira assumed.

"What's going on?" Carlotte hissed.

Narbla shushed her, gave her a hard stare, and placed one large hand on the back of her neck.

Two officers held the sobbing woman upright while the canith who had dragged her out prowled the perimeter of the clearing at the crowd's centre. Livira noticed with surprise that an untidy heap of books lay by the children's feet, as if tossed roughly to the ground.

"Helma and Ivon Gradson!" The canith announced, pointing an accusing finger in the old couple's direction. "Seemingly honest members of our society. They even have the potentate's portrait hanging in their entrance hall . . . but . . ." He spread a hand towards the two pale-faced children. ". . . they had rats in their cellar! Amacar rats!"

The mob sucked in its breath as though this were a revelation. Those with torches pushed to the front, a ring of fire. The canith officer continued with his street theatre. "It doesn't end there. It doesn't end with sheltering the children of those who seek to undermine us. It doesn't end with raising another generation bent on corruption, theft, and moral decay. Impure blood to pollute the lineages of our glorious city." He shook his head and turned his accusing finger on the piled books. "Apparently, the Gradsons are 'intellectuals.'" He put such scorn into the word that the crowd laughed. "Apparently, the library isn't sufficient for them. They need their own collection. And behind the first row of the Gradsons' books, what do we find? Subversive filth by Amacar authors. Pollution between two covers. Wrong thinking that the true library would never allow within its great halls."

He drew a silver flask from inside his jacket and, removing the top, splashed the contents liberally over the books, not caring that the two children were also splattered.

"Light it."

Without further invitation, the torches among the crowd were tossed in, and the pile of books burst into flame with a great whoomph of heat. The children screamed and struggled, allowed a measure of retreat only when the blaze became too hot for those holding them.

Livira stepped in close to Narbla. "How do they know the children are Amacar? You said it was a faith."

"And a culture, shared among a particular race of humans and a particular race of canith," Narbla replied in a low voice beneath the jeers of the crowd as chains were set around the old couple's wrists. "You can tell by looking, if you look hard enough." She turned away.

"What will happen to them?" Livira couldn't look away. The people's faces, lit by the burning books, had a demonic aspect to them, their hate now something visceral, unleashed by the fire.

Narbla turned back, her face grim. "The people who sheltered them will be put in prison, their property taken by the state. Or, if they don't know anyone with any influence, they might just be hanged at the Alarg. The children will probably be sent to Artha Island. It would be kinder to hang them too." She paused, letting the fire speak below the cruel laughter and the insults of the crowd. Fragments of burning pages spiralled up with a smoke that stank of old memories. "Are you in?"

"Hell yes," Carlotte answered without hesitation.

Livira watched the flames dance a moment longer. "I'm in."

Sometimes the best means to secure an invitation is to eloquently express your disinterest. Other times you have to kill a whole bunch of people.
The Debutant's Handbook, by Lady Jane Ashen

CHAPTER 37

Arpix

The dozen fliers were the end of it. Arpix had imagined that a storm of them might descend. He had been attacked on these same slopes by many hundreds of the things. He'd watched colleagues die there: the bookbinders Kleeson and Brigha with whom he'd spent five years on the Arthran Plateau.

But twelve were the limit of the message that the skeer had sent. Twelve to undo any lies that might be told by exhibiting their crippled brethren. Twelve to re-instil any fear that seeing the soldier skeer die beneath a hail of bullets had erased.

Clovis had swung the balance of that equation back towards the city. Her remarkable display of violence had established once more that the insectoids were beatable. It was a lie that might last as long as the skeer's true numbers remained hidden from the potentate's subjects.

For these reasons and more, Arpix wasn't worried that the new waves of soldiers rushing into the square were there to arrest Clovis in connection with the killings from the previous day. The rapturous applause of the crowd might have soured very rapidly if the troops had turned their guns on the only warrior to have convincingly bested a skeer.

Arpix clambered down from his seat and was amazed to find himself not the first to enter the killing ground. He hurried forward amid people who, having seen what they just saw, now wanted to step through the gory remains of the fallen champions to laud the sole survivor. A ring of soldiers formed around Clovis, keeping back the more enthusiastic members of the public who seemed determined to touch her. If not for the shouting, Arpix might have tried to tell them how badly such an invasion of her personal space would end.

While Arpix stood outside the ring of bristling guns, several dignitaries descended from the stands to address Clovis in person. Two lords in plush robes that looked too warm for the day, burdened beneath gold chains, and a tall canith lady with a tumbling purple mane and diamonds around her neck, shattering the sunlight into dazzling pieces. Arpix watched as they addressed Clovis. Words were exchanged, primarily between the two canith, who at least saw eye to eye.

It didn't take long for Clovis to scan the crowd and point Arpix out. More words were exchanged before a group of four soldiers came to secure Arpix's passage within the cordon. The three aristocrats eyed him with varying degrees of disbelief.

"This is the expert?" one of the lords asked, an older man with a greying beard and deep-set eyes.

"He saved me from a cratalac the day after I met him," Clovis said. "The thing was too much for me."

Arpix couldn't help the apologetic shrug that took hold of him, but he didn't deny the story. It was true, after all.

"We'll meet this potentate of yours together or not at all."

Eyebrows were raised, but nobody was ready to argue with a flame-maned warrior still dripping with the ichor of half a dozen skeer.

THE ELEGANT LADY Gharra suffered Clovis's presence in her personal carriage without laying down protective sheets first. She seemed somehow more hesitant to allow Arpix in, despite his relatively unsoiled appearance. Somewhat mortified, Arpix remembered quite how long it had been since his last good wash, and how sensitive a canith's nose was. He felt himself shade to crimson as he squeezed in beside Clovis, wondering if Lady Gharra's nose might provide her with a full account of Arpix's night. Clovis, on the other hand, seemed unconcerned, growling to her new sponsor a comment that Arpix couldn't decipher.

The driver shook his reins and the horses set off, pulling them along at a speed that Arpix had never experienced before. He took the door handle in a white-knuckled grip and tried to pay attention as Lady Gharra continued to quiz Clovis on where exactly she'd come from.

Clovis proved remarkably bad at lying, and uninterested in trying. After failing to deflect their host with "a small place to the east," she turned to Arpix. "You explain it. I'm tired now."

"You're bleeding!" Arpix pointed to a damp patch around a rent in her newly acquired cape, high on her shoulder.

"It's just a flesh wound."

"What other sorts are there?" Arpix looked up at Lady Gharra. "She needs to be seen by a surgeon." He reached for the cape. "Let me see! You'll need stitches at least— Ow!" He snatched his hand back, stinging from Clovis's slap.

"We can deal with it later," she growled.

Lady Gharra smiled. "Wherever you're from, I can see that you've come a long way together."

"We've come from the library," Arpix said, knowing that the questions would not stop. "Things are falling apart. Doorways are opening. We're not from around here. Not this city, not this kingdom, nor continent."

Lady Gharra's eyes widened but perhaps not so much as they might have if this was a complete shock to her.

The carriage rolled sedately out of the square, and Arpix watched a city both strange and strangely familiar go by. A city built of maybes and of different choices, just as every life and every city is. As the driver turned left and right, it seemed to Arpix a portrait of the decisions that, individually and en masse, shaped both people and worlds.

It felt inevitable that King Oanold would be waiting for them in the potentate's throne. Where else would such a man's personal evil and hunger for power take him but across the bodies of the persecuted and defenceless to his own benefit? In this city, just as in Arpix's, Oanold lay at the heart of the disease which time and again dragged his species through cycles of destruction. It was Oanold who, with the library in his grasp, had not merely ignored its lessons, but taken great efforts to paint over them with lies more pleasing to his ears than the inconvenient truths of collective experience.

Anger had long been a stranger to Arpix. He'd lived a monk's life, an austere existence dominated by learning. But as Clovis had opened new chambers within his mind, those discoveries hadn't been limited to new excesses of good feelings. Surrender to emotion carried edges that cut both ways. Arpix's detachment had shielded him to some degree from the horror that Oanold had thrust upon him. Now, raw from the exposure Clovis had drawn him into, insisting with her honesty and appetite that his soul come forward into the light, and be shared . . . he found that anger, rage even, flared when he thought of Oanold's many crimes.

Irad and Jaspeth might be the avatars of some ancient struggle over the alpha and omega of mankind and many other kinds. But the real war was surely the one that Oanold and his lackeys brought with them everywhere they went. The real evil was easy enough to point at, and Clovis's solution, to cut it out with her white blade, felt more reasonable with each passing moment as the distance to their destination narrowed.

CLOVIS HAD TO surrender her sword at the main door. The potentate's palace stood more or less in the space once occupied by the Allocation Hall in Arpix's version of the city. He wondered what Crath City looked like now, two centuries after the canith had sacked it and beneath the vast skeer hive. Were its towers levelled, or thick with the insectoids' eggs?

Such pondering distracted Arpix from the opulence of the hallways and corridors through which Lady Gharra led them, now with a contingent of palace guards to watch over them. Arpix realised how unmoored he'd become from his old life, how adrift on a sea of time and possibility, unable to return to former shores. All that mattered to him now were the friends he'd made, or rather who had made him their friend. They were the foundation that he carried with him. The finding of those friends was the reason he was walking towards the throne room of a murderous dictator. The grand matters of the library's fate, of the futures of the seemingly endless species whose intelligence bound them to Irad's great work, all of that was somehow secondary to securing the safety and company of the people he'd grown with.

As they came to a halt before a towering pair of gold-plated doors, Arpix considered that he had perhaps stumbled across the paradox that lay at the heart of the problem. He lacked the farsightedness required to see past the cycles of destruction to a solution, but the short-sightedness that afflicted him, the focus on friends and family, was at its core what being human was, and without it—

"You're doing it again," Clovis said.

"What?" Arpix blinked and looked around at the servants and guards on all sides.

"Thinking too much. I can hear your brain grinding."

The doors began to open, saving Arpix from a futile denial. Even though he knew the throne room had been constructed specifically with the goal of impressing people, he was impressed. Though far smaller than a library chamber, it somehow made Arpix believe, at least on an emotional level, that it was larger. Pillars of pinkish marble, veined with purple, black, and gold, held aloft a ceiling from which a god and his angelic host peered down through painted clouds.

Armed guards stood at attention within the shadows of each pillar. On a musicians' gallery there would surely be hidden guns aimed at the hearts of any who approached the throne. Arpix resisted telling Clovis of the impossibility of action. She would know already, better than he did. And his comment would see them arrested immediately.

The glitter of courtiers was confined to either side of the throne, where a dozen lords and ladies stood. The floor seemed to have been given over to petitioners, or perhaps to those on whom the potentate was going to pass judgement. Given the swift and summary nature of his own death sentence, Arpix imagined that only the richest or most significant of New Kraff's citizenry got to be sent to the gallows by the potentate's personal command.

Lady Gharra led them to the end of a short line of petitioners, all more grandly attired than Arpix or Clovis. The man immediately ahead of them, whose considerable girth was bound up in purple velvet, and whose obvious wig shimmered with what looked to be gold dust, sniffed loudly, and turned to identify Arpix as the source of his disgust. To her credit, Clovis didn't punch the lordling.

The figure on the throne was still too distant for Arpix to identify as Oanold. The potentate looked like a geyser of costly fabrics, practically imprisoned by the weight of silks and satins that flowed in all directions, and his wig was considerably larger than his head, with oversized grey coils mounded around him. And yet this was the man who had apparently de-monized a sizeable chunk of his population in order to elevate himself to power. He'd plunged the Amacar into a nightmare to provide his people with someone to hate, and to unite them around that common purpose.

One of the courtiers stepped up onto the dais and, coming up behind the throne to avoid the overspill of trailing cape, leaned around the great gilded chair to whisper to the ruler.

The potentate's head lifted and turned until it fixed its shadowed gaze in Arpix's direction.

"Lady Gharra." The man's voice held a familiar croak of petulance. "You may approach with your guests."

The purple-maned lady led the way, and Arpix, shooting a final, furious warning look at Clovis, followed.

"Illustrious Sir." Lady Gharra bowed so low before the throne that Ar-pix finally got his first clear view of the potentate.

Two shrewd, dark eyes met his, underhung with pouchy, discoloured bags of skin. The slightly bulbous nose, pallid complexion powdered to the point at which cracks started to show around his jowls, the loose, wet mouth . . . Arpix knew him in an instant. Oanold, the cannibal king, the man who had ordered slaughter in the library, whose troops had set it aflame. The same venal, cruel, indulgent suppresser of truth who had hunted the weak from the throne of Crath City instead of ensuring the safety of its people.

"I feel I know you from somewhere." Oanold stared at Arpix, then glanced at Clovis with a frown. "The angry one too . . ."

"Illustrious Sir." Lady Gharra straightened, trying to push surprise from her face. "Mistress Clovis here saved many lives, including my own, at the tourney in Blue Tower Square today. She killed more than a dozen bugs . . . with a sword . . ." She still sounded unable to believe it.

"Ah yes." Oanold continued to frown. "That was today, wasn't it? Where's that fellow everyone loves. Looks like a pirate. Golden-something?"

"Erico Goldeye, Illustrious Sir." Lady Gharra winced. "He was the first to die. All of the champions are dead, nearly a score of soldiers too. An unexpected incursion of winged bugs. She killed them all." Gharra spread her hand towards Clovis, who certainly looked fierce enough to make the story believable.

"Remarkable." The potentate sounded less than pleased. "And this one?" He flapped a jewelled hand in Arpix's direction.

"An expert in killing the bugs, Illustrious Sir. Both Master Arpix and Mistress Clovis come to us from the library as a result of recent developments there."

"I see . . ." Oanold narrowed his eyes at Arpix as if trying to see past the barriers holding back the recollections of an alternate life. "Interesting. So, really, they count as my discoveries."

"Indeed, Illustrious Sir." Lady Gharra inclined her head.

Arpix edged closer to Clovis and set a hand upon her wrist, finding it vibrating with invisible but palpable rage. She might be unarmed and surrounded by palace guards, but Arpix didn't entirely trust her not to leap on the potentate there and then. He squeezed and hoped that the squeeze conveyed both his understanding of the depth of her passion, along with the assurance that there would be a better time.

"And you two have come to offer me your services, have you?" Oanold looked from Clovis to Arpix and back again.

"We have," Arpix stated with a surety he didn't feel. He needed to stop Clovis speaking. If she didn't speak, there was still a chance that Oanold wouldn't understand that the reckless hate in her eyes was all for him. "We went to the tournament to prove our credentials."

"It sounds as if you impressed Lady Gharra, at least." Oanold's sour look suggested that he was still chewing over some grievance he couldn't quite put into words. "But the leader of nations can't hand out trust on hearsay." He ran his tongue over yellowing teeth. "You came from the library, you say?"

"We did." Arpix inclined his head, choosing not to elaborate.

The potentate nodded. "Indulge me for a short while." He waved his fingers in a shooing motion. Lady Gharra immediately bowed and started to back away. Arpix followed her example. Clovis, although she couldn't bring herself to bow, retreated from the throne without so much as a snarl.

Gharra took them almost to the ring of pillars that supported the false heavens above them.

"What are we doing?" Clovis hissed through clenched teeth.

"Indulging the potentate," Gharra murmured. "Waiting. Because he's told us to wait."

And so, they waited. The potentate summoned and dispatched a courtier, then turned his attention back to the supplicants before him. Over the course of perhaps an hour he dealt with seven cases, almost all of which concerned land disputes. He ruled on the cases without enthusiasm, ensuring that the state grew richer whatever the outcome. A merchant dealing in imported gun barrels complained that a particular general had dealt with him unfairly. A modest amount of compensation was ordained, but the merchant had to ensure increased supplies in the coming year.

Clovis made no effort to hide her boredom, and even Arpix found himself struggling to hide the yawns that wanted to crack his jaw. It had been a night with far less sleeping and far more exercise than he was used to. Since he wasn't absorbed by the court proceedings, he was one of the first to notice the great doors start to open.

The object that the widening gap between the doors revealed looked familiar. A large rectangular box covered by a black cloth big as a sail. It rumbled forward on poorly oiled wheels, and it was their squeaking as much as anything else that stopped the potentate mid-flow and drew every eye.

"Ah." The potentate waved the guardsmen forward, pointing to where they should position their charge.

Arpix's heart fell. Another skeer. Clovis would have to butcher another maimed soldier to convince the potentate, or perhaps the exercise was simply to entertain the members of court who had felt themselves too lofty to join Lady Gharra at such a spectacle. He steeled himself for violence as he watched the guards manoeuvre the object and a sudden horrible thought clutched at his insides with icy fingers. What if it was *his* alleged expertise the potentate wanted a demonstration of? Would Oanold's evident distaste for Arpix overcome any arguments that his skills were tactical not hand-to-hand, or would he be forced into a hopeless contest?

Oanold rose from his throne, fabric sliding across the floor, a shimmering mass trailing his advance. "Not everything that has escaped the library recently has been deserving of trust, or even mercy." He turned his pouchy stare from Arpix to Clovis. "It seems that some of those emerging from the beyond within—I rather like that one, 'the beyond within.'" He singled out a man near the end of the courtier line. "Jammon, write that one down." Oanold paused a yard in front of his throne. "Some of those emerging from our library in the aftermath of my great work there have demonstrated a natural affinity with the most corrupt elements that plague honest society. Some have no sooner found their way into our great city than they've offered aid to the parasites that drain our wealth and poison our blood."

The potentate glanced around the great cavern of his throne room as if seeking someone, anyone, to challenge his statements. He settled at last on Arpix. "You've won Lady Gharra's seal of approval as a person who knows the bugs. Now win mine as a person ready to bring ruin to my enemies."

All around the chamber's perimeter guards shifted their grip on their weapons. Up in the musicians' gallery, no longer sheltering behind the players, three guards stood, each with a long gun aimed at Arpix's heart.

At the lift of a single finger, a palace guardsman strode towards Arpix and thrust a spear into his hands.

"Really . . ." Arpix stammered. "I couldn't—"

A second guard whipped the cloth from the cage. Rather than the single skeer that Arpix had dreaded, three figures stood inside. Kerrol, Yute, and the child Arpix now knew to be Yute's daughter.

Oanold waved Arpix forward. "Kill them for me."

Eons of biological evolution have shaped us to protect children. Their innocence, ignorance, and helplessness in the face of the world's dangerous complexity call to our protective instincts. But the truth is that we're all children in the grip of the callous indifference existence shows us.

Grimdark, Grimdarker, Grimdarkest, by Michael R. Baked

CHAPTER 38

Evar

O ldo's an idiot, but I don't think he's kidnapping children," Starval said.

"An idiot?" Evar had quite liked the landlord of the Stained Page.

Starval nodded. "A blowhard, a bit of a bully on occasion, a boaster, a fool, in short: an ass."

"You got all that from him delivering two helpings of stew and two plates of ribs?"

"I listen, and I ask questions." Starval shrugged. "While you were out hunting for the latrine, I was chatting with my boys Gothon and Abra."

"Huh." Evar blinked and followed Starval down the street. The mists had all but gone and it wouldn't be long before dawn started to nudge the horizon. He supposed that Oldo, like many people, could present different faces to the world depending on who he thought his audience was. Whatever he'd got hidden in those barrels would reveal yet another face. "Kids? I told you about a sneeze. I didn't say anything about kids."

"You obviously don't have a very good handle on how large humans are." Starval snorted. "The ale barrels I've seen here haven't been big enough for an adult, not even a small human one. If he's transporting something that can sneeze in them, and it's not some sort of animal, then it's children. What his interest in children is . . . I couldn't say. But if it's the most common one in cases like this then I'll stab him myself, no charge. And this time if the first blow doesn't kill him, it really will be because I want to hurt him."

THE STAINED PAGE looked very different, the lights within extinguished. The undercurrent of chatter no longer bubbled through its small windows. Its façade seemed like the face of a friend's fresh corpse: very little changed from when life had animated it, but even so, you could instantly tell that something vital had gone missing.

"Curious," Starval muttered as he led Evar beneath the hanging sign and on past the door they had entered by the previous day.

"What was?"

"Someone forced entry. You didn't see the repairs?"

Evar hadn't. He'd been too wrapped in his musings.

Starval circled around to the rear of the tavern, missing the next alley and taking a longer-than-necessary route down the street after it. When they reached the back wall, he vaulted over it in one fluid motion, finding a foothold halfway up where Evar saw none, and clearing the broken glass on top by a finger's width.

"Come on!" Hissed from the far side.

Evar walked on several more strides, binding a strap of book-leather around his palm several times for protection. With more effort and less grace than his brother he too scrambled over, dropping in perilously close to the latrine huts, and in the other half of the yard to that which Starval had landed in.

Starval opened the door in the wall that separated the patrons' toilet area from the unloading docks and leaned through. "Come on." He beckoned. "Idiot."

Evar hurried to join his brother and came to stand by what he took to be the hatch down which incoming carts unloaded their barrels. With only Attamast's crescent and scattered starlight to illuminate the scene, the place was hard to make sense of. "Locked," he whispered, taking hold of the padlock that secured the heavy chain binding the two handles of the hatch doors.

"It is." Starval nodded. He'd squatted on his haunches, examining a pile of rags by the tavern wall.

"So pick it." Evar's irritation rose. Starval had defeated the lock on the door between the two sections of the yard so quickly that Evar half suspected it had been left open. "Let's get down there and see what we can find."

"Not much, I'm thinking," Starval said. "This place has been raided. My guess is that any barrels we find down there are going to be empty, or full of ale."

"Still worth trying!" Evar worked the largest of his picks from the pocket of his leathers, all made from metal fittings recovered from books. Unlike Starval, he'd never had the chance to practise in the Mechanism, only on locked books in the library. Still, nothing was more likely to motivate Starval to open the padlock than Evar's inexpert fumbling.

"Or we could just ask Gothon here." Starval slipped an arm under the pile of rags. "I don't think he's quite as dead as he's pretending to be."

The figure groaned as Starval lifted it into a sitting position, confirming the assassin's diagnosis. Evar could make out the tangled mass of the canith's hair now, still with the thicket of wooden pegs decorating the many individual locks.

"You're not going to make it." Starval moved Gothon's hair clear of his face. "Best to meet your maker without secrets weighing you down, no?"

A dark patch on Gothon's side bubbled as he coughed and sucked at the air as he tried to breathe. "Go to hell."

"Honestly." Starval shook his head. "You wouldn't believe us if I told you where we'd come from, but you can believe that we've got no skin in this game. My brother is just incurably curious. He heard a barrel sneeze. What can you tell us about that? Before you die would be good, because, like I say, you haven't got long. I mean, it's sad and all that, but you're pretty old anyway. And this way you dodge the bugs."

"Fuc . . . Fuck. You."

Evar pulled Starval back and crouched beside the old man. "I'm sorry about my brother. I'm actually here trying to teach him that people matter. A work in progress, as you can see." Evar tried to pull up his leathers and turn his side towards Gothon. "I was also stabbed in an attempted murder tonight . . . you should—ouch—be able to see the wound? Anyway, I'm sorry this happened to you." Evar met Gothon's eyes. "I can't make any promises. I really have no idea what's going on here. I just heard a barrel sneeze. But I can say that where my brother goes, people have a habit of dying. If you point us towards the person who gave you this injury, there's a good chance they'll be dead before the day's out." He reached for Gothon's hand and held it tight. If Evar were dying, he would want someone with him. Someone who saw him. Less than a day ago they had been sharing ales around a table, talking of the future. Whatever this was, it wasn't right. And the strongest emotion he felt was sorrow.

"Oldo . . ." Gothon laboured for breath. "Hiding Amacar . . . children in the cellar . . . part . . . of a network . . . I was helping—"

"Bullshit." Starval pushed his way back into the man's view. "You hate Amacar . . ." He trailed off.

"Not so sharp . . . as you thought . . . you was." Gothon's laugh dissolved into painful coughing. Blood ran black from his mouth. Eyes that glittered in the starlight looked from Starval to Evar.

"Why would he do that?" Evar asked, Starval's assessment of the landlord still fresh in his mind: a bully, a braggart, a blowhard.

Gothon tried to shrug but abandoned the effort with a gasp of pain. "Bloody-minded . . . he is . . . that one. He'd tell you . . . all sorts of . . . honourable . . . reasons." He panted for breath, trying not to cough again. "Me . . . I think he . . . just wanted to thumb . . . his nose at the potentate." His voice fell to a whisper. ". . . to start with at least . . . Took a shine to some of . . . them kids . . . took risks he didn't have to . . . got . . . them." He trailed off, eyes glassy. Evar turned to meet Starval's gaze. "Got them away." Gothon surprised them both by not being dead. But that, it seemed, was his last gasp, and he slumped against the wall.

Starval stood, wiping his hands on his leathers. "Well. There you are. A heart of gold behind a rough exterior . . . or something. Can we go now?"

Evar released Gothon's hand, setting it across his lap. He stood slowly, burdened with mixed emotions. "'Heart of gold' seems to be pushing it." He felt that the truer assessment would be, like the man in question, complicated. "People can do the right thing for the wrong reasons."

"And the wrong thing for the right reasons." Starval magicked a coin into his hands. "That's why I decided upon a simpler, transactional moral-ity. But you've stolen that from me, brother. You and Mayland." The coin vanished. "So, now we find this girl of yours?"

"Where do you think they've taken him?"

"Oldo? No idea. Some dungeon where they can cut pieces off him, most likely."

"Oldo and the children."

"They send the kids to an island. They don't come back. Worked to death, from what I've heard."

Evar frowned. He wasn't here for this. There were probably atrocities being carried out in the world he'd left behind. There would be murder and mayhem in each of the maybes they had climbed through to reach this one. He felt small and helpless and unworthy of any love that Livira might have had for him. "King Oldo. That's what he said to call him."

"Unless you were his friend."

"And Gothon thought he started this to spite the potentate. A distant heir to the old dynasty, fighting the potentate's core policy." Evar walked towards the street gate. "That sounds like the sort of man who might war-rant a public execution. That sort of man might even get taken before the potentate himself, for judgement?"

"He might." Starval shrugged.

"Ever assassinated a potentate?" Evar dug for the silver he'd taken from Starval. He dug deeper, fingers finding only space. "You stole—" But no, Starval had left him a single coin. Evar held it out to him.

"Emperor, prince, king, sultan, and sultana, magister, queen, overlord . . . satrap . . ." Starval counted them off on his fingers. "But no." He took the coin from Evar's grasp. "I don't believe I've ever ended a po-tency."

Evar lifted the gate bar. "Potency? Is that what they call it? Really?" He pushed the gates open.

"Fucked if I know." Starval walked through. "Maybe we can ask him."

To sneak into a palace was, Starval explained, an extremely difficult thing to do. The methods employed to stop exactly that thing had been evolved over very many years of trial and error, each failure underlined by a dead monarch of some description. To sneak into a palace that one had not observed at length was suicide. Preferably, the assassin would have visited the building in a friendly guise, checking out the interior organisation in a leisurely manner. Ideally, they would possess plans for the structure—ones that included secret passages, hidden doors, and concealed defences.

"You're saying you can't do it?" Evar asked.

"I'm saying that we're going to end up leaving a lot more bodies behind us than just this potentate of yours. I'm saying that the alarm is probably going to be raised, and that you'll be called on to use everything our sister taught you. And that if we're not quick, then the potentate—who could well be this human king we're looking for and have this book we want—will just be bundled off by his guards to somewhere even more difficult to get at. I'm saying that the sensible thing to do would be to observe the place for a week, to find a way to get inside officially, and to plan ahead for as many eventualities as we can think of."

"I'm not waiting. Oldo will be dead or tortured within a day. You said so yourself. And those children—"

"Children you have never even laid eyes on, brother. Children who are part of a stream flowing to this murder island. A place where they've been dying for several years now."

"It doesn't matter. I'm going—"

"And if I told you there were babies being murdered in another land across a wide ocean? Would we set sail as soon as we're done here? You can't save everyone, Evar. When we stepped through that chamber door, the world grew so much bigger. You have to learn when to let go."

"And you have to learn when to take hold." Evar shaded his eyes against the day's sunshine. The city, whose existence he had half doubted in the enfolding fog, now shone before him, its palace a magnificent thing, too huge to find a single man in. "So. How do we start?"

THEY STARTED WITH a fire. Starval had used the last of his stolen money to buy supplies on the way up to the palace early that morning. The process had proved difficult as both brothers were finding it hard to understand the locals, and vice versa. Starval speculated that the Exchange's translation effects, which Mayland had used his knowledge to try to extend, were wearing off.

Their distraction required a distraction. Evar had drawn forth a handful of his blood—a painful and unpleasant process—and fashioned from it a black monster, a miniature cratalac that he set chasing people in the street beside the wall of the palace gardens. The screams and panic drew the eyes of guards in two watchtowers with overview of the road.

Starval took the opportunity to toss a ball of rags over the wall into a place where the green-clad branches of several trees waved above the surrounding masonry. A few minutes later the alchemical wonder he'd buried within the rags ignited, and the device began to emit copious amounts of smoke that billowed out from the tight-packed foliage.

Evar and Starval climbed quickly and dropped into bushes.

"Well, that shouldn't have worked." Starval confirmed that the shrubbery now concealing them was not their first bit of luck.

Evar frowned in concentration, focusing his will until his blood-golem joined them. He gave it the form of a horse now, finding that far less disturbing than a cratalac's nightmare shape. He picked it up and put it in a pocket, unwilling to return the stuff to his veins. "We should have done this earlier, when it was still dark," he muttered.

"There's an entire literature on that, brother. Darkness conceals, but a rich man's house turns in on itself in the witching hours, sealing its points of entry. The palace is expecting visitors. Its doors are as open as they ever get."

And with that Starval began their covert approach through the statue-dotted greenery of the potentate's gardens towards the palace and the invitations of its hundred windows.

"AND THAT WAS TOO easy as well." Starval closed the shutters over the window he'd forced and looked around the empty chamber.

"I can hear a bell." As Evar mentioned it, the distant noise stopped. The room they were in was bigger than some of the houses they'd passed on the way. Large portraits, darkened by age, and bright displays of polished weapons, decorated the walls. More colour and plaster mouldings made a wonder of the ceiling, and the artistry lavished on the furniture dropped Evar's jaw. "Why is no one here?"

"That's palaces for you." Starval moved to the door opposite the window. "More rooms than they know what to do with." He oiled the handle. "I believe that bell was an alarm of some sort. Which might explain why we're getting away with this. Someone else is providing a distraction for us."

"That seems . . . unlikely." Evar joined him.

"As unlikely as meeting Oldo on the day he's taken prisoner?"

Evar opened his mouth to say *Yes, even more so*, but closed it again, realising that Starval's point wasn't to quibble over odds, but to remind him that the Exchange had delivered them with a sense of purpose and timing. Though what that purpose might be, Evar had no idea.

The pair of them made staccato progress, covering entire corridors in a swift advance, sheltering in a doorway for long minutes. Wherever the emergency was it seemed that the problem lay in some distant part of the palace, and was drawing guards from their posts.

"It's here," Evar said. "The book." He looked around as if it might have been carelessly abandoned on a windowsill.

"You can feel it?"

"It's here. Maybe not close."

Evar followed Starval, trying to exercise whatever part of him had shivered with recognition. He hadn't written the book, but he was in it. He had literally travelled within its pages, and somehow those pages reached out for him even now. They reached in some ephemeral way, wound so closely around simple hope, that in the next moment he could convince himself that hope was all it had ever been. But no. It was there.

He wondered if the book had played a role in what had happened to them all, and what now enveloped them. Oanold had fallen, clutching the book. They had all followed through a broken space still churning with the disrupting currents of its passage.

Livira had written her book in innocence, a compendium of her hopes and fears, loves, losses, an account of her life, an aspiration of life to come. But Mayland, and Starval—he had to admit Starval's hand in this—both his brothers, guided by Jaspeth, had fashioned Livira's work into a weapon that could destroy the indestructible library.

Was a weapon all it was now? A burning fault-line running through worlds? Or was it still a book too? Books, in Evar's experience, were always trying to show you something. They might shout it into your face, the author's spittle practically flying from the page, or they might make you work to tease it from a story that seemingly ran in the opposite direction. But whatever their approach, books would, if given the opportunity, lead you to some window in a high tower, or crack open a door you had passed a thousand times and never truly seen, or venture up a mountainside to a rocky shoulder from where an unsuspected vista opened out before you. They would show the reader something, and there, on the edge of some new understanding, small or great, invite another step.

But here, hunting evil, deep in the heart of the potentate's power, what lesson could be learned? Oanold had taken the book, fallen into another life, and here he was, inflicting new terrors on new people. Was that what the book had wanted to show them—that Oanold was somehow the worm at the centre of any rot? That his malignance spanned worlds, time, and possibility? Had Clovis's instinct for revenge been right all along?

"Focus!" Starval yanked on Evar's mane. "This is difficult enough without your mind wandering. Be here. Now. Not off with your girl."

Twice, servants happened across them, but as Starval had moved in for the kill Evar had deflected him. Instead, he'd dazed them with a few blows, then left them bound and gagged behind furniture in rooms that he guessed would receive few visitors.

Starval tutted and shook his head but accepted the added danger as part of whatever lesson Evar was attempting to teach him. It was a lesson that Evar was far from sure of himself. He wanted Starval to share his own instinct for mercy. Softness, Starval would call it. Weakness. And Evar, perhaps agreeing, but convinced there was more to it as well, could, despite all his reading, find no convincing form of words that might change his brother's heart. It seemed to be a thing you just knew or didn't know. Evar couldn't leave it at that though. Perhaps Livira would know a better way. Or Yute, or Kerrol, though he had never sought to change Starval's mind, merely to observe it.

The second servant had been a canith, and in his uniform Evar led Starval through new corridors and up a flight of stairs. One guard, with a long gun at his side, remained at post on the stairs while somewhere below them muffled gunfire could be heard. Some combination of his distraction, combined with the supreme confidence with which Starval followed his "guide," allowed the brothers past without challenge.

"What are the odds?" Evar muttered. "Someone else is invading the palace just when we break in?"

"Long," Starval said. "Astronomical if the events are not connected."

"It's got to be the others, right? Mayland's found an army somewhere?"

Starval shrugged. "We should keep to the mission. Play this to our advantage." He turned another corner into another luxurious stretch of corridor, adorned with paintings, tapestries, and niches in which stood painted vases, marble busts, ornate clocks. "This room." Starval pulled up short before a small, unimpressive door.

"Why that one?"

"It's something functional. We need to get behind the scenes." Starval knelt to pick the lock. The whole time he fiddled, Evar glanced nervously back and forth along the corridor with its many, grander, doors. With each passing moment the risk of interruption grew. Evar would fight, but he didn't want to. His mind's eye saw the walls sprayed with blood, the carpet darkened, and he shuddered.

"There." Starval pushed through.

The chamber beyond was small, smelled musty, and contained only baskets of furniture sheets, and a chute to some level far below where less favoured servants would presumably launder whatever needed laundering.

"Well, that was a waste of time." Evar turned to go.

"You'll notice that someone left a lit lantern hanging in here." Starval made no move to leave. "That lock was a work of art. And the carpet outside is more worn than any other place we've seen. A light, an expensive lock, and a stream of visitors to a laundry chute in this particular part of the palace. None of that makes a great deal of sense."

He went to the wall and began to walk slowly around the perimeter, pushing baskets from his path with his feet while his fingers trailed the stonework.

"A secret door? Really?" Evar looked around. "Here?"

"*Here* to be precise." Starval thumped the wall and a panel swung noiselessly open. "Follow me. Be very quiet."

Evar followed into the tight spaces within the walls. Starval chose not to take the lantern, and its light did not follow them far. Evar fought a newly discovered fear of confinement and squeezed through after his brother.

Quite how Starval navigated in the blackness, Evar had no idea. The space smelled dusty and sour. Things crawled in the dark and scurried there. Starval found a flight of stairs so narrow in places that Evar had to turn sideways to negotiate them, then banged his head, and lacking space to bend, had to lean painfully forward. It would have been uncomfortable even without a fresh knife wound in his side.

Eventually Starval stopped. Evar swallowed the need to ask why. He stood for a long moment with his hand to the assassin's back, listening. The faint hints of a voice reached him.

Noiselessly a long vertical crack of light appeared. It grew no wider than a finger's width. Starval crouched, allowing Evar to lean over him for a look. The sliver of vision revealed a small gallery. A soldier knelt by the balustrade, training his gun down into the space below. Through the shaped columns of the balustrade a throne could be seen, its high back adorned with golden turrets. The attention of the bewigged figure seated there lay upon two large cages, each big enough for a human on horseback. In one, several figures lay sprawled, dead or dying. In the other Oldo stood by himself, gripping the bars, and by the tone of his voice, giving the potentate a piece of his mind.

Behind Evar the sound of boots on stone steps rang out. Many boots. The size of a force that doesn't care about stealth or surprise.

"They've found us." Evar turned with a sinking heart and drew his knife. Better for the confined space, as long as he could avoid the first thrust of sword or spear. Of course, if the guards chose to open fire, then all his skill would count for little.

"I'll take out the man on the throne." Starval pushed the door to the balcony wider. "A good day to die, brother."

"A good day to die." Until Evar said the words, he had stood at the centre of a tug-of-war between faint chances and unlikely options. Now all of that went away. He wanted to live, of course he did, but perhaps it was easier this way, the unresolvable dispute resolved. The looming conflict with Mayland set aside. The library's problems handed back to the library.

The light of a swinging lantern reached up the stairs, soldiers crowding behind it, rushing forward, their cries mixing with the shouts of alarm from the balcony as Starval did what Starval did best.

"Livira." Evar spoke the name he wanted to be last on his tongue. And with that, he threw himself at the enemy.

The sewers of a great city are often feats of architecture that put to shame the homes of many of those living above them. This begs the lie of the claim that our rulers treat the poor like shit. The poor are treated much worse than shit is.
Environmental Agency Report into Unregulated Discharges of Sewage into English Coastal Waters, *Vol. 14, 2023, by various authors*

———————

CHAPTER 39

Livira

"This is all of us?"

The sewer junction chosen might be the largest underground space that New Kraff had to offer, but it wasn't large. The fact that the Saviour's entire assault force was packed within it, or visible in the lantern light extending down the five adjoining tunnels, did not fill Livira with confidence.

"We're talking about reaching the heart of a palace here," Carlotte enlarged. "This lot wouldn't get past the front door of my . . ." She trailed off, probably not wanting to confuse the issue with talk of her recent title and home.

Tremon loomed over the pair of them, her height and width even more intimidating in the narrow confines of the sewers. "The more of us gathering, the more chance of the potentate's spies forewarning him. And even if we had an army, you can only feed it down one of these tunnels at the same rate. If a hundred of us can't do the job, then a thousand would fail too, bottled up at the entry point."

Narbla, taller than Tremon but painfully thin, leaned in, the stink of her absent pipe haunting the air around her, pushing back even the sewer's foulness for a moment. "If we had an army, we'd need you to protect the head and the tail of it from the monsters at the same time. And you don't even seem sure you can protect the people immediately around you."

Livira bit her lip and swallowed her sharp reply. The canith wasn't wrong. She'd struggled against that one Escape at the Gates. Ahead, in the wound made by the potentate's reckless wielding of her book, there might be scores of the things, or more.

People had called Livira reckless her whole life long, whether it be getting into fist fights with boys twice her size, throwing herself into the mouths of monsters, or bringing down the enmity of powerful men upon herself. It had almost never been a compliment. "Reckless" was not a quality valued in a librarian. Job requirements centred on rather different adjectives such as "meticulous," "measured," and "methodical." Leaps of faith were not encouraged.

Now, as she stood knee-deep in filthy water, ahead of her a tunnel full of all the worst horrors that imagination could fashion, and with her retreat blocked by a hundred strangers, she felt that perhaps she should strive to be less reckless in future.

"The blood of the library takes your fear and writes it out before you." Livira held her lantern high and advanced, calling out her words for those behind. She had of course told them this before, but if repetition would imprint the lesson on their minds, then she would say it until her throat ran dry. "Do not give what lies ahead of us any fuel to burn. If you're going to feed it ideas, let them be good ones. Useful ones."

Good thoughts would help, but the blood seemed less receptive to them than to anxiety and distress, perhaps because it was the result of a wound, born of violence.

"TURN LEFT." CARLOTTE had been given a map and had insisted on walking beside Livira. "No, right!"

"Spends half her life in a library—can't read."

"Books, I can read. Maps, not so much."

"You didn't pore over them when you were gloating over your empire?" Livira teased.

"Don't start on me, Livira Page!" Carlotte scowled over her map. "How long did it take you to pull me off a throne into knee-deep shit?"

"I prefer to think of it as water with added shit. Actual shit would be much harder to walk in than this. Plus, to be fair, I am walking you back into a palace. Maybe you can keep this one. The Saviour did say the people could choose who they want."

"Well, that sounds like madness." Carlotte huffed. "You're just going to get the best liar that way."

She had more to say, but Livira held up her hand. "We're close. Let me focus."

Despite her words, the ensuing silence set her mind to wandering rather than narrowing down on the looming sense of untrammelled power lying ahead of them. She thought of her book, and the knot it traced through time, being used to make the library bleed. She tried to visualise the holes that the potentate had already punched through chamber walls, and the harm that might have been wrought upon the shelves beyond.

It had to be Oanold. A man of his avarice wouldn't have lost hold of such a prize however far he'd fallen. And of course he'd fallen into himself, within a different set of maybes, for sure, but it seemed that when fate hadn't seen him born into power, he'd just cut himself a new path to it, careless of who or what had to bleed so that his voice became the loudest.

Carlotte saw it before Livira did. The rapid cessation of splashing beside and behind her brought Livira to a halt. The blackness of the fissure intersecting the sewer tunnel swallowed the lantern light so completely that it might just have been a stain upon the walls.

A long, thin black leg, armoured and jointed, reached out of the fissure almost immediately, seeking purchase on the stone beside it.

"Why are we doing this again?" Carlotte asked in a faint voice.

"For Evar." Livira had never felt less certain of the big picture, the one in which she was a warrior for Irad, a champion of his everlasting, ever-reaching library. Its eternal failure was written into the rocks in geological ages, strata of civilisation and ruinous war, repeated and repeated. And yet were men any more flexible, any more capable of change? Oanold, the bad seed sown through endless perhaps, had brought horror and unbounded cruelty to this city and probably stalked unknown numbers of its shadow cities in similar roles. "For Evar, and for each other." That was what she was sure of.

"Who thought of spiders?" Tremon called out just behind Livira. As the black horror hauled itself clear of the fissure, Tremon turned away, admonishing her troops. "A spider? It's hardly original."

Livira had to admire the woman's courage. Livira had told them what to do, and they had agreed, but to agree and to do were very different things. All Tremon's strength would mean little in the face of what her nightmares might summon from the blood. Her disdain, however, and the scattered laughter among the Saviour's ranks, were better than arrows or spears.

The arachnid horror shrank slightly, even as it tugged free an imperfect back leg from the inky blackness it was writing itself out of.

"Enough. You're mine!" And with a confidence that was nine parts fear and one part reckless self-belief, Livira walked empty-handed towards the creature.

She reached for the memories of her time as the Assistant, and for the timeless recollections that the entity had owned before she ever occupied its shell. The Assistant had never known a moment's fear, and Livira drew on that. The Assistant, however, had also never had any clever strategy for dealing with Escapes. The largest one she had encountered had thrown her around the reading chamber like a rag doll and fractured off part of her near-immortal body. Livira had no such resilience to fall back on.

The spider rushed at her, hind legs thrusting it forward at inescapable speed, whilst an array of sharp-pointed forelimbs angled at her like a thicket of black spears. Every fibre of Livira's being wanted to raise her arms in futile defence. Instead, she kept her eyes open, her body frozen, and her mind searching for that ineffable connection with which she had reduced the blood-skeer at the tavern to a puddle of tar.

She felt the sharpness of the reaching limbs, the impact of her attacker slamming into her, and staggered with it. A moment later she opened her eyes, closed by reflex. The Escape had broken on her like a wave, and now dripped down all around her. She hurt in particular places, more than she should, and the hands that sought the reason came away bloody.

"Livira!" Carlotte took hold of her, searching for signs of injury.

Tremon and others came forward, wary of the glistening pool around her.

"Is it bad?" Livira winced.

"It's not good." Carlotte frowned, hunting out other wounds. "But they're shallow. Like you were stabbed with the world's shortest knife . . . three . . . no, four times." She closed Livira's robe, scowling at the Saviour's men as they edged around. "You're sure this Evar is worth it?"

"He is. But I'd do this just to stop the monster that's seated on this city's throne. Even if it wasn't Oanold."

Livira freed herself from Carlotte's attentions and pushed the fallen Escape back into the fissure it came from. The black blood rolled through the sewer, swirling the water around it and pouring into the darkness.

Livira advanced, trying to avoid doing so cautiously, for with something like the library's blood caution invited in whatever it was you were being cautious about. She stood in front of the glistening black wall, understanding now that the fissure wasn't an impossibly dark passageway, but was full of blood, brimming with it, forming an undulating wall where it met the sewer tunnel. It had looked like an opening before she defeated the Escape, but now the blood deigned to reflect some small part of the light they turned its way, she could see that had been illusion.

Back among the ranks queuing in the tunnel, far enough to be protected but not too far to see, the Saviour stood, watching her through his enigmatic mask. With the blood of the library before her, it seemed that the library's eyes watched her through that white mask. She wondered about the man behind it. He was helping the Amacar, seeking an end to their persecution, decrying the systematic murder of their children on the island that had once been Carlotte's city, and Celcha's prison. Was he doing it for the right reasons, though, or as his own path to power? And did that matter?

Livira sucked in a breath and, in accordance with her will, the blood drew back, creating the imagined tunnel. She stepped in. "Follow me. Don't touch anything. And . . . try not to think."

Livira took firm hold of Carlotte's hand and advanced at a brisk walk. She tried to follow her own instructions and not think about how much like the gullet of some great monster the disturbingly flesh-like tunnel was. At first the passage's floor provided firm footing, but the deeper Livira went, the more two competing thoughts tried to surface from the back of her mind. In one she was walking out onto a frozen lake, and the ice beneath her feet grew thinner with every passing yard. In the other scenario, she advanced through wetlands, and what had at first been soft earth gradually became sucking mud that released her feet with reluctant slurps, muddy lips drawing her ever deeper. The increasing pressure with which she gripped Carlotte was matched by her friend's earnest attempt to crush all the bones in her hand.

In the end, perhaps what saved Livira from crashing through or being sucked down was that she had lived a life out on the Dust and then within the library, a stranger to both ice and mud. Fiction can paint strong images in a mind but is at its most potent when the raw material already lies within you, the writing just a key to turn the lock of memory.

What about a dust-bear?

"Shut up!" Livira found she'd spoken out loud. She glanced back along the line of the Saviour's raiders. The floor of the tunnel had become a writhing mess of entangled black serpents, and from the ceiling fresh horrors were descending, smaller versions of the arachnid that had driven its spikes into her, each dropping on its own thread. Even as she watched, a tentacle wrapped around a broad-shouldered man three places ahead of the Saviour, and in an instant he was gone, hauled away into the liquid wall with barely time to start his scream.

"Close your eyes!" Livira shouted. "Everyone. Close them now." She closed her own for good measure. "A forest. You're in a wood." She imagined the Exchange, its timeless trees, endless pools. "You can feel the roots beneath your feet. The season's turned. Leaves are falling on you."

Livira carried on calling out her vision, subverting the terrors around them. Serpents became the gnarled roots of oaks, questing for water. Spiders became dropping leaves that slid harmlessly away. Unsure of how many of the Saviour's party had bought into her version of the world, Livira could only push on, creating the tunnel ahead of her, and hoping that it resealed itself sufficiently far behind her so as not to trap any of those following.

How far the fissures from the potentate's destruction within the library had spread beneath the city, Livira couldn't say. Nor could she imagine how so little damage had been done to the buildings above. It seemed more like a collision of two overlapping worlds than a process following the common laws of push and shove. The tunnel that opened ahead of her as she advanced would turn left or right at her urging, and however she turned she found no bedrock to block her way, no shaped stone, no sewer bricks. It felt as if she had somehow entered the library's bloodstream, and though it might eventually deposit her at some predetermined spot beneath the palace, there might be no path through the ground that any logical mind would agree she had followed.

The journey seemed endless, not long . . . exactly . . . more as if she had stepped outside time just as she had on her visits to the Exchange. The possibility that the potentate might be long dead when she finally emerged, the crimes of his reign confined to the pages of history books written in now-dead languages, seemed a real one.

With her eyes closed tight she sensed rather than saw when the blood drew back to reveal something new. Ahead, through the tunnel's black annulus, the works of man could be seen again. The walls of another sewer tunnel. And, at the edge, a startled soldier in a uniform too fine for a grimy tunnel.

Livira pushed immediately, driving thick pulses of the library blood ahead of her, letting it gout into the space beyond the tunnel's end. She made no effort to give it form. The defenders' own secret terrors would be far more likely to set them running than anything she could create and running might save their lives.

"Fuck me sideways." Carlotte emerged from the blood-tunnel and fell to her hands and knees, ignoring the filthy water. "Thank all the gods. Even the rubbish ones that look like frogs." Several years as a queen appeared to have coarsened her language rather than refined it.

"Come on." Livira dragged her friend up. She looked both ways down the tunnel, steeling herself against the despairing screams echoing back towards her.

The Saviour's people began to stumble out behind her, some falling white-faced to their knees and retching, not at the foulness of the sewer but at what they had survived. The Saviour came out too, supported by Tremon, his mask slightly askew, a hint of greying stubble exposed.

Once, long ago, Livira had come before King Oanold upon his throne. She had walked away from that encounter as a librarian, despite his strong desire that she be thrown penniless into the streets. If Crath City had owned sewers large enough for people to roam, then no doubt Oanold would have wanted her and all the other "dusters" permanently employed within them, deep in the filth of people they were not fit to gaze upon.

Now she was rising from the sewers of another Crath to face the same king upon a different throne. And though he might wrinkle his nose at the aroma she brought with her to his halls, the true cause of his revulsion would be not the ordure on her robes, or any personal fault his royal eye singled out among her attributes, but instead something a librarian would describe as "categorical." His credo of dividing and demonizing had forever set her upon the shelf of untouchables and rejects, scheduled for destruction.

Livira bowed her head and took a deep breath, acclimatized to a stink that was at least honest. "Come on. Let's finish this."

We are, each of us, a multitude. I am not the man I was this morning, nor the man of yesterday. I am a throng of myself queued through time. We are, gentle reader, each a crowd within a crowd.

                              Arm of the Sphinx, *by Josiah Bancroft*

———————

CHAPTER 40

Livira

"This is what we're here for." The Saviour straightened his mask and addressed the group as the last of his force hastened from the darkness of the blood fissure. They stood in the sluggish flow of the sewer, the thirty or so canith stooped to avoid the ceiling, leading Livira to conclude that humanity had founded the city, and that a peace with the canith, more than that—an integration—had been brokered by one of the monarchs whose line the potentate had ended so bloodily.

"This is where you take back what belongs to the city and not to one man." In the tunnels the Saviour's oratory rolled and echoed, his deep voice drawing the attention of all those who'd made it through the recent horror. "This is where you say 'no' to all the evils this so-called potentate has wrought upon this city and upon our land. Not all of us will make it. But we *will* prevail. We will topple this throne and make a new future for all our peoples. Thank you all for making this stand—for siding with what is right and good."

Livira found herself nodding. Despite knowing the power a skilled speaker could exercise over their audience, she wanted the raiders to succeed, but more than that: she wanted the Saviour's vision to become a reality.

With the talking over, Tremon took the lead, organizing the vanguard, assigning a replacement for one of the Saviour's personal guards who hadn't emerged from the fissure. Guns were readied, knives drawn from their sheaths and replaced, sharpness confirmed.

The big woman seemed to know the way, and her soldiers followed her, eagerness now starting to replace the haunted looks they'd carried from the fissure. Livira recognised among them the two guards from the chamber that Narbla had first brought her and Carlotte to. The younger smaller man she'd named Scar, and the older wider one, both having replaced their crossbows with the weapons the locals called guns, which looked similar to the 'sticks she was familiar with, but more deadly.

THE FIRST SHOT rang out before they reached the palace, but it wasn't fired at the raiders or by them. By the time Tremon led them up the steps from the palace basement levels, the Escapes had already scattered much of the potentate's defence. The library's blood lay here and there in great pools, its potency spent, at least for now. The bodies of palace guards were scattered in greater numbers and more pieces.

When Tremon's vanguard met the first resistance, they found it disorganized, the guards confused about the nature and direction of the attack, unable to focus their numbers against the Saviour's force.

Well protected towards the rear of the incoming party, Livira felt both guilty and relieved. She had no desire to be in the thick of the fight and could contribute little to it. But even so, she didn't want other people dying on her behalf. The Saviour seemingly found it easier to keep his eyes on the bigger picture. The fate of a nation was being decided today and he reminded his followers of it several times.

The back of the force, while safer than the front, turned out not to be safe. Carlotte screamed when guns boomed nearby in quick succession. Plaster and splinters exploded from the wall close to Livira's head. Three raiders behind collapsed, one with an unearthly scream of pain, while the remainder turned and began to exchange fire with the palace guards coming up from behind.

Other raiders hurried the Saviour away. Livira dragged Carlotte after her. Both of them were bloody, peppered with wall fragments, but without serious injury as far as Livira could tell.

The advance devolved into a fractured, vicious series of skirmishes through the sumptuously decorated halls and corridors of the palace. Increasingly scattered and gore-stained raiders pushed on through grand, bullet-splintered doorways. Livira picked her way over the bodies of palace guards in gorgeous uniforms, their colours so vivid that their hearts' blood looked almost drab pumping across them.

"—ira—"

Livira couldn't hear Carlotte even though her friend was shouting at her side. Her ears rang with the explosion of guns on all sides, a high-pitched tone filling the aftermath and drowning out words. Everything felt distant, far away, as if were she to reach out to touch the walls they would retreat from her or break into something as insubstantial as mist. What Livira could feel, with more surety than anything her eyes showed her, was the closeness of her book. She could practically taste it—a concrete presence, more real than whatever stood between her and it.

Carlotte yanked her sideways through a door. Ahead of them Tremon, one arm limp and bloody, was wrestling with a guardsman before huge, ornate doors that had to lead to the throne room. A handful of other raiders slightly outnumbered the remaining guards, and fought it out with knives, swords, and guns that had spat out all their bullets.

The Saviour himself, spear in hand, charged and felled a guard who had been about to strike Tremon from behind. The Saviour stumbled, pulled down by the man he'd impaled.

In the next moment the great doors were booming as a raider, his bloodlust roused, hammered on them with the stock of his long gun.

"Charges . . ." Tremon cast aside the limp body of the man she'd been throttling one-handed. "Charges."

The raiders had come prepared, and a few moments' work saw explosives set in place around the edges of the potentate's last defence. Fuses were lit, followed by a general exodus, and then a blast that renewed the ringing in Livira's ears.

Tremon, sagging and leaving bloody footprints, led the return into the swirling smoke. The doors, already hanging on the ruins of their hinges, fell inwards at the raiders' approach, as if just waiting for the suggestion.

Close to the dais upon which the throne stood was a large cage on wheels, big enough to hold half a dozen full-grown canith. It held only one at the moment, and a slightly built figure. Yute! The librarian stood clutching the bars, eyes hunting the smoke swirls as if he had yet to pick Livira out among the raiders. The other prisoner, the canith, stood behind Yute, contemplating the room with a degree of detachment, and it was that more than the darkness of his fur that identified him to Livira as Evar's brother Kerrol.

The potentate stood before his throne in the echoing grandeur of his throne room. He clasped Livira's book, holding it to his chest as if it were a shield, or a talisman that might protect him from all the ills upon his doorstep. A single defender waited with him, a dark-skinned, shaven-headed warrior in ceremonial armour, a great two-handed scimitar held with the arc of its blade resting against his shoulder.

"But that's not . . ." Livira turned away from the potentate and his throne.

The Saviour, coming in between the fallen doors, had been fiddling with the straps of his mask as if it had been torn loose during the fighting. He stopped now, and let it slide as he gazed upon the man he'd come to tear down.

"Oanold . . ." Livira stared at the man behind the mask. How was this possible?

"You know me?" Oanold glanced her way, eyes narrowing in suspicion. "It's been a long time since anyone called me by my full name . . ." He shook the distraction away and returned his gaze to the potentate. "It's over!" he called out. "The only decision you need to make is whether you surrender with dignity or have to be dragged out screaming."

Livira had never seen the man standing in front of the throne, the bloody-handed potentate who had unleashed horror on his own streets. He was a narrow twist of a man, the kind to pass unnoticed not just through a crowd but through life in general, eyes of an indefinite colour set slightly too close together below a slightly too large forehead. But somehow what lay behind that forehead had set him on a course to write the history of nations.

In answer to Oanold's question the potentate thrust Livira's book out before him in a gesture of negation. A shot rang out, maybe two, but the illusion of flying pages had already filled Livira's vision, and she saw nothing more of the throne room. Pages shot forth, impossibly, pouring through the front cover, flying towards the raiders standing by the ruins of the potentate's doors. The pages rushed forward flat on, untroubled by the resistance of the air, growing larger as they came. An illusion, but one that refused dismissal despite its obvious falsehood. Individual pages wrapped themselves around individual raiders, engulfing them before crumpling into balls that would fit within a fist and skittering away across the floor.

For several long moments the pages veered this way and that, avoiding Livira whilst swallowing away everyone that stood with her. And then suddenly she was dwarfed by a white page overwritten in her own hand, and before she could protest it had folded her within it.

Many readers report becoming lost in a story, the mechanics of reading subsumed in unfolding events. Less commonly noted is the fact that we are all of us lost in our own stories from birth to grave, and likely beyond.
Taking Witness Statements: Metropolitan Police Handbook 6B,
by ChatterPG AI code

———

CHAPTER 41

Livira

Livira blinked. She saw nothing but whiteness. There had been writing too? But the dream left her, withdrawing its roots from her memory. The whiteness was a ceiling. Livira sat up, spilling bedclothes, and found herself alone in a bed in a circular room lined with bookcases.

She ran her fingers up into her hair, trying to squeeze the sleepiness from her head. The dream had seemed so real, and although she could remember no detail from it, a sense of urgency remained, as if she should be somewhere else, doing something important.

"I hate that . . ." She muttered the words to herself, still staring into nothing as if she might force the fleeing nightmare to unveil its secrets. But no, it was gone.

At the back of her head Livira's hair seemed to end in a single shock, as if a great thickness of it had been shorn away with just one cut. Livira looked down at herself. She wore a plain white nightgown, thin with age and reaching down past her knees. It didn't feel like hers. None of this did. The dream appeared to have been so determined to make off with its secrets intact that it had stolen most of hers as well. For the moment at least, Livira couldn't remember what she was doing here, or where "here" even was. She stood, unsteadily, taking some small comfort in the fact that she had woken up with a similar confusion in the past, infrequently, and never this profound, but memory had always returned.

The path to the nearest window required that she negotiate her way over and around several stacks of books that seemed to have no place on the curving shelves.

"A tower . . ." The window afforded her a view of a heath and beyond it a line of sea where white-topped waves speckled beneath a grey sky. The view held her gaze for a long time, at once unchanging but all in subtle motion. At last, she drew away and returned to the bed, trailing her fingers across book spines. That at least felt familiar.

A book lay open on the bedside table, a picture book. The page showed a fairy-tale tower and in the single room at its top, a sleeping princess, a great length of hair coiled beside her bed.

"Sometimes the knight is too late." She ran her fingers beneath the words on the page. "And the princess can't be saved."

The door to the room burst open, taking Livira's eyes from the book. Had there even been a door? Filling the frame stood an armoured figure. A stranger, but one Livira felt she had seen before. A narrow twist of a man despite his blackened breastplate and chainmail sleeves. Eyes of an indefinite colour, and set slightly too close together, watched her from beneath the rim of a helm that doubled as a crown, each of its jagged spikes gilded. Somehow, she knew the forehead hidden behind that steel was large and pale and that behind it cruel thoughts multiplied.

The man took a step forward and she noticed the blade in his gauntleted hand. Soldiers crowded the space behind him as far as the stair's curve allowed her to see.

"Amacar whore!" A snarl twisted the man's mouth, and he advanced another step, raising his sword.

The first scream, distant and echoing up the spiral of the staircase, made him pause. The second and third made him glance towards the door. Sounds of fighting reached them, steel on steel, cries of pain and rage, and above it all, beneath it all, a roaring that made her would-be murderer's snarl seem like a puppy's first attempt.

"Stop him!" The king turned back towards the doorway, urging his troops to stand fast.

Stop who? Surely one man couldn't be fighting his way through the dozens queued behind this familiar stranger who had come to kill her?

One man had no chance. And yet, with surprising swiftness, the clatter and clamour of battle advanced towards them, seeming to circle them, as if a lone wolf were running the perimeter.

Closer, closer now. The soldiers cried out in fear but the presence of the king at their rear prevented them from running.

The king cursed in frustration and ran metal-clad fingers down the length of his blade, setting black flames dancing along the length of steel. Livira felt the sucking void of those flames even from halfway across the room. This was why his men would rather die than retreat. However great a warrior was coming up those stairs, the flame would end them.

With a yank Livira pulled the topmost blanket from her bed, and giving herself no time to reassess her plan, threw herself at the king's back. The jarring collision spilled both of them through the doorway and down the stairs. The king's sword didn't so much burn the blanket as decay it where they touched. The blade hit a soldier's back, reducing him to bones and skin that tore like paper. At that point the king tripped. Both Livira and the blanket-wrapped king went tumbling.

The king, now swordless, crashed into the legs of another soldier and knocked him over just as something large and dark threw itself onto the man. Livira arrested her slide down the stairs with a groan. She managed to focus in time to see the last soldier stabbed half a dozen times before being tossed behind the oncoming attacker.

Uttering a guttural snarl, the warrior reached for the blanket covering the king. When he snatched it away . . . there was nothing, just the stone stairs and an abandoned sword, smoking gently.

The figure looked up. "Livira?" The bloody daggers dropped from his hands. "Livira? How are you here?"

Moments of reunion and parting bracket many relationships. It is not unusual for the punctuation in such love sentences to carry more meaning than the words.
                    The Language of Love, *by Anne Le Knocks*

CHAPTER 42

Evar

E var had thrown himself down the narrow stair to buy Starval time. He hadn't expected to survive. He didn't expect that Starval could free Oldo, even if he wanted to. It wasn't really the point. The point had become lost somewhere along the way. Killing the potentate had become the point. Striking a blow against an obvious evil felt like a relief after the confusion of infighting that had torn his little family open seemingly from the moment they'd escaped the library. The big picture was too big. Evar had been unable to step far enough back from it even to properly see the problem, let alone to divine some solution that had evaded Irad, Jaspeth, Yute, Mayland, and everyone else embroiled in the war.

Evar had thrown himself into the fight on the stairs with an almost-glee that Clovis would have appreciated. He'd needed this release. Even if it killed him, he needed it. He launched the first of the potentate's palace guards back over the head of the second and into the crush behind. He'd slammed the second man into the wall, squeezed past, scraping the brickwork, and stabbed into the space beyond.

His sense of time had escaped him. His world reduced to one of swinging lights, thrusting weapons, the concussive boom of guns, fighting with every part of his body and every ounce of his frustration.

When and how battling down a tight-packed stair had turned into battling up one, Evar couldn't say. How the straight path he remembered climbing within the thickness of the potentate's walls had become an ever-curving stairway, he had no idea.

Was he carving a path back to the balcony he'd left Starval on? Had he lost himself in the maze of secret passages? Were these armoured soldiers the same force as the uniformed palace guard? Was that daylight streaming in through a doorway above him? He was too busy staying alive even to guess at answers.

The opposition thinned, and suddenly he was lifting a blanket, looking for the man who, wrapped in its folds, had tumbled down the remaining steps to fetch up at his feet. The last of the foe? Either way, he'd pulled off quite a magician's trick since only stone steps lay beneath the blanket. The last man? No, someone else had fallen on the stairs ahead and was getting up.

Without his nose sifting her scent from the stink of fear and blood, Evar might have stabbed her. The awfulness of that thought set his blades falling to the floor.

"Livira?" It was her. Dishevelled in a thin white gown reaching to her neck. She picked herself up with a wince, tugging at the nightdress where it had rucked up around her knees. She steadied herself with one hand on the wall. "Livira? How are you here?"

"I'm not quite sure." She straightened, with the sunlight reaching down behind her, brilliant at the margins of her hair, casting her face into darkness. The sunlight made a ghostly nothing of her nightdress, spelling out her shape with sharp delineation. There was less of her than her librarian's robe had suggested, slender curves subtly different from those Clovis owned. Human curves. She stood there, staring at him, her eyes a gleam in shadow.

A moment later he had his arms around her, pressing her to him, careless of the blood that might be his and was certainly others'. The suddenness of it all, the surprise, erased the awkwardness, the hesitation, the worry of overstepping this mark or that mark. It wasn't until her arms tightened around him and she buried her face into his chest with a fierce inhalation that even the possibility of rejection caught up with Evar. They had been so long apart, with such distances between them, and so much had filled the spaces that had opened up.

"Don't. Ever. Leave. Me." Livira's embrace tightened more than Evar had thought a small human female could manage and he gasped. She released him at once. "Are you hurt? You're hurt! Where are you hurt?" She stepped back, gaining another step's worth of height, her touch light, tentative.

"I'm not hurt." Evar closed the gap, gathering her to him again. "Well . . . I was shot. And then Starval stabbed me. And I think maybe I took a few cuts back there—"

"Enough!" Livira broke free and grabbed his hand. "Come with me. Right now!"

Without waiting for an answer, she marched back up the remaining stairs, towing him through a doorway into a small book-lined room at the top. "It's a tower . . ." he murmured.

Livira shut the door behind him and, from one moment to the next, the nightmare on the stairs became something distant. Even though he was still sticky with their blood, he could no longer remember a single face among the many who had opposed him. In fact, as he turned back towards the door, he couldn't even find it, just bookcases.

"I . . . Where—"

"On the bed!" Livira gestured. She started to tear strips from a sheet that had fallen to the floor. "Take those leathers off."

"I really don't need—"

"Bed!" Livira pointed. "Now!"

Evar started undoing the ties and clasps holding his book-leather shirt in place. He felt he might have left some important memory on the stairs, that there was something he should be doing. But Livira's tone brooked no argument. He gritted his teeth against the pain that the necessary stretching caused him, then let the battered garment fall to the floor. It had saved him from a few sharp edges. Others had made it through, and he bled from several nicks and shallow cuts.

Livira produced a large earthenware jug of water and a white cloth. She seemed mildly puzzled by their existence. "And the rest. You could bleed to death and not know it."

"Who told you that?" Evar gripped his belt defensively. "It doesn't sound very likely."

"I read it in a book." Livira swept an arm at the walls.

Evar fumbled with his buckle, feeling suddenly self-conscious. Her nearness had already had an effect on him.

"Hurry!" Livira clapped her hands as if to instil urgency into him.

Still he hesitated, then turned his back on her and started to wrestle with the buckle more seriously.

"Come on. It's not like you've got . . ." Livira trailed off, as if in that moment she had come to the same realisation that Evar had already reached. However experienced she might be—and he expected her to be considerably more experienced than he was, having grown up with the whole world before her rather than one sister and three brothers—it was still a very distinct possibility that he did in fact have something she hadn't seen before.

Evar finally won the buckle battle and got onto the bed, pulling up the sheet before rolling to his back. He couldn't hold back a small snarl of pain. Of all his injuries it was the stab wound from Starval that still hurt the most. If not for the library's blood filling his veins, Evar was certain he would never have reached Livira.

Livira pulled down the sheet that he had pulled up, first exposing his shoulders then chest. She frowned down at him with obvious concern. "What were you thinking?" Finding still more to concern her, she pushed the sheet down further, exposing his ribs, belly, the top of his hips. Evar, conscious of his increasing involuntary response to her curiosity, caught her hand and stopped her further advance with the sheet's folds rucked up over his groin. Livira tutted but relented. She touched a finger to his blood and raised it towards her face, tilting her head in curiosity. The blood that had been red shed its disguise and smoked blackly on her fingertip. "How is this possible?" Livira looked at him with new eyes. "You're full of stories."

"May . . ." Evar had a name on the tip of his tongue, but somehow the memory wouldn't surface. "May . . . Maybe I fell?"

Livira began cleaning a slice on his shoulder, wetting her cloth and dabbing at the wound. "A fall wouldn't have left you like this. So many cuts. How did all this happen?"

Evar started to say, through teeth gritted against the pain of Livira's cleaning, that she had seen exactly how he'd been injured, but found that he wasn't even sure himself.

"You look like you've been dragged backwards through the worst hedge in the world!" Livira continued her ministrations. "How did you get here?"

"Thorns." Evar had other memories, but a different story was coiling through the back of his mind. A tower surrounded by nearly impenetrable thorn bushes, that he had fought his way through. He liked that one better. Nobody died, the only pain was his. "I climbed up." One story felt as real as the next. Livira was the only constant, the linchpin, the reality. "I was looking for you." He closed his hand around her wrist, engulfing it. She looked so frail, though he knew her strength.

Livira drew her wrist, and with it his hand, to her mouth. She set her lips gently to his knuckles, letting him feel their softness and their warmth. He inhaled, slow but deep, drawing in her scent, complex, varied, as uniquely hers as her face, and similarly expressive.

Evar's life had not equipped him with any measure of comparative beauty. He hadn't grown up amid crowds in which such judgements held sway. Livira had been the first human he'd seen. He didn't think in terms of whether she was pretty or whether the black shock of her hair was more or less attractive than the crimson tangle of Clovis's mane. Livira was simply vital to him. His eyes wanted to rest upon her. He needed the living pulse of her body pressed to his. He required that when she filled her lungs, he felt it, and that when she exhaled, that her breath caress his skin.

Livira smiled a slow smile and continued, with her free hand, to clean his wounds. Every place she touched him, the pain ceased. Evar would not have been surprised to angle his gaze down across his chest and discover that each cut had closed behind the passage of her cloth. Instead, he kept his attention on her face, her black eyes, skin still bronzed by the pitiless sun of her childhood, the firm but delicate line of her jaw, the slight asymmetry of her nose, as if it might once have been broken and reset.

Livira, realising herself to be under study, paused and returned his interest with a bold stare. "You don't look so big lying down."

"You don't look so small up there." He released her wrist and traced a gentle finger from the corner of her eye, following the line of her cheekbone, coming to rest at the side of her mouth.

Without speaking, Livira climbed onto the bed, hitched her nightdress up above her knees, and straddled him, the white fabric straining across her thighs. His hips moved, testing her weight.

"Sorry." Evar wasn't sure what he was apologizing for.

He tried to sit up, but Livira pushed him back. Despite her boldness, he could see she was trembling. Fear and desire mixed in equal measure within her scent and lay written less clearly on her face.

Evar might have taken comfort in Livira's nervousness, knowing her as unsure as himself, but somehow, he just added it to his own, wanting to reassure her, but not knowing how. She might share his own fears, of rejection, of having misread the signs even though they seemed so plain, of discovering humans and canith were more different than either of them had thought, more incompatible.

"I—"

Livira planted her hands to either side of his head, just above his shoulders, and leaned in close, sealing off his question with a kiss. Her breasts grazed his chest, nipples firm through the sheerness of the fabric. Evar wrapped his arms around her, pulling her against him, eliminating any space until her body met his along its whole length. Kissing they had done before. Kissing Evar understood. Their questions were silent ones now, asked tongue to tongue.

Despite their phonetic similarities "consummation" and "consume" share no common linguistic root. And yet in the marriage bed there is considerable overlap.
Bedding Ceremonies, *by Prudence Smith*

———————

CHAPTER 43

Livira

L ivira had written stories and become lost in them before. She had not always felt that she was the master of those stories, but she had always known that however deep she might plunge into them she would resurface in time.

The story that held her now, though, was something different, something that twisted, changed direction, tried to shed its skin and abandon its past. She had been a princess, though she was far from that. She had been trapped in a tower with no door, though in truth it had been a wasteland that had first trapped her, and it hadn't been a door she'd needed to leave it, just a push.

A man had come to kill her, but Evar had arrived in blood and fury, and the man had fled into nothingness. Had Evar come to save her, or had she brought him here, written him into her own story?

She had him now, where she had wanted him for the longest time, pinned to her bed by the weight of her body. And it was her body, should she let it, that would write the rest of this story for her. The urgency with which it moved against him knew nothing of the hesitation, awkwardness, and fear that had so often kept her tongue tripping over the easiest of words, skirting around the things she had wanted to say and sidetracking into the pathless wilderness of small talk. Her body knew how this ended. Her hips thrust against him, a stranger to shame, and as she slid down to kiss his chest, her softness pressed against his answering hardness, and her heart's pounding fluttered, losing momentary tempo. His kisses had undone her.

The knowledge that something wasn't quite right had been nagging at Livira. The story wanted her to forget things. To accept changes that didn't make sense. But then Evar had arrived, bloody from his battle with the thorns, and suddenly the rest of it had ceased to matter. The world owed them this moment. The world that had held them apart could now pay off its debt if only it would take itself away for a short time, look away an hour, for a few hours, look the other way and let them be, let them at least reach for happiness. Look away and let them find the comfort and haven of each other's arms.

Look away.

"It's a good thing this tower doesn't have any doors." Livira returned to the bed, tossing aside the cloth with which she'd cleaned herself.

Evar lifted his arm and she laid her head on his chest. He had, she now noticed, six nipples, the top pair most like a man's, the lower two pairs hardly noticeable. But she was now in a mood for noticing the small things about him, having dealt with the big ones.

"Why is that a good thing?" Evar murmured sleepily.

"Imagine if someone came calling." Livira's research and earlier worries had proved to be half-right. Towards the height of their union, it felt as if they had become physically locked together. A state that would make answering the door, or even leaving the bed, impossible. In many ways she had liked it, after the initial surprise. The physical fact carried with it an idea of being bound together, of being a single entity, both parties committed to the act, neither going anywhere until a conclusion had been reached.

Livira hugged him, more comfortable and more relaxed than she could ever remember. It had been more than she had expected. More intense and emotional. More physical. More exhausting. And entirely more wonderful. When he had finally left her it felt like losing some vital part. "I wish this—"

"—would last forever." Evar squeezed her gently and knowing what a tiny fraction of his strength lay within the action somehow made it all the more tender.

"But we need to leave." Livira frowned as she found the unwelcome words in her mouth.

"We do?"

"The others need us."

"Others?" Evar echoed her as though the concept were foreign to him, as if she and he were the whole of the world, and the room was all of space, this moment all of time.

"Others." She wanted to join him in that abandoning of everything that was neither here nor now, but some iron at her core refused to bend to the story's will. She couldn't even name the others, but she could still name the word that tied her to them: "love."

Evar shook his head, confused, and wriggled comfortably into the mattress. "There's only me and you."

Livira kissed his cheek. His blood had been changed. Somehow. The library's essence ran through his veins, and the story had him entirely in its grip. She, however, had written this story and would not allow it to contain her.

"If there's no door then we can climb out."

"That sounds dangerous." Evar squeezed her. "We could stay. I think in just a short while I could do all that all over again."

"Mmmmm." Livira stretched. "But it can't be that dangerous. You said you climbed up."

"I did?" He rumbled in his chest. "That sounds more like . . . more like something . . . something my brother would do."

"You did say so." Livira slipped from his embrace and left the bed. She went to one of the windows with its view of wild heath, lone trees leaning into the wind, and an untamed sea.

"Why doesn't your tower have a door?" Evar sat up and swung his legs off the bed. "Who builds a tower like that?"

"I'm a prisoner." Livira knew it to be true as she said it. She remembered a pale king with a blade in his fist and murder behind his eyes.

"A witch kept you here," Evar said, yawning.

"What? I never said anything about a . . ." But he was right. The story needed a witch. And as the sky outside darkened, and a distant thunder rolled in, Livira knew that the witch was coming.

Rain hit the windows as though the waves had swept ashore and were beating against the stonework, turning the tower into a lighthouse far from land. Within her bedroom the light had grown so dim that a candle would be needed if she wanted to read.

"Get back from the windows." Evar stood and patted his hips before realising his nakedness. "I had knives." He hesitated, then shaking off his confusion, grabbed up his trousers. "I don't need knives. If this witch comes anywhere near you, I'll break their neck."

"The knight can't always save the princess." Livira remembered another time, the same tower. "Generally, princesses need to save themselves."

Thunder boomed, rattling rooftiles. Day became night-time. Shadows flooded the room, and as the lightning struck, its flash painted a figure against the far wall.

The witch was a narrow twist of a man, sinister in the lightning's frozen moments, terrifying in the blindness that followed. He pinned Livira with a hungry stare, eyes a little too close together below a wide forehead.

In the space between one blinding flash and the next, the witch moved. Like a spider advancing every time you looked away. In one hand he held a knife. A small, cruel curve of steel that Livira somehow knew had, from the first moment of its forging, been meant for cutting throats.

Without warning, the storm fell silent, though the darkness intensified, only to be broken by the coldness of witchlight that limned Livira's foe, glimmering around him, making her squint.

Evar had, this whole time, remained by the bed, one hand in the act of hauling his trousers to his hip, seeming mired in some private hell of slowness, all his speed undone, as if the witch had moved him from the current of time and set him adrift in the doldrums, each action taking a hundred times longer than it should.

"I felt you trying to escape," the witch said. "That's not allowed."

"I hadn't even begun trying." Livira pulled a book from the nearest shelf, not taking her eyes from the witch and his knife. "When I start, you'll know all about it."

"You'll do what I say. Stay where I put you. This is mine. All of it. I hold the power here." The illumination swelled around him, a corpse-light not born of flame.

Livira shook off the tendrils of fear trying to invade her. "You tell your story. I'll tell mine." She held the book before her, a shield against his blade. "The foundation of this tower is a page I stole. Its bricks are ink, laid by my hand." In defiance of her fear, she advanced on the witch, and with each footstep the whole structure trembled, more deeply than when the thunder had spoken.

The witch struck as she closed on him, throwing himself forward, his robe a flowing tatter of night. If he had been a warrior, she would have had no chance, but he swung overhand, announcing his attack well in advance. Even so, she barely managed to interpose the book and found herself staring at two inches of bright steel protruding from the back cover just a foot from her face.

With a scream of effort, she struggled to prevent the knife's advance towards her flesh as the witch bore down on her. A moment later she understood that it didn't need to be a contest of strength. She rotated the book, twisting the trapped blade out of the witch's hand.

The pair of them stood at the centre of the room, locked in a struggle for control of the book. Livira snarled, drawing energy into her rapidly tiring muscles, pulling it from the stories lining the walls, from the stones of the tower itself. This was hers. All this was hers. The witch was the interloper here.

The witch, his pale brow beading with sweat, began to lose his grip. In a moment of cunning, he swung his attention to Evar, still mired in slowness, barely two steps from the bed, the horror of his situation beginning to dawn across his face. The witch jerked his head and Evar slammed into the ceiling, rattling the boards, plaster dust pluming around him.

"Give. Me. The. Book." The witch tried to wrest it from her grasp.

Livira felt herself weakening as Evar's pain flooded across the room in waves. The book started to slip from her fingers.

"You can save him." The witch grinned over the cover as they struggled. Evar, still pinned to the ceiling, smashed down. Only a partial collision with the bed saved him from an instantly fatal impact. He broke both the bed's legs on that side, and an unknown number of his own bones, and lay like a rag doll.

Livira knew it was true. She could save Evar. She could write them both into the story they had started here. They could live a life in this tower with the witch banished forever. All it took was surrendering the rest. All it required was that Evar's blood run through the story, and the acceptance that should the fiction be broken, he would die.

"Isn't this enough for you?" the witch panted as he tried to shake her loose.

Wasn't it enough? There was a war outside. She remembered that much. A chaotic, confusing, unwinnable war. One that had swallowed her up and demanded she take sides. One that had broken so much that she loved and was in the act of breaking the rest.

The witch's eyes met her own. They had no particular colour. Like a stagnant pool lingering too long after the rains, they promised a corrupt reflection of anything shown to them. And yet, what Livira saw in them made her grip turn to iron and brought all of her resolve to bear on the matter of keeping the book.

What she had seen in her opponent's unremarkable eyes was a familiar look. This man wasn't Oanold. In the maybe from which she'd been so recently stolen, Oanold had titled himself the Saviour, and whether his motivations were selfish or selfless or something in between, he had placed himself between this man, this witch, this potentate, and the murder of children. But the look—the look in the potentate's eyes—was all Oanold. It was the look Livira had seen when standing with Yute before the throne where Oanold had practised his own tyranny. A tyranny that the potentate's made small, but a murderous, corrupt abomination even so.

"No!" Livira wasn't having it. "No!"

And in that moment of rejection the tower melted away, taking Evar with it. Livira was still struggling with the potentate for the ownership of the book, but now it was very definitely her book, and the stage on which their contest played out was one reclaimed by memory: the throne room into which the Saviour's raiders had forced their way.

Livira stood on the dais, facing the potentate before the throne, both with their hands gripping her book. The Saviour and his supporters lay scattered around the great doors that had fallen in, all of them struggling as if wrapped in invisible sheets, their eyes focused on nothing. Livira imagined that until very recently she too had lain there, trapped in a fiction, albeit of her own making.

And even as she wrestled for her book, Livira wondered if she, along with everyone else, was not still trapped, at least to some degree, in stories of their own design.

Boss levels have become a staple of many first-person shooters. They reflect a conceit that those directing some great obscenity should embody its evil and tenacity. The Wizard of Oz offers a truer perspective. We lift the curtain to reveal hollow gods.
The Winner's Book of Video Gaming, *by Otto Cubed*

CHAPTER 44

Livira

The great cage imprisoning Yute and Kerrol lay five yards from the throne. But of more immediate interest was the potentate's final guard. The man startled, as if Livira had appeared out of thin air to wrestle with his master. His surprise proved short-lived: in the next moment he raised his two-handed blade.

"Livira!" Yute called to her from the cage. "The others are scattered around us. In different maybes."

With a huge effort, Livira wrenched the potentate around, using his grip on the book to turn him and interpose him between her and the man with the big sword.

"I don't know what you're talking about!" she shouted back. More of a scream than a shout. Any moment now the big shaven-headed warrior in his ceremonial armour would work things out and cut off both her arms with one blow of his scimitar.

"The book!" Yute shouted, gripping the bars. "It's scattered. Join the books!"

Rather than let the potentate's warrior gain the initiative, and with it the chance to slice her in two, Livira yelled and drove the potentate back into his bodyguard.

"Join the books!" Yute shouted.

It made no sense. What books? Scattered where? Livira found herself flung to the side. The potentate might not be a large man, but he was taller than her and at least as strong. The bodyguard looked to his master.

"Kill her, you idiot!"

And there it was. No chance of escape. No defence.

Livira remembered in that last moment that the book was a weapon now. It had been used against her. The evidence lay at the entrance to the throne room. She almost wasted her last heartbeat berating herself as an idiot, but managed to hold off that much-deserved upbraiding, and threw her concentration into the book instead.

The potentate might have a tight hold on the physical object but his grip on the text itself was nothing but dirty cobwebs thinking they had tied down a giant in its slumbers. What made the book a weapon was the cycle it had carved through time, a burning loop that could be applied in many ways, from cutting through the titanic walls of the library to trapping a handful of insurgents in story.

Livira sent the potentate staggering back, arms flailing, as the tale of a dinner party engulfed him.

The warrior swung his scimitar, and Livira—now sole owner of the book she had started writing centuries before—hadn't time to turn its power on him. Gleaming steel scythed the air. She lacked the speed or skill to avoid it.

"Livira!" Yute's cry and Kerrol's roar.

The scimitar cut through her, and the warrior, expecting resistance, lost balance, misstepped at the edge of the dais, and fell comically with a yell of surprise.

Livira still held her book despite the fact that she was, once again, a ghost. She met Yute's gaze. No other present could see her, perhaps no other in this world outside the assistants in the library. It had been Livira herself who had shown Evar how in this state the bonds of gravity no longer held sway. She had taught him to fly. It had been Yute's daughter, Yolanda, who had shown Livira there were new directions other than up and down, to move in. Other bonds to break. Yolanda had moved them in time.

Livira had seen too much to believe that she had seen the limit. There were more directions to take, more corners to turn, more dimensions to explore. The book was scattered? The others were scattered?

She reached for Evar first. He needed her. She'd seen him lying there, a broken thing on the floor. She reached . . . and found nothing. Panic seized her. Had he died? Had she let him die? Had they finally found each other only for her to doom him? All she had needed to do was close the door on everything else. To lock them both safe within one story. One maybe. And leave the rest to fall where they might.

One maybe . . . Livira found her new direction. She held her book, her weapon, the book that wouldn't burn, and drew on it, seeking all its shadows and reflections, all its maybes and might have beens.

A vast shadowy multiplicity bloomed around her. The ghosts of ghosts, the walls of the palace repeated and repeated, variations on a theme, growing more and more different with whatever served as distance in this new place. If she reached far enough the throne room might not just have a different design but sit hundreds of yards to the left, or not exist at all, further and the city itself became a question, impermanent against the constancy of the mountains. And perhaps, were she to reach far enough, even the mountains might dance, rising and falling to the tune of different geological refrains.

Stamped clearly through a dozen or so of the nearest maybes were images of her book, all of them in similar variations of the throne room she stood in. All of them close to the potentate who had claimed them.

In one maybe, the potentate really was Oanold, and he faced Clovis, flame-haired and fierce, Arpix at her side looking pale but unusually determined. In another possibility Oanold was a tavern landlord, currently being helped from a cage not unlike the one that held Yute and Kerrol. Starval had opened the door but hung on the bars for support, bleeding from several holes punched through him by bullets. The potentate lay slumped behind the assassin, the hilt of a throwing knife jutting from his eye.

More books, more maybes, more variations of Oanold, more of Livira's friends, more versions of them, a handful of Arpixes, of Clovises. She found Yolanda and Leetar. Even Mayland, hunting the book. In two possibilities he already had it in his hands, and as she touched upon him he looked up, frowning, sensing but not understanding her presence.

In none of these maybes could she see an Evar, though her vision stayed close to the book in each of them, so it might be that Evar was just beyond her sight. Even so, a quiet panic started to close in around her heart. She saw him as she had deserted him, crumpled beside the broken bed where they had shared their love. Abandoned where she had left him. Dying.

Livira shook the feeling off, or tried to. She would find him. She would unite the book and summon Evar into being. Somehow.

Seeing through a god's eyes, Livira understood that all of this had been the work of two mistakes, three if you counted her own and Evar's unsanctioned adventures in and out of the Exchange. Arpix had destroyed a Mechanism, sending Oanold and the book tumbling into possibility, spreading both through a stack of similar maybes. And Mayland had let his own hubris lead him and his family in a chase, where his imperfect understanding had scattered them across Oanold's "landing site."

Join the books.

That's what Yute had said: join the books. Livira saw it now. The book was the common thread. Making the many into one would draw a multitude of threads together. Easily said. Hard to do.

Livira opened her book, the pages fanning in the arc between two covers. Every shadow of the book opened too. The easy part.

Every story wanted to run. They wanted to spread like water spilled upon a slope. They soaked in, trickled here, flowed there, fingered their way into places she never imagined they might go. They took to the very air itself and let the wind have its say. Each story sank its roots deep, dividing, dividing, and dividing again. They resisted direction. They refused instruction. Each character took a voice of their own, and "no" became a favoured word.

To close the book, and with it, each of its shadows, would unite them. Livira knew this. Knowing it made it so. That was part of the lesson. But to close the book—that was the hard part. To close the book was to steer the story towards its end, to weave in or cut short every thread and fibre. To gather the spilled water and return it to the shattered glass. To bottle the genie once more. Ending any tale was an exercise in narrowing possibility, closing off maybes, until in one moment every thread that had been seeded passed through the eye of the same needle.

Livira pressed on the opposing covers, the strength within her arms irrelevant in the face of the forces against her. She brought the whole of her will to bear. She had written this book across two centuries, across a life, and now she came to the sharp point, the place where it would make her bleed. She pushed with the whole of herself, knowing that in the singular result there might be no place for Evar, knowing that what happened when those pages finally came together was not within her control. She could ask. She could not demand.

There comes a point when a mind presses against some immovable thing where either the thing becomes movable, or the mind breaks. Livira wasn't sure whether the *snap* that ran through her, top to bottom, was the former or the latter.

The book in her hands was smoking gently, disproving the old adage, for there was no fire. It seemed somehow more solid, more real than it had before. Livira looked up and found that she was on her knees, still on the dais, still beside an empty throne. The throne room looked much the same, save that the floor was black, a smooth unbroken black like the blood of the library, and every doorway and window showed the same inky night beyond it.

The swordsman who had been about to kill her was gone, the potentate too, the Saviour's people with them. Yute and Kerrol stood roughly where they had been, but the cage had vanished. Starval stood where she had seen him in her vision, patting at his wounds in surprise and finding them gone. Clovis and Arpix were facing the throne, not far from Yute. Clovis looked confused. Arpix even more so, swallowing hard, both hands on his neck as if checking that his head was still on his shoulders.

Yolanda stood alone on the far side of the throne room. Mayland leaned over the musicians' balcony, hands gripping the railing. Leetar was close on Livira's left. Carlotte by the main doorway, framed in darkness, and just ahead of her, Oanold—not one of his alternatives, not the ones who had walked different paths, but "her" Oanold, the venal king who had ordered the slaughter of Evar's people and eaten his own.

"Where's Evar?" Livira turned her back on the bewildered king. "Where is he?" She ran to Yute, her mentor, her master in so many things, Yute who had known the answer that brought them all together again. All except Evar. She took the librarian's white hands in hers. "Evar?"

"I don't know, Livira. The fewer alternatives he survived into . . . the less there would have been for you to take hold of."

"No. I would never have let him . . ." She would never have let him slip through her fingers, she had been going to say. But hadn't she done just that? Hadn't she had him in both hands? Hadn't he been literally locked into her by their passion? And yet here she stood without him. Whose fault was that if not hers?

Starval, black mane at wild angles, pain still on his face despite the absent wounds, took a step towards her. "I tried . . . I tried to kill him."

Livira shook her head violently, sure that Evar's brother had misspoken.

"I stabbed him." Starval looked at his hands. "The last I saw him was when he threw himself down a stairway packed with enemies to protect my back." He turned away and pointed at Oanold. "So I could save this man."

Livira knew it to be true. She had looked upon the scattered maybes and might have beens through the eyes of a god before she brought them together by closing her book. The story of each had been printed upon her mind. Starval and Evar had gone to save Oldo because he had tried to save the Amacar children, and Evar wanted to break through the armour that Starval had placed around his soul. He'd wanted to make his brother step back into the world and be a person in it, not a weapon. He had wanted to show his brother something good, and worthwhile. And that thing had been Oanold, a version of him thrown into different circumstances by chance, faced with different lessons and choices. Not a perfect man, probably not even a good one, but one who had done good, and certainly one who was far from being a terror.

Even if Evar had been in more than one maybe, if he had thrown himself down those stairs in each one of them . . . and fought his way up another set to answer her need and save her in that tower of stories . . . then she had left him there.

Livira's eyes found Mayland, up on the balcony. He looked down on all of them as though they were pieces in his game. "You paid Starval to kill

Evar." She said it loud enough for all of them to hear. Clovis's gasp became
a truly scary growl before it finished.

"I did," Mayland agreed, not looking away from her. "He has the library's blood running in his veins. The destruction of the library would
destroy him too, and it would be an ugly death. I couldn't let him stand in
the way of our freedom from the library's tyranny. The knife was kinder."

"But you saved him?" Livira didn't understand that part. "It was you
who put the blood in him to start with."

"I couldn't watch him die," Mayland said simply. "I wasn't brave
enough. Only Starval could do it. Surprise him so he'd never know. Never
suffer." He glanced at his brother. "But apparently he couldn't either."

"Is he dead?" Clovis snarled her question across both of them.

Mayland shrugged uneasily. "I don't think Evar can fully die while the
library lasts. But, from what Starval says, he might have met a physical
death and been subsumed in the library's essence."

"I can't . . ." The weight of her loss hit Livira unexpectedly, swinging in
from the side beneath her defences. She'd always snorted at the collapse of
the heroines she'd read about in similar circumstances. But here she was,
falling.

Starval caught her, his swiftness a cruel reminder of Evar's. Clovis was
there a heartbeat later, one arm shoving her smaller brother aside as she
supported Livira with the other. Arpix seemed to lumber up by compari-
son, but his hug was both more welcome and even more surprising than
Clovis's concern.

"You don't hug." A whisper as she held tight to her old friend.

"I do change." His voice was choked with un-Arpix-like emotion, as if
his grief for Evar had overwhelmed him nearly as much as hers had her.

Livira understood. She had seen all their stories in the moments she
fought to draw everything together. There had been too many stories to
take onboard at once, but she had seen them all, and now, with Clovis's
arm and Arpix's hug keeping her upright, she remembered that they too
had formed a bond, and sealed it in a manner that Livira would never have
predicted for Crath City's most reserved librarian—a title earned in the
face of stiff opposition.

For a moment all Livira could think of was how the news might explode Carlotte's head, and how pleased Evar would be for his sister and his best friend. The tears started immediately. Ugly, unchecked tears. Grief that shook her body like a flag in the wind and made her depend once more on the support of friends in order to keep her from the ground.

In the aftermath of any great struggle feelings of anti-climax, post-coital tristesse,
hangover, and/or general depression are not unusual. What next? What now?

Potty Training, *by Melinda Rees-Mogg*

CHAPTER 45

Livira

Livira sat on the step of the missing potentate's dais with her head in her hands. Carlotte sat beside her, pressed close, wise enough to say nothing. Leetar perched on her other side, the space of a hand between them. Livira could sense the woman wanted to speak but was abandoning one line after another as it reached her lips.

The rest of her friends, and, she supposed, enemies, stood around the throne room. The blackness, filling every doorway and window, gave the place an unearthly feel, as if it might be some grandiose stage set on which players were about to perform in the roles of ancient gods.

Yolanda was speaking with Yute. Livira saw it as a sign that this really was the end of the world. An estranged daughter talking to her father.

Starval had taken on the job of keeping Oanold under guard. Having the canith hulking over him had kept the man from complaint or snide remarks, so far. It seemed that Evar and Starval had happened upon Oanold in the most sympathetic incarnation imaginable for the man, and since neither of them had ever laid eyes on him before, they had been allowed time to warm to him.

Learning the larger truth had certainly soured Starval on the king who stood before him, but not to the point at which he was going to murder him on the spot. Clovis might have fewer reservations on that score, but Arpix had successfully kept her at a distance, despite his own reasons for despising and fearing Oanold. Even in her distress Livira noticed Clovis and Arpix's new closeness, moving through each other's personal space, one brushing against the other, like sibling cats raised to see each other as extensions of themselves. It made her own loss cut all the deeper.

Evar's absence left Livira hollow. Her moments of near divinity in which she had seen the fabric of not just one but many worlds, laid bare before her, had equipped her with enough understanding to know that if Evar was out there, he wouldn't be able to make it back to her until the small matter of the end of the library was resolved. The experience had not, however, equipped her with enough understanding to know if he *was* still out there in any meaningful sense. And if he had died, then the blame was squarely hers. She had left him when he needed her.

Where the throne had been, a portal now acted as a window to another place. If Livira were to turn round she knew she'd see the ganar Celcha, who had tried for so long to kill both her and Evar. That misplaced effort, based on incomplete evidence, had inspired Celcha to tread another path for the next century and more of her kind's long life. The ganar had somehow reached the centre of the library, a journey that Livira imagined was less about miles covered and more about reaching some elevated state of enlightenment. She also imagined that somehow the destruction that her book was wreaking upon the library had made Celcha's quest easier, opening new pathways for her. Causality rather than coincidence.

On the last stage of her journey Celcha had managed to shed her companions, directing each of them to places they wanted to be. Salamonda and Neera she had sent, along with other citizens of Crath, to a town named Tru where friends, including Jella, awaited them. Lord Algar and a contingent of the soldiers had returned to Crath City shortly after its sacking. Because they had not left the library since fleeing the city's invasion, Celcha's skills were able to return them in full. A dangerous destination, but the pull of the known proved strong.

Celcha was even now employing the wisdom, acquired over a lifetime of study, in an attempt to save the library from the collapse that Livira had initiated with her book. If such a repair could be achieved anywhere then the centre was that place. Thus far, all Celcha had managed was to slow the process's acceleration.

The ganar's position had allowed her to perform other minor miracles though, including finding and contacting Livira. At first the contact had been in the form of the throne tumbling through a newly opened void in the stonework beneath it. Livira's initial thought had been that the book was working its destruction again and that cracks from the library were spreading out through the foundations of not just the city but the mountains themselves.

When it became apparent that a portal had formed, Livira, Yute, Yolanda, and others had come to peer in cautiously. To begin with, Celcha had not been visible. The view moved continuously, as if the other side of the portal were the eye of some questing cyclops. It looked like the library, and yet not like it. Smaller, somehow older, though the library had always seemed both ancient and timeless. The view moved swiftly, along narrow aisles whose shelves were stacked with scrolls, beneath vaulted roofs.

"Remarkable." Yute's voice trembled with awe. "I believe that's Alexandria."

"Where?"

"One of the foundational libraries from the first-cycle worlds." Yute nodded to himself. The view pressed on into a pillared hall where stacks of clay tablets imprinted with innumerable sharp-edged marks rested on stone shelves. "Hanjanika," Yute said, nodding again.

The journey continued and all resemblance to the library fell away as the viewpoint passed into a sequence of natural caves. By the light of fissures in the roof where vegetation trailed in with green fingers, Livira could see that the walls were covered with art, most of it simple and stylized, the shapes of herd animals, their motion captured in a few powerful strokes, the fleetness of a gazelle, the thunder of a buffalo, other objects of the hunt she couldn't recognise, pigments not of her world, daubed by hands that might have shared little in common with hers.

The viewpoint swept on relentlessly into the dark. Here and there were islands of illumination where artists laboured on their endeavours by the smoky light of a single flame. And suddenly out into the blazing sunshine of a hardpan desert across which a near infinity of stones were arrayed with an order that couldn't be nature's work. No two the same, large, small, light, dark, but almost all of them flat, pieces of slate fractured from a cliff face by frost, river stones smoothed by millennia of patient flow, discs of rock fashioned by the sea and thrown upon the beach by a storm's rage.

The point of view's mad rush slowed and as it did so, drew closer to the ground. Livira saw that every stone bore a mark. A circle. A slash. A grid pattern. Two waving lines, one mimicking the other.

"It's the birth of writing," Yute whispered.

Without warning, the march of stones ended and where the next might be expected was a foot. The point of view's advance stopped, lifted, and pulled back, revealing the ganar in a small, circular patch of ground, clear of stones. She stood, looking up at them, leaning on her driftwood staff, her once-golden fur grey with age.

"Celcha." Yute spoke first.

"Yute." The ganar nodded. "Livira."

"We don't have long," Yute said.

"We never did," Celcha replied.

"Is there anything we can do?" Livira asked.

"If there is, then it's here at the end and at the centre that it must be done." Celcha gestured with her staff at the lines of stones radiating in all directions from the centre.

Mayland loomed beside Livira, staring down into the portal. For a moment she remembered another doorway, one he had taken Evar through before locking her out. Part of her wanted to raise her book and drive him back, lest he jump through this portal too and close it behind him, still reaching for the power to make a unilateral choice.

"Jaspeth should be here," Mayland rumbled. "This is too important to be in the hands of . . . us. We're a random, ragtag rabble." He sounded defeated, devoid of the arrogance that had seemed to define him.

"And Irad!" Yolanda joined them. She at least still had passion.

Celcha showed her square teeth in that ganar smile that always looked like pain. She shook her grey head. "There is no Irad, no Jaspeth. They're just the extremes of the argument given form. This matter has always, and will always, be decided by collections of people washed up on this particular shore by chance." She touched the heel of her staff to one of the flat stones around her, and the wavy lines across it lifted into the air, bringing with them the cries of gulls and the smell of the ocean.

Celcha had sought them, needing wisdom, or at least Yute's wisdom. Despite her age and learning, even at the library's heart she couldn't cure its ills. Not alone. Livira she sought perhaps less for wisdom than because of the history between them. If at the end of times one didn't revisit the choices made during a life, then when? And Livira had written the book that was unwriting them all.

In the end no great epiphany was visited upon them. The argument ranged back and forth as it ever did, even without Irad and Jaspeth present as avatars of its poles. Livira had suggested that if any answer existed, it might be more easily discovered if they all joined Celcha at the centre. With the portal at their feet it seemed only a step away. The ganar explained that sight and sound were all that could be shared through the doorway she'd opened. Reaching the centre was difficult—for her it had been a lifetime's quest—and even under the current circumstances the door in front of them couldn't take them to her.

All that resulted from Celcha's great work of magic was that Yute and Kerrol got to return to the place they had been before they fell into Oanold's trail. Yute had no ideas that seemed of use to Celcha, but he felt that in his time with Kerrol, apart from the others, he had missed something vital. The thought that he had unfinished business there possessed him. And Celcha agreed to send him. Kerrol also wanted to return, though he said it was to see a girl. Mayland's asking to go with them had been a surprise, but Yute had agreed without protest.

A vast acreage of parchment has vanished beneath the ink expended upon the subject of growing old. Many cite the benefits of slowing down, gaining perspective, and the like. Others speak of the value added by life's use-by date. But don't believe for a moment that any of them would not wipe away the years if that were an option.

Time to Die, *by Roy Battery*

———————

CHAPTER 46

Kerrol

T his place has changed!" Kerrol couldn't help staring as they emerged from the shop.

"Places do that." Yute followed him into the street. The bookshop door closed behind him, jangling a bell that had the same voice as the one that had hung there when Madame Orlova ran the place. Mayland followed silently, eyes flitting from one thing to the next.

Kerrol let Yute take the lead and followed him along the crowded pavement. None of the humans bustling past, bound within their own business and thoughts, gave even a first glance to the aliens among them, the rear two both head and shoulders above even the tallest of their number. Kerrol mused on their differences, the humans with their delicate teeth unsuited to rending and tearing, with their weak limbs and clever hands. The canith with jaws that remembered the hunt and the kill, and a proclivity for warfare that might even exceed mankind's. And yet these differences had done nothing to stop his brother and his sister finding a match among the human's numbers.

"It's up this way." Yute took a right turn, leaving behind the bulk of the noisy vehicles with their bright colours and fuming engines. He glanced briefly at Mayland, mistrustful. Mayland ignored him. "Not far now."

"Good." Kerrol wrinkled his nose. The town had smelled better when he had left it. Not good, but better.

Yute might be wondering about Mayland's presence, but Kerrol knew why his brother had insisted on accompanying them. Mayland needed control. Despite Evar's obsession with escape, it had been Mayland who first found an exit from their chamber of the library. And he hadn't shared that knowledge. Mayland was here because Yute had wanted to be here. Mayland wanted to see the levers of power that he assumed Yute must be reaching for. That had always been Mayland's failing. He didn't understand the secret hearts of other people. For all the million histories he had studied, Mayland didn't fathom the breadth of motivations that set a person to act. History offered alternatives, an array of possible reasons for any decision. But there was only one reason Yute had come to this place again, despite the danger. And Kerrol supposed that the same must be true of him.

A hundred yards further on, Yute came to a halt before a short wall topped by tall iron railings and split by a double gate that stood open. "Here." He went on through into the tree-lined drive beyond.

Kerrol followed, frowning. "We can just walk in on their young?"

"Apparently."

They emerged into a wide yard paved with some dark, unyielding surface. The uninspiring grounds surrounded what looked rather like a grand house that had been extended several times, each time employing a less ambitious architect and a more limited budget.

A grey-haired man in uniform hurried towards them. Kerrol's fists closed without instruction, remembering the last uniformed man to approach them in the town. Yute took a scrap of paper from an inner pocket of his robe and held it up.

"Ah." The man slowed his approach. "I wasn't told there was a school inspection today."

"It wouldn't be much of a surprise inspection if you were told about it, now would it?" Yute smiled.

"No." The man laughed; it made him look younger. "I don't suppose it would. I'll let you be about your business then, Herr . . ."

"Yute," Yute said.

"Herr Yute." The man nodded. He paused. "We've another visitor today. A scheduled one."

"I know." Yute smiled. "I was hoping to meet her."

The man pointed to one of the newest classrooms.

Yute thanked him and walked towards the door. He waved his piece of paper across a light near the entrance, and the door opened, surprising Kerrol with a strange beeping sound. Mayland started at the sound, revealing his well-concealed tension. He moved on, rumbling in complaint.

Yute followed the corridor and came to a stop before a door, looking into the room beyond through its window. Kerrol joined him and stooped to see. Mayland waited behind them, his mane brushing the ceiling.

The classroom held about two dozen children, all sitting at their desks. They looked more than half-grown, but Kerrol hadn't enough experience with children of any kind to be able to hazard a guess at their age. A fair-haired young teacher stood to one side of the room, her hands knotted together, eyes bright. The children's attention was fixed upon a frail figure sitting at the head of the class, facing them, presenting the back of their head to the door. A halo of wispy hair, as white as Yute's, seemed to float around the person's skull, turned into some kind of aura by the sunlight that slanted in through the far windows.

Kerrol tried to speak, found his throat too dry, swallowed, and tried again. "You couldn't have made it sooner?"

"The efforts that brought us here were immense. To say mountains were moved would not be exaggerating. But the library's sense of timing has always been its own."

The library seldom gave a person what they wanted. Kerrol had to hope that it made more of an attempt to give them what they needed.

Applause broke out within the classroom, the children clapping, led by their teacher who clapped hardest of all. Not joyous applause, Kerrol thought, but the kind offered in respect and gratitude. He hadn't the skill in reading human faces that he had for canith ones, but he thought he saw sadness in the children, shock even.

The figure in the chair looked away from her audience towards the exit. She stood up unsteadily and said something to the teacher. The young woman started to address her class as the old woman picked up her stick and began to walk towards the door.

She wasn't merely old. "Ancient" would be a fairer word. Wrinkled, shrunken, bowed beneath the weight of many decades. Yute opened the door as she approached.

"Anne," he said. "It's good to see you."

"Yute." She nodded, then looked up at Kerrol with watery eyes. "Kerrol. I wasn't sure I would ever see you two again. But I always hoped so."

"We . . . we came back as soon as we could." Kerrol wasn't sure why he had to fight to keep his voice steady. She was just old. The child had become a woman and grown old. Nature's work It shouldn't hurt him like this.

"And you've brought a friend?" Anne peered over Yute's shoulder.

"My brother Mayland." A short introduction, Kerrol thought, but the alternative seemed to be practically a book in itself.

"Come." Anne shuffled past them. "There's a bench in the playground. On the shady side. We'll sit there."

And so they sat, looking out across the empty sun-drenched yard, Yute and Kerrol on either side of the girl they'd left behind yesterday. Mayland sitting on the ground in front of them with his knees drawn up.

Without speaking, Anne reached out with her right arm and took Yute's hand in hers. She took Kerrol's in the other, her age trembling in her limbs.

"You have a number." Kerrol wasn't sure what to say, so he said what he saw, a blurry number tattooed on Anne's forearm, exposed as she'd reached for his hand.

"I show it to the children when I come to schools to talk about what happened. For some of them it's not until they see it that they really believe me. Some of them need to touch it."

Kerrol covered the numbers with one finger. They were ugly. He couldn't read Anne well, but he could read her well enough to tell that the story those numbers told was a terrible one, bad enough that just touching them would fill a person's eyes with tears. He wiped his own with the back of his other hand. "We should have made you come with us."

"No." Anne shook her head, voice fragile with age. "No, you should have listened to me and respected my decision. Which was exactly what you did."

Kerrol opened his mouth but didn't find words there.

"Look at you both," Anne said brightly. "I never realised quite how young you were, Kerrol. You seemed terribly grown-up to me back when I was sixteen. And look at you now, just a boy, with your whole life before you. I do hope you use it well. And Yute, still so handsome, still so serious."

"You could come with us this time," Yute said gently.

"There are wonders to see!" Kerrol hadn't thought of taking Anne back with them. "So many worlds and times."

Anne squeezed his hand. "You came to see me. That's a wonder in itself. And one thing I've found over the years, is that if you stay in one spot long enough, and pay close attention, you'll find that there's magic everywhere."

Yute nodded in surprise as if he had observed the same thing himself, though it had taken him longer to discover that truth. "To be honest, Anne, I didn't come here with high hopes of finding you. I thought we would find a wasteland, still burning with the fires of your war."

"You saw that?" Anne blinked her own surprise. "But you left almost a year before it started."

"I felt it coming." Yute shivered. "Your world then looked close to discovering fire."

"Of course they had fire." Kerrol frowned. "We saw it!"

"I mean the second kind, the burning of star dust. 'Fission' they call it." Yute shaped his mouth around the unfamiliar word. "To look around this city now I can't believe you don't have the third kind." He glanced at Kerrol, then at Mayland, his gaze lingering. "The burning of star fuel. Fusion. That's a fire that will make dust of whole civilisations in a single day." He returned his attention to Anne. "So, I'm extremely glad to find you alive and well." He patted her hand. "And also surprised. Will you tell me all about it? If you have time?"

And she did.

They sat awhile on the bench as the shadows stretched and the children came out to play then returned to their classes. Anne talked, Yute asked questions, Kerrol listened and from time to time clenched his teeth together tightly to keep back the growls, the snarls, and the howling that Anne's story wanted to draw out of him.

Mayland watched in silence, his dark eyes wide and unblinking, rumbling only when she spoke of the camps and the children and the gas.

"And so you come and talk to the children, to ensure that this terror is not forgotten." Mayland was first to speak when at last Anne fell silent.

She nodded. "We humans are very good at forgetting uncomfortable truths."

"And you think this particular truth should be kept forever. Held in books in the library." Mayland didn't voice it as a question, and Kerrol could hear his tone hardening. He could read the distrust on his brother's face, the feeling that he had been walked into a trap of some kind.

Anne looked at Mayland closely, tilting her head slightly, the old intelligence still in her dark eyes. "I hope there will be a time when mankind reaches a point when it can forget such things. As any mother wants her children to forget the fears that torment them. But that time is not now." She smiled, though Kerrol didn't know how after the story she had told them. He assumed she had been gentler with the children or surely they would have been crying and running home to their parents. Unless human young were much sturdier than he imagined. "When you speak of the library, Mayland, I think you must be imagining the library your brother and Yute have spoken of. We don't have that here. We have many libraries, big and small. Most of our books are in people's homes, or on the shelves of shops like my own."

"The library will find you," Mayland said. "Perhaps in the ashes when all this is gone. Holding your books for you, and many others, eternal, unchanging. All sacrifice recorded and kept, all horrors endlessly repopulating the shelves no matter how many times the fire purges them."

"Goodness." Anne watched him closely. "I'm all for thwarting the book burners, young man, but I've always been uneasy with the idea of any one person or any one system reigning supreme. What if it's the wrong one? Who sets these rules for everyone else?" She shook her head. "No, what we have is far from perfect. I don't believe there is a perfect, not in this life. But its strength is in diversity. Its strength, curiously, is in its biases, which lean in every direction. Its strength is in many systems, many ways, the curation of many and varied hands. Whatever hits us, something survives. We adapt, we change, and with god's blessing, we get better. It's hard to become so exercised over what the right answer is when you can have many answers. If you don't like how I run my bookshop, you can take your business across the street, or start your own."

Mayland bowed his head in thought before his next question, and this time it really was a question. Anne gave her thoughts on it, and the next one, a tiny old human chatting to a canith as tall as her when sitting, in the playground of a school to a background of screams and shouts and the wildness of children.

When the school emptied, they let the tide take them too, returning to Anne's home. She lived above Madame Orlova's bookshop, which she now owned, and which her grandson had recently taken over running from her daughter. She served them little cakes in the kitchen at the back.

"The books that were banned are no longer banned. We sell all sorts. You would hardly believe the fiction today." She snorted. "But you can read about Helen Keller too. Madame Orlova would approve, I think. Those nice boys from Weber's too, they write about . . . they call them gay now, yes? I can't remember their names anymore . . ." Anne looked distressed. "They never came back."

"Herman and Carl," Kerrol said. It had only been yesterday. But like Anne's family they had been taken to murder camps and . . . murdered.

"Yes, that was it. Herman and Carl." Anne closed her eyes as if seeing them again. As if Kerrol had given her a gift. "Thank you." She paused. "I *have* grown old, haven't I? It comes to us all, I suppose. Now, where was I? Another cake, Mayland? And one for you, Kerrol?"

"Thank you." He took the tiny, delicious cake and held it close to his heart, and understood why the laws of time should not be broken.

Things fall apart; the centre cannot hold;
Mere anarchy is loosed upon the world,
The blood-dimmed tide is loosed, and everywhere
The ceremony of innocence is drowned.

"The Second Coming," by William Butler Yeats

CHAPTER 47

Livira

N ow they waited for Yute's return as the throne room shuddered around them.

"We can't stay here!" Oanold's cry came after the third crash. Fear of Starval had kept him quiet when the first chunk of plaster had smashed down on the far side of the throne room. And when the second, larger piece had pulverised itself on the floor ten yards from him. But when the growing tremors shook free a whole ornamented section of the ceiling, that had exploded in gilded glory close enough to paint both him and Starval white from head to foot, the king had had his fill.

"Where do you suggest we go, *Your Majesty?*" Carlotte left his title dripping with scorn. All of them had gathered around the portal now, though it offered little by way of escape. They waited for Yute and the two brothers to return, and Livira supposed that, gathered together as they all were, they would die in one collapse rather than piecemeal as the palace fell apart. It seemed the better option. Not good, but better.

The portal had been showing them Celcha's efforts to save the library, but after Yute's departure it had given over to a view that flitted from one library room to another, seemingly at random. The impervious chambers were faring less well than the throne room. Huge slabs of masonry fell from the unfathomable heights to destroy books and shelves by the tens of thousands in great thunderclaps surrounded by a smoke that a closer view revealed as wild storms of loose pages.

"There!" Livira pointed. The view through the portal had changed to one she knew well enough to pick from ten thousand similar scenes. "The labyrinth in Chamber Two!" The place where her book had been born, the source of all its pages. Tremors had shaken books from many shelves, but the place looked largely intact. Even as she watched, the view swooped into the clearing where, on the stained floor, she had first found Edgarallen, the raven who had taken her through the initial steps of her journey to the Exchange. "Yute! Yute's there."

"Kerrol!" Clovis shouted as her brothers came into the picture. "Mayland!"

A titanic groan above them brought Livira's gaze to the ceiling overhead where the cracked architecture of the throne room appeared to be shifting before her eyes, starting to sift great volumes of plaster dust down upon them as it did so.

"Jump!" Starval shouted, and immediately hauled Livira with him as he followed his own advice.

A swirling moment of confusion followed, punctuated by the rapid thump of bodies landing. Livira found herself one of eight people lying on the clearing floor with the shelves of the labyrinth rising above them, and Yute staring down at them in mild surprise.

Starval found his feet first. He patted Kerrol's arm. "We came to you, brother, since you were doing such a bad job finding your way back."

Yute helped Yolanda up, then reached for Livira.

"Are we all here?" Livira looked around for Carlotte, Arpix, and then Leetar, finding them all quickly. Oanold had made it too. Part of her wished him stranded in the collapsing throne room. He might have been capable of better lives, but the fact was that the Oanold she could reach out and touch had committed some of the worst crimes imaginable.

"Yes," Clovis appeared to have completed a head count. "We're all here."

"Where should we go?" Arpix stepped close to the canith as another tremor shook tomes from places they had rested untouched for decades or even centuries, leaving the shelves like gap-toothed smiles.

"We were aiming to get back to you." Yute squeezed his daughter's hand. "Celcha's portal fell short of its promise."

"Celcha!" Livira returned to her earlier idea, though it still seemed no more possible. "I should take my book to the centre. Maybe we can do something there, together, that I couldn't do anywhere else."

"Or collapse the library entirely." Yute frowned.

"It's worth a try." Mayland nodded, his meaning ambiguous.

"It's collapsing anyway." Clovis waved at the ceiling where cracks large enough to be seen from the ground now ran. "The worst outcome is that it happens faster. Let's do it."

First steps are important and are frequently the occasion for celebration. Last steps often go unnoticed. Few of us believe that when we take to our beds we will not rise again.

Cobblers: The Importance of Good Shoes, *by Arnold Shoemaker*

CHAPTER 48

Livira

L ivira's journey owned a great many candidates for "starting point." The door of her aunt's hut on a fateful morning, the steps of the Al-location Hall, the entry to the librarian's complex, or to the library proper. But the black stain at the centre of the labyrinth could also stake a decent claim.

Here she was again, setting out on another journey, expected somehow to find the library's centre when in truth she had spent her whole life exploring just a minuscule fraction of the athenaeum's vast estate and never found even a clue to the centre's location. And now she had to find it before the place collapsed around her. An end that seemed imminent.

Maybe someone else could do it? A guide? She had found the raven here, very long ago, and although it had scolded her loudly and relentlessly, she had come to care for the construct. Part of Livira wanted to speak Edgarallen's name and see if she could summon him. Perhaps he would know where the centre lay. But the bird had always seemed so delicate, at the end of a long, long life, and vulnerable to hazard. Livira wasn't going to call him to face the end of the world with her.

Inspiration struck. "You could call Wentworth?" She turned to Yute.

Yute frowned. "There are certain dangers—"

"Just do it!" Clovis exploded. "Look where we are!" As if to underscore her opinion the distant boom of falling masonry rolled across the chamber, echoing from the walls.

"Still . . ." Yute prevaricated. "We should—"

"Wentworth!" Kerrol called out a loud imperative. "Wentworth! We need help!"

Something huge loomed behind Livira, accompanied by the sound of shelves splintering and falling back. The light dimmed and quailed as if it were being blocked, which was impossible—in the library the illumination bled from the air itself.

Livira hadn't completed her turn before a desperate scream swelled and then cut off with an awful crunching sound.

Wentworth had become huge, larger than a skeer warrior, big as an elephant, Livira guessed, though she had never seen such a creature. More importantly, the cat was less Wentworthy than Livira had ever seen him: his fur had become almost black, mottled with shadow, his claws scythe-like, his eyes lambent amber slits, and his teeth . . . his teeth had just passed entirely through King Oanold's neck.

Wentworth spat out the man's mangled head a heartbeat after his bleeding body hit the floor. Clovis moved with breathtaking speed to put herself in front of Livira who of the remaining party had been standing closest to the beast. She held her white sword between her and the cat, and unless Livira imagined it afterwards, her arm trembled.

"Wentworth!" Yute ran past them both, towards the cat, his voice neither fearful nor angry, but full of sorrow.

Wentworth glowered down at the librarian, jaws dripping crimson, as the man came to him unhesitatingly. Yute's head came only to the cat's great fur-laden chest. He reached out, patting Wentworth while turning back to face Livira.

"I worried this would happen . . ."

"You worried he'd bite someone's head off?"

Yute winced. "It seems he developed a taste for fascists when we were last together . . . But no. This." He looked up at the fang-filled maw and wild eyes pointing his way. "Wentworth has always been attuned to the library. By many accounts he is part of it. As the library fails, so will he."

"He doesn't look happy about it," Clovis murmured, not lowering her blade.

Livira swallowed, trying to see past the teeth and blood to Salamonda's sleepy stair-cat that had so often ignored her, and every once in a while been of immense use. "Wentworth . . ." She swallowed again, and tried with more force in her voice, hoping it wouldn't dry up this time. "Wentworth. We need to reach the centre. I might be able to help you if we can, but I don't know how to get there."

The cat locked eyes with her and suddenly she knew exactly how prey felt. Beneath a weight of fur, muscles tensed, ready to propel Wentworth into motion. For a long moment it seemed that the only question was when he would spring at her, rather than if. The moment passed, and the cat turned away, shrinking as he started to climb the slanting shelves that his bulk had toppled into the next aisle.

"Follow him," Mayland said. Rather unnecessarily, in Livira's opinion.

Wentworth took to the shelf tops, heading west while all around them pieces of the ceiling started to fall. The cat appeared unbothered, though he kept up the dedicated pace of a cat summoned to the kitchen. Livira could tell that he was leading them to the door to Chamber 7. If his intention was to take them to the centre by foot, the journey might be measured in months or years, although the length of the journey felt academic. If it was more than ten minutes, Livira was fairly sure the problem would be solved by them all being crushed by falling rocks.

Before they'd covered half the distance to the door, pieces of the ceiling were falling all around them, a steady hail ranging from fist-sized bits to chunks substantially larger than Wentworth at his biggest. The cat led at a pace dictated by Yute's best efforts at running. He sprinted along shelf tops, effortlessly leaping aisles, then pausing for the humans to catch up. In the old days he would have collapsed in a furry puddle or sat nonchalantly licking a paw. Now he stalked impatiently, agitation twitching in his tail.

Once, when Wentworth had ranged far ahead and was a mere dot atop the shelves at the end of a straight aisle more than a hundred yards long, the place he was sitting in exploded without warning, splinters and pages flying in all directions, dust billowing. Livira screamed despite herself, but a moment later she spotted the cat ten yards closer, stalking the shelf tops.

For a moment she found her heart aching for the lost books. She had never even scratched the surface of what was to be read in Chamber 1, let alone the tomes in Chamber 2, but even so, part of her had always thought that she would have the chance to read any given book here. To see them taken away, not just from her but from humanity, hurt her in ways she couldn't properly put into words.

"How are we not dead yet?" Carlotte panted beside Livira.

"I'm your early-warning system." Arpix spoke up behind them, voice grim.

Carlotte looked back at him, frowning.

"I'm taller," Arpix explained. "The rocks will hit me first."

Behind him, Clovis pointed up in alarm.

Livira had been avoiding looking up, all of them had, not least to keep from getting an eyeful of grit, and also because it was better not to think about deaths that could strike from places beyond their control, but she did so now.

In any normal light the presence of a vast raven high above might have been signalled by its shadow falling across them. Edgarallen—it had to be him—had grown to such titanic dimensions that Livira suddenly knew the truth of the childhood stories Ella had told her out on the Dust. Tales of rocs whose wings darkened the sky and could tear up a hundred trees in their great talons.

Livira hadn't called him. She had no feather. She hadn't spoken his name. And yet here he was, flying as a shield above them, shedding pieces of the ceiling from his flight feathers as his wings deflected an untold weight of masonry from their heads.

"Run!" She shouted it even though they were already running. Surely even on this scale the raven couldn't protect them, or himself, for long.

Even as the thought crossed her mind Edgarallen's whole body shuddered, and a few moments later a huge chunk of ceiling rolled off his back.

WENTWORTH WAITED FOR them by the corridor to Chamber 7. Kerrol ended up picking Yute up and running with him. Starval did the same for Yolanda and Leetar despite their protests. By the time they emerged from the shelves, all the humans were in the arms of canith, Livira borne beneath one of Mayland's arms and uncomfortable about it in several ways.

The stone hail had partially re-established itself as they approached the walls, the raven unable to maintain his position and having to circle over them periodically. As much as having her head crushed by a small piece of the ceiling worried Livira, she also knew that the total collapse that would bring everything down in an unstoppable rush couldn't be far away.

The metal man stood sentinel at the entrance as he always had, the spars of his ruined wings arching above his head. Now however, the strange light that lit when Volente had woken him with a howl was back without the hound's intervention. As the group came forward, the man turned towards them, his whole body moving.

"Livira. Arpix. It is good to see you." He addressed them in deep-voiced sabbertine, the only one of his multitude of languages they shared. "My name, by the way, is Dalion. It has been an honour to share the library with you."

"Hello, Dalion." Livira found no comfort in the metal man's disturbingly final phraseology. Moreover, she wasn't sure how to greet him. He had stood there for a hundred generations and more. He deserved more respect. A thunderous boom close at hand and the encroaching dust billow of the impact overrode her social misgivings and delivered her directly to her point. "We need to find the centre."

The others gathered around, Kerrol and Mayland almost as tall as the metal man.

"That's rather like being impatient to find patience," Dalion replied after a long pause in which more pieces crashed down close by. Wentworth continued to circle, occasionally weaving through the forest of legs to nip at the brownish-gold ankles of the former statue.

"You're not going to give us some mystic mumbo jumbo about the centre being inside us all along, are you?" Carlotte strode up to the avatar with a quick glance at the ceiling. "Because we really don't have time for that sort of—"

"I think what *Queen* Carlotte means"—Livira elbowed her friend aside—"is that unless we get there quickly, we won't be getting there at all."

The avatar rumbled in his chest. "It is a time when many things will end. Me, the bird"—the light in his eyes flickered—"maybe even the old one." He stroked Wentworth's head as the cat grew large and pressed it into his metal hand. "Your lives are not in my gift. I would save you if I were able. But the sacrifice is not mine to make."

"Sacrifice?" Clovis asked.

Livira glanced around, uneasy with such talk. She wasn't sure what else she had to surrender, or how it might help. "Do we have to give something up? To reach the centre? It's a state of mind? Only people who don't want to reach it can get there? What?"

Dalion met her eyes, the glow in his dazzling her. "The world is seldom kind, Livira."

"I'm not . . ." Panic seized her. "I can't give Evar up again. That can't be what you mean!"

"There has to be a sacrifice," the avatar repeated.

Behind Livira Yute exhaled a long, soft sigh.

"I don't understand . . ." Livira looked from Kerrol to Arpix in confusion.

Wentworth suddenly looked up at Dalion, a fresh wildness in his eyes. He surged upwards, growing all the time, lunging at the metal man.

Dalion threw his arms around the cat's neck, grappling with him. "Hurry!" he shouted above Wentworth's yowl. "I can't hold him for long."

"I don't . . ." Livira backed away from the squalling bundle of fury that had been Wentworth, fur flying, scythe-like claws raking across Dalion's metal limbs and torso. "I don't understand!"

As Dalion wrestled with the cat, whose claws were now scoring bright furrows through his bronze-gold flesh, a high-pitched scream dragged Livira's attention from the contest. Starval had hold of Yolanda and was securing her with both arms straining as she started to exhibit a struggle every bit as furious and desperate as Wentworth's.

Livira only caught a glimpse of him. White hair, a dark grey robe. Then he was gone from sight. "Yute!" His name broke from her in a scream and without fully understanding why, she began to sprint after him.

Kerrol caught her and refused to let go. As she beat her fists against him, he howled, not in anger, nor because her blows were hurting him, but in anguish. The same howls that Evar had made long ago over the broken remains of the Assistant.

A swooping darkness descended upon them, and the raven's great talons hit the ground, each toe longer than a full-grown canith, his wings folding about them in a protective shield, his head bowed in so that the point of his vast beak touched the ground close to Dalion, and a single black, unreadable eye watched them all.

A rolling thunder eclipsed all protests or demands. Rock hit rock, the floor trembled and shook beneath their feet. Edgarallen shuddered beneath impact after impact but refused to reduce himself into a smaller target.

Livira kept throwing her strength against the canith's, but it was only when Wentworth tore past them that Edgarallen raised his wing and Kerrol released her.

Dalion lay in scattered pieces, ripped apart by Wentworth's fury. The shelves ahead of them were in ruin, smashed timber, broken books, and shattered stone everywhere. The ceiling continued its collapse, but the hail of pieces had slowed, perhaps as a rainstorm will come in waves, or perhaps the momentary calm before a devastating general collapse.

Wentworth sprang over the first obstacles and charged on.

"We need to follow," Arpix said in a broken voice.

Livira looked back again at Dalion's remains. Edgarallen lay among them, unmoving, back to the size of a normal raven, and more battered than when she had seen him at his worst, his left wing broken, black blood leaking through the sparsity of his feathers. She twisted away from Kerrol, passed an uncomprehending Carlotte, and scooped the bird into her arms. "You don't get to leave."

Yolanda ran on ahead, tearing her tunic on splintered spars, labouring up slopes of books. Starval kept pace, though the main threat came from above and he could do little to protect her from it.

"What has he done?" Carlotte asked, though the tone of her voice indicated that she had already started to understand.

They saw Wentworth first, crouched, his head on his paws. And then a piece of impenetrable blackness, whose silhouette Livira eventually translated into that of a great dog, as large as Wentworth and in a very similar pose, facing him.

"Volente . . ." The library's second-most-accomplished guide.

Between them, a shimmering pool whose uneven edge recalled Livira to that day when the Exchange had delivered her to the mountainside just a little too late to witness Yute's bloody rebirth from the assistant he had once been. He and his wife-to-be had both shed their impervious skins and with them the timeless existence that had held them.

Leetar gave a strangled cry and fell to her knees. Her brother had died in the making of such a pool, that time with the blood of Celcha's brother, Hellet, who had become an assistant in his turn, aimed and engineered by Mayland to begin this whole collapse, tearing down the library from the inside.

"Why would . . ." Carlotte stood, bewildered.

"He sacrificed himself to save us." Arpix choked. "He loved us all. I think. He just never knew how to say it."

Livira looked at her friend while the tears started to roll, hot down her cheeks. Arpix perhaps had understood the librarian better than any of them, bound as he had always been by the same restraint. What he'd just said wasn't something that would ever have escaped his lips before Clovis's arrival. The canith moved up behind him and pressed her forehead to the back of his hair, her mane nearly encompassing them both.

A head-sized chunk of the ceiling smashed down beside them, burying itself in the fallen books.

"Come on," Mayland said, advancing on the blood pool that had been Yute before the falling roof had crushed him. "He did this so we could reach the centre. Don't waste it."

Mayland slowed as he reached the shimmering surface, glancing between Wentworth and Volente who sat like grieving sphinxes, guarding the way. A moment later he gathered his courage, stepped forward and was gone. Kerrol and Starval followed. Yolanda, weeping, stepped after them and let her father's blood take her. Clovis and Arpix shepherded Leetar and Carlotte through, then took their chance too. Before he went, Arpix turned to lock eyes with Livira, paying no heed to the freshening rain of stone around them. "It's time."

Livira, cradling the raven in her arms, came to stand at the edge of what must be her friend and mentor's last gift. She looked from Wentworth to Volente. "I'm so sorry."

Volente whined softly. Wentworth only blinked.

"Will you be all right?" she asked. "You should come with us." But she knew that neither beast would leave their master's final resting place, even if the mountain were to fall upon them both.

Livira drew a shuddering breath and followed the others into the scintillating depths.

To fix something it is sometimes necessary to break it first. Often this goes wrong.
Bone Setting: A Beginner's Guide, *by Bradley Wood*

CHAPTER 49

Livira

Yute's portal, his last act, delivered them all to the centre in one painless step. The clear space in which Celcha stood expanded to accommodate them. When Livira looked back, there was no doorway to return by, no view of Chamber 2, just the hardpan desert stretching away, and the vast spiral of flat stones encompassing them, each bearing the rudiments of writing, a record of the first struggles of many and varied intelligences with the ideas of impermanence, thought, and memory.

Livira went to her knees and lowered Edgarallen gently to the ground. When she stood up she found Celcha's staff levelled at her in accusation.

"You brought *that*? *Here*?" Celcha pointed at the book still in Livira's hands, its cover stained with the raven's blood.

"Kill or cure?" Livira suggested, a little sheepishly. Had she just been running for the last safe haven, like a bug as the water level rises, or had she had a plan?

A tremor ran through the desert, rattling stones. Celcha stumbled as if this had been the first vibration to reach this place. "Kill or cure, if you must, but one merely requires that we wait, and the other I have no idea how to accomplish. Everything I have tried has failed."

"Kill or cure seems a very binary choice." Yolanda sniffed and wiped her nose on the back of her hand, looking very much as if she were a child to match her apparent years, in actions if not in words. "My father died so that we might explore other options."

Mayland took a step towards the girl, then sat cross-legged beside her, still the taller of the two. "I wronged you, and your father. I murdered . . ." He stared at the ground between his feet. "I . . . I have excuses but they are not good ones." Kerrol came to sit beside him. Starval followed, taking his place on his brother's other side. "Your father took me . . . led me somehow . . . to see an old woman who taught me many things in a short time without even seeming to try. She shone a very different light on book burning for me. The destruction of the library no longer feels as palatable as it once did. It hurt me. I wanted to hurt it back. This is not a basis on which to proceed."

Livira stood, slightly stunned. Yute's sacrifice had mechanically moved them all to the centre, of the library, but somehow, more fundamentally, it had shifted the immovable objects that had been his daughter's ideology, and Evar's brother's credo, towards the centre too. Here at the last minute of the last hour of the last day, it seemed that compromise was possible. All that they lacked was a solution.

Part of her wanted to scream at them. They couldn't have done this days ago? Years ago? When there was time left to hammer out the details of an agreement?

Livira advanced on Celcha, pushing her staff aside. "Can you save the library?"

"I don't believe so. Can you?"

"Not if it needs more than wishing really hard in all directions." Yute's death hung behind Livira like an approaching dust storm of earth-breaking proportions. But all of their deaths waited just a step ahead of them, and she had no time for grief. She turned her book over in her hands. Whatever gravity it had carried before seemed absent now. It was just a book. She opened it at a random page, and with a shock saw that it was blank. She leafed through—they all were. "I can't, no." She let the empty journal slip from her fingers, its stories told and gone. It hit the ground and nobody noticed. "We can't stop it."

"And what"—Arpix raised his voice, raw with loss—"what will happen to everything that was the library? I don't just mean the books and the assistants, and the guides . . . I mean all that . . ."

"Magic," Carlotte supplied.

Arpix shot her a disapproving look just as he had when she'd said "magic" on Livira's first day in the library complex. Clovis put her hand on his shoulder. "Magic," he grunted.

Kerrol looked up. "Perhaps you can build something new with it. A new library from the ruins of the old one."

Mayland shook his head without raising his eyes from the dry ground. "And who would fashion its rules? Who would play god for us this time? Will you be Irad, or shall I?" Silence held for a moment, then he spoke again. "The library showed Yute Anne's world for a reason. And Yute led me there for a reason too, though I thought it was my idea at the time. All of us went on our own journeys."

Starval stood up, dusting himself off. "There was a point to all of those Oanolds?"

Livira thought about it. "That we're all made as much by the world we're born into, by chance and circumstance, as by the content of our character? How is that helpful?" Though as she replayed the image of Oanold's head being spat from Wentworth's jaws she had to acknowledge that although the man had been a demon, he hadn't had to be. He could have been a garrulous landlord who risked himself to save children from the engine of state-driven murder.

"And what were we supposed to learn?" Carlotte frowned as if the thought of returning to the classroom were somehow repellent.

"We saw that none of the species were innocent. Even the ganar." Livira shot a look at Celcha, who had been the slave of both humans and canith, witness and victim to enormous cruelties. Her kind were small, not given to violence, so often exploited. "The ganar saw our world in their sky and made war on all of us. They created the skeer through obscenities of science and bred them as slaves of their own."

Celcha's staff slipped from her fingers.

"Perhaps none of us are the worst, and none of us are beyond salvation." Arpix pressed his lips into a flat line.

"We're all imperfect." Clovis backed him up.

The ground shook and the stones danced. In the distance a dust storm threatened. As Livira steadied herself and looked around, she saw that it was coming from all directions, the ground itself being pulverised and thrown against the sky.

"That's it?" Livira eyed the oncoming wave of destruction. "It's all a bit vague and tenuous, don't you think?" She had to raise her voice. A directionless wind had blown up, and the stones' rattling had become an unbroken complaint.

Mayland stood to face the end, dark and thoughtful. "Vague and tenuous can be more enduring than impervious and immovable. I think that's what saved Anne's world. The book burners came, but what they wanted to destroy couldn't be found all in one place. It was there and here and hidden and on display, subject to a thousand different systems, owned, loaned, copied, shared."

Carlotte took Livira's hand. The storm was devouring the intervening distance with remarkable speed. It seemed less like a dust storm now, having grown darker by the mile, to the point of being almost black, as if the floodgates on an ebony sea had been opened, allowing it to inundate the plane. Arpix threaded his fingers with those of Livira's other hand. She looked up at him, Clovis on his far side, and made her bravest smile for him.

"I wish Evar was here." Arpix was barely audible against the thundering approach now. "You two had more stories to write together."

"We did." Livira bowed her head, another tear escaping. The ground vibrated so much with the intensity of the oncoming destruction that dust rose from it, nearly obscuring her feet. Through the haze she spotted her book once more, shaken open, its blank pages fluttering. "We really did!"

Yolanda approached, stooped, picked up the book. She held it out to Livira. "We could try, together."

Arpix and Carlotte released Livira's hands. She reached uncertainly for the journal and its blank pages. The white child did not release her gift as Livira took hold. She glanced around the assembly and at the churning wall rushing towards them on every side. It was jet-black now, the blood of the library rushing to drown them all. "Mayland! We need you too."

The canith shook free of his thoughts and came quickly to join them. He drew a deep breath, looked from Yolanda to Livira, then cupped the book from beneath, his hand almost large enough to encompass both covers.

Yolanda muttered to herself, her eyes red from weeping. Whether it was incantations or formulas or some other ancient wisdom, Livira felt her power. Mayland's rumble reached them even through the building roar, his own education in how to destroy the library now repurposed to different ends. Livira simply poured herself into the pages just as she had spent so many days and weeks and years doing when she first wrote her stories there.

Their workings wound around each other like the threads of some complex melody. The book lay open in Mayland's hand, with Yolanda and Livira each gripping a cover, the pages riffling wildly back and forth in the buffeting wind.

Arpix said something, lost in the howl. Kerrol turned to face the storm. And in the space of one heartbeat everything was spinning, raging chaos.

LIVIRA'S AIM, AND, she intuited, the aim of her two accomplices, had been to draw down the thundering sea of the library's blood into the unwritten book. The book itself had become a hole in time, and what was a hole if not a way to reach one thing from another?

Livira's teacher, Master Heeth Logaris, had once held up a bottle of black ink, and declared, "This, Yuteling, is the blood of the library. It contains vast power, so treat it with respect. The manner of its application is unimportant, the groove of a quill, the aperture—that's hole to you, Yuteling—of a push pen, the brush of a Henlo-scribe. But what it sets upon the page may be wisdom that will build or topple empires." At this point he had returned the bottle to its high shelf and tapped a blunt finger to the as-yet-unadulterated page. "The ink is potent, but this"—he tapped the page again—"this is king. The blank page. Unlimited possibility. This, Yuteling, is where the future lies."

What she had not forgotten was the love that had first taken root in the timeless soil of the Exchange, or her first meeting with the young, handsome Evar Eventari.
The Book That Held Her Heart, *by Mark Lawrence*

CHAPTER 50

Excerpts from *The Traveller's Guide to Tru*

They say that the whole forest of Tarjal was once a lake. Many find it hard to believe, but time plays its own games, pushing the scenery this way and that, so who knows, maybe it was.

Speaking of time, it's something that's easy to lose track of when you wander among the trees. People like to speak of enchanted woods, of fairies, talking animals, and darker denizens coiled amid the briars. The woodlands that surround the town of Tru have a different type of magic though, some distillation of peace. As you weave a path around the many pools and listen to the pulse of the place, you might feel that you've somehow stepped out of time's flow, and that if you were to take a nap, years could slide past unnoticed.

Thankfully, it's just a feeling. Nobody has been lost for more than a day, and all you'll find on your return to the world is that you've misplaced your troubles.

The town itself is known for several things, but prime among them is the broad spread of its people, the number of humans nearly matched by those of both canith and ganar, with others who have journeyed even greater distances. Some joke that one day a skeer will move in and open a bookshop. And that does lead us to another local industry. Tru is a hive of learning. Its library, run by the famed academic Arpix Eventari, is a place of pilgrimage for many scholars.

A host of bookshops support this economy of education and cater to the tastes of many visitors who stop by on their way to the cities of the east coast.

Perhaps the most charming of any of Tru's bookshops is to be found off the lesser market square. You can navigate to it quickly by looking for the well. The locals say that the well predates the town by several centuries and harkens to a time when the alleged lake was an even harder story to believe. The well has its own wall to prevent the loss of careless children, and a small roof to shelter it. The drop to the water is scarcely more than a yard, but legend has it that the shaft reaches down deeper than anyone could sink and still find their way safely back to the surface. Much deeper.

The store that lies behind the well was perhaps named ironically. The Blank Page does not in fact deal in stationery, and all its pages are well covered. Be warned, as well as an addictively varied stock of rare tomes and popular literature, the place is also home to something of a menagerie. Or at least it was when this author had the pleasure of visiting. All its residents are somewhat elderly though, so I can't guarantee they will still be there to greet you on your arrival.

The first I encountered was a particularly big, ancient, and dare I say it . . . raucous . . . raven, perched on the post supporting the shop's nameboard. He's a talkative fellow, though neither he nor the proprietor seemed willing to give me his name.

Inside, expect to be greeted by a surprisingly large black hound who, despite age touching his curls with grey, will be extremely interested in the contents of your pockets. He struck this author as a very good boy, though sadly his eyesight appears to be failing . . . that or he thinks he can walk through walls, as he does quite frequently bump into things.

And the final member of the collection is what must be the largest of all domestic cats, and very definitely the sleepiest of the trio. This colossus among felines can be seen lying upon the shelving units and cannot be less than two yards from nose to tail tip.

As to the owner—

———

LIVIRA SAW THE young man to the door. He left clutching his new books and promising a glowing write-up in the pamphlet he was working on, a guide to the town for passing trade.

She stroked Volente's head as she watched the man cross the square.

"Hack! Hack!" Edgarallen cawed after him.

"Now, now, bird." Livira shook her head. "Be kind. He was nice."

She turned back into the shop and looked at it, trying to see the place with fresh eyes. She hoped it had made a good impression on her visitor, just as she hoped it did on all her customers. There was a magic in the place after all. More than just the tendency for people to lose themselves among the aisles and exclaim on leaving that they never realised quite how far back the shop extended.

"How far does it go?" the young man had asked, a look of mild confusion on his face.

Livira had given him the same answer she gave everyone. "All the way."

She had an urge to explore her shelves herself this afternoon. You never really knew what you might find back there. When they had siphoned down the library's magic, all three of them, the inheritors of Irad, of Jaspeth, and of Yute, they had agreed on a plan. They had sent the magic out into the world with no direction other than it should gather in any place where books gathered. The blood of the library wrote itself into every volume on every shelf, permeating, perhaps replacing, the ink that marked their pages. The magic wove itself into the walls of libraries both public and private, pooling in the quiet places, flowing along the shelves. It gathered in bookshops and bathed both the proprietors and customers, so that someone with the eyes to see would note it in the footprints leading away from the shop door.

Diluted by distance and space and numbers and time, the library's magic played more subtle roles than it had in the monolithic vastness of the athenaeum. It was a gentler enchantment, more given to whimsy and unpredictable results. Sometimes it made itself known by drawing the right eye to the right spine, making an auspicious marriage between reader and book. Sometimes it was a tingle in trailing fingertips, causing the browser to stop and examine the novel her touch had found.

Occasionally, rarely, it built to something of more grandeur that might draw notice and even find its way into a book of its own, a new story spilling unchecked across blank pages . . . until finally . . . it met the back cover and washed against it.

"I'M OLD," LIVIRA muttered as she walked the aisles, her touch lingering on old friends all the way. Gone were the days when she had sprinted at tree-top height across the shelves of the great library, leaping aisles, hunting . . . what had she been hunting? There was a time when she never forgot anything. She had forgotten what that felt like.

What she had not forgotten was the love that had first taken root in the timeless soil of the Exchange, or her first meeting with the young, handsome Evar Eventari. How tall he'd been, how athletic. How sweet, innocent, and how brave. She blinked away a tear for days gone by so long ago and muttered at herself for her foolishness.

The brothers still stopped by to see her, Kerrol most often, an elderly statesman now, always so kind when he called in, bringing with him a box of the little cakes he adored. Starval would appear unexpectedly from time to time, his mane still black, though she thought he must dye it. He spent most of his time fussing Volente and saying little, but never left without giving her the fiercest of hugs, taking her by surprise every time.

Mayland came once a year on the winter solstice, so bent beneath his years that she felt each visit must be his last. He spoke to her gravely about matters of politics and policy, his voice nearly as creaky as the rest of him, and when he'd departed, she would find a small book left for her on the table at which they'd taken their tea. Always poetry, often ancient. Clovis had once surprised her by saying that she believed her brother spent far longer choosing the book to bring her than he did on the lengthy journey from Crathe.

They spoke about Evar of course. All of them. Sometimes indirectly. Mayland had, in all of his conversations with Livira, spoken his brother's name only once. On his most recent visit. A fact that had left Livira with the conviction that he thought it would be his last.

All of them had loved Evar best. Even Mayland. All of them missed him. And all of them had a secret, one they wouldn't speak for fear that doing so might undo the magic of it. Livira had seen it in their eyes and kept her own secret close for the same reason.

"Ah, there you are."

Livira turned the corner to discover the reading table and her comfortable chair. They existed in a clearing among the aisles, but no customer had ever remarked upon them, and even Livira could wander for a while before she found the spot. The coil of a long tail gave away the presence of a large cat snoozing beneath the table.

She settled in her chair, sighing as the worn leather accepted her ageing bones. "I needed this." She kicked off her sandals and set her bare feet on Wentworth's furry belly.

Her book lay on the table, and she picked it up, running her fingers over the faint design on its worn covers, a ball of wind-weed, a thousand swirling lines that somehow wove the shape of a canith from nothing, a figure approaching from a dust storm.

She opened it to her favourite page and began to read.

And amid the warmth and comfort of the bed they shared Livira awoke once more from the dream of her life, turning with a yawn to find Evar beside her.

The blood of the library ran in his veins and while he walked the pages of many stories, visiting friends both old and new, it was here in the tower she had built for him that Evar Eventari laid his head.

He reached for her, smiling, and slid his hand from her shoulder to her hip, before pulling her close. A moment of perfect union when every star aligned. Gently, he kissed her forehead.

"Hey, sleepyhead. What shall we do today?"

ACKNOWLEDGEMENTS

As always, I'm very grateful to Agnes Meszaros for her continued help and chapter-by-chapter feedback as I write. She's never shy to challenge me when she thinks something can be improved or I'm being a little lazy. At the same time, her passion and enthusiasm made working on the book even more enjoyable. Under the pen name Mitriel Faywood, she is now an author—go check out her excellent debut, *A Gamble of Gods*, for which I was a beta reader. It's one hell of a story!

I should also thank, as ever, my wonderful editor, Jessica Wade, for her support and her many talents, as well as Jessica Plummer, Stephanie Felty, Gabbie Pachon, and the design, sales, marketing, and publicity crews at Ace. And of course my agent, Ian Drury, and the team at Sheil Land. Plus, a shout-out to all the good people on my Patreon whose support is invaluable and who provide welcome distraction on our Discord.